Caffeine N

C000232962

When the Killing Starts

RC Bridgestock

Fiction aimed at the heart
and the head..

Published by Caffeine Nights Publishing 2016

Published in Great Britain by
Caffeine Nights Publishing
4 Eton Close
Walderslade
Chatham
Kent
ME5 9AT
www. caffeinenights com

Also available as an eBook

British Library Cataloguing in Publication Data.
A CIP catalogue record for this book is available from the British Library

ISBN: 978-1-910720-51-6

Cover design by
Mark (Wills) Williams

Everything else by
Default, Luck and Accident

Also by RC Bridgestock

The D.I. Dylan Series

Deadly Focus
Consequences
White Lilies
Snow Kills
Reprobates
Killer Smile

All available in paperback and eBook

Deadly Focus is available on MP3 CD audiobook
and as a downloadable audiobook

Consequences is available to download as an
audiobook

White Lilies is available to download as an
audiobook

Acknowledgements

We both feel very privileged that our police and writing careers have both been eventful and fulfilling. We couldn't have done either without so many kind, dedicated and professional individuals who have walked into our lives and left footprints on our hearts...

Our special thanks go to our publisher Darren Laws, Caffeine Nights Publishing and our literary agent David H. Headley, DHH Literary Agency for their continued support and encouragement.

Thanks too, to Lisa Rothwell, Tactical Flight Officer (TFO), West Yorkshire Police and Sarah Dodsworth, West Yorkshire police mounted section for their advice in this novel. Factual knowledge that can only be told by someone who does the job, helps us to give our readers the most realistic experience possible in our fictional tales.

To those who bid at charity auctions to name a character in this book, we can't thank you enough. We hope you enjoy how we have utilised the information that you supplied about your character.

We will be forever thankful for the love and support of Betty and Ray Jordan (Carol's Mum and Dad) who have looked after us when we 'forget' to eat, the ironing pile is growing or Belle and Vegas need walking whilst we endeavour to reach a deadline.

And to our children and grandchildren who remain in our thoughts every hour of everyday for their love and support in what we do, even though this means we get less time with them...

Finally, but by no way least to our followers #TeamDylan

Thank you all from the bottom of our hearts...

To

All emergency service personnel and first responders around the world for putting us all before themselves to make the world a much safer place.

A special mention to charities that we support in the hope that in a small way this gives them the exposure they need for much needed promotion and funds.

We are proud to be Patrons for: -

B.A.S.H Local
www.bashwy.co.uk
B.A.S.H provides an outreach service that connects those in need with the charities and services they may not have otherwise known about whilst offering food, clothing and friendly faces, located in Brighouse, West Yorkshire.

Isle of Wight Society for the Blind -
www.iwsightconcern.org.uk
The Isle of Wight Society for the Blind provides information, practical help and emotional support to approximately 1,000 people living on the Isle of Wight.

The Red Lipstick Foundation –
www.theredlipstickfoundation.org
The Red Lipstick Foundation offers support and links for those whose lives have been affected by suicide, located in Southampton

We are proud to be Ambassadors for: -

Bethany Smile
   www.bethanyssmile.org
   Bethany's Smile - aim to raise a minimum of £300,000 to build Smile Cottage – a holiday/respite home, in Yorkshire, where families can go and spend quality time plus build happy memories, when they are faced with the news that their child has a very short life expectancy.

Supporters of: -

Sunshine & Smiles
   www.sunshineandsmiles.org.uk
   Who organise groups and events to improve the lives and opportunities of children and families living with Down Syndrome in Leeds, UK.

Last but not least a charity that is close to our hearts.

Forget Me Not Children's Hospice, Huddersfield is a special place that supports children with life shortening conditions and their families throughout West Yorkshire.
   www.forgetmenotchild.co.uk

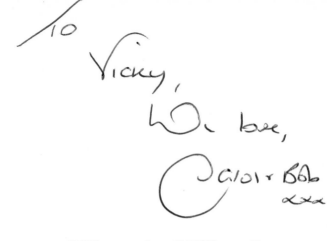

To Vicky,
We love,
Cailir Bob
xxx

When the Killing Starts

Chapter One

Jack Dylan's daughter Maisy draped a chubby little arm around his neck and put the tip of a finger under his chin, to gain his attention. The shopping centre was busy and Jen was constantly reminded that her husband was on-call because of the habitual checking of his mobile phone. His tour of duty didn't stop their normal routine, as long as Jack stayed in the Force area. However, from past experience she knew if a call came in she could be abandoned – anywhere, anytime. After all, Detective Inspector Jack Dylan was the man in charge of Harrowfield CID and the responsibility for serious crime in the area fell firmly at his feet.

Shopping was finished and they had achieved a quick look round the shops that sold prams; happily with no interruptions. Dylan planted a fleeting kiss on his daughter's forehead and he was rewarded with a loving smile as he carried the tired three-year-old back to the car. Jen hooked loosely on to his arm. They had almost reached their destination when she felt a cramp grip her stomach. Doubling up she halted and Dylan turned to see his wife's panic-stricken face look up at him. The hot street ahead appeared to waver in the sun and the feeling of nausea came over her.

'You okay?' Dylan said. Jen's lips were pale.

'Give me a minute, I will be.'

Jen climbed into the passenger seat of the car and Dylan put Maisy in the rear. Jen's chin was to her chest when he climbed in next to her and it was apparent she was breathing through the pain.

Dylan opened her a small bottle of water and she gratefully took it from him. Putting the vessel to her lips she took a few sips of the cool liquid. Her eyes stared at him in a colourless face. 'Get me home,' she said.

Dylan started the car engine. Jen wound down the passenger door window. 'Oh, no.' she whispered as she felt a warm gush of liquid between her legs.

'Promise you'd tell me if you weren't okay?' Dylan said as he parked the car in the driveway. Scooping Maisy deftly up in his arms, he hurried to open the house door. Jen went directly to the bathroom. Dylan settled Maisy at the kitchen table with her new sticker book and put the kettle on.

'I knew I should have eaten something,' Jen said more cheerily when she joined them. Her colour had returned.

Dylan's face was one of relief. 'You frightened me.'

'I'm sorry,' Jen gave him a brief kiss on the cheek as his mobile rang. He snatched it up from where it lay on the table.

Dylan and Jen's eyes locked as he listened intently to the caller.

'Yeah, okay, I'll turn out. I'm about half an hour away from you. Will you ensure they preserve the scene?' Dylan put his phone in his pocket.

'You've got to go?' said Jen.

Dylan nodded his head. 'It looks like someone's either been thrown off a building, or they've jumped.'

***

Crime was their way of life; Declan and Damien Devlin's loyalty was to each other.

At a glance, the twenty something-year-old steroid enhanced, muscle bound, shaven headed, tattooed bodied brothers could quite easily be mistaken for twins and often were, but Declan was the elder, and the aggressor.

The brothers hadn't had much of a childhood. The stolen video of Oliver Twist was constantly played on the stolen TV because their father proudly likened himself to Fagin. They, their father said were in 'Fagin's gang' and every woman he took up with was known to them as Nancy. It made their unusual existence seem somewhat normal and fun, to two small boys, who, as they grew up favoured a relatively nomadic lifestyle.

Unlike their late father; well known to the police as a petty thief and brace and bit burglar, entering premises as a trespasser, quietly, and to the best of his belief when they were unoccupied, his boys acquired a liking for creating fear, ensuring compliance of the victim by being armed.

The pair had one macabre pact; arrested, to be caged like an animal, was not an option.

The mundane pick pocketing and robberies the two had cut their teeth on, no longer fed their addiction. Nor did it satisfy their hunger, or bring in the coveted bounty that enabled them to live the lifestyle they had come to enjoy. But, would the crime they had spent all summer planning have been a step too far for their good-for-nothing wrong-un of a Dad; more often in prison than not when they were growing up, and dead from alcoholism before Declan's eighteenth birthday?

***

Rich, golden flora, various shades of red and brown littered the car park. The dappled early morning sunlight spotlighted those leaves on the branches of the Ash tree that dominated the central reservation of the busy trading estate. It was warmer than of late, especially for September.

The Mercedes-Benz alloy wheels crunched their way on the gravelled driveway as it exited Redchester Regal Hire Cars. The man acknowledged the owner with a slight nod of the head, as he closed the huge metal gates behind them. It was eight-thirty on Monday morning as the brothers headed out of the city towards the M65.

One might say a hire vehicle was an unnecessary expense. But Declan, the brighter of the two, knew it was far better to be legit on the road. They didn't need some eagled-eyed cop pulling them over because of a dodgy light when they were tooled-up.

Vandalism was apparent in the town, graffiti dominated the walls, floor and ceilings of the buildings in the notorious red-light area, where drug pushers and pimps were known associates. Rubbish, mostly disregarded junk mail, takeaway boxes, flyers and newspaper, blew carelessly in between parked vehicles and into the royal blue Mercedes' path.

In a holster tied about Damien's torso he felt the hardness of a handgun. This morning the Devlin brothers had business to attend to and nothing nor no one would be allowed to get in their way. The plan was to travel a hundred miles across two counties, their intended destination was Merton Manor, Harrowfield.

Several visits by the pair to recce the site over the last few months had seen it transformed from a partially renovated building, into a family home. Most recently it had been painted a distinguished Olde English white and before the present owners of the artwork empire moved in, the front door, lovingly restored by traditional craftsman had been given a coat of black gloss paint and adorned with period door furnishings.

It was easy to see what had drawn the wealthy couple to the countryside location. But they didn't need an estate agent to disclose the property's history as it was well documented. It was often said to the new owners. 'A good job you're not superstitious!'

The house held a tragic past. Sir Edward Crowther (Teddy), who had commissioned the house, died before it was finished. His son completed the project his father had started; after which William (Bill) Crowther and his eighteen-year-old bride Isabel commissioned the ornamental gardens in a Capability Brown style. At the time it was reported that the most eminent figures of the age were entertained in the then fifty acres of adjoining land. However, the couple's marriage didn't last long when a child, a boy died suddenly in infancy.

Troops were billeted in the house during both world wars. In more recent times, the house had been subject to several renovation projects but for one reason or another, other than the opulent bespoke kitchen and dining room, commissioned by Jake's father, the rest had never seen completion. It had long since been rumoured by villagers to be cursed with several ghosts running amok - rumours probably started by Jake's father to keep unwanted opportunists away. Jake told Leah he was unsure how his family had come to own the property, although his father had confided it was by way of a gambling debt. He'd had hours of fun playing in the grounds in his youth, and he'd never seen a ghost.

The house stood on the lower slopes of Beacon Hill, facing south west, which meant it caught the best of the sun. It had tall period sash windows to the front with a paved terrace wide enough to house a small pond. The veranda was edged with plants and bushes and giant wreaths of rhododendrons stood aside patio doors which, when opened, announced the dining room.

Beyond the terrace there were two lawns of bowling-green grass, joined in the middle by way of a newly laid asphalt driveway.

Near the Freemantle Gate, adding grandeur to the entrance, stood eight weathered staddlestones.

***

Jake Isaac walked up behind his wife as she stood at their bedroom window, looking idly out at the beautiful view. 'There you are Leah,' he said softly, before laying his hand gently on her shoulder. Without turning around, she put her hand over his and their fingers entwined. Silently, they appeared deep in thought. Jake's eyes found an old Ford Popular car travelling gaily along the meandering lane which led from Merton Village into Harrowfield passing the entrance to the manor house. The quiet road was used mostly by the locals or the odd lost Sunday driver who stumbled on it unwittingly.

'We could be lucky enough to be stuck here for weeks during the winter.' said Leah, with a contented sigh.

'What a lovely thought,' he said. 'Just you, our baby and me hostages to the elements.' For a moment or two they were content to be still until Jake broke his wife's reverie. 'Are you glad we decided to take on the old place, even with its torrid past?' he said.

Eyes fixed on the view, Leah took a slow, deep breath, rested her head back on his firm chest and closed her eyes, she nodded. 'Yes of course. How could anyone in their right mind believe this beautiful house is cursed?'

Jake chuckled. 'Me and our kid used to spend hours making up ghost stories to scare our friends. I don't believe we could have found a more idyllic spot if we'd chosen it ourselves do you?'

'All the plans to make the house into our home,' she said, tilting her head backwards to receive his feather-light kiss, 'is all I dreamed it would be. Thank you.' Leah turned her head slightly to look up into his face. Jake bent down to kiss his wife, this time firmer on her parted lips.

'Don't thank me, thank my father for leaving it to me in his will. I always thought he favoured my brother. How wrong could I have been? Leslie is more than welcome to the penthouse in the big city. I love it here. Saying that, with my father gone now my love, the family empire does rests heavily on our shoulders,' he said with a grave expression that held a tender smile. 'I just hope this little one,' he said, as he patted Leah's tummy, 'likes art!'

'Can't you just see our children running bare foot together on the lawns in the summer?'

'Steady on,' he said. Jake rubbed his wife's very rotund stomach. 'Let's see how we fair with this little-one first before we begin to talk of having a football team.' Jake gave a little throaty cough but his laughing eyes were suddenly bright, moist, and his voice eager.

'How about I build them a tree house in that grand old Beech,' he said, pointing straight ahead to the South lawn. 'I wanted my father to build me a tree house. He was always too busy.' Jake was thoughtful.

'Now whose imagination is running wild?' she said looking down at his leg that was strapped in a bandage at the knee.

'Alright, I'll get my man to build it for my son,' he said.

'Or daughter,' she said with a cock of her head. 'And my maid will live in the cottage out back.'

'Hold on a minute we'll need that cottage for the gardener,' he said.

Leah smiled sweetly. Then looking suddenly puzzled she showed her husband a frown. 'Where on earth is the nanny going to sleep?'

'If you want a nanny, she'll have to sleep in the nursery.'

Leah went into her husband's arms and held him tight for a moment then draping her arms loosely around his neck she pulled away. 'You make me so very, very happy.'

Jake followed his wife's eyes to their four poster bed.

'Shall we?' she giggled.

'Go on with you,' he said tapping her lightly on her bottom. 'You've only just got up. And the doctor said you should rest!'

'I will. I promise. Later,' she said, with a flick of her hair. 'But first I want to do a little more work on the nursery mural -make my tree branches look less swollen and diseased as you kindly pointed out.'

With supplies from the shop and paint brush in hand Leah was soon using long, sweeping brush strokes. Oh, to be married to an artist and a perfectionist at that! She stopped to peruse her work from time to time and watch the painted owl come to life opposite the bright yellow bird that had just taken flight. From where she stood at the nursery window, at the rear of the house, she saw hilly farmland. Each field framed with a Yorkshire stone wall and rock fencing, her inspiration for the animated woodland scene sketched by Jake, that she worked from. The deeply set window frame that the drawing was pinned to housed a thick cushion for a window seat. When she sat, she could see down below the back yard, stables, outhouses and a dilapidated servants' cottage that would indeed be a nice project for the future. Gazing beyond the farmland, her eyes rested on a green valley rising on a gradual incline of newly planted trees to the age old oaks of Oakhurst Wood. In her mind's eye there was many a family picnic planned on that hillside. Leah had chosen this particular room for the nursery because she had seen sheep, cows and horses grazing from the window when Jake had first brought her to the house. It had a nice, warm, welcoming feel. Sometimes in the bedroom she smelt the sweet bouquet of apples and pears. As opposed to the stench of boiled animal fat and lye in the dark, dank cellars. Oddly enough, she had noticed her sensitivity to different smells increase as her pregnancy progressed. Some rooms were pleasantly scented, but others made her feel instantly dizzy and nauseous, such was their overpowering odour - unfortunately that often happened in the kitchen and dining room, when sometimes she could only liken the smell to a butcher's shop. Jake thought it highly amusing but the doctor said it wasn't uncommon.

***

Declan and Damien had been northbound on the motorway when Declan noticed the blue lights of the emergency vehicle rapidly approaching in his rear view mirror. He steered the car swiftly to the central lane, allowing the police car unrestricted access ahead.

'Why do all Coppers drive like fucking Twats?' Declan muttered as the uniformed passenger in the police car looked their way.

'Let's hope for their sake they keep moving,' Damien said, through clenched teeth. As the police car came along-side he leaned forward and raised an eyebrow at the police officer. Damien stroked the tips of his fingers over his weapon.

'Don't panic,' said Declan. 'You heard what the Pigs were saying in the pub. With police cuts they're dependent on the 'hobby bobbies'.'

'The public would have a heart attack if they knew how many officers are working this week in Harrowfield,' said Damien a little less anxious as the police car sped ahead. 'Merton's cop shop is up for sale and Tandem Bridge is only open a few hours a week - we've done our homework. Lucky for the likes of us the force is on it's fucking knees.' Damien paused for a moment. 'Listening in on the coppers conversation is much easier now the shiny arses have shut the cop shop bar. All any villain needs to do to get the low down is go to the nearest pub to the police station at the end of a shift and they're all in there moaning.'

'You listen to the Pigs that much you're beginning to sound like one of 'em - no manpower, coppers on shift, the public. Whine, whine, whine.'

Damien crossed his arms over his chest, 'Ah but, all your moaning about me spending time at the Pig and Whistle has paid off hasn't it?' The corners of his mouth were turned up in a grin.

'Why did you call them, shiny arses?' Declan pulled a face at his brother.

'Shiny arses, that's what the cops call the bosses that never go out of the station: sit behind the desks all day.'

'That's why we have to do this job now.'

'They're gonna have no bugger to come out to our job today are they?' Damian sniggered.

'Well, a robbery isn't exactly going to be top priority, is it?'

Damien studied his brothers strong tattooed hands that gripped the black leather sports steering wheel. He reached inside his jacket and wrapped three fingers around the magazine well of the handgun securing his grip with his thumb. He watched Declan's unblinking eyes shoot from rear mirror to side mirror as another police car came up their rear. Releasing the gun slightly from the holster enabled Damien to lay his forefinger straight along the side of the barrel. 'If they don't go past, the public will be having a parade,' Damien said in a whisper, with a lopsided smirk on his unshaven face. He stared straight ahead.

Declan's jaw twitched. His knuckles were white. Suddenly there was nothing more than a quick flash; seconds later the police car had passed and disappeared in the chaos ahead and all that remained was the distant wailing of a siren.

Damien took a deep breath in and whistled on the breath out. He lay his weapon, in his limp hand, upon his lap and studied it.

'Put it away,' said Declan.

Damien lifted his head towards his brother and four brown, staring eyes locked. Damien lifted the gun to his jaw, ran it across his lips and dropped a feather-light kiss on its barrel.'

'What the fuck did I tell you?' said Declan, his eyes flew quickly back to the road ahead as he put his foot down hard on the accelerator.

Damien paused, raised an eyebrow and only then did he do as his elder brother said.

'Those Pigs, they must have been doing well over a ton.'

'It's not us they're after. That's all I care about.' A smile spread across his face. 'Mind you, they wouldn't catch us if they were,' he said laughing like a madman as he put his foot to the floor. 'They'll never, ever catch me.'

'Open her up. See what she can do over the moors,' Damien said as they reached the markers which directed them onto the slip road and off the motorway. 'Three, two, one.' Damien looked at his watch. It was 10.15 a.m. as they approached Saddleworth Moor which would take them over the Pennines to the A6162, Harrowfield Road towards Merton village. There was a fine, grey mist hanging in the sky which soon became steady rain as the car climbed to the moorland summit. From there they would see their destination in the distance, sat in the picturesque valley.

The heather clad moorland, peat bogs and rough grazing land was all that they surveyed for a few miles. Hill-cloud induced its fair share of drama as the brothers were forced to slow down for patches of over-zealous fog. Emerging from one such instance there appeared to be islands of moorland floating ahead of them. Dean Reservoir was now within sight. The adrenalin started pumping.

'Do you reckon that's what heaven looks like Dec?'

'How the hell would I know,'

'Don't suppose it matters, we're never gonna fucking find out are we?'

Chapter Two

Detective Inspector Jack Dylan stood looking down at the crumpled dead body of a man he knew well. He felt his lips slowly turning up at the corners. Detective Constable Ned Granger from Harrowfield CID, stood beside him. His phone rang insistently but he appeared to not hear. 'Well, you know what they say boss, if you live by the sword, there's a good chance you'll die by it.'

Dylan turned his head sideways and looked at his officer whose eyes were still on the corpse. Ned's phone stopped and immediately started to ring again. He ignored it. After a while it stopped.

'They also say, what goes around, comes around,' said Dylan. 'And on this occasion I've got to say that "they" whoever "they" might be, are right.'

'Trouble is,' said Ned with a sigh. 'That suggests this one isn't going to be easy to detect.'

'How do you work that out?' said Dylan?

The portly, smaller Detective Granger lifted his head to look up at his boss. 'Well, even if someone did see what happened, they're hardly likely to shop the culprit are they? In fact, I'd go as far as to say there might be a few who'd buy the murderer a pint.'

Dylan raised an eyebrow at his Detective Constable. 'What do I always tell you? Never...'

'Never assume. But, bloody hell boss, come on, name me one person who is going to care that that scroat's had his lights put out?' said Ned pointing his latex-gloved finger at the dead body.

Ned's phone rang again. He took it out of his jacket pocket this time, looked at the screen and dropped it back in his pocket.

'Will you answer that darn thing or turn it off. It's doing my bloody head in,' said Dylan.

Ned fumbled in his pocket, turned off his phone as requested, and put it back.

Dylan's face was expressionless. Freddy Knapton, it was true, was the scourge of the local Community. He was laid on his back, his left leg twisted in a contorted way beneath him. It was obvious from looking at the deceased that the once intimidating, aggressive twenty-year-old had had his throat cut, and the person who had cut it hadn't intended him to live. Without speaking, Dylan looked skywards to the top of the adjacent building, already aware that the multi-storey car park spanned the roof of the town's indoor shopping complex. 'By the state of him, my guess is that that's where he's come from.'

'Well, that's a bit of street cleansing that'll no doubt come as quite a relief to a lot of law abiding residents, I'd have thought.'

Dylan scanned the crime scene looking puzzled. 'Where's Satan?'

'If he were here we wouldn't get anywhere near Knapton.'

Dylan gave a slight nod of his head. 'Exactly, so where is he?' His brows furrowed. 'That dog's dangerous so we need to locate him, and quickly.'

'I'll never know why the magistrates allowed him to keep the friggin animal.'

'It never attacked a human being, or not one that complained, that's why.'

Ned's eyes widened. 'How many dogs have been viciously attacked and their owners reportedly petrified by it though?'

'It's hardly the dogs fault. But with Knapton dead who knows what it might do without him to keep it under control,' said Dylan.

'Wherever it is it must be scared,' said uniform Inspector Peter Reginald Stonestreet who on approaching the two men heard part of the conversation. 'I'll send someone to speak to the dog warden to see if he can us help locate it.'

Dylan bent down on his haunches. Inspector Stonestreet turned to speak over the airways. The hood on the SIO's coverall tugged at his hairline and his mask became taut. He put a gloved hand to the elastic and released it to help him breathe easier as he leaned over the body to study it closely.

Knapton's heavily tattooed right hand was clenched tightly. At the base of four of his fingers were what looked like initials. They were blue and faded and the staining had been done in an amateur fashion. 'A.C.A.B,' Dylan read out loud.

'All, Coppers Are Bastards,' Ned said, bending down beside him.

Dylan looked up at Ned Granger and pointed out the remnants of a leather strap that could be seen trailing from beneath Knapton's hand. 'The remains of Satan's lead?'

Dylan and Ned turned quickly at the sound of female voices. 'I look like a chuffin' Teletubbie in this damn suit.' Vicky Hardace was speaking loudly over her shoulder to Sarah (Jarv) Jarvis the Crime Scene Supervisor who was stood, hand on her hip at the open doors of her van; typically marked Crime Scene Investigation.

'It's not my bloody fault,' Jarv replied to Vicky. 'You should fetch your own. I can't help it if I've only got extra-large,' she said, with a hint of amusement in her tone.

'It's about time you lot bucked your ideas up.' Vicky mumbled to herself as she lifted the tape to the inner cordon.

'Rumour has it they're changing the colour to blue if that would suit madam better?' said Jarv as she caught up with Detective Sergeant Hardacre at the inner scene.

'Better,' she said. 'Don't you think?' She pondered the fact as she stood between Dylan and Ned.

'Better than what?' asked Ned.

'Blue's a better colour than these white polar bear suits.' Not waiting for an answer from her colleague her eyes were drawn to the face of the dead man. 'Ooo Freddy Knapton. It's the first time I've known him to be quiet in my presence. Didn't recognise you when you're not shouting obscenities!' she said loudly at the body. 'Ah, he looks quite angelic,' she said turning her head this way and that. Her smiling face turned into a grimace. 'Looks like someone has had a go at taking his head off. Pity we haven't still got the gibbet in Harrowfield. It would have been a lot less messy, don't you think?'

Dylan shook his head slowly from side to side.

'A guillotine?' said Ned.

Jarv tutted. 'Vicky, really!'

'What's wrong with you? I'll never forget our school trip to see the Halifax gibbet – I'd have been about eight years old. Just short of a hundred people were beheaded in Halifax between the first recorded execution in twelve-eighty-six and the last in sixteen-fifty. And, it is reported that in twelve-seventy-eight there were ninety-four privately owned gibbets and gallows in Yorkshire, bet you didn't know that? Now that's what I call bloody justice,' she said turning to look at Ned.

'Impressive.' Ned smiled.

'Everyone says that,' she said. 'I've told them two before,' she said nodding in the others direction. 'I had a crush on my history teacher.'

'That figures. They wouldn't have used it on a petty criminal like him though would they?' suggested Ned.

'Too bloody right they would. Any thief caught with stolen goods to the value of thirteen and a half old pennies or who confessed to having stolen goods to that value. Not only that, once the felon was caught they were put in the stocks for three market days, before they beheaded them.'

'So who sentenced them to death then, because presumably someone was judge and jury?'

'The lord of the manor's bailiff, would summon a jury of sixteen local men, and the jury had only two questions to decide on: were the goods stolen in the possession of the accused, and were they worth at least thirteen and a half pennies? There were no judge or defence council present; each side presented their case, and the jury decided on the verdict. Halifax had a reputation for strict law enforcement and was noted by the antiquary William Camden and by the poet.' Vicky stopped and frowned. She looked at Dylan.

'Jon Taylor's the name of the poet you're looking for who penned the Beggar's Litany: "From Hell, Hull, and Halifax, Good Lord, deliver us!"' answered Dylan.

Dylan and Ned looked up to the top of the building.

'So, we think he's come from up there do we?' Vicky said following their gaze.

'It's a probability,' said Ned.

'It's a possibility,' said Dylan.

'Well, if he has, it proves one thing boss.'

'What's that Vicky?'

'Shit really can fly. Or maybe not in this case,' she said.

Chapter Three

A wave of fatigue swept over Leah Isaac, as it often did when meal-time approached.

'It's nothing to worry about,' the midwife had said on her last visit, with a comforting smile. 'Blame it on the extra weight you're carrying.' Leah put her hand to her waist and arched her back to stretch out the ache. Standing straight, she bent her head towards her chest and looked down at her feet, her ankles were swollen. She sat down on the bed. The feeding pillow moulded itself around the bottom of her back, she gave a little moan of brief respite. Surrounded by baby paraphernalia, she unfolded the freshly laundered baby clothes into piles. Snowballing the fluffy soft towels into one soft mass, she couldn't resist lifting them to her face and inhaling the magical aura of love that babies evoke. With neatly folded clothing in one hand she hoisted herself up. Overwhelmed by the heat, a dizzy turn knocked her off balance. She grabbed the corner of the bedside table and stood perfectly still. She found closing her eyes made the sound of the music coming from downstairs appear louder. Jake had put a CD on. Les Miserables was their favourite. Wonderful memories came flooding back of a date with Jake at the West End premiere. That night he had asked her to marry him. After a couple of minutes of daydreaming Leah opened her eyes, gave her head a little shake, blinked her eyes to become accustomed once again to the bright light, and continued to pad across the bedroom. She stopped to hang muslin cloths on the nappy changing station and nudged off her shoes, all the while humming to the lyrics that she knew so well as they bellowed out loud and clear from below. Jake's favourite song, Master of the house. He sang the words at the top of his voice. In stocking feet, she felt the comfort of the soft, cream, shag pile carpet. With a contented little smile upon her face she fondled each tiny vest and sock in turn before placing them, neatly in a drawer, and when the drawer was full - she snapped it shut. A flicker of excitement rose within as she felt the baby move. She put a hand to her belly. 'The next time I open that drawer little one you'll be in my arms,' she whispered to her unborn child. Leah looked up and saw her face in the mirror. The baby hiccupped, Leah giggled. 'I dreamed a dream.' She sang out loud to the tune.

It was midday. Jake was stood at the central island workstation preparing a light lunch; chicken salad with lashings of mayonnaise and extra cherry tomatoes that Leah had a craving for. Leah headed for the shower with her husband's whistling in her ear.

Jake looked over the solid oak breakfast bar through into the dining room and shook his head, still unable to believe his good fortune. After the traumatic start to his married life to a beautiful woman ten years his junior, the subsequent numerous miscarriages they blamed on her age, and the death of his parents in a hit and run road traffic accident, things were at last starting to come good. With the return of his estranged brother to the family business, something he could have only dreamed about at one time, things were returning to a relatively normal family life. He had begun to think that having a family of his own had passed him by at forty-seven, and he and Leah would live the rest of their life never being blessed with a much wanted child to seal their love, but how glad was he that he had been wrong? His commitment to the artwork empire had not wavered but his obsessive passion, brought about by him being what he thought of as the sole heir, had eased with his brothers return. Being a father and having a family of his own meant everything to him; his priorities had changed. He pressed replay on the CD player and smiled contentedly to himself as he sliced with the care of a surgeon the organic chicken, and with his large hands he tenderly cut the tomatoes into the shape of a goldfish and the cucumber into the shape of a flower. 'Master of the house.' He sang, 'keeper of the zoo.' He plated up lunch. 'Perfection!' he said. Nothing was too good for his wife and their unborn child.

The Mercedes occupied by the Devlin brothers had reached its destination. There was a slight pause before Declan turned the car between the two large stone pillars leading into the long driveway that led directly to the front door of the manor house. He swerved onto the grass verge, almost hitting one staddlestone, then another before careering back onto the tarmac.

'What the fuck are you doing?' Damien shouted as his hand shot out to steady himself on the car's salubrious console.

Declan laughed swerving again and again, this time running over a couple of grazing rabbits.

'Clever twat!' said Damien. 'There's a squirrel, bet you can't catch that fucker?'

Declan screeched like a banshee, skidding and swerving the car, and, in the process tearing up the bowling green grass lawn. The terrified rodent legged it up a tree. 'Loser!' Damien shouted.

Very shortly the banter would stop. They were nothing but professional when it came to their work.

The wet room was filled with steam. The extractor fan made a low burring sound. Leah wallowed in the humidity and the heat, soaping her body. Millions of tiny effervescent bubbles released Lavender oil and when the scent met her nostrils she devoured the heady perfume. Turning her back on the pummelling jets of water she delighted in the feeling of tiny needles, pelting her skin. Her breasts hung heavy, sensitive and sore. Nipples that had once been a light shade of pink were now red, large and dimpled - they were getting ready for nursing, there was no doubt. Leah turned off the water and walked around the bath tub that fitted snugly in the corner of the room. Drying herself was difficult given that she couldn't see the top of her spindly legs that supported her swollen high rounded belly. She turned to face the full length mirror and oiled her stomach, inspecting it as she did so. There was no way she wanted stretch marks, god forbid, she had a drawer full of designer bikini's. Leah was sure she was carrying a girl - she'd done the wedding ring gender test. Was the dangling of her wedding ring over her belly on a string accurate - that was up for debate? She'd know soon enough. She stood and stared at her bump. Everyone said it was a girl. A daughter to dress up in beautiful dresses, pretty hats, shiny shoes and frilly socks. But, they hadn't been told it was a girl, not for sure. Deep down she knew Jake would like a son as his first born. She opened the door and tiptoed into the bedroom. The mystery they had created by not finding out the sex of their baby would add to the excitement at the birth, Jake said, and she was hopeful he would be caught up in the moment and not be too disappointed at the birth of a daughter.

Leah sat at her dressing table in just her panties. Wearing clothes had become uncomfortable and the hour a day when she allowed herself time to bathe was exhilarating as much as relaxing. 'After lunch I'll have a little rest,' she thought. She yawned. As she turned on the hairdryer she looked towards her suitcase that stood by the door - all packed and ready for the hospital. The hospital; she squirmed in her seat. They had been given a tour of the birthing room at the final antenatal class. It had reminded her of a torture chamber complete with high metal stirrups to hold her legs in the air. She shuddered, reached for her bra and lifted one large, heavy breasts after the other into the enormous cups. Veins had appeared upon the top of her breasts. But they were now 'to die for' Jake told her. 'They're painful,' she'd said. Thirty-six weeks had passed - the rest would be a breeze now she had stopped work. 'And relax...' she said with a sigh - the bra fastened.

Leah could hear the buzz of the juicer downstairs. When it stopped she heard what she thought was car tyres crunch to a standstill on the gravel outside. She tiptoed over to the window. The car had pulled up directly underneath it. Pulling back slightly so as not to be seen she saw her own puzzled face looking back at her from the mirrored wardrobe. Jake hadn't said he was expecting guests. Inquisitively she leaned forward and peering down from behind the curtains. She saw the driver's door open and a smartly dressed man alight. The driver strolled around the front of the car. His mouth open and closed, speaking to someone, but she couldn't hear what was being said. There was a tip tap of footsteps on the stone steps that led to the front door and whoever it was rapped on the wood. She went out onto the landing. The music from Les Mis was still playing merrily away, but presuming Jake had gone to the door as the knocking had stopped. Unsuitably dressed to greet anyone in her semi-naked state, she scurried back into the bedroom as quick as she could and closed the bedroom door behind her.

'An unlocked door. An open invitation. What do you say?' Declan winked over his shoulder at Damien, who followed him sheep-like into the house.

The smell of cooked chicken filtered into the hallway. Declan and Damien walked across the marble foyer in the direction of the music - each eyeing the splendour of the original curved oak staircase. At the foot of the stairs were paintings reminiscent of tapestries, complete with rich borders and fringed edges. 'Suggested confidence, stability and prosperity,' Jake had said to Leah.

Unsuspecting of the intruders, Jake Isaac was drying his hands on the kitchen towel. He wiped his little finger over the edge of the side plate that had been touched by the whipped cream. Hearing a noise in the adjoining room and, assuming it was his wife, he shuffled along in his slippers to meet her, humming as he went. At the door to the dining room he was stopped in his tracks. Hand still on the door knob he took a step back. 'Who the hell?' he started to say, but before he could finish Declan had pinned him against the wall with the barrel of a revolver rammed up his left nostril with such force that it caused Jake's nose to instantly pour with blood. Looking directly into the intruder's eyes, Jake could see they were slightly bloodshot. A muscular body and a firm hand was pressed against Jake's mouth which meant he was having to fight for each breath. The perpetrator's face was so close to his he could see the spittle at the corner of his gregarious, mouth. His breath came in rasps. With nothing said, but with an expert's skill, Jake was turned around by the second intruder, the gun now to his head, and his hands were tied securely behind his back with cable ties. He heard the tearing of tape from a reel and a strip was slapped on his face which sealed his lips. His eyes felt as if they would burst from their sockets, such was the pressure in his head. Totally incapacitated he had to admit to himself that he was no longer a free man.

'Where is she?' Declan demanded. There was an unusual fragrance to his clothing. Jake, wide eyed, looked at his aggressor questioningly through squinting eyes. He'd smelt it before, a long, long time ago. An earthy, burning smell. It turned his stomach. Weed, Marijuana, Cannabis?

Declan, grinning, smeared the bloodied barrel across the distressed man's face leaving a trail of blood.

'Your wife, asshole?' he hissed through bared teeth.

With eyes that were full of fear Jake unwittingly indicated upstairs.

'Anyone else here?' demanded Declan. Jake shook his head in little, jerky movements. A cluster of sweat beads appeared on his forehead.

Declan raised his head slightly. 'I'll see to him. Fetch her.'

At the foot of the stairs Damien bent down and ripped the telephone wires from the socket as he passed. He took the stairs two at a time. His size twelve feet made no noise on the sumptuous pile of the floor covering. Quietly and quickly he peered into each room in his search for Leah Isaac. Eventually satisfying himself no one else was home, he headed in the direction of the noise of her hairdryer.

Leah had her head down as she tussled her locks. Sensing the bedroom door open behind her she threw back her head, and raising her eyes to the level of the mirror her face was one of horror as she saw the giant of a man with a chest the size of a heavy weight boxer filling the doorway.

'Jake!' she screamed. 'J a k e!' she screamed louder and with more urgency. Leah's heart banged in her chest. Her continued calling became gradually no more than a whimper. 'There's a man. In our bedroom.' Leah's last words were spoken softly.

Damien assertively walked towards her. She froze. Recoiling her body, as far back as her pregnancy would allow, without falling from her chair, she let go of her hair dryer and it fell from her limp hand. Hitting the floor, it rolled on its side and for a few moments it rattled against the dressing table. There was a smell of burning - the motor stopped and smoke emanated from the appliance. A deathly silence ensued. For a brief moment the room was still. Leah's eyes darted from side to side looking for a way out, but knowing there was none other than passing the heavyweight. With a shaking hand she picked up her hairbrush and threw it at the slowly approaching Damien. But, so feeble was the throw that he lunged forward and caught it with the ease of a cricketer in mid-field. He held the brush in the air, a serene, almost religious smile lit up his face.

Leah's mouth was dry her eyes unblinking. Damien lunged his head forward at hers. His staring eyes were the colour of flint. She was in no doubt who was in control. Reaching out he grabbed her and his large hands spanned her forearm. She yelped in pain. From her sitting position she could see white powder around the intruders' nostril. She held herself rigid but such was his strength that he lifted her from her sitting position and she had no option but to do his bidding and stand upright in front of him. Swiftly, he put her arm behind her back; and with ease he manoeuvred himself into his favoured position behind her. He bent to breathe in the Lavender smell of her damp hair. Tears fell from Leah's eyes and she cried out as he forced her arm further up her back.

'You smell nice,' he whispered into her neck.

'Please, please don't hurt me,' she begged arching her body away from the heat she could feel from his body at such close proximity. 'I'm having a baby.'

'You don't say,' he said, scanning her half naked body.

'What do you want?' she said to his mirror image. My husband; he's downstairs. He'll give you whatever you want. Just take it and leave.'

'I know exactly where your husband is. Let's hope he does give us what we want because believe me, it's the only way he can help you.'

Leah briefly closed her eyes, her body tensed. She could sense his appraisal of her in the full length mirror. He turned her to face it.

'You're lovely, you are. Far too young and good-looking for that old git downstairs.'

Leah could feel his warm breath on her forehead. 'Please let me go,' she said, trying desperately to hide her semi-nakedness with her free arm. Damien pushed her gently in her back, in the direction of the door and towards the stairs. She felt disoriented, wobbly, sick; she felt faint. Her heart was racing at an incredible speed as he pushed her from the top step and she feared she was going to fall. She stumbled and he steadied her. Her thoughts turned to her baby as she precariously hobbled down the steps. The baby was unusually still, as if it sensed they were both in danger.

As they neared the foot of the stairs Damien let go of her arm momentarily, however, instantly he grabbed her hair and with a backward kick knocked a tall Japanese vase against the wall. The sound of it smashing rang in her ears. Leah was stretched onto her tiptoes. The giant of a man was a lot taller than her. With each step they took, his grasp of her hair felt like it was being ripped from her scalp. More hot, stinging tears emanated from her eyes, fell readily down her cheeks and dripped off her chin onto her bare chest.

'Please, stop, you're going to hurt my baby.'

Damien gave an ironic laugh. He turned her face towards his, with hands that were scabbed and looked sore. Seeing she had noticed them he rubbed his unshaven bristles roughly against her cheek. 'Chin pie the Guv used to call it,' he said, as if she would know who the Guv was. Again she cried out and, in response, he licked the tears from her face and then lowered his tongue to her chest. A tongue that had strange blue patches upon it. 'Salty, I love salty. You're good enough to eat,' he said as he bit the top of her breast. Leah screamed out her husband's name but no one came.

Damien slapped her across the face which silenced her, instantly before leading her across the hallway at pace. Her elbow caught the wall and she flinched. At the opening to the dining room, the Lincrusta wallpaper that her and Jake had lovingly chosen felt like sandpaper chaffing the skin on her shoulder as she was dragged against it. She almost missed the step into the dining room that she'd skipped up a thousand times before, stumbling, she lunged forward. Her right leg collapsed under her but Damien's tight grip on her hair stopped her from falling.

'Whoo, that was a near miss wasn't it? You should be more careful in your condition,' he said, dragging her by her hair to her feet. He looked at her. His face took on one of mock concern. 'If you're not careful you'll seriously harm yourself and that baby of yours.'

'Let me go,' she said in a whisper.

'Walk on,' he said pushing her into the dining room with the palm of his hand to her back.

The sun shining in through the large windows meant that the carpet was warm to her bare feet. But her body turned cold to see a man, not unlike the one that was behind her, stood over her husband who was bound up, bloodied and laying face down on the floor. Jake was trussed up so tightly that he could barely lift his head.

'I'm okay.' Leah mouthed. Unchecked tears spilling down her face. A loud sob caught in her throat at Damien's touch.

'Look what I found,' Damien said to Declan. 'Isn't she a beaut?'

Without words or emotion Declan took Leah's hands in his and tied them in front of her rotund belly. His hands, that were neither nervous or hurried, were clean and soft, his fingers stumpy with square nails. So proficient was he in the act of bondage that at all times he stared into her face. His eyes were shining, like glass. She averted her gaze. Stood very still. Her hooded eyes were accepting. Flat and dead like a dolls. The inside of his arms, she noticed, were peppered with injection marks veiled mostly by his tattoo's.

The task completed, he raised a flat, firm hand and gently putting it on her chest he pushed her down without saying a word. She fell backwards onto the soft leather sofa with a thud. Jake was picked up from the floor effortlessly by Damien and unceremoniously transported to join her. The action of him falling down like a sack of potatoes beside her, made her suddenly conscious of her superficial injuries and she flinched. Her eyes prickled and a fire burned inside her. She tasted the salt in her tears but not a sound escaped from her lips. Although not religious she prayed, 'Please God make them leave us alone.' Frightened for Jake, whose nose was disjointed and bleeding, she stared appealingly into his blackening eyes that were increasingly closing because of the swelling, they darted from side to side and eventually fixed on the doorway. The tape on his mouth was taut but his eyes yelled at her a loud and clear message from within. But, even though her legs weren't shackled she knew she wouldn't be allowed to leave, as his eyes suggested to her that she should try. After a moment or two of silence, the sound of one of the hostage taker's voice made Leah jump.

'Listen to me. This is purely business. It's nothing personal. It's just about the money.' Declan held out his hand, palm up and shook his head slowly. 'Give us the money and then we'll leave you be.' Declan spoke calmly and with authority.

Leah scanned the muscular men before her. The shaved heads, the tattoos on their skin. They both appeared to have difficulty remaining focused.

Damien started to hop from one foot to the other when neither her or Jake responded. 'Come on. We're not going anywhere until we get it.'

There was silence.

'Put the kettle on,' said Declan to Damien. He didn't take his eyes off his hostages.

'You want a brew?' said Damien looking bemused at his brother. He wiped a hand under a runny nose.

'Just do it,' Declan said.

The switching on of the kettle was louder than Leah had heard before. Minutes later white billowing steam gathered on the ceiling. Damien stood looking questionably at his brother whose eyes had not left the couple. The kettle automatically switched off.

'Bring it here,' Declan indicated with his outstretched arm and clasping hand.

Jake began shaking his head from side to side in a frantic fashion. His whole body trembled. Declan leaned towards him in a menacing fashion, ripping the tape from his mouth. Jake groaned momentarily. His swollen eyes barely able to see. Time seemed to stand still. Leah, eyes were wide, staring and pleading silently for Declan to stop, but he was not to be deterred.

'Where is the money?' said Declan. The kettle held threateningly in his hand. It's spout facing Jake.

'We don't keep money here.' Leah blurted. 'Tell them Jake, tell them,' she screamed.

'And you've underestimated us if you think we're stupid enough not to have done our homework.' Declan said raising an eyebrow at Jake. Declan snarled. 'Happy families eh? You obviously don't tell the missus everything, do you Mr Isaac?'

'You've been watching us?' said Leah.

'For months' love,' said Damien. He winked at Leah.

Jake's sight was on Declan's hand as he moved towards Leah. Jake blinked away the sweat from his forehead that had mixed with the blood from an open wound and ran into the slits that were his eyes.

'Your wife is very beautiful Mr Isaac. It would be really naughty of me to leave her scarred for life, now wouldn't it?'

Jake remained silent. Leah's eyes darted from one to the other of the hostage takers, then her eyes settled on Damien. The panic rose in her and the comfort that she sought in the younger brother's face was not found.

'Jake?' she said, urgency in her voice. 'Please Jake?'

'But if you're going to be stupid Mr Isaac.' Declan nodded his head at his brother. His eyes turned back to Jake. Damien grabbed hold of the man's bound hands and lifted him to his feet. Jake fought with the younger man but his strength was no match for Damien and with ease he held Jakes arms out in front of him. Without taking his eyes off Jake's face Declan poured the boiling hot water slowly and deliberately over his forearm until the kettle was empty.

The scream that emanated from Jake's lips was a sound like Leah had never heard before. She saw her husband's head jolt backwards and when he shuddered, his jaw line ridged and tight, he slumped forward. He'd passed out.

'Please, no, no, no.' Leah sobbed.

Damien grinned an open mouthed grin that showed Leah his gold fillings.

Declan got down on the floor next to Jake. 'I'm boiling the kettle again; except next time it won't be you who gets it. The next one is for her.' He passed the kettle to his brother as his eyes flew towards Leah. Damien obediently walked to the sink and, taking the lid off the kettle, filled it with water and proceeded to plug it in. The switch went down. Leah's eyes hung on the little hand of the dining room grandmother clock.

'You've got seconds,' Declan said, grabbing Jake by the hair and yanking his head viciously backwards. Raising his arm Declan slapped Jake hard across his face with the palm of his hand. Once, twice, three times. His lip split open and blood oozed from the wound. The bruising on his face was developing into a rainbow of colours. Blisters were forming rapidly on his pink hands and arms. 'Stop pissing us about. Don't you know by now we mean business?'

Jake opened his eyes, as much as the bruising would allow. 'We don't keep any money here,' he said. Blood splashes from his mouth peppered his shirt.

Declan grabbed hold of Leah by her arm and pulled her to her feet. He indicated to his brother. 'Do you want her?'

Damien left the kettle and strolled over to the pair. Standing beside her he put his face close to hers. 'Urm.' He screwed up his face. 'Go on then.' Declan turned to Jake and raised his eyebrows.

Leah shrank back, trembling. She looked at Jake who was semi-conscious on the sofa. 'Do something, please Jake, please, I'm begging you.'

'Don't bother love,' said Declan. 'He obviously ain't going to help you or he would've done by now.'

'Look, I'll give you my purse, my credit cards, what cash I have.' Leah's lips were trembling so much that she could barely talk. The kettle was boiling, a steam-cloud wafted towards them, calling to the hostage takers.

'I need the toilet, please?'

Declan nodded to Damien and on shaking legs Leah stumbled towards the door.

'Go with her,' ordered Declan.

Leah turned quickly. 'No, no, It's okay.'

Damien looked at her trussed hands with a furrowed brow and then back to her face. 'Really?'

'If you'll just undo my...' Damien grabbed her hands and she screamed. 'Jake! Jake! Give them the money, please!' she called out as she was led away.

Leah sat down on the cold toilet seat, only to look up into the cold staring eyes of her captor who stood directly in front of her.

'Let me get my clothes?'

'No chance, I'm enjoying the view.'

Leah looked down at the floor.

'Finished?' he said. She nodded.

From the downstairs toilet she could hear scuffling in the hallway and when they returned to the dining room Jake and Declan had gone. Leah sat on the sofa and Damien pulled up a dining chair so that he could sit opposite her. They waited.

From upstairs Leah could hear muffled voices that suddenly became desperate and loud. 'And the rest?' Declan could be heard shouting. Damien stood up and looked towards the doorway. Nonchalantly, he walked towards the kitchen worktop where the kettle stood. Leah saw him reach out and her heart skipped a beat, but instead of picking it up, as she feared he would, he grabbed a handful of food from the plate. He glanced at Leah each time he put more food in his mouth, chewed it and swallowed with a hint of satisfaction. He looked at her in a way that sent shivers through her body. She hoped and prayed that Jake had given the hostage taker what he wanted. If cash was truly all they were after, and her husband was giving it to him then they should be gone soon. A feeling of relative calmness came over her as Damien smiled at her in a human like way. He strolled over towards her. 'Want some?' he said as he pushed a cold chicken leg to her lips. Leah opened her mouth to comply but the smell made her gag. Involuntary her stomach heaved. She turned her head, coughed and promptly, threw up on the settee.

'Gross,' he said as he cupped her chin in his hand and squeezed it tight. Clear spittle dribbled down her chin and her eyes swam with tears. He turned her face to look up at him. 'Don't you ever, ever, turn away from me you bitch. Do you hear?'

Leah nodded.

'I might not be as la-di-da as him,' he said with a toss of his head towards the upstairs. 'But, I've earned respect and now I do what I want, when I want, do you understand?' He put a finger in his mouth and not taking his eyes off Leah's face he released her bra fastening and ran his finger around her bare nipple. Damien's lip curled. Splaying his fingers to cup her breast he pushed her away from him and she breathed an audible sigh of relief.

The tears that came burned in her eyes and her head throbbed at the temples. Leah swallowed hard and rested her hand flat to her stomach and the baby moved. 'I'm sorry. I'm sorry, please, please. It's my, our, first child. I'm so scared.'

A loud bang from the stairway stopped them in their tracks and they both looked towards the door. The noise that ensued was one of someone being dragged down the stairs, thud, thud -one step at a time. Declan was laughing as he entered the room pulling Jake by a noose he had made to put around his neck with a bed sheet. He carried a blue, cloth bank bag and a metal cash box that Leah knew Jake used for petty cash. Jake's face, so bloated and bruised was hardly recognisable to her.

'What are you looking at me like that for sweetheart?' Declan said. 'He tripped. Didn't you mate?' He threw Damien the bag that was plumped up full with notes. 'Count it,' he told his brother as Damien slammed the bounty down on the table. 'I still think he's holding out on us. There's more. I know it.' He turned and kicked Jake in the shin with force. 'I'm fucking sure there's more.' Jake keeled over. 'Another safe?' As Jake stood upright Declan punched him in the stomach.

'It's not enough,' said Damien holding the bank notes in his hands. 'A couple of grand. It's not enough.'

'Big mistake, big fucking mistake.' Declan shouted at Jake. 'Come on! Come on! Where's the rest?'

Damien walked towards Leah, he pulled her to her feet and dragged her in front of her husband. 'Look at her,' said Declan. 'Do you love her?'

Jake's head bobbed slowly up and down. The most he could do with the injuries he had sustained. Leah shoulders slumped.

'Be assured, unless you come up with more, a lot more, very, very quickly you can say goodbye to your wife.' The gun Declan produced was held to her forehead and then menacingly, he ran the barrel very slowly down her body, between her naked breasts and he stopped as it reached her swollen womb. He looked across at Jake.

'There's another safe.' Jake panted. Leah slumped to the floor. Declan grabbed Jake by the throat, tightening the sheet around his neck as he did so. Jake made a gurgling sound.

'That's good, good. Take me to it then and let's stop fucking about,' Declan said in a whisper, close to his ear.

Leah looked puzzled. 'For god sake,' she screamed. 'How could you? If you've got money, give it to them. Give it to them now, you stupid idiot!'

The audience to Jake and Leah's conflict watched on with amusement. Jake staggered a few yards towards the oak panelling in the recess of the dining room. He turned and held out his hands indicating to Declan to untie them. Once released from his shackles, he dragged a small footstool a few inches towards the fireplace and stepped up onto it. Leaning heavily on the mantelpiece enabled him to reach the first book from the right hand side of the fifth shelf down from the ceiling. Surprisingly, the wooden surround to the bookshelf opened to reveal a safe. Leah's jaw dropped and her eyes were unbelieving. With bloodied, shaking hands Jake retrieved a bag. Damien grabbed it.'

'There must be near on fifty grand here,' he said, peering inside at the tightly rolled notes.

Jake stepped down with a thud on the wooden floor. Satisfied, Declan re-tied Jake's hands, put tape over his mouth and tossed him, like a mannequin back onto the sofa.

Damien put his arm limply around Leah shoulders and stared down at her breasts. 'Do it again,' he said to Declan.

'Do what again?'

'The thing you did to her with the gun.' Damien raised one eye brow at his brother. The elder grinned.

'You dirty twat,' Declan said with a sneer.

Leah looked from one to the other. 'Please! He's given you what you wanted.' Leah could barely say her husband's name.

Declan pointed the gun at Jake and then at Leah.

'Upstairs both of you, we'll ring the police when we're away,' he said matter-of-fact.

Compliance seemed to be the best option and Leah led Jake, with a gun to his back and as little fuss as possible, up the stairs. Damien joined Leah on the top step. He nodded towards the bedroom giving Declan a lopsided grin. Declan took Jake into the main bedroom and instructed him to lie face down on the bed. He tied his legs together.

Damien took Leah into the nursery and instructed her to get down on the floor.

'Can't you leave me with my husband, please?' A dry sob caught in her throat at the sight of the emptiness behind his eyes. His breathing was heavy and quick. She could see the adrenalin pumping through his veins at his temples. 'On your hands and knees,' he commanded. The softness of the carpet in her clenched fists and the smell of baby powder filled her nostrils - it gave her some comfort.

She heard him undo his belt which he did without any hurry. A feeling of foreboding washed over her. She was hot, she was cold, she felt sick to the stomach. The noise of him undoing the trouser zip was short but the shuffle of him dropping behind her was quick. As he entered her from behind she heard the firing of a gun.

'Jake!' she lifted her head and screamed.

Chapter Four

'She's all yours.' Damien said releasing Leah's hips from his tight grip as he withdrew from her. Without his support she fell on her side whimpering. Leah sensed the two men standing above her but she daren't open her eyes. Screaming as hard and as loud as she could she curled into the foetus position. 'No more, no more,' she sobbed.

With the quickness of an animal jumping on its prey Damian picked up the duvet from the cot and the musical mobile sprang into action. As it merrily danced to and fro he threw the cover over Leah's head. Lunging towards her Declan tossed the gun in Damien's direction and held the duvet down as she struggled beneath. 'Do it,' Declan yelled at his brother. Damien looked at his brother panic written all over his face. 'Shut the bitch up. Shut her up now!' The younger brother didn't question the command. Three shots rang out before the sound of silence. The cot mobile cut the silence with one musical note. All was still. There was no rush, panic, or emotion from the men, just a need to ensure there was nothing left to link them to the crime.

'We need a fire?' said Declan.

'We don't need to search for an accelerant. Look, over there, turps.'

'An explosion?' said Declan with a glint of mischief in his eyes.

Quietly and with expertise they poured the contents of both the bottle and the can over the bodies. The little that remained they sprinkled on the beds and carpet before casting aside the containers.

'Get the money. Leave it by the door. We'll set both of them alight. Then we'll go downstairs and turn the gas on in the kitchen. That should give us an explosion.'

'It should also get rid of any evidence,' said Damien.

'There you go again. Been listening to them Pigs down the boozer! You'll be wanting to join up next.'

'Yeah, whatever.' Damien looked about him. 'Shame really.'

'What is?'

'To fire it. I could live here,' Damien mused.

Declan handed his brother a lighter. 'Ready to go?'

Damien gave a nod of his head.

Both fires in the bedrooms were lit simultaneously on the count of three. The brothers hurtled down the stairs. An alarm began to ring, then another, a third, a fourth. High pitched screeching alarms. The brothers raced to the kitchen. 'For fuck's sake, how many smoke alarms can one house have?' shouted Damien as he covered his ears to the deafening sound.

Quickly the two brother's worked as one turning on the gas taps. As Damien passed the kitchen worktop on their hurried exit he swiftly picked up the cooked chicken laden plate. As the brother's fled the house, the cash haul was scooped up where it had been left at the front door. They ran away from the house, leapt into their car seats and Declan jammed the key in the vehicle's ignition. It was speedily driven directly down the driveway. When the car came to the gateway Declan slammed his foot unexpectedly on the brake. Damien looked across at his brother questioningly. Then as Declan turned his head back towards the house he followed his gaze. Damien lit a joint. Declan reached out for a drag. The sickly sweet smell of weed filled the air. Momentarily, they watched the flames lick the panes of glass like hungry fingers, and as the fire grew, so did the billowing noise. One almighty boom saw the upstairs windows blown onto the terrace, the splinters cascaded so far they could be heard hitting the tarmac on the ground nearby. Damien opened the passenger door, slid the plate of food onto his brother's lap and, before Declan could ask why, was throwing a staddlestone into the boot of the car.

'Come on you fucking idiot.' Declan shouted before snorting a line. 'Trumpton will be here in no time. We're not exactly in the middle of the bloody desert.'

Damien let out a groan as he slumped back into his seat and slammed the car door. Declan threw the plate back on his lap. 'Okay, okay. I didn't realise how fucking heavy, them fucking mushrooms are,' he said, leaning back in his seat.

'Why the hell did you want one of them?'

'Grandad always wanted one for his garden?' His grin was wide.

'You're going soft in the fucking head.'

'Come on. What you waiting for? Let's get out of here. Go, go, go.' Damien rammed a chunk of chicken into his mouth. 'I'm fucking starving.'

Declan shouted. 'That's the fucking weed...' He put his foot down on the accelerator and the car made a huge roar as it screeched on the tarmac and leapt into action. His eyes were not on the road ahead but on his brother face. 'You're a fucking, mental twat!'

'Look out!' Damien shouted. Squinted eyes were suddenly like saucers.

Declan stamped down on the brake. Damien's head found the windscreen. The car tyre's screeched and they were thrown to and fro as Declan tried to gain control of the swerving vehicle. But he wasn't quick enough, or in a fit state, to make sure it entirely missed the stone pillar.

'You're alive then?' Declan, reversed the car from where it come to rest against the stone pillar. 'I've heard it's the quite ones you need to worry about.'

Damien raised an eyebrow at his brother and his lips were pursed. 'What the fuck?' he growled. 'Are you trying to kill us?'

'Lack of concentration our kid. It won't happen again,' Declan said.

'Jack arse - you've been snorting?' Damien grabbed hold of his brother's chin and turned his face towards him. This time Declan's eye's remained on the road ahead. White power residue was apparent on his upper lip. He ripped his face from his brother's grasp and started coughing. 'That'll teach you, you fucking smack head.'

Sirens could be heard in the distance as Declan drove faster and more erratically along the country road towards Saddleworth moor.

An explosion in the distance sounded like one almighty crack of thunder. Declan pulled the car into a small lay-by at the side of the road, at the top of a hill. 'We can watch the circus arrive from here,' he said pulling out of his pocket a small, see-through bag containing white powder. He threw it at Damien and in exchange took scraps of food from the plate. Through drugged crazed eyes the brothers watched the ball of fire that was surrounded by torrid plumes of smoke. 'Always finish what you start, that's what the Guv used to say didn't he?' Declan said.

Damien blindly ran his flaccid fingertips over the grease on the plate. The feast done, he opened his window and threw the plate out, just as a fire engine whizzed past.

'Bloody hell,' said Damien. 'There are Dennis's coming from all fucking directions.' His laughter was loud and uncontrollable. 'They'll put it out.'

'You're paranoid – they're not quick enough,' said Declan with a lazy smirk. Morton Manor could not be seen for the dense blanket of black smoke.

Damien wrinkled his nose and sniffed loudly at his fingers.

'Turpentine?' Declan said. His head lolled to one side.

Damien sniffed the other hand sharply this time. 'I can smell her.' His neck twitched repeatedly. As he watched the blaze from afar he could barely keep his red eyes open. 'I wish I could fly right up to the sky, but I can't.'

Neither brother mentioned the kill, or the child that would never be born as they travelled southbound: job done.

Chapter Five

On a tree stump, in a cool, shadowy corner but clearly visible to anyone entering Groggs Park was the decapitated, scorched head of a dog on a pole.

Vicky cringed. 'I've been to some pretty horrendous barbie's but that takes the biscuit.'

'Worryingly, whoever did that appears to have taken great pleasure in also displaying their handy work,' said Dylan.

'I feel sick. Whatever we thought about Freddy Knapton, whoever did this to his dog is severely disturbed. He wasn't a murderer.'

Dylan took a moment. 'As far as we know.'

Vicky's expression hardened. 'I always thought the scroat would end up dead by the hands of someone with a short fuse. He could be a vile git. He'd spit in people's faces and tell them he had AIDS you know.'

Dylan shrugged. 'A good egg then?' he said sarcastically with a nod of his head.

Vicky didn't answer. Her thoughts were elsewhere. 'Who do you know that is capable of this?'

Dylan's face was optimistic. 'We can't count anyone out; it could be a long list of suspects.'

Vicky gave Dylan a knowing look.

'Make a note. In the first instance we need to dig deep into Knapton's background and look at his recent movements and acquaintances. Look at any reported incident that involved him. Take hair samples from the dog,' he said with a nod of his head towards the decapitated head on the spike. 'As well as swabs from its mouth.'

'Mmm. You never know the poor animal might have managed to bite it's killer I suppose?'

'Exactly, and what we do know from experience is that most dogs only need brush past us and they'll leave hair on our clothing. That evidence might just tip the balance of the case when we find the culprit.'

Vicky appeared to be weighing up what Dylan had said. 'Do you think he was born evil?' she said.

'What the dog?'

'No stupid! Knapton? As long as I've been in the job he's kept turning up like a bad penny. Any hint of trouble and you can bet Freddy Knapton would be involved in one way or other and those vile tattoos of his, they've given me bloody nightmares.'

'Nightmares?' said Dylan with a furrowed brow. On seeing the question linger, in his eyes, she quickly went on.

'You've no idea how many times I've had to count them tattoos and list them to update his personal record,' she said. 'Every one of them related to hate, killing or something evil.'

'What his past arrest history tells me is that he was put up for adoption at birth. His adopted parents, they couldn't cope and he was put into care. Where he remained until the state deemed him old enough to go-it-alone. Who are we to judge? Being violent, a bully, might be the only way he survived.'

'Or a reaction to the way he was treated?'

Dylan tutted. 'Life certainly wouldn't have been easy for the young Freddy Knapton. But, that doesn't justify the way he went on to treat people as a grown-up.'

'Any relatives still alive do you know?'

'No. There is no information to suggest there is.'

Vicky's eyes looked downcast. 'He'll have a pauper's funeral. A simple service, conducted in a vacant slot, probably early one morning; transported in a van, not a hearse, and his ashes will be scattered across the crematoriums grounds. Vicky raised her eyes to Dylan. 'Could we at least ask them to put his dog in with him. In the cheap box?'

'You big softie?' said Dylan, turning to her.

Vicky's heart and her head were at odds, 'Well, what harm would it do?'

'Ask if you want. They can only say no,' Dylan said with a wink of his eye. 'Come on, let's get back to the nick; get the incident room up and running and I'll let the press office know what we've got so far. Take this down.'

Without words Vicky flipped over the cover of her pocket book and her pen was poised.

'I want any CCTV in the area collated and those car park ticket machines,' he said, pointing in the direction of the entrance to the park. Dylan looked thoughtful. 'I wonder how many vehicles were in the car park at the time? Let's see if the pay stations can prove useful, for once. And, we will need Knapton's last known address.'

Vicky was subdued. 'I'm sure that's not going to be hard considering how frequently we had him in for questioning.'

'Let's hope his killer or killers aren't hard to get hold of either,' said Dylan abruptly. The fact that the attack was violent, planned and the perpetrators appeared to have taken pleasure in it concerned him deeply.

As they walked together back towards the car a glance at the park wall showed Dylan some graffiti which grabbed his attention. Vicky followed his gaze. 'Kids with spray paint in this park, a problem do you know?'

'Don't think so. I've never heard anything to suggest that it's a problem.' Vicky showed Dylan her bottom lip.

The spray painting was of a bald headed man looking over a fence. He knew from school that the cartoon had become prominent during the second world war in America, before it came to England. 'It was known as Chad and it appeared all over the place when I was a kid. It had several tags, the word what, spelt W O T. Like "WOT NO CIGS" or "WOT NO SPUDS" or any commodity that was scarce at the time.'

'Never heard of it.' Vicky's face looked puzzled.

'You're too young.' Dylan carried on walking.

'You're not that old surely,' she said as she caught up.

Dylan couldn't help but raise a smile. 'I don't actually remember it being used. But I know it stopped being used as soon as things were no longer rationed.'

He strode towards the wall, across the grass, and Vicky followed close behind.

'Look at this one it's not been here since the war,' he said. 'Could this be the killer's tag do you think?'

'Cool bananas. That's good. Whoever's done that spray painting is pretty damn talented.'

'Let's have it photographed and paint samples taken.' Dylan looked around him. 'Get the bins checked in case there is any discarded aerosols that we might get prints from.'

'You must have been reading my mind,' said Vicky looking amused.

'God forbid that should ever happen.'

The setting up of an incident room was routine for the head of a major incident team. The main focus was to be moving the investigation forward at all times. Dylan drafted the press release to be given out by Harrowfield Headquarters press office for immediate release:

'A murder investigation has been launched in Harrowfield after the discovery of a young man's body in Union Street, close to the multi-storey car park, in the town centre, this morning. The deceased who is known to the police suffered a serious wound to his neck. The man's pet dog was also found dead in the nearby Croggs park. It had been subjected to a sustained brutal attack. Police are appealing for witnesses who may have seen anything or anyone acting suspicious in, or around these areas. The deceased's identity will not be released until family members have been traced and notified. Detective Inspector Jack Dylan is leading the investigation and he said, "The attacker or attacker's clothing would be heavily bloodstained and I urge anyone with any information to contact me or a member of my team at Harrowfield police station, in confidence." A post-mortem will be carried out and further information will be released in due course.'

Dylan knew full well that the little, young blue-eyed, blonde Connie Seabourne from the press office would be on the phone for more information as soon as she received the update. For now, that would have to do, to help her keep the media happy while the team gathered more information they could share with the press.

'Boss, according to Shooter...' Dylan's look caused Ned to offer an explanation, 'Community Bobby, PC Sharpe – sharp-shooter, he used to be in Firearms' Dylan's blank expression didn't change.

'Well, he tells me that Knapton was squatting in the semi-derelict Old School House, less than a mile from where he was found.'

Vicky watched Dylan who was still looking at Ned.

'What are you standing around for?' said Dylan, 'Go!'

Ned was heading for his jacket draped over the back of his office chair.

'Uniform are already en route to seal the area off, and I'm arranging for Sergeant Clegg and his search team from the support unit to attend,' said Vicky.

'Well done. Don't forget the risk assessments.'

'Seriously?' she said. 'As if we haven't enough to do!'

'Your job, your shout Sarge.' Dylan's manner was abrupt.

'Don't you just love Health & Safety? What's wrong with plain and simple common bloody sense?' Vicky muttered under her breath as she followed him into his office.

'It's no use moaning. Litigation is the last thing any police force needs, risk assessments have to be carried out, recorded and retained as part of everyday policing nowadays, and you know it.' He sat behind his desk.

'No wonder Stonestreet talks so fondly of the good old days,' she said sitting down opposite Dylan. He picked up his pen and put his head down as if to write, but the pen only hovered over the blank piece of paper. After a moment or two he sat back in his chair and appeared deep in thought. 'Yes, well it wasn't a bed of roses then either, believe me,' he said solemnly. Dylan sat up swiftly and leaned forward towards her pointing his finger. 'Those forms,' he said nodding in her direction. 'They won't fill themselves in.'

Dylan picked up his mobile to ring Jen, it was the first opportunity he'd had to see how she was. There wasn't a cat in hells chance he was going to be home in time for tea, just as DS Jon Summers walked in to his office. 'Boss, Control have been trying to contact you over the radio. I've informed them you're in the station.' The words had hardly tumbled from Jon's mouth before the office phone started to ring; Dylan picked up.

'Jack Dylan, just give me a moment.' He placed his hand over the receiver. 'Put the kettle on Jon will you, we need to discuss staffing levels for the Knapton murder.'

Vicky stood up as if to leave.

'Stay where you are,' Dylan said. 'I might need you to get things off the ground with the Knapton murder if I'm required elsewhere.'

Jon left the room in haste. Vicky sat back down.

'Sorry, I'm back with you now,' said Dylan his eyes still on Vicky's face.

'Force Control Sir, Duty Inspector is requesting your attendance at a double fatal house fire at Merton Manor. Apparently all early indications confirm that we have an arson attack.'

'Okay, let those in attendance know I'm en route.'

'For your information Sir, the fire brigade are still on site.'

Dylan texted Jen as they waited for Jon's return. 'Picked up a murder and en route to what appears to be another. I'll be in touch, love you. Are you feeling any better?'

Jen clutched onto the fact that the test taken after the bleed told her she was still pregnant. However, she had a niggling feeling that something wasn't right.

'We're fine. Make sure you get something to eat. Love you too,' she texted back.

Jen, in Sibden Park was distracted by her daughters cry. 'More! More!' the child was shouting as the swing slowed to a stop. Affording herself a smile Jen pushed her once more. A warm breeze was playing with the hem of her skirt. 'Just a few more minutes, then we really must go.'

She turned at the sound of their Golden Retriever barking, and in doing so only just stood clear of her daughters kicking legs. Max ran excitedly from the nearby copse. Reaching her he leaped up and down nuzzling her leg. She greeted him with a stroke of his soft, honey coloured head but he continued to jump up and down. 'Look out, you daft animal. You're slobbering all over my trousers.' Max had been chasing around all the while they had been at the park and his tongue was hanging out, saliva running from his jowls. Jen walked grinning towards Maisy, whose smile had turned into a frown at her mother's cross tone. Jen put out her arms when she reached her daughter and scooped her out of the swing. Popping the tired little girl in her pushchair with a kiss on her cheek, Jen put the dog on his lead and headed homeward.

Before the three reached the gate at Sibden Park she saw Maisy's head flop to her chest and a few seconds later to one side and she knew she was asleep. Taking the bridle path Jen found the going hard; one minute she was pushing the pram and the next pulling it over the uneven pathway. As she struggled on, her arms hurt from shoulder to wrist. Tired as she was her eyes began to sting with unspent tears of her growing frustration. Once at the top of the hill she stopped to catch her breath and admire the view. Far enough from the road she could hear the sound of the birds. Below her, she could see the river flowing over the boulders jutting out of the water. Only in the distance could she hear the hum of the traffic. Max sat down at her feet. The wooden bench beckoned her. Her quick bright smile at the dog belied her feelings inside. She sat. Her thoughts deepened. As if sensing her sadness Max moved closer to her and rested his body comfortingly against her leg. Tears threatened. She stroked Max around his ears and bit her lip hard. The disappointment of Dylan was still in her and, for all she was worth, she could not let it go. The more she thought about Dylan's commitment to his work, the police promotion system, and how it had let her husband down once again, the more upset she became. There was no doubt about it, the Police promotion system stank nearly as much as the lip service given to the grievance procedure and the equal opportunities they boasted about.

Those who presided over these things never took into account the demands and pressures of the individual's daily role. It wasn't about how good a police officer you were, but the courses you had been on and the company you kept. What she found hard to understand was why an intelligent man like Dylan believed otherwise? And he did. 'Why are you bothered?' he would say to her. 'The higher up the tree they go the more of their arse they show.' And he'd laugh. A sob caught in Jen's throat and she choked back her tears. She presumed that after being a member of the establishment for so many years he had been hoodwinked and brainwashed by those that he took his orders from; for she could only assume that if he didn't believe in their integrity how could he possible put his life in their hands on a daily basis? Her present role as personnel clerk had truly opened her eyes. The likes of Chief Superintendent Walter Hugo-Watkins and her own supervisor Avril Summerfield-Preston spent their time openly courting the people they thought could give them a leg up in their careers. They didn't care one jot about the public or the victims of crime, they only cared about themselves, for the higher up the pecking order they got before they retired meant they'd get a bigger pension. Jen took a deep invigorating breath that filled her lungs as she stood up. She shook her head and wiped her eyes whilst considering her descent. The path ahead was well worn by dog walkers and travellers alike.

'We'll be off now,' she told the curious magpie who had been watching her for the past five minutes. She took the brake off the pram and, pushing it towards the bird, watched it take to the skies. 'Fly away you coward,' she said though gritted teeth. 'Although,' she sighed as she pushed the pram down the hill. 'If I had wings, I'd be off too.' She looked down at Max and he looked up at her with his big, brown, sad eyes. 'Don't worry fella,' she said. I wouldn't want to go it alone, not without Maisy, Dylan and you.' Max forged ahead as if consoled. She pushed the pram faster down the hill after him, until she was almost running. Feeling the sweat forming on her face she stopped at the river to wipe her brow. She let out a deep breath through pursed lips. Luckily for the public, the majority of officers got on with the job they were paid to do. The only status she wanted Dylan to achieve now was retired; if the workload didn't retire him first. She was angry, she was emotional, what the hell was wrong with her? Oh, yes, she was pregnant, she was anxious, she was frightened; why in god's name did her mum have to die so young? And why did Dylan have to work such long hours; she felt alone, very alone.

**

'More bodies?' said Vicky. 'You're never satisfied with just the one are you Dylan?'

'If only! The story of my life. You okay keeping hold of the reins on the Knapton murder for the time being whilst I go with Jon and assess what's been discovered at Merton?'

'Sure. Before you go though, just so you're aware, I've been informed a call came in yesterday from an irate man complaining about Knapton.'

'Go on,' he told her as he grabbed his shirt cuff in a fisted hand before putting his arm into his suit jacket.

'Basically, he was claiming Knapton had almost given his mother a heart attack when his dog attacked her Yorkshire terrier. The Yorkie had to be treated at the vets for shock. He ended the call with a threat. Just the norm. If we didn't do something about Knapton, he would. Control passed it for the attention of the local community officer, no instant response required, and let's face it with Knapton's behaviour, calls like that about him are two-a-penny.'

'All the same, make sure someone speaks to the caller as a priority. Anything that comes in that you think I should know about, ring me. I'm on my mobile.'

He stood quietly for a moment studying the implications of what she had said. 'That incident, see if you can find out the time it happened, it may be the caller or his mother was the last person to see Freddie Knapton alive.'

Chapter Six

The emergency services responded quickly to a three nines call alerting them to the fire at Merton Manor. However, their progress was impeded by the rural locality. The police helicopter had been directed to attend.

'I want aerial photographs. Whose working in the air support team?' said Dylan.

'PC Rothwell confirmed the helicopter airborne sir and you can speak to her on channel 2.'

Dylan breathed a sigh of relief, 'Good. ETA?'

'Travelling approximately two miles per minute, as the crow flies. Taking into account the tail wind, which will speed them up, it'll take them around nine to ten minutes, sir.'

Flying high and keeping a safe distance, it was deemed by the helicopter crew that the neighbouring properties were not at risk and suggested the country road nearest the manor house was cordoned off accordingly. Because of the quick response, Dylan was told en route that the fire brigade had the blaze under control. The house however, had suffered serious damage. So much so that there were concerns for its structural stability and the safety of the personnel in attendance at the scene. Fire scene investigators were on site, routinely called for fires as severe as this. The initial assessment of the situation by the fire crew suggested an explosion had occurred in the downstairs area of the home but they were satisfied that there was more than one seat of fire, due to the intense burning of areas on the upper floor.

The only means of access to the upstairs of Merton Manor was by way of the fire brigade's ladders due to the fact that the staircase had perished. Parts of the upstairs floor were deemed unsafe. Wesley Crutcher, the fire investigator on site, took careful steps throughout the smouldering building. His tour halted by the sight of human remains. A charred skeleton lay amongst the remnants of the bed in what was thought to be the main bedroom because of its position in the house and its size. Wesley glanced around him and considered his route amongst the debris before carefully moving into another room where the remains of another badly charred skeleton, this time bent and twisted in what looked like a foetal position, was found.

The body, although unrecognisable, had a bullet hole in the skull. In his experience, he was aware that this fire was most probably a deliberate attempt to hide the fact that a person had been killed, and to destroy evidence. His job now was to keep the scene as sterile as possible until the police evidence gatherers arrived.

Dylan was the first to receive this information via the Control Room operator. Merton Manor was approximately thirty minutes' drive away from Harrowfield Police Station and while Jon drove, Dylan was occupied issuing instructions over the airways. 'It's very important that the details of everyone who's attended the scene, and where they've been within that scene, is recorded,' he said. 'I want the time of their arrival, and their departure noted.' Mentally he prepared himself. He needed a loggist: a running incident log that would record everything in chronological order. He repeated the importance of this to the operator as Merton Manor was a crime scene and it needed to be treated as such, as per Home Office guidelines.

Jon's foot was pressed flat down on the accelerator and the car picked up speed as they hit the moorland stretch of open road. The siren's activated when necessary to alert motorists ahead that they were required to move out of their path.

'Call the crime scene supervisor and crime scene investigators. I want them to meet me at the scene as soon as possible. The rendezvous point will be the road outside the entrance to the grounds,' said Dylan.

Jon was quietly concentrating on the job in hand to get the Senior Investigative Officer to the scene of the incident safely and as soon as humanly possible, because nothing would move now until he was on site.

'To save lives and make the property safe I know it's unavoidable that the emergency services are all over the scene without giving the contamination issue a second thought. But, in all probability it means vital evidence, that may help us convict the offender is lost forever,' said Dylan to Jon. He dialled the number for the CID office and waited for the pick-up. The hedges on the country lanes were high and Dylan was tossed from side to side in the passenger seat of the police car.

'Harrowfield CID. DS Rajinder Uppal speaking.'

'Raj, good, they called you in. Get me any intelligence you can on Merton Manor and its owners will you?'

Dylan grabbed hold of the door handle at the sight of the sharp bend. Jon drove the car into it at speed and narrowly missed hitting an oncoming tractor on the other side. Dylan was thrown towards the console with some force, his seatbelt saved him from hitting the windscreen but he continued issuing orders to Raj, his mind locked into the process of dealing with the initial stages of a major incident.

As Jon stopped the car outside the entrance of the manor house, Dylan could hear the drone of the helicopter circling above them. Jon had completed the task of getting Dylan to the scene as he did everything else, with his unique ability to make everything look effortless no matter how stressful.

'Overhead,' said PC Rothwell via Channel 2.

'Are you getting the aerial shots Lisa?'

'Yes, I'm up front doing the camera work sir. Leave it to me.'

Dylan turned to Jon. 'Feel free to add your two-penneth if you think I've missed anything,' he said, his brows knitted together.

'No sir,' Jon said, his mouth turned up at one corner. 'I think you've covered everything and you'll find I never waste time voicing an opinion unless it's asked for.'

The art of being a good supervisor in Dylan's eyes was knowing the strengths in others, and in Jon Summers he knew he had the mind of an officer who could spot a pattern, and draw accurate conclusions where others would struggle. A characteristic most useful that had helped him obtain a degree in applied maths followed by a PHD and a previous career as a university lecturer at one of the top engineering departments in the UK. 'Why in God's name did you decided to jump ship and do this god-forsaken job, I will never know,' Dylan said as he opened the car door and alighted.

Jon looked slightly bemused, but followed his boss. He slammed the door behind him as he stepped out onto the grass. 'Probably for the same reason as you, sir,' he said. 'I want to see wrong doer's punished.'

The men looked around them as they stood on the grass verge, the house was half a mile up the driveway. 'Tell me, why did you decide to have the rendezvous point so far away?' asked Jon.

'I want to survey the scene from here. We'll need a uniform officer at this entrance. Nothing enters without my say so from now on. Can you get on to control and tell them we've arrived and I want this entrance protected as soon as possible? I'll be back in a minute,' he said as he walked a few yards towards the stone pillars. He took a three hundred and sixty-degree view as he went. When he reached the pillars he noticed that one was engraved with the word 'Merton' and a fallen pillar to the right 'Manor'. He noted the absence of working gates. There was nothing suggesting that the gated entrance had been fit for purpose for some considerable time.

A rusty, metal, link chain was hanging precariously from the right pillar 'Private,' he read on this weathered sign and 'No Through Road on another.' Just below, his eyes were drawn to a dark paint mark that ran down the edge, just above knee height. Dylan bent down to his haunches on seeing debris also scattered at its base. 'Relevant?' he thought. 'What vehicle might have caused that was the question, and although the debris looked recent, how recent?' he wondered. He made a mental note to check what colour the cars were that belonged to the owners of the house? Or was it possible that it was one of the emergency vehicles in attendance at the scene that had collided with the pillar in their haste?' His investigative mind questioned the discovery. Purposefully he strode the few yards back to Jon, who he saw was back inside the vehicle, putting his phone away.

'What's the ETA for the extra uniform?' Dylan asked, sitting in the seat beside him.

'Looks like they're here.' Jon's eyes upturned to fix on the rear view mirror. Dylan eyes flew sideways to the wing mirror to see a marked police car heading towards them. He opened his car door and alighted. Jon joined him to greet the two officers.

PC Shelagh MacPhee and PC Tracy Petterson were out of the car swiftly. There were no pleasantries at their meeting with the men but an acknowledging nod of the heads. Dylan took no time in explaining to the officers exactly what he wanted them to do, which he would reiterate to their supervision Inspector Peter Reginald Stonestreet once he was located on site, to ensure compliance with Dylan's specific instruction.

'Most importantly we need a log of every person entering or leaving the scene. Nobody enters without my permission and their vehicle details, make, model, colour and registration number etcetera must be recorded. The right hand pillar,' he said turning his head to point to the offending stone, has damage. It looks to me like it's recent. There may be chance for us to collect a paint sample. There's debris at the base. Can you put police cones around it for now to protect it until scenes of crime have examined it? I'll ensure CSI do it as a priority.'

The uniformed officers spoke sharply, in unison, 'Yes sir.'

The police officers leaned into the car and busily collected what they required to complete the task they had been given.

Jon walked alongside Dylan to their vehicle. It was now apparent to him what his boss had been doing at the entrance. Without Jack Dylan's investigative experience it may have been overlooked by others who would have travelled directly up the driveway to the scene of the fire.

'I'll drive slowly. We don't want to miss anything.'

Dylan smiled. This quiet and gentle talking man, Dylan began to feel, would be an asset to his team, not just this enquiry; he learned fast.

They had driven but a few feet beyond the gate when Dylan slammed his hand on the dashboard. 'Stop!' He got out of the car and Jon went to stand by his side.

'See those recent tyre tracks on the lawn?'

Jon nodded.

'We need castings and soil samples taken.'

Jon drew a notebook from inside his jacket pocket and scribbled the action down.

'See that Jon,' said Dylan now pointing his finger to a patch of earth where something, until very recently, had obviously stood. 'Another staddlestone, do you think?' he said observing the others.

'Whatever it was, it was heavy, but it must be worth something for someone to go to the trouble of stealing it. Maybe all will be apparent when we see photographs of the house.'

The two men's looked directly up towards the house. 'I don't think we'll be lucky to find anything intact in there, do you?'

'Maybe they've staff who might tell us?'

'Good point, it's not an opportunist job this, you can guarantee that looking at the location,' he told Jon. 'I think we'll walk from here to be on the safe side.' Dylan paused at more upturned turf. 'If I were a guessing man I'd say someone's either a crap driver, or under the influence.' Dylan stopped at several more points to examine the skid marks that had chewed up more of the beautiful lawned garden. 'Sacrilege,' he said shaking his head. 'Let's have those tyre marks checked too, to see if they belong to the same vehicle?'

Again Jon noted his request for the action in his notebook. 'And the dead rabbit, do you want that too?' said Jon, pointing to the dead animal at his feet.

'Yes, make a note; blood samples, DNA and soil samples. There is no doubt in my mind it's recently been mowed down. It might help us place a particular vehicle here, you never know, stranger things have happened.'

The men moved forward their senses heightened. 'Would you mind talking me through your approach to the scene sir?' said Jon.

Dylan looked at the officer and nodded. 'A good investigator will always consider the approach to a crime scene; that of the emergency services already in attendance and their subsequent path,' he said. 'Never, ever leave anything to chance. Don't always take the obvious route. That'll give you another opportunity to secure uncontaminated evidence.' Dylan stopped and looked up towards the smouldering building whose black smoke and scattering embers blighted a view of the beautiful countryside ahead of them. 'I know what you're thinking Jon.' Dylan took a few steps to the left and carried on. 'Those tyre tracks, the paint and the debris on the stone pillar, they could belong to any vehicle friend or foe, but as investigator's we can never take the liberty of assuming. Everything that we see as "out of the norm" at a scene has to be questioned and acted upon to be sure it isn't connected or, if eventually the evidence proves to us that it is, and helps us in some way. It's all part of the incident jigsaw puzzle which usually starts with the SIO being handed a rogue piece of blue sky.' He stopped and once more did a scan of the scene from the location.'

As they got closer the scene looked busier and was noisier. Jon was very quiet. 'You okay?' said Dylan.

'Actually, I was just thinking about the rabbit. There's another one. My boys used to have rabbits. Salt and Pepper.'

Dylan looked down at the ground. Jon Summers was known for adopting trousers that were too short for his legs and, when off duty, shirts with vivid and flowery patterns. It made Dylan smile. 'I'd like a son.'

Striding over the rabbit and onto the final hundred meters to the house, Dylan discreetly took stock of the new detective sergeant on his team, and he liked what he saw and heard. At just over six feet tall, he had a smooth face with small, deeply set hazel green eyes and mole bumps on his cheeks. His fine hair was thinning on top. He'd first met Jon briefly when he had unintentionally landed in CID on a job, where his skill of making bad news sound palatable, combined with a flair for negotiation between waring fractions in uniform, was required. He was commended for finding common ground, highlighting benefits and keeping the communication lines open at the time. Dylan was told by his peers that Jon would make an excellent negotiator and they wanted him to be his mentor. That was some months ago now and he recalled at that time Jon had sported a beard which, to all intent and purpose, had disguised his double chin. The facial hair had made him look younger, in contrast to most other beard wearers. Dylan had dabbled with growing a beard himself once. It made him look like his father.

Jon had a fractured turned up nose that somehow gave him an incongruous, nasty look, on an otherwise harmless looking face. He had a scar above his lip. His first job when he'd left school had been a baker. He told Dylan that he wished he could have claimed that his scar and fractured nose had been from duelling but they had been achieved whilst cycling home on the first of many night shifts in the bakery. He was still a keen cyclist however, an indication to Dylan that this man was no quitter.

'I remember one of my colleagues getting up in the middle of the night because his son's rabbit was making so much noise in the hutch, that it was keeping him and his wife awake. The fool didn't bother to put on any clothes.' Dylan chuckled. 'Walked outside bollock naked, to shout at the animal but he got more than he bargained for when his neighbour's daughter, arriving home from a night out clubbing, walked down the adjoining path with all her mates.' Dylan glanced across at the older man as they walked, and saw his features crinkle into a wry little smile. What the two of them were about to witness in the following hours, they both knew, was going to give them nothing to smile about, but they had much in common, and their camaraderie was to be more closely cemented that day because of it.

'Well, from wild rabbits to wild fires Jon. Let's see what amount of damage the fire has done,' he said climbing flagged steps that would take them to what would soon be known as the inner police cordon. Their eyes lowered to scan the ground beneath their feet.

At the front of the house, Dylan counted three fire engines, turntable ladders aloft, a gas van and a marked police vehicle. Black, yellow and red hoses of different sizes littered the ground. Sporadically they slithered, as if they had a life of their own, making a crunching sound on the saturated gravel as they did so. Puddles of water of various sizes and depths were dotted amongst the little stones. A number of fire officers sat on a long, low brick wall, most in the process of shedding items of outer protective clothing and breathing apparatus. The image of the exhausted looking, soot lathered emergency service workers before him, who had risked life and limb to put out the flames, reminded Dylan of scenes on a spent battlefield. It was time to find out where those in charge were and where possible evidence could be preserved. 'Where are Uniform?' wondered Dylan as, at that very moment, he caught sight of Inspector Stonestreet standing talking to a member of the fire crew under the arched entrance of the property's walled garden.

'What on earth have you got there?' asked Dylan as he approached the men. Peter Reginald Stonestreet was cradling a baby rabbit in the palm of one hand and stroking it with his other.

'Abandoned we think,' he said almost apologetically. 'I couldn't leave it to die now could I?' Dylan closed his eyes momentarily and shook his head. Such an act of kindness to small animals was not unusual for Peter and Dylan should have known that by now.

'I think we may have seen more of the warren near the bottom of the drive' said Dylan.

Peter looked hopeful only to have his hopes quickly dashed.

'Road kill,' said Dylan.

Fire officer Bill Dixon introduced himself to Dylan and Jon.

'We need to know everything you can tell us, from the thread to the needle,' Dylan said to both men.

Inspector Stonestreet related concisely the circumstances and facts of the incident as he had found them. Dylan trusted him implicitly to give him a full and detailed account. Many years after Dylan had ceased to have the older man as his mentor, he found himself at a scene thinking how Peter Reginald Stonestreet would tackle the job himself.

'Emergency services responded to a call from a passing motorist of a large fire at Merton Manor, the exact times are recorded but it was around lunchtime. The fire crew and ourselves were on the scene in less than fifteen minutes.'

Bill Dixon carried on. 'We've tried our best to limit foot traffic and cordon off the scene whilst extinguishing the fire. The house was well ablaze when we arrived. Initially we responded with two tenders believing that to be sufficient to deal with such a fire, but I very quickly realised we needed another. The partly thatched roof caused a vast amount of acrid smoke and fierce flames. It appeared there had also been an explosion, hence the gas services presence. Eventually, once the fire was under control we managed to get a team inside with breathing apparatus. Quite quickly we came across two bodies in upstairs rooms.'

'Are the bodies still in situ?' asked Dylan.

'They are. The staircase in the house, however, isn't. Well, not so as it's fit for purpose. Access to the upper floor is only possible by ladder. It's pretty unstable in places so great care will be required by anyone going up there.' Bill's eyes sought the upper floor window frames. The glass in some of the windows, as you can see, has been blown out.' Shards of glass lay scattered about them amongst the gravel, water and other debris.

'Paramedic's attend?'

'Yes, but there was nothing they could do,' said Bill. 'Names and contact details have been taken for you to get statements.'

Dylan was thoughtful.

'It's not going to be easy to recover the remains of the bodies Dylan,' said Peter.

Dylan gave a lop sided smile. 'I was just thinking the same.'

'Well, there's just a bit of damping down to do. Then our job's done here,' he said. 'I've been told that the team have done a full search and there are no more bodies on site, but it's pretty obvious to us that the fire wasn't accidental.'

'Why's that?' said Dylan.

'A brief look around the manor by my officers has shown up a number of things for you to be aware of. Number one, in the kitchen all the gas rings on the stove were turned on. Now they either knew it was an older stove and had no flame safety device fitted, or they just got lucky. Two, there are two seats of fire in the upper floor, one in each of the bedrooms where the remains of the bodies were found. Although they are burnt beyond visual recognition, what is clearly visible are bullet holes in the skulls. On your colleagues' instructions once that had been ascertained, we came out of the premises to await your arrival. I can show you, from the fire investigations approach my findings and those of my colleague Wesley Crutcher when we go back inside together, if that helps?'

'That would be great, once our crime scene investigators and the exhibits team arrive. We'll need to get suited up and then we can go inside together. I may require a forensic fire expert. But, it could be sometime before I can get them on site,' Dylan turned to Inspector Stonestreet. 'What do we know about the people who lived here, anything?'

'The Isaac Art Emporium, they own it. It's been in the family for donkey's years. It was in need of modernisation until fairly recently when it was left to Jake Isaac in his father's will, and Jake, who is quite a bit older than his wife Leah, had it renovated into a modern family home. Quiet couple by all accounts, he's seldom seen other than going to and fro to work in the upper floors of the Art Emporium in town. They aren't ever seen on the social scene; he doesn't give interviews - appears that they prefer to keep their family life private. Mrs Leah Isaac again, keeps herself very much to herself, although the people we have spoken to say she's friendly enough. Apparently Detective Constable Rupert Charles paid them a visit a month ago. I'm making enquiries into what for. This certainly has all the makings of robbery gone wrong, doesn't it?'

Dylan knew Peter was probably right in his judgement, but he didn't respond. He needed to make up his own mind once he had seen the inside of the crime scene, held all the information the professional experts at his disposal told him, and took heed of his instincts.

The additional officers requested to present themselves at the site were now beginning to arrive. As the SIO, Dylan's first job was to ensure that everyone knew what they were doing. He needed an officer to take charge of gathering evidence outside the property, such as the dead rabbits, and to look at what the tyre tracks could reveal. Dylan was more than aware that blood or fur from a dead animal may easily be found in the wheel arch of any subsequent connected vehicle found. These samples would be what were termed controlled samples. This was no time to be sensitive. The animals were dead and they could ultimately help put the offenders before the courts. Soil samples needed to be collected, as did the paint Dylan had spotted on the stone gate pillars at the entrance. Video footage from the fire-engines on their approach would need to be retrieved as well as tyre tread marks of emergency vehicles that were had been present; for elimination purposes.

'Bill,' Dylan said. 'Before I forget. Have you or any of your staff taken any photographs?'

'Yes, it's routine for training purposes. Is there a problem?'

'No, but I need them - all of them. I've got to have the originals and any copies for future disclosure to the defence teams, along with any notes, logs etcetera that the brigade may have, and that also includes the recordings of the emergency call reporting the fire.'

Bill's shoulders dropped. 'Of course.'

'I know it's a ball ache. But it's an absolute necessity otherwise any future court case could be thrown out if we don't comply with disclosure.'

'I know I understand,' he said. 'I'll ensure everything is collated and passed to your exhibits officer.'

Dylan continued to listen intently to what he was being told by the Inspector and the fire officer. Jon took notes in his pocket book. Reticent of Jon's character he didn't interrupt, or waste time voicing any opinion but methodically noted details to share with his colleagues at a later time in the debrief.

'Please pass on my thanks to the team for their gallant efforts,' said Dylan to the fire officer. Turning to Jon, Dylan instructed him to take charge of the outer cordon of the crime scene, with respect to the evidence gathering. The update on the radio announced the arrival of on duty Crime Scene Investigator Supervisor Sarah Jarvis and Mark Hamilton in the next convoy of emergency service vehicles. All were being directed to the rendezvous point.

Jarv threw Dylan a package as he walked towards her. He caught it in both hands and immediately tore it open with the ease of someone who had done the act a hundred times before.

'DI Jack Dylan,' she said to Mark Hamilton. 'Dylan, Mark Hamilton, Crime Scene Investigator latest edition to our team.'

'Pleased to meet you Mark,' said Dylan offering his hand to the six foot, athletic looking man. Mark was clean shaven with a pale complexion and blue eyes. He bent down to put a leg into his coverall. His head was shaven and showed a cut to the top.

'That looks nasty,' said Dylan, observing the wound.

Mark put his hand directly to his head and laughed. 'Worse than it looks sir. At forty-six I should know better than to still be playing footie for my local, on a Saturday afternoon.'

Jarv cocked her head at her colleague. 'You'll get on you two,' said Jarv. 'He's as OCD about orderliness as you are, sir.'

'Nothing wrong with that Jarv,' said Dylan who was now suited and booted apart from the gloves, which he took from a paper tissue sized box, offered to him by her.

Detective Sergeant Jon Summers, satisfied he had organised the necessary actions to be carried out by others on the outer cordon, joined them at the CSI van and also put on his protective gear.

Dylan took his mobile out of his pocket and telephoned the office to ensure the local intelligence officers had started researching the Isaac family, reinforcing as he did so its urgency. 'We need an exhibits officer,' he said in what was almost a whisper, and at the same time as he finished putting on his gloves he saw Detective Constable Andy Wormald talking to PC Shelagh MacPhee. 'Andy, you're exhibits on this one,' he shouted. 'Get booted and suited, quick as you can mate.' Andy Wormald raised his hand in acknowledgement.

The small team including the fire fighter Bill Dixon walked as quickly as their protective coveralls would allow back into the mutilated shell of the manor house. A solemn look upon their faces. There was a feeling of anticipation in the air and words were not spoken as their senses began to heighten and adrenaline pumped through their veins.

Astonishingly the exterior front door and door frame were still intact. The door was unlocked.

Amid echoes and periods of eerie silence Dylan could hear the slight burring of the Crime Scene Investigation camera recording. Still photographs, he was well aware, were being taken at the same time.

The kitchen, Dylan was told could be accessed directly through the hallway door but there was an entrance nearer to the right of the front door, situated at the bottom of the staircase. This route would take them to the kitchen via the dining area.

Everywhere Dylan looked there were charred remains. The walls were blackened from smoke which was only broken up in a few places by blobs of melted wall lights. Part-burnt picture frames hung in a haphazard fashion. The subject of the images too damaged to tell what they had once portrayed. Bits of material draped from the furniture of which most were now just a frame, a shell. He could still feel the heat inside the building and the smell of the smouldering, damp wood was prominent.

In the kitchen, the large stove oven was the next area of attention. Although there had been an explosion and intense heat, the mangled shell revealed the melted gas hob switches were all indeed switched on, as he had been advised previously. There were no visible utensils on top of the cooker.

'Classic deliberate act, don't you agree?' said Dylan to a group of nodding heads.

The team were led to the ladders that the fire brigade had put in place to give them access to the upper floor.

Bill Dixon led the way. At the base of the ladder he turned to those that followed. 'Be careful. Follow me, and keep as close to the walls as possible and we should be okay.' The fire officer's face was semi-concealed by the lack of light in the hallway. He put his foot on the first rung of the ladder. He carried with him a large Dragon lamp that illuminated their way into a dark chasm.

It was bad enough climbing up the ladders for Dylan. At the best of times he didn't have a head for heights, but in the ill-fitting coveralls and cloth boots the short journey was treacherous and very slow work. Climbing back down would be just as difficult, if not worse, he feared the nearer the top he got.

The fire officer had been in the scene before so it was sensible for him to lead the team into what he believed had been the main bedroom. On entering the room, the smell changed dramatically. Dylan's tongue instinctively rolled to the roof of his mouth as if to block his gullet. The sickly, sweet odour was a 'lingers in-your-nose-forever' smell that was never to be forgotten. He'd smelt burning flesh before on occasions. It could be likened to beef fat cooking in a frying pan - but this was not a pleasant odour.

Jon looked across at Dylan. 'I used to wonder why burning human flesh smelt so different. Then I researched it. Processed meat from animals is relatively free of blood and other fluids. Human flesh still has all those things floating around in it, and that makes the smell much worse.'

'So strong that you can almost taste it,' said Bill.'

Mark gagged. 'Always makes me feel nauseous,' he said. 'Can't eat for hours afterwards. The sensation it gives you, stays in your head.'

'You'll get used to it Mark,' said Jarv hovering closely over the blackened burnt shell of a body with her camera. The charred remains lay sprawled out on what was clearly once a bed. Visible on the skull was a hole to the rear.

In the second bedroom was another burnt body. There was less flesh on this skeleton but like the first a bullet wound could be seen on the skull.

'These are your two seats of fire,' said Bill. 'And we know some kind of accelerant was used. I suggest what happened is that these two were killed upstairs first, the fire was started to try and conceal their deaths as murder, and on leaving the scene the perpetrator turned on the gas downstairs which led to the gas explosion to further guarantee there was as little evidence as possible left for you guys to find, in order to trace them.'

'That seems like a reasonable assumption to me,' said Dylan. 'Could you liaise with our forensic officer who is experienced in arson investigations? I'll let you know when we have an ETA.'

'Sure,' said Bill. 'This one's a first for me; I've been to a lot of fatal fires over the years but never any where the occupants have been shot as well.'

'Executed, these two were executed. For now, we have to presume that the badly burnt bodies are the owners of the house and we'll have to prove their identities. Which by the looks of it may be down to the examination of their teeth as we don't seem to have much more than burnt skeletal remains.'

Satisfied there were no other bodies upstairs, the police team gingerly stepped down the ladder back to the ground floor. Bill slid down the ladder with ease, showing his years of experience with the fire brigade. Dylan took a step at a time, just pleased to reach the bottom rung without any mishap.

Outside the house, the smell of the smoke filled the cool air.

'That smell. Always reminds me of bonfire night,' said Andy.

'Bonfire night reminds me of a burned tongue, from hot booze,' said Jarv, sticking her tongue out slightly whilst firmly holding it between her teeth.

'Squeezing hot dog mustard down my jeans,' said Mark.

'Toffee apples.' Jarv licked her lips.

'The Robert Catesby failed gun powder plot to blow up the Houses of Parliament,' said Jon.

'Robert Catesby?' said Jarv.

'Yes, it was his idea; he led the group.'

'Guy Fawkes was in charge of guarding the thirty-six barrels of gunpowder in the cellars of the Houses of Parliament,' said Dylan.

'Well, you learn something new every day,' said Jarv with the toss of her head.

Dylan strolled around, a little away from the others. Questions chasing each other around in his head. He answered them in order of priority. He needed time to gather the large amount of information that he had taken on board and to think about the way forward. The priorities were clear enough to him. Arranging and ensuring that a careful and thorough search of the building was paramount. He was well aware that there may be a weapon inside, hidden amidst the burnt timbers and pile upon pile of debris. He considered what specialists were available to him to assist Would the forensic specialist in arson be able to tell him anything more than the firefighters already had? He was well aware, depending on the experience of the person called upon, that their knowledge would be paramount to helping him identify the accelerant sooner rather than later.

The recovery of the two bodies was causing him to feel anxious. They needed to recover the spent bullets and the casings if they were on site. He wondered if the Isaac family were firearm's licence holders? A check back at the station would quickly give him that answer. His immediate job was to establish the second incident room and then speak to Connie Seabourne at Headquarters press office. This was going to be a high profile investigation and the media would be all over it like a rash. He could see the headline now, 'Couple Executed Before Mansion Destroyed by Fire'. His mind was buzzing. He knew a few minutes with his mind focused on something else would allow it to settle. Strolling yet further away from the others gave him a moment of privacy he sought to gather his thoughts.

Dylan held his mobile phone in the palm of his hand. He was about to dial when the quickness of a squirrel running up a tree a few feet away from him, grabbed his attention. He stopped and looked about him, Inspector Stonestreet had clearly seen the rodent too. Their eyes met across the debris and they smiled at each other. The Inspector saw how tired Dylan looked and knew only too well the pressure he was under. 'Peter, have we arranged to get flasks and doggy bags out here for the troops? I need to top up my caffeine level and something to eat wouldn't go amiss.'

'En route. Say hello to Jen for me,' Peter called back.

Dylan's head was bent as he tapped numbers into his mobile phone but his eyes were immediately raised to his elder. Peter knew Dylan well.

Chapter Seven

Jen watched Maisy sitting upright asleep in her pushchair in the kitchen. She loosened her outdoor clothes but her daughter didn't wake. The little girl's soft snoring and the way her hair curled into damp tendrils at the nape of her neck reminded Jen so much of her father. A comical little laugh escaped from her lips.

Jen busied herself heating soup for the child's dinner and made ham and cheese sandwiches to share. Eventually she lifted her out of her pushchair to wake her, so exhausted was she from playing in the park she was lethargic. She kissed her sleepy head and sat her on the toilet for a moment or two, talking to her softly as she did so. Maisy, still drowsy, raised her little eyes to Jen and smiled wanly. 'I'm done,' she announced a few minutes later with a widening grin. Maisy jumped down, rolled up her sleeves and pulled her step out to enable her to wash her hands and when she had dried them she ran to sit on her seat at the table. Jen sitting next to her took a hearty bite out of her sandwich and Maisy was spooning a helping of soup into her mouth when the phone rang; it was Dylan.

'What you up to?' he said with a smile in his voice.

'Just having lunch. You?'

'I'm at Merton Manor, or should I say what used to be Merton Manor. There's been a fire, the house is gutted and as if that's not bad enough we've two bodies.'

Jen looked down at the sandwich she held in her hand as he spoke. Her stomach heaved. She pushed her plate to one side and, gagging, she reached for the biscuit tin and took out two ginger biscuits. She snapped one in half, 'An accident?' she said, popping it in her mouth.

'No, arson. It looks like someone has tried to cover up the murders.'

'More murders?'

'Yes, both bodies have bullet wounds.'

'Oh my god.'

'Yeah, so I'm up to my neck in the proverbial again. Remind me, why I do this job?'

Jen nibbled at the biscuit. 'That's simple Jack, you enjoy a challenge and the thrill of the chase. Me, I'm just looking forward to your retirement, and hoping you're not too knackered to enjoy it.'

'Me? Knackered? Never!' he said.

'You going to be late tonight?'

'Not too late I hope, but tomorrow I'm likely to be busy once we've recovered the bodies.'

'Lovely. Something for you to look forward to then?' Jen proffered a groan.

'What's that?'

'A day in the mortuary, I wouldn't sleep tonight if I were you knowing that.'

'It's all part of the job. Hopefully we'll get some clues as to how the fire was started and recover a bullet at the PM. Which may help us nail the killer...'

'I wonder how many hours you've actually spent in a mortuary over the years?'

Jen watched her daughter intently as she concentrated hard on eating her sandwich while her parents talked. Jen offered her another spoonful of soup. Her little mouth opening expectantly reminded Jen of a little bird being fed.

'I dread to think, but it makes me very grateful.'

'What for?' Jen wiped Maisy's mouth with a piece of kitchen roll.

'I walk out at the end of the post-mortem, and not many people can say that.' Dylan chuckled. 'How'd you get on at the hospital?'

'I'm fine.'

'Really?'

'Okay, if you don't want it sugar coated I feel like S. H. I. T. E.' she said. She gave Maisy a wide false smile. In return she saw two little bright eyes smiling back at her.

'And the baby?'

'Stop fussing, it's all good. It's my hormones, they're all over the place.'

'Good,' he said distractedly. 'Maybe we should think about getting a bigger house now that we're having another?'

Jen felt an overwhelming feeling of panic wash over her. 'Maybe,' she said abruptly.

'That reminds me, work wise, have you informed all those that need to be aware that you're pregnant?'

'I had to because I had to ask for some time off today. Beaky looked at me as though I'd thrown a rotten egg at her, but that's the kind, considerate supervisor Avril Summerfield- Preston is and we're not going to change her now, are we?'

'Better the devil you know, as they say. Peter Stonestreet sends his regards. I'll have to go. Give Maisy a big hug and I'll ring you, as usual, when I'm heading home.'

Jen's eyes found the hospital paraphernalia over spilling out of her handbag. She plucked out her appointment card and threaded it through her fingers. It was a different size and colour this time round. Being Consultant led was going to mean a different approach for this pregnancy she had been told. As she looked at the date of the next appointment it filled her with trepidation; she didn't know why.

***

The much awaited catering van arrived at Merton Manor. The thick brown paper Doggy bags of food for the officers on site were unpacked and handed out to eager outstretched hands. Dylan felt more in need of liquid refreshment. He looked inside the bag he'd been handed which revealed a chocolate bar, an apple and a salad sandwich made with brown bread. A small bottle of water was concealed by a thin white paper napkin. A healthy lunch, and not one he would have chosen, but enough to sustain him. He listened intently to the peace of the countryside, pondering how idyllic the setting was for a family home. Sadly, all that glistened was not gold here though, and the words from one of his favourite Shakespeare plays rolled off his tongue. 'All that glisters is not gold; Often have you heard that told.' Did the large house and its location play a part in the crime? He shuffled off the wall impatient to move forward with the job. He walked towards Jon. 'Anything for me?' Dylan said, looking over his shoulder at the building.

'There doesn't appear to be any security as such, sir.'

'No, I must admit one of the first things I'd have had done would be to have electronic gates at the bottom of the driveway,' he said nodding his head towards the police circus that was gathered there. Dylan looked into his paper cup, drained the remainder of the hot beverage and threw the dregs to the ground. He rubbed the apple on his jacket sleeve, considered its shine to be as good as that of a cricket ball, then took a bite. Juice ran down his chin and he dabbed it with the napkin. 'I'm going back to the station to get the press release done, and while I'm there I'll try get an update on the Knapton murder. Keep an eye on things here will you while I'm gone?' Jon nodded his head. 'I'm on my mobile if you need me.' Jon watched his boss walk towards Inspector Stonestreet.

'Thanks for everything Peter,' said Dylan. 'I always know that if it's you and your team that's working when I get called out to a job nothing's left to chance.' Dylan patted his colleague on the back.

'How's Jen doing? A little bird tells me she's in the family way again?'

'Nothing gets passed you does it? She's emotional.'

'Ah, and it's at times like this she'll miss her mum being around. That was a bad job. She was taken far too soon. Look after her. This is just a job remember. Work to live, don't live to work.' He wagged his figure at Dylan. 'The youngsters have a habit of growing up quickly. I often look at pictures of my girls and say to them, 'You were so cute, what happened?''

'And when you pick yourself up off the floor?' Dylan laughed.

'They know I'm only joking. I might not say it often, but it's all in here,' he said, patting his hand on his heart.'

'But when the job's running what are we supposed to do?' said Dylan.

'I know what you're saying but, I've said it before and I'll keep saying it until you listen, while we must work to live...'

'We shouldn't live to work.'

'That's it son, now look sharp and get this one sorted. It's a bad 'un.'

'Aren't they all?' said Dylan.

'You're not wrong. I didn't think I'd ever say it but I don't miss CID and the long hours. Once my eight-hour shift is done in uniform, it's done, and I'm off home.'

'I'd settle for a twelve hour shift these days and I know Jen would too. I'm just nipping back to the station. I won't be long.'

As Dylan walked away he heard Peter whistling as he knew he often did when he was thinking. Dylan took off his coverall's on leaving the scene and handed them in to be placed in an exhibit bag that would be tagged, for future disclosure, should they be required.

Dylan spoke to Connie at HQ press office about the distribution of the facts he was able to share with the media and what intention he hoped the press release would achieve before he wrote it. 'The fire at Merton Manor, that occurred earlier today, in which two people are known to have died is being treated as murder by the police. An investigation is underway, led by Detective Inspector Jack Dylan. The deceased have yet to be positively identified. We are appealing for anyone who was in the Merton Manor area at the time of the fire, or has any information, no matter how trivial they think it maybe, should without hesitation contact the incident room at Harrowfield police station.'

The CID office was quiet, which meant hopefully that everyone was out and on enquiries. He glanced at his office clock. There had been no update from Vicky regarding the Knapton murder. Dylan decided to quickly check his emails and sift through his in-tray of everyday paperwork which didn't stop because he was dealing with a murder or two. He ensured the cogs were in motion to get the two incident rooms up and running.

On arrival back at the scene of the fire, Dylan's footsteps quickened towards Jarv who told him she had completed the photography and seized relevant samples. CSI Mark Hamilton and Andy Wormald were standing with Jon discussing the large amount of parcelled exhibits that had been collected, bagged and tagged. It appeared, much to Dylan's delight, that Jon was coping admirably. As he suited up for the second time at the scene, he could see that there was only one fire tender now present, which had remained as a precaution, but now they were also preparing to leave.

Jarv, still booted and suited went over the list of what she had done and why with Dylan. She had been extremely thorough. 'We've located two safes in the house sir, both are open but what is unusual for a robbery is that jewellery remains inside. They were opened prior to the start of the fire, confirmed by the pattern and extent of the carbonising within. Forensics are in attendance. It's a David Walker, I don't know if you know him, but he's pretty switched on.'

'Thanks.'

'Moving to the outside of the building, the tyre marks are all cast. The first impressions are that they're all the same type of tyre. The paint sample and debris, as well as photos of gatepost are done. Sergeant Clegg and his team from the support unit are searching the grounds but they've found nothing of note, as yet.'

'Now where's Jon gone?'

She nodded her head in the direction of the detective and forensic expert who had just left the building.

'Bill Dixon said he'll get us full details of his staff compliment on site and the recordings you asked for, along with duty statements from his colleague Wesley Crutcher.'

'Good, if we haven't got them by the first thing tomorrow, get the incident room staff to chase him up will you?'

Dylan left Jarv and walked towards Jon and David. He proffered his hand to the arson specialist. 'The accelerant, I'm certain it's not petrol. I've taken samples.' He held the nylon bags aloft. Dylan looked at him questioningly. 'We use these now to deal with the inevitable evaporation. This will give me best possible chance to trace the origin of the inflammable liquid. Whatever it was, it'll have been extremely diluted due to the amount of water about. I've also found the remains of a plastic bottle,' he said holding up another nylon bag with the vessel inside.

'Looks like a lump of melted candle wax to me,' said Dylan,

'No, it's good, we should be able to do something with that,' said David handing the bags to Andy, the exhibits officer. 'Like Jarv and the fire officer have probably already told you, there's more than one seat of fire on and around both bodies. It's obvious the fires were started to destroy evidence connected to them. The gas taps, all being turned on, inevitably caused the explosion and a secondary fire. Again, to ensure destruction of any evidence and, perhaps whoever started the fires expected the bodies to go undiscovered.'

'Thank you for your time. You've corroborated what the fire officers have already told us.'

Dylan needed a motive. What had been stolen from the house? The safes were open and jewellery remained inside that he would expect to have been of value. He wondered if the bodies had any jewellery on them? Had one of the deceased been forced to open the safes? If the perpetrators had got what they came for, why were the occupants then killed? Did the deceased know the robbers? Or had the robbers been careless enough to let them see their faces? Although Dylan's mind continued to race ahead, his next job was to have the fragile remains of both bodies moved to the mortuary, and the immediate area where they had lain then searched.

'I want the spent bullets,' he said to Jon. 'If we retrieve them ballistics will be able to tell us the type of weapon from which they were fired. It'd be good evidence if we also recover the weapon but even without it they'll be able to tell us if it's been used in other crimes.'

It took a further hour before the two bodies were finally carried from the house in body bags to the awaiting private ambulance that had been sent from Harrowfield coroner's office. They would now be taken to the mortuary.

The search had initially proved negative for spent ammunition on the upper floor and the familiar pang of disappointment replaced the earlier upbeat, positive gut feeling Dylan had initially had.

'I really wanted the shell casings,' he said. However, having seen the destruction inside the house that the fire had caused the fact that they hadn't been located shouldn't have surprised him. On the positive, they had been lucky to recover the bodies in their entirety.

It was late and the team looked done in. He knew it was time to finish for the day. Uniformed officers would remain at the entrance to the driveway to keep the area secure for a few days yet, or until Dylan felt there was no longer a need to protect the scene. He informed those still working that he would brief the enquiry team in the incident room at eight a.m. the next day. The search team would continue to sift through the debris searching for clues. The post-mortems would also take place tomorrow. The thought of the smell of the burnt flesh, in the confined space, on top of the smell of the mortuary did nothing for his stomach, but that was another day. He looked at his watch and contemplated whether to ring Jen to tell her he was on his way home but decided against it. If she had any sense she would have gone to bed and be fast asleep. Maisy had a habit of rising before six o'clock and once she was awake, no one else in the house slept. Little monkey. His face broke into a smile at the thought of her little smiling morning face when she wandered into their bedroom teddy in tow.

It was around ten-thirty when he drove down the cul-de-sac towards the house. He passed a lone man walking his dog, but other than that all was quiet. Physically he could now rest but, mentally his mind, he knew from experience, would be working throughout the night, like it or not. Luckily for him there had been nothing that required his immediate attention on the Knapton murder enquiry and Vicky was proving to be a real asset to him.

The house was in darkness as he stepped out of the car and onto the driveway, apart from the lamp in the hallway that Jen switched on for him if she'd gone to bed before he arrived home. His earlier instinct had been right not to ring her.

It was three o'clock in the morning when Jen woke bleary-eyed. She rolled onto her back, reached out and felt the bed next to her empty. She saw Jack sat by the window. 'What on earth are you doing? Are you okay?'

'Just writing a thought down before I forget it, it was keeping me awake,' he whispered. 'Go back to sleep.'

'I can't, not until you come back to bed.' She gave a long agonising groan.

Dylan went to the bathroom. She heard him flush the toilet and was hopeful Maisy did not wake. He managed the few steps to the bed in the dark but stumbled as he reached the ottoman. Feeling his way up the bed he eventually climbed in. 'Now, will you go back to sleep,' he said, wriggling under the bedclothes. He turned away from her but instinctively Jen rolled onto her side and wrapped her arms around his stomach. 'You're freezing,' she said. 'How long have you been up?'

'Not very long,' he lied.

Now wide-awake, worry chequered her voice. 'You sure you're okay?' she said.

'Fine.'

'Are you worried about the investigations? Two murder scenes in one day can't be easy. Can't someone else…?'

'I've told you I'm fine,' he said abruptly. 'Go back to sleep.' A few minutes later there came a sigh and Dylan shuffled irritably to rearrange the pillow. 'I'm warm that's all,' he said dismissing her arms that were still about him. Jen rolled away and Dylan sat up putting the TV on. Jen screwed up her eyes to shut out the light. But she knew watching the silent motion of the programme would help take his mind off the horrors of the day. Within five minutes she could hear the change in his breathing. He was asleep. Only then could she rest too.

Dylan didn't sleep for long. He slipped out of bed and went to sit on the easy chair where he remained restless, his eyes wide and to the ceiling until the sun came up. He crawled back into bed where he fell into a shallow, unsettled slumber and he dreamt of being a child again and his earliest memory of coming face to face with his grand-father's bull and staring into the murky depths of its big brown eyes.

He woke with a start. Maisy was standing silently by his side of the bed and it was her soft, smiling eyes that he saw when he opened his.

'Wake up! Wake up sleepyhead,' she shouted. As she did so, she did a little jig. Jen was up and dressed and just about to leave the bedroom.

'Come on Maisy, let's get Daddy his breakfast before he goes to work.' She gave Dylan a faint smile.

Maisy dropped a kiss on Dylan's cheek and ran from the room. He heard her small, steadying footsteps on the stairs and her counting of them down. Max was waiting for the little girl at the bottom and she squealed with delight as she jumped over him with a bang.

For a few moments, his semi-lucid state allowed his childhood memories to return. When he was a child, the highlight of his year was going to his grandparents' farm. Those carefree days of summer when he would ride on the back of granddad's open cart to feed the cattle, herd the sheep off the moors, return from the haymaking to cheese and pickle sandwiches in homemade bread. Those times were among the happiest of his life. His eyes were still closed but his mind once again was brought back to the present on waking, and the job in hand, the recent brutal killings.

The little girl's endless chatter took Dylan's mind briefly off the day ahead, and he ate a hearty breakfast. The eating over, Maisy was soon restless, and Jen chastised her.

With military precision the pots were tidied and the dog was about to be walked as Dylan put on his suit jacket. He picked up his briefcase, gave Jen and Maisy a peck on the cheek and they walked to the door together.

'I'll see you at work,' he said to Jen giving her a parting wink. 'You be a good girl for Chantall,' he said to Maisy.

'I will,' she said rolling her little eyes up to the ceiling, a trick she had just learnt to do that she knew made Dylan laugh.

Chapter Eight

It wasn't unusual for him to be the first person in the office. He looked at the documents that lay on his desk and used the quiet time to write down some of the necessary actions he wanted carrying out. These would be the priority for the day utilising the notes he had written during the night. He wanted to know about the workmen who had worked on the recent renovations of the house. There was bound to be more intelligence gained by now on the history of the Isaac's.

Once he had confirmation from the coroner's officer of the times for the pending post-mortems of the murdered victims, including Freddy Knapton, and then he could arrange his diary accordingly. Dylan would never send another officer to the mortuary on his behalf. He knew other senior officers that would and did, but being at the mortuary for the post-mortem of a victim, he felt was priceless. To be able to speak and ask probing questions and to see first-hand, the evidence that the dead body gave them. He wanted to be there to understand the injuries and have the exact cause of death explained to him. The images he would take away with him from the examination, he knew, would speak a thousand words more than a report written by someone else.

The family history of the owners of Merton Manor would take many man hours of investigation. Dylan had already identified Detective Sergeant Jon Summers to champion this, and selected a small team to assist. While it was obvious that the Isaacs had been targeted, it was not known by whom or why? He wrote a list of questions he wanted answering. How many people carried out the murders? Why did they need to kill the occupants? Did the Isaacs know their attackers? Who was the heir to their assets and, was this a possible motive? 'Early days,' thought Dylan as he considered his suspect strategy. The investigative net would be cast far and wide. He penned another media release for the daily newspapers, morning television and radio. His mind circled like an aeroplane awaiting permission to land. The information he would give press officer Connie Seabourne to release would still be limited, which would enable him to drip-feed more information periodically throughout the day, in the hope that this would keep the incidents in the public eye. The recent killing of a wealthy couple would overshadow the Knapton murder.

'Emergency services responded to a report of a fire at Merton Manor yesterday. This resulted in numerous fire officers and tenders responding. To their credit, they managed to bring the fire under control quite quickly and subsequently it was extinguished.

At the first opportunity officers with breathing apparatus entered the building and found the badly burnt bodies of two people on the upper floor. A major investigation is underway led by Detective Inspector Jack Dylan, as it was apparent from the outset that the two occupants had been murdered. Once the identities of the victims' are confirmed, further details will be released. The manor house itself is severely damaged. Anyone with any information, no matter how slight, should contact the incident room at Harrowfield. It is believed that the deceased are husband and wife, Jake and Leah Isaac, who are the owners of the Isaac Art Emporium, Harrowfield. Visual identification is not an option to the investigation team, therefore formal identification will be done by other means. The victims, we can confirm, were shot prior to the house being set alight. Another update will be released after the post-mortems.'

NB: NOT FOR RELEASE AT THIS STAGE (Connie, I'll call you once we know for sure to give you the green light).

Dylan's experience meant he wouldn't second guess anything. He wanted to be accurate about the injuries to both parties and wanted confirmation that the bodies were those of Jake and Leah Isaac before that information was released to the public. Dylan was thoughtful, 'Was there any significance in them being found in separate rooms?'

Dipping into his in-tray he found confirmation that the post-mortems for the Merton Manor victims would commence at one o'clock, he immediately sent an e mail to DC Andy Wormald, the exhibit officer, Senior CSI Sarah Jarvis and CSI Mark Hamilton to inform them that they would be required to attend.

Dylan read on. Immediately after the conclusion of these post-mortems there would be a short break followed by the post-mortem of Freddy Knapton. Dylan sighed. It was going to be a long day without daylight for company.

At 1 p.m. Dylan arrived at the mortuary and was greeted by his team. Professor Bernard Stow was also present. The detectives knew him well. As a would-be comedian, he made an exceptionally good pathologist.

'Good afternoon everyone,' he said with a hearty slap to Dylan's back and a theatrical bow to the ladies. Stow was partly gowned. 'Smile,' he said as he watched the others prepare to gown-up. 'It could be worse; it might be one of us on the slab.' Stow laughed heartily.

Dylan looked at the rotund figure of the pathologist, his thick brown wool pullover looked extremely worn and it hung over his midriff.

He completed his dress for the post-mortem by putting an apron over a gown and pulling on his stocking feet, waterproof short boots. Then with his half-moon spectacles on the end of his nose and his unkempt curly hair tucked into his head cover he tugged on his plastic gloves letting them twang dramatically against his wrists. 'Right shall we get straight on with it?' he said.

'Ready?' said Dylan to the team. With a nod of the head and the rise of the face masks they followed Professor Stow into the mortuary theatre.

The professor stood at the head of the corpse on the mortuary slab. 'We'll deal with the male first,' he said as his eyes took in the uncovering of the body. 'Did I tell you the story about our local vicar who was in charge of the barbecue at the village fete this year?' Dylan slowly shook his head. Stow looked over his glasses at the rest of the team. His eyes were sparkling with mischief. 'He served up burnt sacrifices.' Professor Stow chuckled heartily, at his own joke. Unfazed by the lack of reaction his face became serious, he looked back at the corpse and stopped to consider, 'He's one bad cook alright. Saying that he's not much cop as a vicar either.' The tools of Professor Stow's trade were handed to his outstretched hand. Dylan smiled beneath his mask. He was a kindly soul, and his joviality was his way of coping with his job, no doubt. It also put the team at ease, stopping them being sucked into the sadness of the event.

The mangled charred remains of what was believed to be Jake Isaac's body didn't resemble a human being. It was a blackened mass that lay out on the stainless steel table. Black skeletal bones with a few areas of pink flesh stuck to them, along with fragments of cloth. A clump of singed hair was visible on one side of the head. It looked idiotic. Dylan outlined the circumstances of the discovery of the bodies, before offering everyone extra strong mints that he quickly withdrew from his pocket when the smell became too much for him. He filled his own mouth with the sweets to try to eradicate the putrid odour that travelled up his nostrils and formed a distinct foul taste in his mouth.

The professor began his examination by taking samples of flesh and hair for DNA purposes before he moved onto the skull. Two clear and perfectly rounded holes at the back and side of the head were photographed and measured. Impressions were taken of the victim's teeth with the hope that this would give a further chance of identification.

Using both hands, he stood behind the body and shook the skull. He looked at Dylan with raised eyebrows. 'You might be lucky inspector. There appears to be something...' He turned his head as he peered inside. 'I'm sure I heard a little rattle. A bullet? Didn't you? The death rattle,' he growled. Again his eyes danced above his mask mischievously before they turned serious. 'Death would have been instant. Two shots to the head when actually one would have been sufficient to kill him. Someone was making doubly sure this guy was dead as a door nail.' With little that remained of the victim, Stow quickly examined the rest, before asking the mortuary attendant to remove the skull cap, even though it was already fragmented.

'Tweezers please,' he asked his assistant. With camera in place to capture a picture of the exhibit, a spent bullet was plucked from inside the skull and dropped in a tray. 'That's one bullet for ballistics to examine for you Dylan,' Stow said.

Dylan's eyes widened. 'It's surprising what they'll be able to tell me from that,' he said as he eagerly popped another mint in his mouth.

'Right let's see if we can find the other little blighter, just a minute,' Stow said, as he tentatively probed about inside the skull. 'I think I may have located it wedged in the spine at the top of the neck.'

Dylan could see beads of perspiration forming at the professor's temples. He paused for a moment when he turned, and located a saw. A knife in the hand of his assistant was considered. He looked back at the skull and finally accepted the knife to help him ease the ammunition from its lodging place. He gingerly poked and cautiously probed. Stretching his aching neck, he took a moment to nudge his head cover upwards from his sweating brow. It seemed to Dylan that everyone around the table was holding their breath. The tension was culpable until suddenly he turned sharply towards Jarv and her camera was instantly pointed in the direction of the bullet. Snap! There was an audible group exhale.

'Take as many shots as you like, if you pardon the pun,' he said before pulling the second bullet from the corpse. 'I say, two-for-one even in the mortuary. Two-for-one,' he said smearing the moisture from his pink cheeks with the wrist of a gloved hand. He adjusted his glasses on his nose with the tip of his finger, paused and looked at Dylan with satisfaction in his eyes.

'Excellent,' said Dylan. 'Now we will be able to find out if the shots were from the same weapon.'

To everyone's relief Professor Stow called for a break to outline his findings.

'The victim was shot twice, once at the side of the head and once in the back.' Stow stopped and appeared to be collating his thoughts. 'And, while the bullet hole at the side of the head...' He pointed to his temple, 'Could have quite easily been done by the individual himself - the bullet to the rear, because of its positioning and the direction of entry, would have been impossible to self-inflict. This death, in my opinion, was nothing short of an execution. The bullet administered to the side of the head may well have been the first bullet and when the victim fell flat, the gunman took a further pop at him to ensure he was dead. Death, caused by a massive fracture to the skull by a firearm. In simple terms he was shot! Now...' Stow looked around him, put his hands flat on the table and eased himself from his sitting position. 'Comfort break I think, and time for a cuppa before the next?' he said, motioning towards his assistants. 'It'll give them a chance to clear away,' said lowering his voice.

'Any chance of a slice of toast with that tea?' he said a little louder.

'Of course,' said the mortuary assistant. 'And I'll put a broom up m'arse and sweep the floor at the same time, if y'like,' he said.

'Just make sure you don't burn mine like you did last time Bert,' Stow called over his shoulder. He walked towards the door as Bert headed in the other direction to the kitchenette mumbling. Stow chuckled to himself, his stomach moving beneath his gown in unison with his chin. 'Such is life,' he muttered. 'Such is life...'

Fifteen minutes later the team were back in the mortuary. It felt cooler this time, but the smell of burnt skin was just as overpowering.

'The body is believed to be that of Leah Isaac,' said Stow.

The almost skeletal, burnt carcass was a lot smaller than the first corpse. Stow automatically obtained the relevant samples for identification purposes before moving onto the more detailed examination stage.

'Well, this one is very obviously female to me Dylan. The lady wife you think?'

Dylan nodded.

'Did you know she was with child?' Stow looked at Dylan over his half-rimmed glasses.

'No, I didn't,' Dylan said sombrely. His jawline tensed and twitched, immediately thinking of Jen and the baby. He put his hand into his pocket pulled out a bottle of water, flipped the lid and put the nozzle to his mouth. He drank heartily, relishing the cold liquid, the action taking his mind off the feeling of being kicked in the stomach.

'There seems to be excessive burning around the groin and lower abdomen,' Stow continued totally unaware of how Dylan was feeling. 'Was someone wanting to destroy the evidence of the child, I ask myself? Why would accelerants have been deliberately used in this area?' Stow looked up. 'I'm just speaking my thoughts aloud. What remains of the unborn child, due to the intensity of the heat, means that the foetus has fused with the mother's pelvis.' Stow's gloved hand spanned the skeletal stomach, 'I'll have to do some further tests to determine the age of the foetus. You may have a feticide on your hands too.'

'Child destruction: The crime of killing a child capable of being born alive, before it has a separate existence.' said Dylan. 'Crime Act 1958 deemed that to be twenty-eight weeks' gestation, later reduced to twenty-four.' Dylan's mood had changed, as had Professor Stow's – no longer the comedian.

'Never had a chance, this little one...' Stow said with a sigh. 'I'll do the necessary tests but I'm sure your enquiries will confirm that Mrs Isaac was over two-thirds of the way through her pregnancy.' Stow took the samples in silence. Jarv was close at hand taking photographs.

Stow moved to the skull. 'Two shots to the head,' he said. 'The one here,' he said pointing to the side of the head. 'I suggest this long groove, is a slight skirmish. Then, as with her husband, the killer directed a bullet into the back of the head. The pathologist searched within the skull but this time he could only locate one bullet. The female skull was badly damaged - broken like a boiled egg shell being forcefully hit with a spoon. 'The second bullet could easily be in the debris at the house but I guess searching for that really would be like searching for the proverbial needle in the haystack.'

Dylan took another mouthful of water. He stooped to rub his calf muscle.

Stow looked at Dylan, who had gone decidedly pale. 'You okay?' he said.

'Yes,' said Dylan. 'The cold tiles, they give me cramp.'

Stow continued. 'The only reason we found this bullet.' Stow held the offending item aloft. 'Was because it was lodged in her upper jaw bone.' Stow tutted. 'Another execution.' Stow looked puzzled. 'One thing I don't understand is that there are no remnants of clothing. That tells me that she must have been wearing very little, or been naked. The couple; they were found in separate rooms you say?'

Dylan nodded. 'No clothing, intense burning to the groin area and she was discovered in a different room from her husband. Could Stow be right, had there been an intention to destroy the unborn child?

Waiting for Dylan in the kitchenette at the mortuary was DS Vicky Hardace whose attendance was required for the third post-mortem which Dylan was also to attend that day - the post-mortem of Freddy Knapton. She was sitting at the table with her head resting on her arms. She looked up blurry-eyed and her face broke into a wide sleepy smile. As he sat, she stood and without speaking filled the kettle. Opening the cupboard, she retrieved two mugs off the shelf. 'Drink?' she said, yawning. Her hand hovered over the coffee jar. He looked across at her. 'As if you need to ask?' he said. 'Make it a strong one.'

'That bad?' she asked, with a grimace as she poured milk into the cups and spooned sugar into Dylan's mug. She slid into the wooden chair opposite him and pushed the hot drink towards him.

'You look as if you've been up all night?' said Dylan.

'Most of it.' Her eyes held a twinkle.

'I don't want to know.'

'No, you probably don't.' Vicky touched the plastic bag with tentative fingers. 'Aren't you going to see what I've brought you?'

Dylan put his hand on the bag but his fingers fell short of opening it.

'Come on. Jen sent it for you. She said you wouldn't have eaten, so there's bound to be some goodies inside. Shares?'

'She knows me.'

'She loves you.' Vicky put her hand to her mouth; this time the yawn was wider and noisier.

'She sees me through rose-tinted glasses. I don't deserve her.'

'I wonder if I'll ever find anyone who deserves me?' Vicky put her elbow on the table and her chin in the palm of her upturned hand, she dragged the bag towards her and unwrapped sandwiches and cake. Her eyes grew big and round. She took a gulp of her coffee and sunk her teeth into a piece of Yorkshire Parkin. 'By, your lass doesn't half make nice cakes,' she said, smacking her lips together.

Dylan was solemn. 'She does.'

'Hey, you,' she said. 'What's with the long face?'

'The woman's body.'

'What about it?'

'She was pregnant.'

'Good God! Is it a feticide?'

'That depends on the age of the unborn child doesn't it? We have to specifically show that the baby could have had an independent existence of its mother to charge.'

'So if the baby were less than twenty-four weeks, what would the charge be?'

'It would likely be wounding with intent or child destruction. But the two counts of murder of the child's parents would take precedence. The barristers can fight over that.'

'Life imprisonment for the scum when they're caught anyway.'

'Poor little mite. We take it for granted, don't we? We get pregnant. We have a baby. It brought it home to me in there just how fragile an unborn baby is.' Dylan shook his head, cleared his throat and took a bite of his sandwich in silence. He chewed the mouthful as if it were cardboard. He considering another and looked at the sandwich intently before dropping it back into the bag.

'What's wrong?' said Vicky, her head tilting to one side? Are you ill?'

Dylan was so deep in thought that he had not realised how long they had been sitting there until he heard Vicky slide her chair away from the table and his eyes went to the clock. 'I have this overwhelming feeling that something bad is going to happen,' he said quietly.

'Well, it is.' She pulled a face at him. 'We're about to go into a bloody post-mortem.'

With Vicky's injection of humour the sombre mood was broken and Dylan gave her a little smile. 'You're right,' he said getting to his feet. 'I'm just tired.'

'You're a big softie if truth be known Jack Dylan,' she said putting an arm around his shoulders and squeezing him tight. 'You're lucky to have each other, you and Jen.'

'Hey, don't you go spreading that rumour young lady. I've a reputation to keep,' he said giving her a fleeting wink. 'My nickname didn't used to be *Basher* for nothing.'

***

'Professor Stow is ready to start the post-mortem of Mr Knapton if you'd like to get your aprons on,' said Bert the mortuary assistant when he popped his head around the door.

'A bit of a local celeb this one isn't he Dylan?' said Stow.

'Let's say he was well known, but for all the wrong reasons,' said Dylan.

'It's quite exciting isn't it, you never know what a body has to offer in terms of evidence to capture their killer?'

'I wouldn't quite put it like that but whoever murdered Freddy probably dismembered his dog too, that's more upsetting,' said Vicky who dragged her feet into the examination room behind the two men.

Dylan and Vicky stood on the periphery. They shared knowing looks as the body was uncovered. Vicky took a packet of mints out of her pocked and offered them round. Finding himself without mints Dylan was pleased his mortuary survival regime was rubbing off on his protégé.

Knapton's clothing was bagged and tagged on removal by Ned. Being exhibits officer at a post-mortem, Dylan was aware there was little time to think about one's surroundings. Professor Stow pointed out cuts in the material of Knapton's clothing, holding his sweatshirt up to the artificial light on the ceiling to see clearly where the knife had penetrated the cloth. Once the dead man's body was naked, Stow counted eight stab wounds to his trunk and legs. Some of them were superficial but Knapton had also suffered a deep cut to his throat.

The professor measured precisely the width and depth of each wound before moving on. Next he opened the body cavity to examine what damage the penetration of the knife had caused to his internal organs. He continued this post-mortem quietly, methodically and at pace. He too, Dylan thought, feeling the ache in his legs, must be getting tired. Two hours later and it was over.

'The cause of Mister Freddy Knapton's death is due to the wound to his neck. Which in turn caused extensive damage to his jugular vein and carotid artery. He would have been unconscious in a couple of minutes after this wound was inflicted, and dead within ten due to the loss of blood and oxygen to the brain. He has six stab wounds to his legs, some are deep but none of these, or the more superficial one to his trunk, would have been immediately life threatening.'

'And the weapon?' said Dylan.

'The weapon? A knife with a double edge blade. From the deepest wound I would suggest you're looking for a knife with, at the very least, a four-inch blade. The wounds to the legs are of interest to me. These show me that it is most probable the attacker was sitting down when they were inflicted. The blade has gone into the thigh horizontally. The deceased, I suggest was stabbed in the back, before his throat was cut.'

'What you're suggesting is that our murderer has been calculated in their action, and knew exactly what they were doing?'

'That's exactly what I'm saying.'

'Do you believe it was one person who inflicted the wounds or maybe more?'

'The wounds suggest to me that the same type of weapon was used, that's all.'

'But, we never assume do we?' Vicky took a sideward glance at her boss.

'Exactly,' said Professor Stow. 'It is always a possibility that an identical knife was used in the attack. It's not too difficult these days to buy two, three, four of a kind. Moving on, Knapton has scuff marks to the skin, which indicate to me he was dragged. He pointed to bruises to his body. 'These suggest he was kicked.'

When the examination was over Stow recapped his findings.

'In brief, he was stabbed, had his throat cut. He was kicked and dragged before being dumped off the car park roof. Of course there are other bruises and injuries to his body which were clearly sustained after falling from such a height and these are consistent with them occurring after he had died.'

'After he died? So what you're telling us is that he was dead before he was thrown off the car park roof?'

'That is exactly what I'm telling you, Dylan.'

It was dark and the overflow car park to the hospital where Dylan had parked earlier in the day was now almost empty. His car stood alone by the exit to the stairs. Vicky's car looked abandoned on the top of a concrete island.

'How the hell, did you manage to get out of the driver's side?' said Dylan eyeing the driver's door inches away from a stone pillar.

'I didn't,' she said, opening the passenger door and climbing across it to slid in behind the steering wheel.

'If only I were that agile,' he said shaking his head. Vicky laughed aloud as she turned on her engine and opened her window.

'Fancy a drink?' Vicky's eyes were wide and bright. She released her hair from her hair grip and she instantly looked younger than her years.

Dylan shook his head. 'Not tonight. I'm off to my bed. 'We'll discuss the findings tomorrow. Enough is enough for today.'

'Lightweight,' she said with the flick of a hand tossing her blonde hair over her shoulder.

'My office at eight o'clock lady,' he called out as he walked to his car. 'Don't be late.' He pulled his tie loose and opened the top button of his shirt.

'Don't worry. You know me. I'll be there all bright-eyed and bushy-tailed,' she said. Dylan heard the car reverse and land with a bump as it dropped down the kerb. Vicky revved the engine as she pulled alongside him. He opened his door and flopped down into seat. 'Give my love to Jen,' she called. He nodded and watched as the tail lights of her car vanished towards the exit at speed.

***

His drive home was a quiet one. The car's headlights guiding him along the pitch black, long, winding roads of the Sibden Valley as he left the bright lights of Harrowfield town centre behind. With his car windows open he inhaled the fresh, cold, night air into the depths of his lungs. Would the Merton Manor enquiry now be deemed a triple murder? Was the unborn child capable of existence independent of its mother? Could the pregnancy be a motive? Several possibilities for murder bounced around his mind like a pinball, and the night air gushed in. He shivered with cold, his eyes watered but still he didn't shut the window. He tried unsuccessfully to close his mind to the killings but, deep down, he knew his mind would be like a submarine, running under the sea, pushing onward, never stopping until it reached its journey's end. Dylan needed a distraction, he needed Jen.

He let himself into the house and shut the door behind him. Standing quietly at the bottom of the stairs he listened intently for a sound that told him Maisy or Jen may be awake. All was silent. Max rose to greet him from where he lay at the bottom of the stairs. Dylan patted him. The dog followed him down the hallway and into the kitchen. Dylan threw his keys on the table, took his mobile phone from his pocket, turned it off, and laid it face down next to them. He walked to the fridge and took out a can of lager. Max sat next to him as he drank.

The long hot soak in the bath did nothing to turn Dylan's mind off the events of the day. He climbed into bed and hoped that sleep would take him quickly into oblivion. Jen stirred, and although he was hopeful that they would talk, she did not wake. He leaned over to kiss her warm cheek, but instead of turning off the light he lingered for a moment or too, leaned on his elbow and viewed her sleeping face. 'You are beautiful,' he said in the softest whisper.

'You're biased,' she mumbled. Tenderly he kissed his finger and put it to her lips. She opened one eye slightly, smiled, moaned and turned away from him. He switched off his bedside light and snuggled up behind her feeling her warm body next to his. As he did so, he purposefully lay his hand on her rounding stomach. 'You'll always be beautiful to me.'

Jen grunted. 'Have you been drinking?' she said, sounding more awake.

Dylan chuckled softly. 'Just a lager, why?'

Her answer was to put her hand over his. All was quiet for a moment or two.

'I love you so much,' he said. She could feel his breath on her shoulder before he kissed it.

'I love you too,' she said opening her eyes. She turned facing Dylan and the light from the nick in the curtain allowed her to see the depth of emotion in his eyes.

Jen eyebrows came together. 'Whatever's the matter?'

Dylan shushed her as he stroked a stray lock of hair gently from her eyes. He took a deep breath. 'I just had a reminder today of how fragile life is. I don't know what I'd do without you and our...'

'Well, we're not planning to go anywhere,' she said, gently closing her eyes. 'So, you don't have to worry.'

He surprised her by kissing her on the mouth, long and passionately. There was no need for words. She responded with an eager naked body against his, and after they had made love it was Jen's turn to wrap her arms around her husband's girth and he slept, a peaceful sleep of a contented man.

***

It was half past six when they woke. Maisy could be heard chatting away. Dylan didn't attempt to get out of bed so Jen laid her head on his chest and wallowed in the few minutes they had alone, before their daughter decided she had occupied herself long enough. Jen felt a stirring in her stomach.

'I can't bear to think what that poor couple went through. She was pregnant you say?'

Dylan was silently looking wide eyed at the ceiling; images of the post-mortems flashing through his mind. He nodded.

'Me neither.'

'Did you put yesterday's clothes in a black bag for the cleaners? I don't think I could stomach the smell of the mortuary this morning?'

Dylan smiled. 'I did.'

'I'll take them to the cleaners.'

Maisy's chatter became a shout – then a cry. Jen rose. Another day had begun.

Chapter Nine

Dylan sat in his office gathering his thoughts. Who stood to inherit the Isaac's fortune? Jon Summers tapped at his door. Had he read Dylan's mind?

'Take a seat. What can you tell me?' Dylan looked at the paperwork in his hand.

Jon sat on the edge of his chair. Dylan sat back in his, his face serious.

'The Isaacs; nice couple by all accounts. No apparent enemies. Feedback from the Isaac's Art Emporium staff tells us that Jake Isaac was good to work for, valued his staff, and rarely had to advertise. There are no incidents of note that anyone is aware of, and we have nothing on our police systems about them or their properties that is of relevance.'

'The Emporium doing well?' asked Dylan leaning forward to rest his elbows on his desk. He put his fingers together in the shape of a steeple and rested his chin on his thumbs.

'Yeah, sales figures are up on last year, but as a matter of course I've asked the financial investigation unit to put him and his business under the microscope.'

'So basically the only irrefutable info we have on the case so far is that the Isaacs are nice couple, violently killed in their own home, for no apparent reason?'

'Ah but they were a very wealthy couple too sir.'

'But there was jewellery still in the safe and I imagine other expensive items in the house. So if it was a robbery why leave so much behind?'

'Unless they were looking for something in particular?'

'Right enough, Jake Isaac would be in the arena to pick up valuable collectables. Do you think he'd be so naive as to keep a large amount of money in the house?' Dylan scowled.

'Who knows, the interest rate for savers is rock bottom. Did the intruders kill the couple because they knew they'd recognise them?' said Jon.

'Otherwise why was it necessary?'

'If only we knew the motive? You don't think that we are being led to believe it's a robbery when it was a contract killing and murder was intended by the perpetrators from the outset?'

'Dunno. What about family? Any news?' said Dylan.

'Both parents are dead but he has a brother – he's single. We are still trying to locate him through their solicitors. It's only since Jake's father's death that they have been reunited so we are told. Their father left the brother a flat in London and Jake the house. The brother, he's a bit of a playboy by all accounts and he's well-travelled. So, sadly, it appears Jake and Leah pretty much just had each other, and a child on the way, which of course would have been the one to inherit the Isaac's fortune eventually.'

Dylan's eyebrows rose. 'Well, at this moment in time we'll stick to the basics, systematically go through the information that comes our way and wait to see what the experts can tell us. Who knows where forensic results etcetera, will lead us?' he nodded at Jon. 'Thanks for that. Let's keep digging and we'll have a debrief at five.'

***

The Devlin brothers were still in possession of the hire car. They'd spent the evening at Redchester's Casino with a couple of escort girls, then they'd taken them back to the executive suites of a five-star hotel in Harrowfield.

Declan and Damian were sitting scanning the morning newspapers in the breakfast room. Damien lifted his chin to his brother. 'It's York races. We could've taken the girls.'

'The girls have done what they were paid to do and gone,' said Declan not looking up from the newspaper.

Damien sought the betting odds on his mobile phone. 'I liked Shani. She was cute.'

'Get real, will you. Shani isn't her real name.'

Damien scowled at his older brother. 'Why would she lie?'

Declan shook his head and his tight lips turned up at the corners. Still he didn't look up but his hand found his coffee cup and he put it to his mouth, took a sip, and put it back down on its saucer

'You saying I'm stupid?' Damien lowered his voice and leaned into the table.

'If the cap fits.'

Without saying a word Damien pushed his chair backwards on the wooden floor and threw his napkin on the table before marching out of the dining room.

Declan folded his paper slowly, looked around the room to ensure that his brother's quick departure hadn't drawn attention to them and, gently wiping his mouth with his napkin, placed it on his plate and followed Damien out of the room.

Damien was standing beside the entrance, a sullen look upon his face.

'Okay, okay, give them a call to see if Shani and Nancy are free.' Declan was growing impatient.

'Really?' said Damien his eyes brimming with child-like excitement.

'Why not if it makes you happy?'

The brothers walked across the foyer amiably towards the elevator. 'Did you win last night?' said Declan.

'I'm a couple of hundred up.' Damien had a spring in his step as he lunged forward to press the elevator button.

'Good, that means you can pay for today,' said Declan. His eyes on the elevator lights that counted the lift to the ground floor. The lift opened and the brothers stepped in.

'I will.'

***

The Devlin brothers stepped out onto the stone steps at the front of the hotel dressed in matching Italian, designer suits. Declan asked the doorman to get their car brought round to the entrance. There were large news placards on show outside the newsagents opposite.

'See that,' said Declan. 'While we have been enjoying ourselves the police have been working around the clock. Tick, Tock, Tick, Tock.'

'More fool them.'

The elder brother laughed. 'Yeah, well not everybody is lucky enough to have a brother like me to look out for them.'

'What do you mean? We're a team. We get on alright, don't we our kid?'

'I told the Gov I'd look after you, and if you get us caught, I for one aren't ready for the alternative to going down - just remember that.'

A crafty smile flickered over the younger brothers face. 'Me neither. Those ladies last night, they were just begging for it weren't they?' he said with a twinkle in his eye.

Declan laughed out loud at the very idea.

'Ladies? They're bloody prostitutes!'

'Whatever,' said Damien. 'Shani said she'd have done anything for me and I believed her. I could do worse than settle down with a girl like her.'

'And me with Nancy.' Declan sniggered. 'And before you say anything, that's not her real name either.'

'I don't know what you mean?' Damien looked puzzled. 'Why wouldn't you believe her?'

'Nancy? Just Nancy? Nancy is the name of the bloody character from Oliver Twist and Shani Wallis, for your information, is incidentally the name of the actress who played her. Didn't you learn anything from dad's obsession with Fagin? Cause she'd have done whatever you wanted her to do, you were paying her!' Declan paused and lowered his voice. 'Just so happened that she didn't have to because you were stewed.' Declan raised an eyebrow with a knowing smile.

Two leggy blondes in short, tight skirts and strappy high heels climbed out of the red flash car that pulled up at the foot of the steps. The doorman obviously knew the lady driver and didn't intervene but instead signalled to the brothers that their car would be arriving imminently. Declan secreted a large tip in his hand - which the doorman gratefully accepted with a bow as he stepped forward, seeing the royal blue Mercedes draw up at the bottom of the steps, he opened the car doors and shut them when they were all seated.

'For the ladies and gents,' he said tongue in cheek and a tap of the hand on his breast pocket where he had covertly secured the monies.

***

'Will you be wanting me to park your car Sir?' said the car park attendant when they arrived at York Races.

'Declan looked at his brother, frolicking with Shani. 'Yes,' he snapped. Alighting from the vehicle he opened his wallet, handed the little man in the ill-fitting uniform a few notes and passed him the keys.

He looked up at Declan with a shocked expression on his face. 'That's very kind Sir. You sure?'

'Go on,' Declan said eventually. 'Get yourself a ticket, have a bit of fun why don't you?'

Declan and Nancy followed the younger two.

'You're my lucky girl,' Damien told Shani as they walked through the big metal gates. He looked about him, and content he wouldn't be heard he whispered in her ear and gave her a wad of notes. She giggled like a child.

In the club lounge Declan silently studied the form. Nancy poured herself another glass of champagne from the bottle in the ice bucket on the table. She looked extremely bored.

'There are people who do that for you here,' Declan said to her without looking up.

'Oh, I don't mind,' she said nonchalantly, looking about her then proceeded to hiccup.

'I do,' said Declan. His eyes found hers and she noticed they were like steel. Hastily she put her glass down on the table, crossed her legs and sat back in her chair.

Damien and Shani continued to giggle like school children. The money Damien had given to her was on show, stuffed in the garter at the top of her stocking.

Declan looked irritated. 'Know anything about horses Nancy?' he asked, frustration with his brother growing in him.

'I like a ride. But not on a horse.' She gave a slow suggestive wink.

'That's good since it's in the job description.'

Enjoying the fact, he was making an effort to at least engage with her she leant forward, showing him ample cleavage. Seductively she rubbed the inside of his thigh. 'Ah, so you have read the services on offer?' she said with a smile as she licked her glossy red lips with her tongue.

Declan swiftly pushed her hand away. His patience was wearing thin with Damien whose behaviour with Shani was attracting attention.

Sulkily, Nancy slouched back in her chair and purposefully picked up her champagne flute and downed the contents in one. She slammed the empty glass on the table. The action brought no reaction from Declan. After a moment or two she picked up a beer mat, read the information upon it and turned it around slowly, in a limp hand. From her bucket leather seat, she surveyed the other guests until her eyes met those of an older gentleman at the bar who raised his brandy glass to her. The group of tweed-clad men in his company, apparently from the horsey set it was deemed due to their attire, became suddenly very raucous. Sensing Nancy's distraction and thankful it had taken the attention off his younger brother and the prostitute, Declan followed her gaze.

As he leaned forward and beckoned her, the red-faced Nancy leaned very slightly back.

'Know him, do you?' he asked with the flick of his head in the direction of the bar.

She nervously cleared her throat. 'No.'

'A customer is he?'

Nancy was silent.

'You wouldn't tell me if he was, would you?'

Declan could see the fear in her eyes and a thrill ran through his loins. He lifted his brow and his face broke into a reassuring smile. 'That's okay,' he said softly reaching out to take her hand gently in his. She flinched initially at his touch, but he caught her hand at the fingertips and held them tight. 'He could be useful. Go on, to work, let me see how good you are. Use that charm of yours. See if he'll give you a tip,' He encouraged her to stand. She looked about the room nervously.

'Don't worry there are no Pigs in here,' he said. 'If there were I'd smell 'em.'

Hearing Declan's aggressive tone, Shani turned to look at her friend. Shani's face was full of concern. With questioning eyes, she followed Nancy's footsteps as she walked to the bar. Not liking the fact that her attention had been re-directed, Damien put his large hand about her face and squeezed her cheeks between his finger and thumb. He turned her head back to face him with a rough hand. 'No girl of mine looks at other blokes when they're with me,' he said through gritted teeth. 'Do you understand?' Shani nodded her head in small jerky movements and he rewarded her with a hard kiss on her lips.

When Nancy got to the bar, the drinks waiter was absent. She stood on her tip toes. Tapping the tips of her false nails on the bar. She loosened her bracelet and when it dropped to the floor and she bent over to retrieve it she knew she had the tweed-clad men's attention.

'Oh, let me get that for you,' said the older gentleman beside her. 'I don't want you having to bend down in that dress my dear,' he said struggling to reach the floor to pick it up with his aged hand. 'They might fall out.' The other men laughed and all attention was on her.

Taking a moment to look at Declan she saw him give her a reaffirming wink and with a nod of his head prompted her to carry on. 'That's right lass, "where there's muck there's brass," or so they say in Yorkshire,' he said under his breath.

'Why, thank you, kind sir,' Nancy said to the old gentleman as she placed a beautifully manicured hand on top of his. She moved in closer. The old man's eyes were on her breasts, exposed through her see-through blouse, unashamedly she played to his weakness for a pretty young girl. She rewarded his attention with "oo's" and "ou's" that came thick and fast. Soon she had the old gent under her spell; laughing at his jokes. Frequently she reached out to touch his jacket lapel, finger his tie, stroke his arm. Turning to face the bar laughing, they appeared deep in conversation - their heads together over the same racing paper that Declan had been studying. The old man pointed to this and that with a shaking hand and before she left him she leaned in to kiss his cheek. His friends collectively commented on his prowess, loudly, as she prepared to leave him at the bar. Unperturbed, she moved in at his request and he whispered something in her ear. She whispered something back and he turned to look at Declan. Giggling she returned to the table.

'I told him you were my cousin,' she said before turning around to smile at the man through thick, mascara lashes. He blew her a kiss. She blew him one back.

Declan raised his glass to the gent and unsmiling he nodded; coughed into a fist and returned to engage with his friends.

'So?' Declan raised his eyebrows to her.

'His name is Cedric Oakley and he lives at Welford Grange, near Wetherby.'

'Any tips?'

'Firepower in the three-thirty. Apparently, it'll walk it.'

'What a coincidence.' he said with a wicked smile.

'A coincidence?'

'Nothing,' he grinned. 'Guess if he's going to walk-it that means it'll come last then?'

Nancy kicked his shoe playfully under the table. 'Are you for real?' Nancy laughed out loud.

Declan sat up and took a bundle of twenty pound notes from inside his jacket pocket and handed them to her. 'Put a grand on its nose will you,' he said, giving the all-seeing gent at the bar a wink.

Confirmation of his bet in his hand, he stood up, grabbed hold of Nancy's hand and bending down reached out to punch his brother on the arm. Damien wasn't pleased to be interrupted from the fun he was having with his playmate.

'Firepower,' Declan said. 'We've got odds of five-to-one. Come on, they'll be under starters orders in a minute and I want to see this one pass the post.'

Chapter Ten

With Dylan otherwise engaged on the Merton Manor Fire investigation, DS Vicky Hardace had quietly and efficiently succeeded in setting up the Freddie Knapton murder incident room. DS Raj's influence, organisational skills and tidiness was evident.

'Priority enquiries are out with the investigative teams' boss,' said Vicky nodding in the direction of those busily inputting on their computers, speaking on the phones and in conversation with colleagues. She pulled out a chair for Dylan, looked around and called out to Ned. 'Get the boss a coffee will you?'

Ned sat staring at a piece of paper that he had extracted from an envelope. His face was pale. He was hunched in his chair, appeared unshaven, unwashed and with his shirt crumbled and his tie loose, he looked as if he'd not slept.

Ned snorted, pushed back his chair and sluggishly dragged his feet towards the kitchen, stuffing the correspondence in his back pocket.

'What's up with him?' said Dylan.

'Life's tough but it's tougher when you're bloody stupid.'

'What's he done now?'

'The Mrs', she's gone to her mothers with the kids. Need I say more?'

Dylan shook his head but DS Raj approaching them turned his frown into a smile. As always she was smartly dressed, her dark shoulder length hair coiffured in a neat chignon bun; her light olive skin glowed. She looked down at Dylan with her big brown eyes, giving him her warm friendly greeting. 'The girl's done good,' she said, screwing up her nose playfully at Vicky.

Vicky's cheeks reddened.

'I can't help feeling very proud of her,' said Raj, emotionally.

'And she reckons to be tough, but we all know she's not,' said Vicky. Suddenly her smiling mouth turned down at the corners, and she frowned. 'That's as long as you don't leave dirty dishes in the sink, and remember to clean up your clutter.'

Raj laughed and when she laughed she looked far younger than forty.

'Seriously though, that call I've just taken was from a very angry man,' she said, perching herself on the edge of the desk. 'He said he'd threatened Knapton recently. Here's his name and address. You might want to speak to him,' she said handing a piece of paper with her neat, bold writing on it to Vicky.

Vicky took it from her and read it out loud. 'Arthur Carson, Flat Five, The Maltings.' Vicky raised her eyes to looked at Raj. 'That address, is within walking distance of Groggs Park.'

'Exactly! He did apologise for his outburst, but it appears he heard that his elderly neighbour, who's apparently nearly blind and hard of hearing, was knocked over by Knapton's dog in Groggs Park: and to add insult to injury, Knapton called her a silly old cow and told her to fuck off. Mr Carson said he was unaware of what's happened to Knapton and Satan until now. But, who knows he might be able to tell us more.,'

'I dare say there are a lot who threatened Knapton,' said Dylan. 'With no direct line of enquiry we'll just keep eliminating people, who come forward, wherever possible.'

'Forensics say they've found fibres in Knapton's dog's mouth, which they think are possibly denim,' said Raj.

'Satan bit his attacker?' said Vicky her eyes opening wide, momentarily. 'What strikes me is that Knapton has been a scourge on the community for as long as I've been in the job and I guess people have somewhat accepted that he's, well, Freddy Knapton. He's just a twat.'

'What you getting at?' asked Dylan.

'I think he's done something that's pushed someone over the edge to commit murder.'

'But why would someone do it in such a violent way?' said Raj.

'Find out what he did and to whom and we might find out who murdered him,' said Dylan.

Ned pushed a tray of cups ungraciously across the desk. The dark, hot liquid splashed about in the half filled mugs. 'In God we trust, all others are suspects,' he said under his breath.

Vicky's mouth opened and closed. 'That's a bit profound for you isn't it? Have you sugared?' she said reaching out to pick up a mug.

'I'll drink it for you as well if y'like,' he muttered. Ned sloped back to his desk hoisting up his belt that held up his trousers. He slumped back in his chair, put his elbows on the desk and rested his chin on his fist.

'Pull up a chair Raj,' Dylan told her. 'Ned,' he called. 'Come and join us. Let's have a brainstorming session while we can.'

'This should be funny,' Vicky said to Dylan quietly. 'According to your missus Ned, your brain's are in y'trousers aren't they?' she continued in a much louder voice.

Ned showed her his middle finger and the tip of his tongue.

'Vicky,' growled Dylan.

Raj gave her a withering look.

Sulkily Vicky threw Ned a pen and paper. 'Oy, *Lump* you'll need these.'

'This is not the time or the place,' Dylan scolded, as he shuffled to the edge of his seat and leaned over the desk. Pen in hand, he hovered over his open notebook. 'Right, first off, make enquiries with the RSPCA, PDSA and local vets to see what information is available to us regarding treating dogs with attack injuries.'

'And perhaps complaints about dangerous dogs?' said Raj.

'Yes, good,' said Dylan, putting pen to paper.

'Local dog owners?' said Vicky. 'There should be a database for the dogs that are micro-chipped.'

'There's a microchip register.' Ned told them.

Vicky turned her head towards Ned. 'As they say, we'll leave that one with you then kid,' said Vicky cheerily.

Ned groaned.

'Fell for that didn't you?' said Dylan.

Ned's already rounded shoulders dropped. 'Have we thought the killer might not own a dog and, not all dogs are microchipped.'

Vicky rolled her eyes and tutted. 'Okay, then find me an alternative more promising line of enquiry?'

Ned frowned and remained silent.

Dylan turned to the others. 'Dogs are like children to their owners, don't forget sometimes they're all a person has for companionship.' His thoughts turned to his meeting with Jen. New to the area, and with only Max to keep her company. How things had changed for her and him since that fortuitous day.

'From previous enquiries,' said Raj. 'I found dog owners don't tend to know fellow dog walkers, or necessarily the dog breed, but they might know the dog's name. It might be worth having a category for those dog names that are given to us during the enquiry, which may ultimately help us match them with their owner?'

'Yes, I can relate to that,' said Dylan. 'I hear a woman calling Sonny and Peaches regularly in the park when I walk Max but I've no idea what the dog owner's called.'

'I bet Jen does,' said Raj.

'Yeah, because she's more sociable than you,' said Vicky.

'Me unsociable?' Dylan raised his eyebrows. 'I bet she doesn't,' said Dylan.

'Ask her.'

'I will.'

Satisfied the subject had been covered Dylan moved on. 'It would be useful for us to work on the timeline for Knapton's movements over the past week. Do we know if there is CCTV in the vicinity of where he was sleeping rough, or his usual haunts? If so, seize it; it's a laborious task I know to watch the footage but it may help us trace, and eliminate people he was acquainted with.'

'I'll look at that boss,' said Vicky raising a hand in the air.

Dylan stretched his aching back. 'So, we've plenty to keep us busy. Until we discover something else that either leads us down another path, or shows us another motive to investigate. So, we'll stick with this approach, agreed?' The team agreed. 'Hopefully gathering this information will establish facts on the database worthy of cross referencing to ultimately help us catch the killer'.

'Assuming his murder was dog related...' Ned's voice was a slow, low drawl. Elbow on the desk he looked down and combed his fingers through his thick, greasy hair. When he sat back in his chair he looked like he'd been dragged through a wind tunnel.

'Ah, but we never assume do we boss?' said Vicky with a cock of her head.

'No, and Ned, you should know better,' Dylan said, collecting his paperwork together. He stood to leave. 'Ned, my office, now.'

Ned looked up at Dylan his hooded eyes widened.

'What?' he mouthed as Dylan walked away. He dropped his pen and stood, dragging his feet as he made the lonely walk to the boss's office.

Dylan was sitting behind his desk. 'Shut the door behind you and sit down,' he said sternly. Momentarily he was distracted by papers that had been left on his desk. He signed them and cast them into his out tray before he turned his attention to Ned. He leaned towards him. 'What's wrong?'

'Nothing sir,' Ned stuttered. His red rimmed eyes looked down at his hands.

'Nothing?' Dylan nodded and pursed his lips. 'Okay, let me rephrase that. Look at yourself? No-one's denying you're a bloody good detective. But, just look at the state of you?'

Ned glanced up to the ceiling, took a deep breath, and looked back at Dylan with puppy dog eyes. He slouched in his chair, sighing.

'You've a choice, you either tell me what's going on so that I can try to help, or carry on as you are and you'll be off the enquiry and out of CID before you can say Sir Robert Peel!'

Ned's eyes stared at Dylan, unblinking, he looked as if he might cry. Knowing he was in a mess was one thing, but having the reality of the consequences of his actions spelt out to him, shocked him. 'Sir, I need your help. I'm in a bit of bother.'

Dylan eyed him suspiciously. 'What kind of bother?'

'Women trouble.' Ned leaned forward and shuffling about on his seat he produced the envelope he'd stuffed in his pocket earlier. He withdrew a piece of paper, unfolded it and handed it to Dylan.

When Dylan had finished reading the letter he looked directly at Ned, questioningly.

'A policewoman I slept with, she sent it to my wife,' he said quietly.

'Is it serious?'

'Is what serious?' Ned looked puzzled.

'The affair?'

'God no! A drunken grope in a car park one night.' He looked sheepish at Dylan's raised eyebrow. 'Well, you get the picture.'

'And this, policewoman, she's obviously read more into this coupling?'

'She's bloody obsessive. Rings constantly. The calling at the Freddie Knapton murder scene that you witnessed, that was her. She wants me to leave my wife.' Ned had a look of desperation. 'I've told her. I love my wife. I love my kids. I have no intention of leaving 'em.'

'Okay okay, look,' Dylan said looking down at the piece of paper that told Ned's wife her husband was playing away from home. 'You need to go see this woman.'

Ned opened his mouth as if he was about to say something but Dylan silenced him.

'I want you to go see her and tell her what she has done by sending this to your wife. This is misconduct in a public office.' Dylan told him flatly. 'Tell her if this harassment continues,' he said shaking the letter in mid-air. 'If she doesn't stop playing with fire, let her know you've told me and you'll also tell her supervisor if it doesn't stop.' Dylan's voice thickened with anger. 'Then go and see your wife; get down on your bloody knees if need be, and ask her for her forgiveness.'

'Yes sir,' Ned said. He stood to take the letter that Dylan offered. 'What shall I do with it?'

Dylan considered the detectives question then shrugged his shoulders 'Whatever you like.'

Ned seemed reluctant to take it from Dylan's hand. His eyes went to the filing cabinet.

'Do you want me to keep it locked away, just in case this doesn't go away?'

Ned nodded. 'Yes,' he said quietly. Standing to leave he smiled wearily. 'Thank you, sir.'

Dylan waved a hand. 'Get out and don't come back until you can give me one hundred and ten percent. I've two major investigations on the go and I could well do without the added drama.'

'Right sir. Er... Thanks.'

'And remember,' Dylan told him when Ned put his hand on the door handle. 'If you can't cut it, I have officers only too willing to step into your shoes.'

The Knapton investigation was up and running smoothly. Dylan needed to concentrate on the shootings at Merton Manor and bring some urgency to the investigation. It had been the headline story on the front page of every national newspaper.

***

'Come on Firepower!' Damien screamed at the top of his drunken voice. His face was almost the colour purple. His eyes bulging.

The commentator was shouting five words a second over the tannoy, and Firepower was in the lead; one furlong from home. Arms raised, sweating profusely and waving frantically with the abandonment that comes with great excitement, Damien hurled himself through the crowd, who seemed only too pleased to step out of the lunatic's way. Finally, he was at the front of the enclosure.

Amid the jostling of the five thousand-strong crowd, moving forward upon a wave, trying to get closer to the track, Declan glanced down at the betting slip in his hand and held it even tighter. Then there was one almighty cry. A Mexican wave of a groan, amongst an almighty cheer.

Firepower had been pulled up two lengths ahead of the others and Declan could only listen to the verbal diarrhoea of the commentator relaying the facts. Annoyed and angry, Declan looked towards the club lounge balcony to see Cedric Oakley looking down on him. Eyes brimming full of cheer the old man raised his glass. Declan knew he'd been had. 'You don't know who you're dealing with,' he mouthed at Cedric Oakley.

Declan was unsmiling. Damien noticed his brother's anger but he wouldn't let it spoil his day. 'Come on bro,' he said swinging his arm around Declan's neck. 'You'd already chosen that horse. You win some, you lose some.' Damien lowered his voice. 'Let's face it, it's the manor house money, not ours. We're at the races and he's taken you for a ride.'

Declan appeared to process the information and his mouth turned up at the edges. 'You're right. We'll sort him later.' His eyes raised towards the balcony. Cedric Oakley had disappeared inside.

'Which horse shall we bet on in the next race?' Damien said digging his newspaper out of his pocket with a sweaty hand. 'Did m'laddo give you another tip?'

Nancy's face blanched at the cold look on Declan's serious face.

'No, I'm sorry. Firepower, he definitely told me to put money on Firepower – I know I didn't mishear him.'

Declan put his arm around her shoulders and gave her a brief squeeze. 'Hey don't apologise. I'm a patient man me.'

'It was a lot of money,' she said her eyes wide brimming with tears.

'Doesn't matter Nancy,' said Damien. 'Win or lose we'll have some booze.' And with that he grabbed Nancy around the waist and, lifting her off the ground, he spun around and around until dizzy they fell onto a heap on the grass laughing.

Chapter Eleven

Dylan was on the telephone being updated with regard to the ballistics findings; the science that deals with the motion of projectiles - not just bullets but also shells, rockets and aerial bombs. For now, he was only interested in certain bullets, the ones recovered in connection with the murders of Jake and Leah Isaacs and their unborn child.

'All the ammunition was nine millimetre,' said Clancy Mason. 'The rifling, however, on the recovered casings, was different which shows us that two different semi-automatic weapons were used to fire the shells. Both weapons are believed to be Smith and Wesson though, and enquires are in progress to see if there is a match on the national database.'

'Which may tell us if either of the guns have been used on any other crimes,' said Dylan.

'Exactly,' said Clancy.

'Well, that's a step in the right direction and it makes me believe that at least two people were involved.'

'Looks that way Dylan,' said Clancy.

For a few minutes after he had put the phone down to Clancy, Dylan considered the implications of more than one murderer and proving who had done what.'

There was a tap at his door and seeing his Detective Sergeant through the glass he motioned for Jon Summers to enter.

'Doctors have just confirmed to us that Leah Isaac was thirty-six weeks pregnant, sir.'

Dylan made the comparison with his and Jen's babies gestation. Vicky came to stand at Jon's side.

'Would you like a coffee boss?' she said holding up a mug in her hand. Her presence broke Dylan's reverie. At his nod she walked in and put the drink on the corner of his desk.

'Also, I am told the Isaacs didn't want to be told the sex of their child but her recent scan confirmed it was a boy,' Jon continued.

Vicky stopped as she walked back towards the door and looked from Jon, back at Dylan.

'The child was capable of being born alive and to be independent of its mother.' Dylan said softly.

'Yes, sir,' he said in a quiet voice.

'So, we now do have a triple murder investigation on our hands.'

'Not that it will make a difference to the determination of the team sir,' said Jon.

'You're right there. But whoever they are they've stepped up into a different league. I fear we won't have heard the last of them. By the way did we manage to get any uniform seconded to any of the teams?'

'Yes,' said Jon.

'Without an argument?' Dylan asked with a look of surprise.

'Inspector Stonestreet let us have PC Shelagh MacPhee, sir. He thought it would be good for her development as she has shown an interest in joining CID – he rates her.'

'Shelagh MacPhee?' said Vicky. The tone of her voice sounded unusually high to Dylan's ears.

'Why? What's wrong with MacPhee?' said Dylan.

'Nothing,' said Vicky, a big grin appeared on her face. 'She's a canny wee thing is our Shelagh.'

'You've worked with her before?' said Dylan.

'Yes, she hadn't been in Harrowfield long when I was called to the address of a suspected sudden death. You know the usual,' she said, her head swaying to and fro. 'An old lady hadn't been seen for a number of days. It was early turn, seven o'clock and Shelagh was in the company of a police cadet.' Vicky chuckled.

'Get on with it,' said Dylan, leaning back in his chair. 'We haven't got all day.'

Jon leaned on the door jamb and Vicky quickly sat down.

'It was hilarious. The house was a terraced. There were no lights on and all the curtains were closed - basically, there were no signs of life. The milk on the doorstep had stacked up for days and the post could be seen on the door mat, through the letter box. The only option, as Shelagh saw it, was to break in. So, using the mighty rubber torch,' Vicky said, raising her arm, 'Shelagh smashes the kitchen window and gets a leg-up from the cadet. Shelagh, by the way happens to have stockings on at the time, according to the cadet's version of events. She told him to cover his eyes.' Vicky giggled. 'She climbed in at the window and put her foot straight into the kitchen sink.' Vicky looked at her audience's blank faces. 'Come on! Imagine the scene, we've all been there. It's pitch black, shards of glass everywhere. Next thing Shelagh jumps down onto the kitchen floor and she hears a low, deep, groan.' Vicky put her hand to her mouth to stop herself laughing out loud. 'She's only landed on top of the poor woman hadn't she?' she laughed out loud before becoming more serious. 'Fortunately for Shelagh, the woman was dead and it was the air trapped in her body that she had disturbed. The smell in the house was horrendous.' A grimace crossed her face and she gagged. 'I can still smell it now.' Vicky's eyes lit up again. 'Anyway, it gets worse. Shelagh opens the door to the cadet and they call CID, me, out. This old lady turns out to be a hoarder and Shelagh and the Cadet are there for a couple of days counting over two thousand pounds in cash that she has neatly folded and put into crisp packets.' Vicky appeared to reflect. 'Good things sure come in small bulk, as Shelagh would say. You'll like her – she's top bollocks, as Ned'd say.'

***

For Dylan to be satisfied that they were on top of things there was a lot of information that he required. He sat opposite Jon Summers, DC Wormald and PC Shelagh MacPhee.

'Take this down. We need to chase up who the Isaac's contracted to do the renovation work and that means, builders, joiners, painters and decorators. You get my drift?' Dylan counted on his fingers. 'Number one, what do we know about them? Number two, have we traced them and if not why not? Number three, when were they last at the house?' Dylan's hand fell to his lap. 'I've been told the crime prevention officer visited the Isaac's. I want to know why and what advice he gave them.' Eagerness, and the need to move the enquiry forward thickened his voice. 'These are basic enquiries in these early stages of the murder and they need completing quickly. My advice to you is never assume anything -rely only on fact. For instance, while it appears that Jake Isaac is the father of the child; and there is absolutely nothing at this time that suggested otherwise, we need to be a hundred per cent sure he is. DNA for comparison has been taken from the remains. Of course if it turns out that the baby isn't his then we must consider whether his wife had an affair. Is there anything else?' The rest of the group shook their heads and got up to leave. 'Close the door behind you,' he said. Dylan picked up his telephone, 'Dylan, I want to speak to crime prevention officer DC Rupert Charles as a matter of urgency.'

Within thirty minutes Detective Constable Rupert Charles appeared at Dylan's office door. He was in his late forties, dressed in a custom made suit, Windsor knot to his striped tie, a tip-up matching handkerchief in his breast pocket, and engraved cufflinks to finish off his dapper attire.

'Good morning sir. Frightfully sorry for the delay. A meeting with the crown.'

'The Crown?'

'Oh, no, no, no, not royalty sir, the dentist. I've become what they call "long in the tooth."' Rupert laughed at his own joke.

'Better late than never,' said Dylan taking a sip of his drink. He looked at Rupert curiously over the rim of the mug. 'Take a seat.' Dylan gestured towards the chair opposite and when Rupert sat he rubbed his hands together. 'Now, I want you to tell me everything you know about the Isaac's.'

Rupert took a deep invigorating breath. 'Just over two months ago I was contacted by Jake Isaac who asked me if I would could call to see him at his home address.' He looked away momentarily as though remembering the visit. 'Beautiful, beautiful property it was. He and his wife had recently finished the renovation of the manor house and they were excited about the birth of their first child, which had prompted them to review their security.' His eyebrows knitted together.

'So what were they looking for?'

'Jake Isaac showed me around the property, his wife left more or less as soon as I arrived for a hair appointment. He pointed out to me two safe deposit boxes. One concealed, using the facade of books on a shelf near the fireplace in the dining room area that his father had had installed some time ago. He was thinking of electronic gates, and cameras at the bottom of the driveway. They were looking at CCTV around the exterior of the house. He also wanted a panic room and was quite willing to forgo a bedroom to accommodate it.'

Dylan blew a slow, low whistle through his teeth. 'Pretty serious stuff then? Was there any reason given that would make him need to go to such lengths for their safety?'

'No, not that he made me aware. But, he was striving to have the work completed before the baby was born. I'm surprised that the work was not in progress.'

'Do we know what security consultancy he was instructing?'

'No, unfortunately I don't. However, the document I'd prepared does include a few local companies that I recommended. Now, whether the local contractors might have found one or two of their requests a bit ambitious I don't know.'

'I guess there isn't much call for panic rooms in Merton,' said Dylan.

'No sir,' he said popping the paperwork he had prepared on the edge of Dylan's desk.

'Thank you. They will all be subject of a call from us.'

'In the document I have also included a copy of my report to them and advice given.'

'Did you take any photographs?' said Dylan.

He gave Dylan a self-satisfying smile. 'In the appendix,' Rupert Charles said. 'Two dozen to be exact. These include images of the exterior and interior of the house which I have marked with suggested possible locations for the alarms, cameras etcetera.'

'Interesting,' said Dylan, picking up the file. He flicked through it before looking up at Rupert. 'This may be the most up-to-date imaging record we get prior to the fire.'

'In all honesty sir I cannot understand why the Isaac's hadn't moved forward on the security plans. Money didn't appear to be an issue.' His eyes grew round. 'The interior of the property was awash with luxury fittings and antiques.' Rupert's face suddenly paled. 'If only they'd acted sooner.'

'Maybe it wasn't their fault. Maybe they had agreed the work with contractors with a future date to proceed?'

'Of course that's a possibility,' said Rupert studiously. 'Mr Isaac didn't give me the impression that he would sit on the project. His mind was most definitely made-up. If only...'

Dylan thanked him for his time.

'Just glad to be of some help sir, best of luck with the investigation and if I can be of further assistance please let me know.'

'If only,' Dylan said with a long, deep sigh as he watched Rupert Charles leave his office. Those two little words he had heard used by so many victims and their families. 'Hindsight – a wonderful thing.'

***

The office seemed exceptionally quiet when larger than life character DC Charles left Dylan alone with his thoughts. Dylan picked up the copy of his report from the desk and carefully considered each photograph within. Dylan's perception of how the house looked before the devastation was never greater. DC Charles was right, these photographs showed him a luxury home. The gardens were neatly manicured, even the staddlestones stood proudly like soldiers on sentry duty. The more he looked at the pictures the more he was drawn to the staddlestones. Dylan was almost sure that one of those was missing when he'd attended the scene after the fire. He rummaged around in his in-tray for the pictures he knew had been taken by the crime scene investigators and, locating them, he pinned them together. Now placed side by side, he attempted to spot the difference on the two near identical images. Feeling excited by the realisation that there was indeed a staddlestone missing on the day of the fire he wanted to know when and why? He was aware it wasn't uncommon for criminals, or indeed police officers to take trophies away from crime scenes. He recalled a crime scene investigation officer who happened to be a keen gardener. He'd created his own crime scene rockery at his home address after taking stones from crime scenes he'd

116

examined. He even knew exactly which stone came from which enquiry. There was 'nowt stranger than folk', as Dylan's old mum would have said. Now what he needed to know was were there any identifiable marks on those particular staddlestones. Anything that would mean that if they found the missing object it could be positively identified and connected to Merton Manor. He typed an action for a member of the team with the relevant expertise to visit the remaining stones and offer advice. It may be a little piece in the jigsaw to solve this puzzle, but it could be an important one. As he pressed 'send' Dylan's mind moved on. He wondered who the Isaac's solicitors were and if the couple had made a last will and testament. 'Who would benefit from their deaths?' he typed. The incident room staff would input these 'actions' into the database and then raise the necessary paper enquiries for the team to carry out the investigations.

Dylan gave Jen a quick call. She was in the admin office on the floor above him. 'I've just bumped into Dawn Farren in the corridor,' said Jen sounding bright and breezy. 'It's ages since we've met up. Would you believe that her little girl Violet is four years old next birthday?'

Dylan chuckled. 'Time flies doesn't it? I was sad to lose her from the team when she went to 'act up' as Detective Inspector on the Child Protection Unit as it was then, but she's so well suited to her role I can't imagine her ever coming back to division can you?'

'No,' said Jen. 'She sends her best and we've a lunch date for a catch up.'

Dylan groaned. 'Baby talk if I know you two.'

Jen went silent. 'You still there?' Dylan looked at the telephone receiver in a puzzled way after a moment or two.

'Yes, yes, I'm still here,' she said but her voice was quieter and she now sounded sad.

'You okay?'

'Yes, I'm fine, tired, nauseous, sore boobs, constipated, but ... I'm just not looking forward to the thirteen-week scan, that's all.'

Dylan's smile softened his face. 'You're a worrier.'

'Come with me, please?' she said softly.

'Wild horses wouldn't keep me away.'

'I know that, but criminals might.'

***

Vicky's arrival in Dylan's office was a noisy one. A large smile was pasted across her face.

'Well, you've either detected the murder or your love life is on the up,' he said without looking away from the document he was typing. 'Where's my coffee?'

'It's not the former, although I'm working on it,' she said with a wink. 'I've just ordered two coffees and asked for biscuits.'

'So, go on then, who is he?' Dylan raised his eyes over his computer screen at her.

Cheekily she tapped the side of her nose. 'Wouldn't you like to know,' she said cocking an eyebrow. 'I'm using my right to remain silent.'

'Seems like the only words in the defence team's dictionary at the moment,' he grumbled as he carried on typing.

'That and, no comment.'

Dylan finished what he was doing and refreshments were put on the corner of the desk. He turned his chair to face Vicky, picked up a mug of coffee in one hand and scooped a ginger biscuit from the plate with the other. 'Whoever you're seeing appears to be making you happy, so that's good enough for me. Let's talk about the Knapton murder,' he said leaning back in his chair and putting his coffee cup to his lips.

'Arthur Carson. I've been to see him.' Vicky nibbled on her biscuit. 'Lovely elderly gent, bless him. He got himself so wound up when he was speaking to us that he kept losing his top set of dentures.' Vicky chuckled. 'He might have liked to give Knapton a good hiding but he's far from capable. He lives in a nice little sheltered housing bungalow in a quiet residential cul-de-sac near Groggs Park.'

Dylan nodded. 'He couldn't help us any further?'

Vicky shook her head.

'What else have you done since our last meeting?'

'We've set up a database for all things dogs, owners, etcetera and we're building a time line for Freddy Knapton's last few days on this earth.'

'Once we find out what he was up to and with whom that'll generate more leads. Any joy with CCTV?'

'Nah, not yet, we've seized it from the local garage and several shops to see who was about at the time but it's not proving useful at the moment.' Her eyes caught sight of the photograph on Dylan's desk. 'Wow, that's Merton Manor before it was destroyed by fire I presume?'

'You presume right,' said Dylan, turning them around to face her.

'What a beautiful place.'

Dylan pushed two photographs joined together in front of her. 'Notice something missing?'

'One of them giant mushrooms?' she said looking up at him with raised eyebrows.

'Staddlestones, and I would make a guess that they're the real deal.'

'If they're antiques, are they worth a bob or two then?'

He nodded. 'You can buy cheap ones at garden centres and the like.'

'Who took the pictures?'

'Crime Prevention Officer DC Charles went to see the couple to give advice, and the other from CSI after the event.'

'When was the stone removed I wonder? It's positioning in the grounds, the size and that, you're hardly going to miss the fact it's gone are you?'

'I'm hoping the gardener will be able to help when we get to speak to him.'

'Staddlestones, they're like buses and police officers,' she said putting the pictures back down.

'What do you mean?'

'The old guy we went to see Mr Carson, his neighbour had one in his garden. The only reason I noticed it was because it was next to the bird bath and a Blackbird was having a right old splash about.'

'Replicas are ten-a-penny.'

'They were originally used as supporting bases for granaries, hayricks, game larders, things like that, protecting the stored grain from vermin and water seepage.'

'Do you know, Vicky, you never cease to amaze me with the things you know.'

'It's surprising how much crap you can store in your head isn't it. For some reason I have always had this knack of remembering the most bizarre facts. Was you good at school?'

'I hated it. Left school the night before the mock exams.'

'So how did you...?'

Dylan shrugged his shoulders. 'End up as a DI? I guess I just picked up the life skills I needed along the way. Tell me more about these staddlestones?'

A bemused look crossed Vicky's face. 'Well, the buildings at the time had wooden feet but stone was so much stronger and lasted longer and before you ask the name comes from the old English word stathol, which meant a foundation support or trunk of a tree. As time went on the name became staddle, or stathel.'

'Remind me to be on your team at the pub quiz,' Dylan said laughing. 'Anyway, interesting as the history lesson is we're detracting from the murder.'

'Photographs,' she said with reverence. 'They're always distracting aren't they? You managed to catch up with Lord Charles then?'

'Lord Charles?' Dylan looked baffled.

'He thinks he's royalty. Have you been to his house though?'

Dylan shook his head.

'Put it this way, you wouldn't stay for a cuppa.'

'Why? They use expensive bone china cup and saucers?'

'No. It's a shit hole the rumour squad say,' she said in a hushed tone. 'He's got a problem. He's a gambler, lottery tickets, the horses, the dogs, you name it, he's backing on it.'

'I wish the rumour squad worked for a living, they can get the word out quicker than any intelligence bulletin.'

Vicky shuffled the paperwork in her hand.

'So what else have you got for me?' Dylan said picking his pen up and threading it through his fingers.

'Two days before his death we know that Freddy Knapton was in Tesco, Argyle Street. Just after nine o'clock he was creating havoc because staff wouldn't sell him any booze. We have the incident recorded on CCTV. In his usual pleasant manner, he's 'effing and blinding, before he walks out giving it, 'You fucking bastards I'll take my custom elsewhere.' I bet the poor young girl behind the counter that he stuck his fingers up to hoped he'd stick to that promise. Bless her, her face was ashen.'

'Any sign of his dog, Satan?'

'Yes, he's caught on the camera outside the shop, tied up, jumping, snarling and snapping at everything that comes within striking distance.'

'Good. So we know they were both alive and kicking and wreaking havoc as usual two days before they're found dead. Anything on the spray paint or the tag?'

'Not yet, but according to intelligence and the locals say it's a new one for them.'

'Okay let's keep digging, tracing dog owners and hoping we get a bit of luck thrown in the mix.'

'To kill so brutally, surely it's something more serious than a skirmish and anything other than that we would have heard about, wouldn't we?' Vicky's eyes were unblinking.

'I don't need to tell you about man's inhumanity to fellow man. And, don't forget like we said before people's pets are family, and in some cases the only family some folk have. Animal antics may well feature on the motive list.'

'I know our job is not to reason why,' she said with a sigh. 'We just need to find the bastards.'

'Couldn't have said it better myself. Now, see if you can find out what the rumour is on the street, at the vets, and don't forget to make enquiries at the pet shops.'

'I have a meeting at the vets later today to see if they have any idea how best to proceed with enquiries that are dog related, and we have their authority to look through their files. I've asked for information regarding dogs that have been treated or had to be put to sleep because of an attack recently.'

'Somebody knows something. What we need to do is make them feel confident enough to talk to us. I'll get Connie to release a press appeal now I'm able to name Knapton. We'll be appealing for anyone who had seen Knapton, spoken to him, or had a run in with him in the last couple of weeks to contact us. Have you got the phones covered?'

Vicky stood to leave. 'Yes. How's things on the Isaacs' murder?'

'Slow.' Dylan shrugged his shoulders, his expression bleak. 'We have two or more armed men who execute people, I'm trying to step it up a notch by increasing staffing levels.'

'By the way, I hear congratulations are in order. I understand Jen is pregnant?'

'What did I say about the rumour squad?' Dylan's face softened to a smile. 'Jen wants to keep it quiet for the time being - it's early days.'

'Would you like a boy this time?'

The look on his face told her all she needed to know.

Chapter Twelve

Detective Inspector Dawn Farren approached the quaintly furnished table in the cafe where Jen sat waiting. Her eyes were downcast but as soon as she looked up to see her friend walking towards her she instantly smiled standing to embrace her. Jen quickly sat back down and Dawn's wide grin turned to a frown when she patted Jen's pregnancy bump and she saw the tears well up in Jen's upturned eyes. She sat down opposite her, reaching across the pretty tablecloth, to squeeze Jen's hand. 'Hey, what's up?' she said scowling at Jen through her straight cut, thick fringe of her newly bobbed haircut.

Jen could hardly talk for the lump in her throat but she shook her head and the tears she'd held back for so long began to fall. Dawn felt in her jacket pocket and pulled out one of her beautiful hankies she was renowned for carrying. Rising swiftly from her chair she handed it to Jen and promptly travelled around the table to sit at her side. Dawn put her arm around Jen and squeezed her tight.

Wiping away her tears Jen spoke of her fears. 'When you miscarried,' Jen's sob caught in her throat. 'How did you know you were going to lose the baby?'

'What do you mean?' said Dawn looking concerned.

'Stomach cramps, bleeding, nauseous?'

'Don't you remember me fainting at work and them having to cart me off to hospital in an ambulance when I was carrying Violet? And look at her now.' Dawn's eyes misted over and Jen couldn't miss the haunted look that appeared within. 'I bled when I lost the babies, before,' she said softly. 'Why?'

'The baby,' she said putting her hand instinctively to her stomach. 'I've had the most awful stomach cramps.' Jen's voice lowered to a whisper. 'And I've been bleeding.'

'Does Dylan know?' she said looking shocked.

'He knows I've not been well.' Jen chose the words carefully. 'I went to the hospital,' she smiled weakly through her tears at Dawn who had automatically gone into professional mode.

'And, what did they say?'

Jen swallowed hard. 'They listened to the heartbeat and told me to try not to worry. They're arranging a scan.'

'Let's hope that it's sooner rather than later. How far gone are you?'

'Twelve, nearly thirteen weeks.' Jen raised her eyes to look into her friends, as keen as they were kind that twinkled restlessly above the wholesome russet-red of her chubby cheeks.

'Listen to me lady,' Dawn said softly. 'There is no one knows how you're feeling more than me, but that little one inside you is fighting for its right to life. You have to do all you can to help. Do as you're told and put your trust in the doctors. Do you hear me?'

Jen nodded her head and gave her a wan smile.

'Now, where's that waitress? I'm going to treat you to the biggest cream cake they have.' She patted Jen's knee. 'That'll cheer you up,' she said beckoning as she did so to a young girl in a white pinafore.

'Trust you,' said Jen wiping under her eyes.

***

Dylan had just written the latest news bulletin and sent it to Connie for immediate release. It was with reference to the murder of Freddy Knapton. He'd spent the last half an hour talking to the press officer outlining the purpose of the statement, Knapton's background, and why he was well known in the community.

Police name man found murdered as Freddy Knapton. Mr Knapton was a local man seen regularly in the community, usually accompanied by his black Pit Bull Terrier called Satan. Detective Inspector Jack Dylan, who is leading the investigation said, 'Freddy and his dog were both well known. Although he was known to the police, neither him nor his dog deserved to be brutally murdered. I am appealing to people who have seen, spoken to, or have been spoken to by Freddy in the last two weeks, or indeed anyone with any information about the murder, to get in touch with me in confidence at Harrowfield CID, or ring Crimestoppers. These were particularly sadistic killings and, as always, we are appealing to the public for their help to trace those responsible. Please don't assume someone else has given us the information you may hold.'

As soon as she received the press release Connie was directly back on the phone to Dylan. 'When is it likely you're going to be ready to do an appeal in relation to the murder of the Isaac family at Merton Manor?'

'Shortly,' he said. 'The last thing I want is for the murders to be competing with each other for the headline on the news.'

'Understood,' said Connie.

***

Dylan marched into the incident room like a man with a purpose. He saw Detective Constable Wormald and DS Summers at their desks. 'I need to know if there is any more news on the Isaacs' next of kin?'

Jon Summers put the telephone phone down. 'Just on with that now sir, Mark Haywood the family solicitor has traced the brother to a hospital in Switzerland where, apparently, he is recovering from a broken leg from a skiing accident. This happened before the fire and he is still there. Wealthy in his own right and devastated by the news. The Will is quite straightforward. They've no other immediate family. Jake Isaac has very recently been in discussion with Mr Haywood, the intention being to make amendments to bring his will up to date after the birth of their child, to incorporate an heir.

'Get the intelligence unit to ring the national crime faculty to see if there have been any similar robberies around the country.'

'I've already contacted them sir,' said Jon. 'Nothing to note of any interest yet but they're still digging.'

'Good man.' Dylan knew only too well that if anyone had discovered a link, as the head of the enquiry, they would be telling him as a matter of course. But he was frustrated and he wanted to remind them he was on their case, he was feeling starved of any new developments and the clock was ticking.

The suspect criteria for the Isaac murders was wide open. Dylan needed something, anything that would make enquiries more focussed, to reduce the parameters but, although it wasn't ideal for the team, the net had to remain stretched to its limits for now.

Dylan's phone was ringing and he moved quickly into his office and slid swiftly back behind his desk to answer it. A press conference was to be held at Harrowfield HQ at eight o'clock the following morning Connie told him and he agreed that he would confirm the identities of the deceased at that time. Dylan sat with his head in his hands.

Jon knocked at his office door and walked in. 'We have DNA confirmation that Jake Isaac was the father of the unborn child.'

Dylan breathed in deeply. 'Well, I guess that answers one question.'

Since enquiries didn't seem to be moving forward at a pace he decided to finish work on time for once.

***

The welcome he got from Jen, Maisy and Max when he walked through the door made up for all the trudging through paperwork he'd done, the repetitive phone calls and frustrations of the investigations. Maisy launched herself into his arms before he had time to put down his briefcase. Max fussed around his legs vying for his attention and Jen's face looked more relaxed than of late.

'Lovely, you're home early,' she said, standing on tiptoe to kiss him on the cheek.

'The day was going nowhere. You know the sort, when you can't cross anything off your job list but yet you're working flat out?'

'Great, so we're second choice?' she said flatly, but her eyes danced playfully.

'Never,' he said with a smile. 'You look a lot brighter? Had a good day?'

'I met with Dawn and well, like she does, she put everything in perspective, and we had cream buns.'

'Cream buns? Cream buns?' Dylan squealed turning his attention to Maisy. 'Your mummy had cream buns Maisy. I hope she brought some home for us!' He put Maisy on the floor and she ran into the kitchen.

'I wish cream buns could solve my problems.'

'You just need a break. It'll come. It always does.' Jen gave Dylan a fleeting smile.

Suddenly there was a scream from the kitchen and Dylan and Jen rushed towards the door to see Maisy with an empty plate upturned in her hand and Max lapping cream from the floor. Dylan reached out to grab Max's collar and Jen bent down to scoop up the remaining crumbs. Max barked his disapproval.

Maisy's tears soon turned to laughter and her giggles were infectious. 'Well, we will never know if cream buns could help although Dawn swears they solve everything.' Jen was on her hands and knees wiping the floor. 'It was Dawn's present for you.'

Jen winced and Dylan noticed her put her hand to her side when a stitch caught her breath as she stood.

'You okay?' said Dylan, just as the phone rang. Jen nodded reassuringly and hobbled towards the hallway to answer it. Her voice was stilted and serious. 'Yes. Thank you. We will be there tomorrow,' she said looking at Dylan who stood at the kitchen door with their daughter in his arms. Maisy had her finger on his lips as if to quieten him. She giggled. Dylan nodded unsmiling at Jen.

***

The room where the press conference was to be held was buzzing, with standing room only. Dylan looked at the microphones which adorned one side of the desk where he was sitting. They reminded him of snakes ready to pounce. Connie was present, looking radiant as ever. At 8 a.m. sharp the clicks and flashes of cameras commenced and broke his reverie. Momentarily he was blinded.

After outlining the circumstances of the Merton Manor murders, he told the audience that he was satisfied that the house had been targeted and at least two armed and dangerous criminals remained at large. He reassured them that there had been an increase in the number of trained firearms officers drafted into the area. He appealed for help from members of the public, who may have passed the house on the day of the fire, or for anyone with any knowledge of those who may be responsible for the crime to contact him by way of the incident room, or Crimestoppers.

After he had finished speaking, the questions from the floor came thick and fast. They covered all aspect of the incident. Dylan answered them as truthfully as he could. There were questions he couldn't answer because enquiries were ongoing. If he was unable to comment he explained this to the audience.

The conference over but the pressure was not off as he was immediately escorted by Connie, to undertake one-to-one interviews with the various television, radio and news team presenters who were all clambering for that bit of extra information, or another angle on which to write their story. He told them that Mrs Isaac had been carrying their first child which had also been killed. He revealed this in the hope that it would keep the investigation at the forefront of people's minds and hopefully tug at someone's heartstrings, and encourage them to come forward with information that they were presently withholding.

Two hours out of his day had passed by the time he returned to the incident room. Dylan knew the power of the media and was grateful for the attention that both enquiries were getting. He was very aware how short their attention span might be, should another incident occur. Hence Dylan always tried to be accommodating. They had brought him rich rewards in the past and he knew how much the reach of an appeal could suddenly move an enquiry forward.

Back in his office a cup of coffee was put before him on his desk. Detective Sergeant Jon Summers was ready with an update. Sitting quietly, sipping the hot drink, Dylan listened with interest.

'I've been talking to the Isaac's gardener. He came to see us directly he returned from holiday and was told about the fire. His name is Phillip Munroe, he's fifty-five years old and he has worked for the family for a long time, previously at the gallery. On average he spends two days a week at the Manor. He tells me that the Isaacs were a pleasure to work for and a genuinely nice couple.'

'Nothing out of the ordinary that he picked up on recently?'

Jon shook his head. 'No, absolutely not. He says he remembers DC Charles going to the house to offer them crime prevention advice because he spoke to him on his arrival, saw him taking pictures of the house and the grounds, and waved goodbye to him on his departure. Mr Isaac spoke to Phillip after DC Charles left and told him of their plans.'

'Funny, DC Charles never mentioned speaking to him,' Dylan said.

'Maybe, he didn't think it was relevant?'

Dylan appeared thoughtful.

'Mr Munroe told me that apart from the decorators, Mr Isaac used Nigel Earley to pollard trees recently.'

'They'll all need checking out.'

'You might be interested to know that although he was devastated about the fire he was terribly upset to find that one of the original staddlestones had gone missing.'

'It was still in situ when he went on holiday then?'

'Yes sir.'

'Confirms what we already thought from images taken before and after the fire. I don't suppose he told you if they were identifiable?' Dylan raised an eyebrow.

'They were carved on the underside and it's a unique mark created by the stonemason back in the day.'

'Is it visible to the naked eye?'

'Yes, if you tip the staddlestone upside down and look closely under the mushroom, near the stem. He said he would send us a picture of the marking as it is identical to the others. The letters being M M followed by what he says is a serpent.'

'That's good news.'

'It is if we find it sir.' Jon looked downcast.

'Positive! When we find it.

Andy Wormald came to stand at the door and the men's attention turned to him. 'Sorry to disturb you but I've had a message from a Detective Inspector Terry Hawk from North Yorkshire who has asked me if you would give him a call sir? Apparently he's dealing with a murder where the deceased was shot in the head and wonders if there may be some connection with the Merton Manor murders?' Dylan reached out for the piece of paper he held in his hand which had a telephone number thereon.

'Thank you,' he said before turning to Jon. 'Have we finished?'

Jon nodded.

'Then I'll give Terry a ring.' Dylan picked up the phone immediately, curiosity getting the better of him. 'Jack Dylan, Harrowfield,' he said. 'I understand we might have a common interest?'

Terry Hawk chuckled. 'Well, we've got a wealthy landowner that's been shot in the head and ballistics tell me it's got links to your shootings at Merton Manor.'

'Bloody hell, that's music to my ears,' said Dylan.

'It could of course be a pool weapon,' said Terry. 'Are you about this afternoon? I'm thinking of having a trip down to see you?'

Dylan's heart sank to his stomach. 'Terry, that's really good of you but my wife and I have an appointment. You couldn't possibly make it tomorrow could you?'

'I'll see you tomorrow morning and we'll have a talk about linking our databases. Make sure you have the kettle on.'

Dylan put the phone down, breathed deep and closed his eyes. How his priorities had changed he thought to himself as he studied the photo of Jen and Maisy on his desk. He called Jon back into his office.

'I've got a meeting tomorrow morning with DI Hawk and I'd like you to be present. Feed the information into the incident room will you and see if there is any intelligence links to North Yorkshire. I'll be out of the office this afternoon so if anyone is looking for me I'm on my mobile.'

Chapter Thirteen

The old lady, who had followed Jen onto the bus and sat beside her, tapped her gently. 'Excuse me, I think the next stop is yours Love,' she whispered. Jen turned towards her. She smelt of lavender, her eyes were grey and watery, her cheeks over powdered and her lips red and loose. 'You looked miles away,' she said as she stood to allow Jen to pass her on to the platform. Jen stared at her, appearing to have no idea of her surroundings. 'The Hospital,' she said.

'It is,' Jen smiled at her weakly and rose from her seat. 'Thank you.'

When the bus stopped Jen quickly clambered off. Perhaps it was a good job Dylan would be taking her home in her present state of mind. There hadn't seemed much point trying to park two cars in the hospital car park when Dylan was joining her there.

The bus journey had been relatively quiet and surprisingly comforting, affording her time to rest, but as she set off in the direction of the hospital building, the noise of the traffic and the bustle of people became quickly all consuming. Entering the hospital, she found the smell to be a mixture of mouth wash and body odour. She walked down the long corridor with the shiny floor. A door suddenly flew open on her approach and made her jump. Hospital personal staff ran out. The overpowering smell was of stale urine. Jen walked on, up the rise toward the maternity unit. The level of sound came in waves; telephones ringing, people chatting, and the clatter of trolley's. Reassuringly, people in uniform were busily going about their business. Then there were the patients, on every corner, every landing and in the lift. The visitors amongst them, some walking around aimlessly, others stood quietly comforting, some laughing, whispering, weeping.

Patients passed her dressed in hospital garb wheeling themselves and their intravenous drips towards the nearest exit. Were they trying to escape? No, they were desperately clutching packets of cigarettes. The hospital visit was as important as it was surreal and Jen found herself thinking that she could easily have been in the middle of a TV drama and she wished with all her heart that someone would shout 'Cut'!

Leaving the hustle and bustle of the main building behind she walked through the doors of the quieter maternity wing, to see several women with sizeable bumps heading towards reception. Jen held the door for a couple carrying a newborn baby proudly in a car seat. It was apparent by their smiles and chatter that they were going home. She held her breath when they passed and prayed. This building was newer, cooler. The walls painted pastel colours and here and there were murals depicting children's fictional characters. Standing alone now at the reception desk, she was conscious of the quickening of her heartbeat and for the second time that day she felt a tap on her shoulder, but this time when she turned she saw Dylan's smiling face. He put his arm around her shoulders and pulled her close, planting a kiss on the top of her head.

The receptionist sprang up from behind the desk. 'Jennifer Dylan? The sonographer will be with you soon, if you'd like to take a seat in the waiting room.' Jen followed the direction of her pointing finger.

'Come on, the sooner done, the sooner over so you can stop your worrying,' said Dylan as he took hold of her tremulous hand and pulled her along.

Jen's hopes rose at the positive tone of his voice. She leant her head on his shoulder and forced a smile. The couple sat quietly waiting. Jen picked up a magazine from the rack. New born babies. She snapped it shut, put it back and picked up a Scallymag. Dylan mulled over what Jen had told him about the bleeding, and deep down he had to consider that it could be serious - far more serious and worrying than he had led her to believe. Instinctively he reached out to lay his hand reassuringly on her leg.

At the sonographer's request, Jen climbed on the bed and lifted her top to reveal her stomach. She chatted away as she squeezed gel onto Jen's stomach, laughing as she did so at Jen's reaction to the coldness of it. Jen lay perfectly still, turning her head to Dylan. He held her hand, she squeezed it tightly. Her heart raced now as if it would burst from her chest. Her stomach turned, panic rose in her throat. Dylan nodded reassuringly and their eyes turned to the screen and then to the sonographers face. She put the transducer onto Jen's stomach. 'Don't look so anxious you two,' she said with a chuckle.

As soon as the baby's image flickered into view the sonographer's smile dropped from her lips. Her eyes stayed glued to the screen, pushing the transducer firmly into different locations on Jen's stomach. 'If you'll just wait here I'll go and fetch my colleague.' The sonographer disappeared quickly.

'I knew it. It's bad news,' said Jen through trembling lips. As the words tumbled from her mouth a tear squeezed from the corner of her eye and ran down the side of her cheek on to the pillow. She swallowed hard. Dylan tenderly brushed the tear away but it was rapidly followed by others. He handed her his handkerchief.

'Let's wait and see.'

The second sonographer's smile was not reassuring; instead, to Dylan, it appeared to be more of a consoling one. 'I'm sorry this wasn't what you were expecting.'

The next morning was tense. Make-believe enthusiasm was never harder but they both knew their daughter was much too young to understand what was going on and they had to try as best they could to keep to the routine.

***

Dylan found work, as always in times of past personal angst, to be a distraction, and he and Jon Summers looked forward to listening to what Detective Terry Hawks from North Yorkshire Police had to say.

Waiting for Jon to join them, Dylan and Terry moaned, groaned, smiled and shared stories about their years in the job. They also put the world to rights regarding the changes in modern policing and the dangers now facing front line officers.

'Too many Chiefs and not enough Indians is always going to be a problem,' said Terry whose attention was drawn to a picture on the office wall.

'By 'eck that takes me back, Jack Warner.'

Dylan turned his head to face the picture of a uniformed police officer who was stood saluting. The peak of his cap was covering the bridge of his nose, shielding a winking eye.

'Even wore his chin strap correctly. Between the bottom lip and the point of the chin,' added Terry.

'My hero,' said Dylan. 'Dixon of Dock Green.'

'Evening all,' said Terry in a deep voice as the door opened and in walked Jon carrying a tray of drinks.

'The father-figure. The protector,' said Dylan quietly.

'Right Dylan, let's get down to business,' said Terry taking his paperwork from a blue, cardboard folder. 'Our victim is a proper old country gent. His name is Cedric Oakley, seventy-eight years old. He owns the very grand estate at Welford Grange, Wetherby. He's stinking rich. Last week he was found dead by the side of the road in his Range Rover registered number CO 1. The car was found in the lay-by of a narrow country lane, approximately three miles from his home. It looks like he'd pulled off the road to, I don't know, allow another vehicle to pass maybe? Driver's side window was partially open, and the engine was still running, suggesting to us that he may have spoken to someone just before he died.' Terry shrugged his shoulders. 'He's been shot not once, but twice in the head. Nothing else was disturbed, nor is there any damage to the vehicle, which makes us think that he was the target.'

'You've recovered the ammunition?'

'Yes, one from his head and the other from inside the vehicle. They have been checked and confirmed as being from a nine millimetre Smith and Wesson revolver.'

'The same gun that was used at Merton Manor.' asked Dylan.

'An exact match, is what ballistics are telling me.'

'The most exciting thing here for me is that we have another opportunity to trace the killers,' said Jon. 'I'll get both databases checked to see if any other links can be established.'

'Although it might be pure coincidence,' said Terry. 'You wouldn't believe how many enemies an old guy can have.'

'What do you mean?' said Dylan.

'Let's just say he isn't very popular with locals. He's sold off parcels of land to developers for affordable housing and more recently for a wind farm development. It has been brought to our attention that he's also a bit of a lady's man - upset quite a few husbands in his time.'

'Recently?' said Dylan.

'Oh yes, let's just say Oakley, we are told, was a very sociable sort of bloke, according to his acquaintants. Never missed a party. He also liked throwing his money around, a flutter on the horses and he has his fingers in all sorts of investments projects. The last race meeting attended was at York races. Does horse racing feature in your job?'

Dylan and Jon both shook their heads.

'Not that we're aware of,' said Jon.

'We're in the process of scrutinising the CCTV footage from the VIP lounge that he frequented on race days, in the hope that it confirms to us who he was with, and of course if anything untoward occurred that day. The word is he was a heavy gambler and apparently a very successful one.'

'Not content with the office sweep on Grand National day then?' said Dylan.

'Nah Jack, this guy was in a very different league to you and me.'

'I wouldn't mind a copy of the York races CCTV to let our team view it to see if they can identify anyone sir,' said Jon.

'That's not a problem. We also have some stills we can share. We're in the process of identifying the people he was with so we can speak to them.'

'I presume we are not letting the media know about the connection we have made regarding the murders yet?' Dylan asked.

'No, definitely not. You and I know that the gun would never be seen again. While at the moment it's highly likely, even if it is a pool weapon to be still in circulation.'

'I totally agree,' said Dylan.

The facts regarding the two murders and a strategy for liaison between the two forces incident rooms was discussed at length.

Agreement was made for the two databases to be linked and available at all times to the respective teams.

'How times have changed in respect of databases between forces that actually 'talk' to each other,' said Terry. 'Remember the huge round index card systems we used pre-1985?'

'Do I? We had to have the floor reinforced in the Yorkshire Ripper enquiry incident room due to the weight,' said Dylan. 'That enquiry brought in the computerised data base HOLMES, and wasn't that a giant step forward?'

'But that wasn't totally compatible between forces was it? Not until they brought out HOLMES 2 which links all the UK police forces, Northern Ireland and the military police,' added Jon.

'I couldn't care less what they use as long as it makes me less likely to overlook vital clues in complex cases,' said Terry rubbing his hands together briskly. 'Right, I'm off.'

'Shall we have a bite to eat together before you leave?' said Dylan.

'Why not?'

'If you follow me to Prego in Brighouse you're straight back onto the M62 from there,' said Dylan.

Shortly after eating, DI Hawk headed back to North Yorkshire and Dylan found himself driving back to the incident room. The incidents, for now, were being investigated independently, with close links to each other's databases. While the same weapon was used in both incidents, it didn't automatically follow that it was the same person using it. He'd speak with his counterpart to ensure each other's policy log reflected the same reasons for independency.

On arriving back, he liaised with the HOLMES team sergeant ensuring that the links between each enquiry database were kept up to date with information.

There would be a massive amount of time dedicated on both enquiries to viewing CCTV images, but they were all aware the killer(s) may be thereon.

Dylan was conscious he had to balance his own time between the Harrowfield incident rooms. Fortunately, Vicky was doing well handling the Knapton investigation, and he was due another update.

**

The next day the devastating news came that Dylan and Jen's baby had a series of serious health problems which meant the child, a boy, had but a one percent chance of living. Talking, sobbing and hugging each other until they were exhausted, Jen pleaded with Dylan to leave her alone and she was promptly sedated, falling into a deep sleep. Chantall had been looking after Maisy while they had been back to the hospital. Dylan told her he was needed at work, and asked if she was able to continue looking after her until he returned. Fortunately, it wasn't a problem. He drove towards the station but, as he reached the top of Sibden Valley and looked over the town of Harrowfield he stopped the car and walked across the heathland. Facing into the wind his shirt billowed about him. He stood for a while, his mind numb and his heart heavy. When the doctor's words came back to him, he turned his face up to the sky that was threatening rain, and with tears streaming down his face, he screamed a scream that sounded as if it didn't belong to a human but an animal, an animal in great pain. Anger raged through him. 'What had his unborn child done to deserve this when there were murderers walking free?' Sobered by the fact that he had to go to tell the team, he needed their help to keep the plates spinning, he pulled himself together.

Vicky was sitting at her desk with Detective Inspector Dawn Farren when Dylan walked in to the office. They had nearly given up hope that he'd be in and, with no contact at all, they were both worried. Dawn was in the process of advising Vicky how best to proceed in his absence. Relief showed on their faces when he walked in the door, and then they saw his rounded shoulders as he walked towards them, his face the colour of milk, his eyes dark and hooded.

'Bloody hell boss, we thought you'd abandoned us,' said Vicky.'
Dawn put a hand over hers to stop her.

Ten minutes later, the devastating news imparted, tears shed and strong coffee administered, Dylan turned to Dawn with great sadness in his eyes.

'And there isn't a chance the baby could be born alive?' Dawn brought out a handkerchief and wiped her teary eyes.

It was Vicky's turn to put a hand out to Dawn.

'No. Well, one percent they said,' said Dylan with a glazed expression.

'It's going to hit Jen hard. She's going to need all the support you can muster.'

'Yes.'

'Be assured everything's ticking over fine here boss, so don't worry about anything this end.' Vicky told him.

As Vicky spoke his eyes left Dawn's face and he turned to the younger woman. He gave her a tired half-smile. 'Thank you,' he said. 'I'll be back for the debrief. 'Please can we keep this between us for now?'

Dawn slumped forward with her head in her hands on Dylan's departure.

'Dawn?' said Vicky questioningly.

'I can't do this now.'

Vicky saw Dawn's demeanour was grave. She lifted her head, her face was haunted.

'You've no idea what it's like to lose a child,' she said as she pushed her chair backwards and stood up slowly. Turning, she left the office without a backward glance.

'Or maybe I do...' Vicky said quietly. 'Never assume...'

***

Two murder enquiries and each one just as important for Dylan to solve. On a daily basis, it was about making decisions, what lines of enquiry were a priority. This was also a factor determining which enquiry takes precedence for the SIO's immediate attention. The Merton Manor murders were certainly more high profile.

Dylan walked into a packed briefing room and all eyes were on him.

'Due to personal circumstances I may not be around much over the next couple of days. But I am more than confident in each and every one of you that you are capable of keeping the murder enquiries moving at pace, without the need to bring another SIO in. What is of paramount importance is that you keep your supervisor up-to-date with any developments at all times. I will endeavour to get to at least one briefing a day. These briefings are, at this time, more than ever of the utmost importance to keep everyone working on the enquiries up-to-speed. Please ensure you are in attendance.'

The sea of faces before Dylan were serious. All was silent. 'We all need to keep our eye on the ball, look out for each other and keep digging. We will get there.' Dylan's voice changed to a more upbeat, encouraging tone. 'Tell me, what results have we got to date?'

Starting to feature, and becoming more of an interest to the Freddie Knapton murder investigation, was a group of hoodie wearing youths, perhaps six or more in number who had been reported to congregate in Groggs Park.

'Identifying them has got to be a priority,' said Dylan.

'Dog walkers have apparently become intimidated by them,' said Andy.

'And so have the younger kids walking through the park on their way to Harrowfield Academy,' said PC Shelagh MacPhee who had settled into the CID office well under the wing of Vicky.

'Do we not have a school liaison officer? There's a good chance that some of them may be pupils, or ex pupils. We just need the name of one or two and then we can do the rest.'

Shelagh put pen to paper.

'I understand we have actioned a search of the drains in the area?' said Dylan.

Vicky nodded her head.

'Have we got any results?'

'No sir,' said Vicky.

'Why not? That should have been done within the first forty-eight hours. If a murder weapon has been dumped in a drain, we want the best possible chance to secure evidence before the weather intervenes. Accelerate the enquiry as an absolute priority and any further delays I want to be informed about immediately.'

Dylan sat down to drink coffee at his desk after the meeting. Vicky was seated opposite him. They discussed the Knapton murder enquiry. The mood was sombre.

'It's got to be someone with local knowledge' said Vicky.

'Maybe,' Dylan said absentmindedly as he checked his e-mails. He stopped what he was doing and looked directly at her. 'Graffiti. A kid's thing these days would you say?'

'Depends how you categorise "kids". I'd say it's a younger generation thing. But the "wot no" Chad art work isn't. I didn't know what it was until you enlightened me, which suggests to me that if it is kids then someone has got some background knowledge of the cartoon from somewhere.'

'Maybe the tag is to throw us off the scent? I wonder if the pupils at the school have been doing a second world war project.'

'Mmm. We need to trace those that have been hanging around Groggs Park.'

'And we need to speak to them fast to eliminate them, or find evidence to connect them to the incident. Once you've identified the members of the group I want you to do a mass arrest and if need be carry out searches of their homes the same day. That would send out a clear message to the public that we mean business.'

'The numbers may make it impractical, so we may have to cherry pick to make the raids manageable.'

'Tracing and speaking to them is top priority and so is getting those local drains checked. I want you to keep me posted on any news. If you need me to add some weight to the actions being completed, let me know. Remember, I am on the end of the phone.'

'That it?' Vicky said collecting her paperwork together on her lap.

'Yes, I think so.' Dylan's eyes went back to his computer screen and he commenced typing. Vicky stood up and walked towards the door.

'Vicky,' Dylan said before she opened the door.

'Yes?'

'You're doing a great job. Don't think I don't appreciate it.'

'Thanks boss,' she said. 'And I hope it all goes well. Well, I hope you and Jen and...'

'I know what you mean, and thank you. It's a difficult time.'

'Who else knows?'

'Just you, Dawn, Raj, Jon, the Chief and Avril Summerfield-Preston.

'You told Beaky?' she said. Her voice rose and she pulled a face.

'She's Jen's line manager, we had no choice. I've told everyone who knows that I don't want it to go any further. Hardly anyone would suspect Jen is pregnant, and we want it to remain that way. It's going to be hard for Jen losing the baby without all and sundry questioning her.'

'Yeah, well good luck with keeping it under wraps if Beaky knows,' she said.

'Even she can't be that cruel?' said Dylan.

Vicky raised an eyebrow. 'Can't she?'

Chapter Fourteen

Jen loved autumn, and this year Maisy had been able to, for the first time, run with her mother holding her hand through the fallen leaves. The crisp, clean air that rushed up the valley on days like this, pinched her face and usually made her feel alive, but today she found it all too much. Her whole body ached, her heart was like a brick in her stomach and for the first time she felt the need to sit on a bench and watch as her daughter jumped, threw, and kicked the fallen foliage. Max, unusually quiet, came to sit by Jen's side. She wrapped her arms around his thick, furry neck. He turned to her. Her face crumbled and she buried her head in his soft fur. 'It hurts Max, it hurts so much,' she cried. Tears fell onto his hairy face and his long pink tongue whipped up to his nose to lick them away. She gave little sob. 'I feel so hopeless.'

Lost in her own world, she didn't hear the footsteps that came nearer from behind. Maisy saw Chantall and her friends Hermione, Annabelle, Cameron and Frankie before her mother did and she ran squealing past the children and into her childminder's open arms.

'Hello Jen?' called Chantall cheerily. As she got near she saw Jen's red eyes and mottled colouring of her face. 'You okay?'

Jen wiped her eyes. 'I will be.'

Chantall smiled down kindly at the excited children circling her and carefully steered them towards the swings. 'I was worried when you weren't home,' she said as she returned and sat beside Jen. She put her arm about her shoulders and briefly squeezed her. 'Then I thought, where would you be on a lovely autumnal day like today? So we came to find you.'

'Am I that predictable?' said Jen giving her friend a faint smile.

'Oh Jen, Love, I wish I could do something.' Chantall reached out for her friend's hand that held tightly onto a well-used tissue.

'There's nothing anyone can do.'

'And there's no chance the baby will live?'

Jen shook her head slowly. 'If he manages to hang on to full term it would be near-on a miracle.' She sat up straight and took a deep breath in. Her teary eyes wandered to Maisy playing happily with her friends, blissfully unaware of the turmoil and the unknown fate of her unborn sibling.

Chantall's slight, sharp intake of breath and tighter squeeze of her hand made Jen turn towards her. 'If I can do... well, you know where I am.'

'Thank you. That's very kind. Trouble is there is nothing anyone can do. I don't know what to say even to my husband. And, I'm sure as hell that he doesn't know what to say to me.'

***

Dylan was in no mood for excuses from the team.

'Have we traced and interviewed the decorators who worked at Merton Manor Jon?'

'We're interviewing them today sir.'

'Whose interviewing?'

'Andy and I sir.'

'I want to catch the bastards who did it before North Yorkshire do,' he growled. 'Terry Hawk won't let me forget it if they do the job for us.'

'As long as the killers end up behind bars sir, I'll be happy,' Jon said.

'What do they call 'em?'

'Who?'

'The decorators?'

'Would you believe A. Painter & Sons?'

'No? Really?' Dylan said smirking.

'Yeah,' Jon said, allowing himself a little titter. 'Alan Painter and his sons George and Patrick; at first I thought it was a wind up, but no, the guys are genuine.'

'Find out if they work outside the county, and if so where? Also of major importance, where were they, all three of them, on the day of the fire?'

***

Detective Inspector Dawn Farren popped her head round Dylan's office door. She looked sheepish 'You free?' she said.

Dylan unsmiling, nodded his head. She closed the door behind her.

'I'm sorry I was so pathetic yesterday,' she said sitting down to face him across his desk. 'How's Jen?'

'I didn't get in till after she'd gone to bed.' Dylan was thoughtful. 'She was asleep, or if she wasn't she pretended to be so she didn't have to talk to me.'

'You don't know that.'

'Yes, I do.'

'And this morning?'

Dylan looked awkward. 'I was in work early.'

Dawn frowned 'You can't go on avoiding each other. You two need to talk.'

Looking down at his hands, Dylan nodded. 'I know. In all honesty I don't know what to say. Why can't I find the words to talk to my own wife?'

'You've got to face this head on Jack. Jen needs your strength right now.'

'Don't you think I don't know that?' Dylan argued. When his voice began to waver he stopped and composed himself. 'Truth is I feel bloody useless.' Dylan felt the pain in his chest. It felt like two strong hands squeezing the air out of his lungs. His face paled and his mouth half opened as if he was having trouble breathing.

'You okay?' said Dawn.

He nodded, got out of his chair, went to stand by the window, opened it wide and drew a few deep breaths of crisp, cold air before sitting down, his colour returning.

They sat in silence for a moment, Dawn filled with sadness, and Dylan hurting like he never had before.

'I'm so sorry,' said Dawn.

'So am I,' he said. Dylan sighed deeply as he put his hand to his sweating brow.

Dawn got up to leave. She leaned forward and put her hand over Dylan's. 'Just don't leave it too long to speak to Jen and tell her how you feel.'

**

Detective Sergeant Jon Summers and Detective Constable Andy Wormald had caught up with the decorator in the process of painting the exterior of a detached property called 'The Norland', in Tandem Bridge.

Alan Painter was a silver haired gent, balding and bespectacled. In his late sixties, in white overalls that were splashed with every colour paint under the sun, or so it seemed. He had a paint brush in his hand. He looked like he had the world on his shoulders, but he had a friendly if not a tired smile. He shook his head in despair at his sons who were chasing around after each other. 'I don't think they'll ever grow up,' he said.

'How many times do I have to tell you; you can have your fun when the work's done!'

The two younger men laughed and took their fathers telling off with good-nature.

The family-oriented decorator told the officers how he had been thrilled to hear that Leah Isaac was pregnant, and excited to be asked to help her create the nursery. Their involvement at the Manor however, some seven days prior to the fire, was finally over and they had left Leah to add her own personal touch to her much wanted unborn child's room.

'We left some turps, and a couple of brushes,' Alan said.

'What were the couple like to work for?' asked Andy.

'Leah brought us sandwiches and homemade cakes,' said George.

'Did they have any visitors whilst you were there?'

Alan scowled. 'Not that I recall,' said Alan scratching his head.

'Have you spoken to their gardener? He was the only person who we saw on a regular basis. He was forever pottering around the place doing odd jobs.'

The two Painter boys came to sit on the bottom platform of the scaffolding.

'Those the two vehicles you've been using?' said Jon noting the registration plate numbers, make and model in his pocket book.

'We need new ones but dad won't hear of it,' said George.

Andy walked around the vehicles observing closely every scratch and slight dent.

'What you looking for?' said Patrick who was close behind him.

Andy turned to see his inquisitive face. He smiled. 'Just making sure you've not had an argument with anything lately.'

'Always wanted to be a police officer did our Pat,' said Alan.

'Ey too bad he's as thick as pig shit,' shouted George.

Patrick screwed his face up at his brother. 'Why don't you go for a long run on a short pier!' he said, throwing the briefest of threatening glances in his direction.

'Do you work out of the county?' Andy asked Alan.

'Sometimes, but the cost of the fuel and travelling time doesn't usually mean it's viable these days.'

'Where else have you worked before?'

'North Yorkshire, South Yorkshire, East Yorkshire, Lancashire.'

'Recently?'

'No,' said Alan. 'Not in a long while.'

***

The afternoon was filled with telephone calls and scrutinising automatic number plate retrieval information. Any vehicle recorded in both areas would be flagged up to the enquiry and registered on the databases. All the personal details, along with vehicles used by the people being seen by the team of detectives were being fed into the HOLMES system.

All the people spoken to so far had alibis for the day of the fire, including the tree surgeon Nigel Earley. Him and his gang had been on an emergency call-out working in Marsden, twenty-five miles from the scene, where two large fallen trees were threatening the main trans-Pennine train line and all trains had been stopped until they had been removed.

Dylan looked around the briefing room and he felt for the team. They looked dead beat and with no positive lines of enquiry on either murder investigation moral was getting low.

'Don't forget every phone call made, every enquiry completed means we are a step closer to the killers. I know from experience that sooner or later we will get a breakthrough and the investigations will become more focussed. However, for the time being the nets have to remain wide-spread.'

Dylan had questions for the Merton Manor murder enquiry team: 'Did the Isaacs have any connection with North Yorkshire? Did Jake and Leah know Cedric Oakley? Had they got the telephone analysis? Was there anything forthcoming from it?' Dylan's eagerness was met by a lot of blank faces. 'Our killers will have made mistakes and it's our job to find them. We know the same gun was used to murder the Isaac family and Mr Oakley, if it was the same person, people then I feel sure they are not going to stop killing until they are caught.'

The working copy of the disc for York Races had arrived on his desk while he had been in the debriefs. It was six o'clock when he opened the brown envelope that contained the stills of those identified. It felt like something positive. Being given something visual to look at brought the murdered victim to life for him. He was now real. He saw for the first time footage of the deceased Cedric Oakley. Instead of going home he put the disc in his computer and sat down. Sitting on the edge of his chair, he fast forwarded every image hoping something would catch his eye.

Race courses had somehow withstood the passage of time and still drew in massive crowds. With the stills available to him he was quickly able to recognise the victim Cedric Oakley in the VIP lounge. To say he was one who was known for being a lady's man there was only one lady that he appeared to have eyes for. He raised a glass to the stunning young woman sometime later. The young woman who hadn't been identified was with a man and another couple. The men could have been twins.

He stretched his back, loosened his tie and opened the top button of his shirt. Turning off his computer he was in the process of locking his desk draw when his phone rang. He considered letting it ring but thought better of it. He snatched the phone, 'Dylan,' he said abruptly.

'Boss, thought you'd like to know we've had some success with the drains. Some four streets back from the park, they've found a knife. CSI Mark Hamilton is photographing the exhibit in situ as we speak.'

'That's great news Vicky,' he said. Adrenalin rushed through his veins awakening his senses. 'That's got to be more than a coincidence hasn't it?'

'Hopefully. It's a hell of a weapon from what I can see, a real nasty looking blade.'

'Thanks for the call, let's get it examined forensically as a priority.'

'Will do boss, speak later.'

Dylan butted in. 'Unless it's urgent Vicky, leave it until morning will you. I'm going home and Jen and I need to talk.'

'Of course,' she said quietly.

It was eight o'clock when he looked up at his office clock. It was dark outside. Dylan picked up the phone and rung his home number.

'Hello?' Jen's voice was weak and hesitant.

'I'm coming home,' Dylan said. 'I think we need to talk?'

'Have you eaten?'

'No, you?'

'No.'

'I'll make something.'

'I'll pick something up?'

'You can for you, if you want but I'm not hungry,' said Jen.

'Me neither.'

'Don't bother then, just come home.' Jen's voice was almost inaudible to him.

***

The house looked cold and uninviting as Dylan pulled up in the driveway. The curtains were not drawn, but there were none of the usual welcoming lights shining from within. He let himself in the house and, putting his head around the lounge door, he saw

Jen sitting in the dark, her face lit only by the flames of the log fire. Max flapped his tail slowly and it brushed rhythmically against the wall, but he didn't move from where he was at Jen's side. She was huddled in his sweater amongst cushions and Maisy's toys. His eyes found hers, words were unnecessary as tears rolled down her cheeks unchecked. Dylan dropped to his knees. She went gladly into his open arms and they cried, but this time together.

Chapter Fifteen

CSI Mark Hamilton had a see-through plastic tube in his hand, it contained the knife recovered from the drain in Curzon Drive. He brought it to Dylan.

'That is one hell of a weapon.'

'It's cleanliness suggests it hasn't been down there for long and fortunately the drain was dry,' said Mark.

Dylan studied the large sturdy knife which had a yellow handle and jagged blade of, he guessed, around fourteen centimetres, seven inches.

'That blade would cut through flesh like butter,' said Mark.

'Why something so sinister is available to the public at large is beyond belief. It's an instrument of death,' said Dylan.

'Let's hope they find something on it when it's examined, linking it to Freddy Knapton, or his dog,' said Vicky.

***

The teaching staff at Groggs school were helpful and accommodating, providing opportunities for officers to speak with pupils in attendance. The Head was very concerned that a brutal killing had taken place so near to the school and appalled that someone had beheaded a dog, and displayed it in the adjacent park. Apparently he telephoned Chief Superintendent Hugo-Watkins office and asked what the police were doing about it.'

'The school are not aware of any of their pupils using graffiti similar to that daubed on the wall in the park, boss,' said Vicky in the morning briefing.

'They've developed good intelligence about those using graffiti as an art form, which fortunately has become less of a problem recently I'm told, due to the students being given supervised allocated places to display their art without causing offence,' added Ned.

'The art teacher knows the tags used by his pupils because most of them can't resist using the same logo to identify their work books,' said Shelagh

'With regard to the group of hoodies that have been hanging around the park, we have a name of two ex-pupils, two girls, who have been seen there. It is believed they have been hanging around with some older lads and those have yet to be identified,' confirmed Vicky.

'The art teacher told me that the school was aware of the group and were intending to make a report of nuisance to the police because of their behaviour, that had become abusive and intimidating, with recent threats directed towards younger children as they passed to and from school. There had also been demands made for cash. However, since the finding of the dog they appear to have moved on, and the report hadn't been deemed necessary,' said Ned.

'Do we have the names of two girls?' asked Dylan.

'Farah Ruwal, who's eighteen and her friend Tara Cabe sixteen. Both live on the Meadow Estate,' said Vicky.

'Farah has previously been cautioned for possession of a small amount of cannabis and both her and Tara have been recently caught shoplifting, which is still pending process,' said Ned.

'We have got them on our list to see as a priority,' said Vicky.

***

It wasn't long before DC Ned Granger and PC Shelagh MacPhee were knocking at the door of flat 4, Pan House, Meadows Estate.

'Fuck off! I ain't got no money!' came the hurried reply.

'Well, at least we know somebody's in,' said Ned quietly.

'It's the Police,' called Shelagh through the letter box. 'We'd like a word.'

'You've had a word, now fuck off,' came the reply from a girl within.

'Allow me,' said Ned. Raising his arm and pulling back his jacket sleeve. He made a fist and bringing it down hard on the door he hammered three times. His booted foot made contact with the wood and it cracked.

'Okay, okay, I'm coming! Don't smash the fucker. Council will go ape,' the girl shouted.

All was quite in the concrete clad corridor but for the key being turned in the lock. The door opened slowly, an inch at a time and stood before them, shadowed by the dingy hallway, was a large, heavily tattooed, obese young woman. With red rimmed eyes, she looked into PC MacPhee's face as if searching for something. She pushed her hoodie sleeves back to her elbows as if up for a fight when her eyes found DC Granger's.

'What do you want?' she said scratching the back of her lank black shoulder length, mattered hair. 'Should be a law against people waking folk up at this time of day.' She yawned.

'It's nearly lunch time,' said Shelagh pushing past her.

'Exactly,' she said. Her hand still on the door her eyes followed the police officers up the corridor. 'I don't think I invited you in but, come in why don't you?'

Farah stood with her back to the door, her eyes now alive with anger as she stared at the police officers.

'We're here about Freddy Knapton's murder,' said Ned.

There was no reaction.

'You knew Freddy Knapton didn't you?'

'Might 'ave,' said Farah, head down, kicking the carpet with her grubby, bare, stumpy toes.

'Do you live here alone?' said Shelagh.

'Did you say you were from t'police or social?' Farah said, with a sideways glance.

'Police,' Ned said as he held out his warrant card for her to see.

A sly smile crossed her lips. 'I know who you are. I was joking.' she said throwing herself down on the mattress which lay on the floor. 'I live on me own, me mates just stop over for a sesh now and then.'

Farah sprawled out and reached for a cigarette packet at the side of her bed. 'I'd offer you a seat but, well, you can see there's nowhere to sit,' she said with the unlit cigarette bobbing up and down in her mouth. She propped herself up against the wall and lit the cigarette, puffed on it once and threw the match across the room where it lay on the carpet. 'Unless you want to sit on the floor?'

'Is that wise? You could start a fire,' said Ned.

Farah raised her eyebrows. 'It's okay, landlord's insured,' she said putting a lager can to her mouth and taking a gulp of it. She screwed her face up. 'Flat,' she said by way of an explanation.

'Freddy Knapton was murdered. This is serious,' Ned said.

'Good fucking riddance to bad rubbish is what I say.'

'Okay, we get it. You didn't like him?' Shelagh retorted.

'Like him,' she squealed. 'I fuckin' hated him,' she said, labouring on her words. 'He were a complete Twat. Look, if we saw him coming down the street me and me mates would cross over and then he'd shout and spit at us. He'd even started setting that vile dog of his on us.'

'When did you last see him?' asked Shelagh.

'Jesus, I don't know, maybe a week, ten days before he got what he deserved.' Farah stubbed her cigarette out on the wall beside her that was already full of round, burn marks. She continued to play with the stub, rolling it around in her fingers and eventually peeling the paper from its filter. Tossing the filter paper, she reached over her head put the tip on the windowsill.

'Can you remember where that was?' asked Ned.

'I think it might have been in Groggs Park. I don't remember.'

'Were you with anybody at the time?'

'I don't know,' she said shrugging her shoulders.

'Take your time. It's important,' Shelagh asked.

'It could've been Tara. Yeah, me and me mate Tara. I remember, she fancies this lad who hangs about in Groggs Park and we were waiting for him when Knapton went in t'park.'

'Good, that's good. So who else was there?' Ned's voice was more urgent.

'There were a few people there because I remember Tara...' Farah's face broke out in a wide grin. 'Tara'd promised this bloke, the one she fancies a blow job.'

If she was trying to shock the officers she was disappointed.

'So, who is this bloke then, does he 'ave a name?'

'You'll know him, Macca, Dean McIntyre.'

***

When Shelagh and Ned reached the car park leading to the semi-detached that was 256, Gregory Avenue, Meadow Estate, they sat for a moment to evaluate. Farah Ruwal hadn't enlightened them much but they now had the name of Dean McIntyre, a local robber, burglar, drug user and scourge of the community. They sat looking directly at Tara Cabe's home where she apparently lived with her mother.

'I hope Farah hasn't spoken to her,' said Shelagh as she climbed out of the car.

'If she hasn't, you can bet your bottom dollar she'll have texted her.'

The exterior of the property gave them a clue as to what mess they were to encounter inside.

Shelagh was on pins. 'We're going to need a responsible adult present, she's only sixteen. Fingers crossed mum's in.'

Ned put his foot up onto the broken decking and taking Shelagh's hand he helped her up onto the platform, guided her past the raised planks of wood and finally they stood side by side at the back door. He knocked on the hardboard that covered the broken pane of glass.

Mrs Cabe's willowy figure was wrapped in an expensive looking cardigan with a fur collar and deep fur trimmed pockets. Her face made up, her hair held three large strategically placed rollers, one either side of her head, and the other in her platinum dyed fringe. She clutched an e-cigarette in a Gatsby-style holder between the second and third finger of her right hand and held a tumbler in the other, on her feet were fluffy mules.

'We're investigating the murder of Freddy Knapton and we'd like to speak to your daughter please,' said Ned, smiling pleasantly at the woman.

Mrs Cabe looked dubious.

'And, of course because of her age we'll need you to be present.'

'I've always told my kids to give him a wide birth. He wasn't all there you know,' she said tapping her nose. 'Tara!' she shouted. Her eyes never left the officer's face. 'Why do you want to speak to her?'

'We are led to believe she belongs to a group that hangs around in Groggs Park?'

'We're just trying to build a picture of Freddie's movements,' added Shelagh.

'Come in.' Mrs Cabe beckoned the officers into the kitchen and they followed the woman, unsteady as she was on her feet, into the dining area. 'Tara! Get your pretty ass down here pronto! The police are here to see you.'

Mrs Cabe moved a stack of newspapers from one chair and various items of clothing from another, and invited the police officers to sit. 'She's still in bed,' she said with a shake of her head and a click of her tongue. 'I'll go get her. She should be out looking for a job,' she said as she left the room.

'Do you think she's been drinking?' whispered Shelagh.

'I don't think. I know,' said Ned nodding in the direction of a bottle of vodka with its cap missing and a half empty bottle of lemonade on the table directly in front of him.

Other than the overflowing ironing basket on the floor and the table scattered with cups and boxes from the nearby Indian takeaway, the room was not in bad order.

Tara Cabe was a tall, slim, attractive girl, who appeared before them dressed in an overlarge tiger-skin print, fluffy onesie. She looked considerably older than her age. 'Farah texted me.' She held her mobile phone at shoulder height. 'You've just been to her flat.'

'Farah Ruwal?' Mrs Cabe turned on her daughter. 'What have I told you about knocking around with her?'

Tara looked bored. 'What does Auntie Joanie say mam? Keep your friends close and your enemies even closer.' She turned to the police officers. 'Living on this estate it's better to have her as a friend than an enemy.'

'Did you know Freddy Knapton?' asked Shelagh.

'Tell me someone around here who didn't? Him and his dog, they terrified me. Another reason for having Farah as a friend, she's twice the size of him. You don't argue with her.'

'She tells us you were one of the group who used to meet in Groggs Park. Tell me, why don't they hang-out there anymore?'

Tara shrugged her shoulders. 'I don't know. They're just a bunch of losers anyway. Dean McIntyre, he's top dog. Farah fancies him,' she said with a little smirk.

Mrs Cabe turned on her daughter. 'You've not started going around with him too? God, give me strength Tara. You know he was the one who robbed your gran's flat.' She turned to the police officers. 'Another that was at the back of the queue when the brains were being handed out.'

'It's called survival mam. Don't you know?' Tara rolled he eyes.

'Who else is in this gang?' Mrs Cabe demanded.

'Harry Withers, Martin Lister, Joe Grayson, I don't know them all, they're all older than me.'

'That's what worries me.'

'Oh, mam.'

'What did the group get up to in the park?' asked Shelagh.

Tara's eyes flew to the ceiling. She pondered a moment or two. 'They just hang around.'

'And do what?'

'Smoke, drink, climb trees, mess about, talk. There's always one of them up there to hang out with if you're bored.'

'Did you see Freddy Knapton often in the park?'

'Quite often,' she said with a little chuckle. 'Freddy used to come through Groggs with Satan, screaming and shouting, throwing stones at us. One day they decided to bombard him with used bags, from the dog bin.' Her lips formed a smile that immediately turned to a frown. 'His dog attacked Courtney though. Luckily he managed to free himself, get through the park gate, shut it and leave the bloody lunatic attacking the gate. Courtney stopped coming up after that.'

'Did the gang and Freddy ever come to blows?' asked Ned.

Tara shook her head and screwed up her face. 'Not actually blows.'

'Okay put it this way, do you know of anyone who has been physically attacked or had any reason to attack Freddy Knapton?' responded Shelagh.

'No.' Tara sighed.

Ned took a deep breath. 'Who's the artist?'

'Artist?'

'The graffiti in the park?'

She took a bit of time to consider her answer. 'I don't know.'

Ned bent his head towards Tara, 'Well perhaps you might know why the gang are known for wearing hoodies – is it so that people can't recognise them when they're up to no good?'

'Hoodies are fashionable didn't you know?'

'Farah told us it was you who had a bit of a thing for Dean McIntyre?' Shelagh said. 'That true?'

'No way! It's her that's trying to get his kegs off. She'll catch a dose one of these days the way she puts it about.'

'Tara! I won't have you talk like that,' Mrs Cabe interrupted. 'Not even about Farah Ruwal.'

'Well, it's true,' said Tara sulkily.

***

The officers drove back to the incident room for the debrief. 'There's no accounting for taste. Seems to me like the girls are vying for Dean McIntyre's attention,' said Ned to Dylan.

'We asked Tara why the group stopped going up the park. But the only explanation she could give us was that it might have been because they knew the police would be all over it,' said Shelagh.

'Let's face it we know Farah Ruwal is two sandwiches short of a picnic but I got the feeling that Tara Cabe was also telling us what she thought her mum wanted to hear,' added Ned.

'The soldiers weren't all marching in line then?' remarked Dylan when he heard.

'Huh?' said Shelagh.

He smiled. 'My dad used to say that when we were kids if we didn't all sing from the same hymn sheet.'

Shelagh still looked blank.

'Telling the same story to get them out of a fix,' said Vicky. 'It'll be interesting to see what Dean McIntyre and the others Tara named have to say to us.'

'Gather the intelligence we have on this Dean McIntyre and let's put these named others in or out of the enquiry as soon as we can. I wonder where they're congregating now? Speak to the local support officers, they should know,' said Dylan.

'Or the PCSO. They're getting paid overtime these days. And what do we get?' mumbled Vicky.

'Fuck all,' said Ned.

'My mate earned nearly twice as much as I did last month,' said Shelagh. 'Tell me what's the point of a PCSO getting more overtime than a PC when they don't have the powers that we do? It just doesn't make sense.'

Vicky shook her head. 'The Government are bloody colour blind? How else can they justify not seeing the Thin Blue Line disappearing?'

'I've heard we're getting a lot of nuisance reports from Tandem Bridge railway station that began shortly after Freddy Knapton's murder, so I made some enquiries while you guys were out and Dean McIntyre features among others known to us,' said DS Raj. 'The usual, bad language, rowdy youths, broken bottles and rubbish bins fired. My suggested plan would be some discreet observations there for a couple of evenings, which may see the majority of the group together. Then with the assistance of uniform we do some stop checks and find out exactly who they are, and what they were doing on the day Freddy Knapton was murdered?'

Dylan didn't hesitate. 'Do it!'

'I also took the initiative to do a bit more digging into Dean McIntyre.' said Vicky. 'He's got previous for robbery at knifepoint and, as luck would have it, at present he is the main suspect for a robbery where a knife was used at the Elf Filling Station, about two miles from Groggs Park. The one witness we have for this attack is waiting to do a visual ID.'

'Let's see if we can get that accelerated by the VIPER unit. It shouldn't be difficult for the computer suite to facilitate it, they don't have to go out and get volunteers to stand on an identification parade anymore now they're computerised. When I think back, the number of times we turned a whole office out, to find look-a-likes for a parade. If I heard a prisoner say, "It's not me. Put me on a ID parade," my heart would sink. Their solicitors knew how hard it was to get look-a-likes and therefore we usually had to bail their client to a suitable date when we could pull one together. Hence the defendant had more time to come up with a likely story. We only had a fiver to give to a member of the general public that we could find to stand on the parade. Students and pensioners loved us, but for the others we'd have to go stand outside the benefits office. Any problems with the computer suite let me know.'

'Will do.'

'From our point of view if McIntyre is already in it makes it much easier for us to speak to him,' said Dylan.

'And once other members of the group know he's out of the way, we may just find some of them with squeaky bums,' Vicky said with a grin.

Dylan shook his head and a smile crossed his face.

'Don't look at me like that, it's true.' She wagged a finger at Dylan. 'If the group think he might be talking to save his own skin then they might speak to us too. Going back to our attendance at the murder scene though, you said you thought someone had pre-planned the attack. Do you really think the likes of Dean McIntyre, Farah and Tara are capable of being so clever?'

'We'll only know that when we've interviewed them won't we? One thing's for sure, there won't be any short cuts, the interviewing and elimination of suspects will need structure. The usual attention needs to be set on clearing the ground beneath our feet before moving on.'

***

'Tomorrow is another day' – Dylan read out the wording on the sign in his office. He turned off the light and headed home.

Jen awaited Dylan with the news that she had been to see the consultant at the hospital. Her voice was shaking.

His mood changed. 'Why didn't you tell me you were going. I'd have gone with you?'

'Don't be cross. It was something I needed to do on my own.' She reached out for the leaflets she had been given, gathered them together in her hands and dropped them like a hot potato in front of him. 'I will be given medication that will trigger off my labour. I will deliver our child naturally.'

Jen saw Dylan's face pale and she know it was more than he could take in. Sitting down with a thump on the chair, he put his briefcase down on the floor and put his hands to his face.

'There is no room for discussion,' said Jen softly. 'We can't hide from it anymore. We've talked about it. There is nothing else to say. We've spoken to doctors, nurses, the charity who supports couples like us and we both know there is nothing else to be done.'

Dylan nodded his head sadly. 'I know, you're right. What's next?' He looked defeated.

'I would like to name our son.'

'You would?'

'Yes, and I want to hold him in my arms, I want to know what he looks like, I want to feel close to him even if it's only for a while. I want him to know we love him and we will never forget him. I want to say hello; I want to say goodbye.' Tears streamed down Jen's face.

'And when can this happen?' Dylan was resigned to the fact.

'Tomorrow. Unless.' she said, her voice faltering. 'Unless you can't make it.'

Dylan shook his head and reached out to hold her hand. 'I'm sorry. If I seem to have been pre-occupied. I didn't know what to say to you. How to say it. In true Dylan style I've been keeping myself busy, on purpose, so I didn't have to think about, the inevitable. I would like to do all the things that you want to do. I'd like to call him Joe, after my dad.'

'Joe, that's nice. Joe it is then.' Jen touched her stomach.

For the first time in days he saw a brief glimpse of a smile pass Jen's lips. 'Joe Dylan,' she said softly. 'I like that.'

Bone-tired, Jen washed up the pots and said good night to Dylan who she left staring at the TV screen in the lounge. The room was silent. Dylan often watched TV without the sound to detach his mind from recalling terrible images that he had witnessed during the day but she knew this time it was different. Jen climbed the stairs with a heaviness in her heart that she had never felt before but the weight on her shoulders was lesser. She stood at Maisy's bedroom window, looking at the night sky and she prayed. Where was her mum when she needed her? The brightest star in the sky twinkled brightly and with tears in her eyes she sat down beside Maisy's bed and put her hand on her little girl, feeling her warm body through the sheet. She listened to her rhythmic, shallow breathing. Sleepily, she put her head upon the duvet and softly cried herself to sleep.

When Dylan went to bed some time later, he saw by the light of Maisy's night light that Jen lay there. Softly, he padded in his stocking feet across the little girl's bedroom carpet and gently lifted Jen up into his arms. In her sleepy state she didn't object but allowed him to take her to their room and lay her down on the bed. She was cold to his touch. He climbed into bed fully clothed and drew Jen towards him. In a matter of minutes, he was asleep.

Chapter Sixteen

After a couple of fitful hours Dylan woke to hear the handle of the bedroom door being turned. Jen looked to see Dylan rise up on his elbow. 'Go back to sleep,' she whispered. 'It's only half past five. I'll bring you a coffee in an hour.' With that she crept out of the door. He heard her footsteps on the landing. Max greeted her at the foot of the stairs with a low, gruff bark. Following her into the kitchen he stood by the back door. She opened it and let him out. Dylan lay still for a while but his mind was active. He went to the bathroom, got dressed and went downstairs. There was a pleasant aroma of baking.

'What on earth are you doing?' asked Dylan wearily noting the scones and buns covering the worktops. Jen turned suddenly, her hands full of dough. She wiped her cheek with a floury hand and went back to the job in hand without speaking, threw the dough on the worktop and kneaded it with her knuckles as fiercely as she could.

'Bread, I'm baking bread,' she said eventually.

'But you don't need to make bread Jen, today of all days.'

'That's where you're wrong, I do!' she said clapping her hands together to release a flurry of flour. Jen went to the tap and filled the kettle. She noticed Dylan's strained face. He gave her a knowing smile. 'Eggs and bacon for breakfast?' she said.

'Whatever you want to give me,' he replied. When Jen had made her mind up he knew there was no stopping her. If this was how she was to cope with what was facing her today he would not interfere. 'You okay?'

'If you mean do I feel okay?' she said sitting down next to him as he drank his coffee. 'Yes.' She shrugged her shoulders. 'What choice do I have?'

Saddened, Dylan didn't taste the hearty breakfast but was thankful for the sustenance. 'If it's okay with you I'll go in to work this morning, see what's happening and pick you up at lunchtime to take you to the hospital?'

Jen looked across at his attire. 'Well I didn't think you'd be wearing a shirt and tie if not,' she said, as a sleepy Maisy, teddy under her arm walked through the door. Jen rose to pick her up. She sat her on her knee and cuddled her tight. Maisy wiggled in her mother's arms. 'And you little lady are going to stay at Chantall's for a sleepover.' She tickled her daughter. 'How exciting is that?' she said to the now giggling little girl.

'Are you sure?' said Dylan.

'I'm certain. When Maisy comes home, it'll all be over and we will be back to normal.' Jen was busily preparing Maisy's breakfast.

'And you're sure you don't want me to get your Dad and Thelma to come up from the Isle of Wight for a few days? They'd be here like a shot if we asked them.'

Jen came to stand at the foot of the table. 'I know they would.' She expelled air from pursed lips. 'But how many times do I have to tell you I want as few people as possible to know about the baby and most definitely not my Dad.'

'Okay, okay,' Dylan held his hands up in the air. Jen gave him a gentle shove.

'Now get off to work and out from under our feet while we get Maisy's overnight bag ready. What do you say Maisy?'

Maisy nodded her head and with a squeal ran towards the stairs.

***

Dylan walked like a man on a mission as he entered his office. The phone was ringing. He answered it.

'Dylan, it's Terry Hawk,' the North Yorkshire DI said. 'I want to release some stills of the people we've got on CCTV seen talking to Cedric Oakley at York Races. Have you got a problem with that?'

Still standing Dylan flipped through the paperwork in his tray and pulled out the stills of the race meeting. 'No, that sounds like a good idea to me.'

'We've got some information from a friend of Oakley's who tells us the girl at the bar, seen flirting with the old man is believed to be from an escort agency. Any intelligence on your enquiry that suggests any involvement with escort girls?'

Dylan scowled. 'Not that I'm aware of.'

'Didn't think so but I thought I'd check. We're scrutinising Oakley's bank records, credit card usage and his mobile, but as you know only too well, to get results takes time.'

One of the problems with the investigation at Merton Manor was that the fire had been so intense and destructive that Dylan and his team didn't have the luxury of documents to seize and examine as did their colleagues in North Yorkshire. All that remained at the home of Jake and Leah Isaac was a pile of blackened debris. The majority of which was ash. Even the Isaac's cars, housed at the time in the attached double garage were burnt out shells. The fire had done what the perpetrators had hoped it would do – destroyed evidence but, thankfully, not all the evidence.

They were in the process of creating a pen picture of the couple from knowledge gathered from work colleagues, accountants, solicitors, doctors, dentists. The list was seemingly endless as the officers would ask questions of anyone they felt could assist in the enquiry, whether they wished to speak to them or not.'

Dylan was in no mood for talking. His office door firmly shut, a sign that staff knew meant he didn't want to be disturbed. He looked up from his computer screen to see through the glass in the door, DC Wormald hovering. He beckoned him in. 'Did you want to speak?'

'Yes, sir but I didn't want to disturb you,' Andy said noticing Dylan tapping his desk with his fingertips. He looked wary. Dylan reassured him. 'The closed door is because I won't be in this afternoon and I have a lot of work to get through before I go. Jon will be taking the debrief. Will it wait?'

'DS Summer's is working lates sir and we've just had a call into the incident room from a motorist who had been driving past Merton Manor at the time of the fire. I thought you might like to know about it?'

'Go on.'

The caller tells us she saw a blue Mercedes pull out of the driveway. She remembered the car for two reasons, one because it was clean, bright, new looking, and the other because she had to slow down as it pulled out in front of her, in haste. She was one of a number of people who telephoned the fire-brigade.' In Andy's eyes Dylan could see a glimmer of excitement. He quickly moved on. 'Another caller tells us that they saw a vehicle in a lay-by overlooking the manor house from the top road. He remembered the car because the fire came into view below in the distance, as he passed it. This vehicle was described as a blue Mercedes saloon.'

'Both positive lines of enquiry. The lay-by where the car was seen. I want it searched. A sighting of the car leaving the scene at the time of the fire – Excellent! Which way did the witness say the vehicle turned on exiting Merton Manor?'

'To the right sir, towards the moors and the motorway network.'

Dylan's spirits were lifted. 'So the car in the lay-by could have been one and the same. There will be cameras on the approach to the motorway. Find me a blue Mercedes with a showroom finish and get me that witness statement to read asap. Ask both witnesses if there is anything else they can remember, no matter how trivial it may seem.'

'Yes, sir.' Andy turned to leave.

'While you're on it, is someone checking to see if there have been any reports of a Mercedes being found burnt out, or stolen? If so where, when and what colour?'

On Andy's exit, Dylan could hear the buzz of the incident room outside, Vicky had just walked in with Shelagh. The familiar banter brought him out of his despair for a brief moment. 'Leave the door open, and thanks Andy,' he said, needing normality.

'Fancy a brew?' called out Vicky. Dylan couldn't help but smile as he watched her throw down her shopping bags and sit at her desk.'

'That would be great,' he shouted back.

'Ned!' Dylan saw her calling over her shoulder. 'Put kettle on. Boss wants a brew and mine's a black coffee. Two sugars. No make that three,' she added. 'I need the energy.'

Vicky staggered into Dylan's office. 'Andy called me about the Mercedes so I've been to the garage off the slip road to the MI on my way in.' Vicky dropped down onto a chair. 'The girl behind the counter, she can't half talk. And, I've got a throat like bloody sandpaper.'

'Have they got CCTV?'

'Yes, requested,' she said, with a grin. 'We're hoping we might pick up the blue Merc refuelling or the occupants using the loo.'

Dylan smiled.

'Why are you smiling? I always stop there to use their loo before I go onto the MI.'

'You remind me of Jen. She plans our journeys around the toilets en route, especially when she's preg...' Dylan stopped, his face saddened.

'When's it happening?' Vicky's voice lowered. Her eyes were downcast.

'This afternoon.' Dylan's voice cracked with emotion. Ned walked in with two cups of coffee and put them down on the corner of Dylan's desk.

'Milk?' Vicky turned abruptly to her colleague.

Dylan immediately picked up his cup and put it to his trembling lip.

'You said black?' said Ned. 'Make up yer mind.'

'Women's prerogative to change her mind, especially when that woman is your boss,' she said winking at him.

Ned stamped out of the office grumbling under his breath.

Dylan's eye's met Vicky's over the rim of his cup. 'Thanks,' he said, appearing more composed.

'The woman witness recalling a Merc coming out of the driveway at the time of the fire... Isn't it strange how some people recall something like that happening well after the event?' said Vicky.

'Yes, but she might have noted it at the time and thought little of it, a minor detail, until we asked if she remembered anything else. Now to us, that minor detail could be of significant importance, but to her it was just a car leaving the driveway of Merton Manor that she may have seen happen a hundred times before.'

'Or it could have been something in particular that triggered her memory, like the speed?'

'I remember a job some years ago when a woman was the subject of a vicious cash point robbery, she gave us a great description of her attacker and we did an e-fit. On the same day we locked someone up. Officers went to inform her of the arrest and tell her that they had recovered her credit card. They also wanted to inform her of the fact that he had a tattoo on his face which was readily visible and ask her why she hadn't mentioned it? Would you believe that her immediate response on answering the door to the officers was, "He's got a swallow tattoo on his right cheek. I remembered seeing it when I saw you at the door."'

'I've taken statements to similar effect. In that instance was the guy found guilty?'

'Yes, but the defence claimed he had found the woman's credit card and they went overboard about the fact that she hadn't mentioned the tattoo at the time of making her initial statement, and in fact not until their client was arrested. The defence alleged that the witness was shown a picture of the offender. Therefore, they wanted the judge to exclude her evidence, but he wouldn't, and he left it to the jury to make their mind up as to whether she was telling the truth or not.'

'And was she?'

'She certainly was and he was proved to have previous. Although that couldn't be revealed to the jury at the time. He got put away for four and half years.'

'And that's why we interview witnesses more than once.'

'In my experience it appears people remember all sorts of things when we, the interviewers start talking about sounds, feelings on the day, the weather, how they think other people would describe what had happened and getting them to start at the end of the incident and work back.'

'Cognitive interviewing; let's hope she suddenly remembers the registered number,' Vicky smirked.

'And then where would the challenge be for us?' Dylan cocked an eyebrow.

'It appears, according to her statement, that the only other thing the witness could tell us about the Mercedes was that the blue was a royal blue,' said Vicky, wafting a single piece of paper in her hand. 'And we are lucky because she was more aware then most, having previously worked in a car showroom.'

'And we're sure she doesn't suffer from colour blindness?'

Vicky looked puzzled.

'It doesn't occur often these days but Faulty Trichromatic Vision is the technical terminology. Reduced sensitivity to green light is the most common, followed by red, and blue being the rarest. So if you ever get major discrepancies between witnesses on a colour, that could be the reason.'

'That could be so unintentionally misleading.' Vicky's eyes grew wide.

'Exactly.'

'Talking of what they saw, neither witness can say anything about the occupants of the car,' said Vicky.

'Not unusual, but what I think needs to be done now is for them both to point out a car which is the exact same colour, don't you?' added Dylan.

'And the model they had seen if they are confident in doing so?'

'Yes agreed. I want to be absolutely sure about the description of the vehicle before we appeal to the public for more information. I've asked Andy to get the lay-by searched where the car was seen by the second witness, any waste paper, cigarette butts, cans, bottles collected. If we are lucky enough to get a registration number from the CCTV available in the area...'

'Then our task is to locate it.' Vicky said matter-of-factly.

Dylan was pleased with the progress on both enquiries, each had started gathering momentum and were focussed. Vicky updated him on the Knapton enquiry.

'By the way, the witness from the Elf filling station is coming in to the VIPER Unit tomorrow to view the suspects. Wonder if she'll pick out Dean McIntyre?'

'Time will tell.'

'At least the poor woman won't have to go through the dreadful scenario of having to walk down a line-up and touch the shoulder of the one she recognises as the person she saw committing the crime. Can you imagine what that must have been like for a rape or an attempted murder victim in the past?'

'No, the computerisation of identification parades, with its visual suspects, really does test the witnesses but in a safe and none intimidating environment.'

'Do you remember the two way mirror they used at one time?'

'I remember it well. At that time the witness or victim could view the suspect on the line-up without them being able to see them.'

'Trouble is nowadays the computer images available are so strikingly similar I don't think I could pick out the real Ned.' Vicky leaned forward and looked out of the window in the office door. She waved at Ned Granger from where she sat. She turned to Dylan and screwed up her nose. 'Oh, I don't know though. There could never be another Ned Granger, could there?' she said with a laugh. 'More?' she said lifting her cup. Ned stuck a middle finger in the air. Dylan and Vicky shared a smile.

Chapter Seventeen

Jen sat nervously waiting for Dylan to arrive home, clutching the forever baby blanket she had made to wrap their son in. She looked down at the closely knit wool. Oh, how she had never wanted it to be finished, for as long as she was making it her baby was still alive. She rubbed her finger gently over the delicate sky blue, silk stitching of his initials and lifted it to her cheek to feel it's softness. How many tears had fallen on it she did not know, and could not tell, but they were there woven into the fabric as was her love.

Her eyes were drawn to her small suitcase that stood upright at the front door.

Max lay beside her on the sofa, his sleepy head rested on her lap. She ruffled the fur behind his ears and his big, brown, trusting eyes opened wide, rewarding her with a look of unconditional love.

The sound of silence that ensued was calming and with it she was lulled into a sense of peace. She sat back, put her hand on her stomach and closed her eyes. Suddenly Max flinched, his's ears shot up at the sound of a vehicle approaching and Jen leaned forward to see out of the window. Was it Dylan? Her heart began racing. This was it. But it was the red post van that pulled up outside. She saw the postman get out of the van and stroll across the front lawn. She heard a knock. Max barked twice but didn't bother to get up. The milkman parked up when the postman drew away from the curb and, jumping off his milk cart whistling, she heard the patter of his feet that quickened to a run down the path to the back door. A clink of bottles meant he had taken the empties. Everyone around her was going about their usual business but her day was far from normal.

Jen sat on the edge of the seat and looked around the room - she took a deep breath. Her very first home of her own. The place where she had found sanctuary, fleeing the Isle of Wight after being dumped by her childhood sweetheart. Shaun had decided he couldn't live with a woman who had been told she would never have children. She had thought at the time she would never feel happy again. But this house held so many happy memories. In this room she and Dylan had shared their first kiss. There had been love, laughter, Christmases, and birthday celebrations shared. And then Maisy had come along quite unexpectedly; Maisy filled Dylan and Jen's lives with insurmountable joy. Swallowing a sob, she leaned forward and puffed up the cushion behind her ready to leave everything in its rightful place when she left for the hospital.

Although she had told Dylan that she was okay, he needn't worry about her, inside her heart was breaking.

Dylan gazed across at Jen's pale face when he entered the lounge. Feeling her pain, he walked across to her, she stood as if in slow motion, not a scrap of emotion on her face. He opened his arms and she walked into them. His heart swelled with love for her. He so badly wanted to tell her that everything was going to be okay, that he could make it all better. But he couldn't. Instead his expression stiffened and he found the strength as he always did behind the mask of the detective. Without speaking, Jen pulled herself away from him and picking up her coat that lay on the arm of the settee, next to the door, she walked into the hall. She bent down to pick up the suitcase but Dylan, coming up silently behind her, snatched it up. He opened the front door for her and she stepped over the threshold. She heard her own footsteps clip, clip, on the paving stones and the rhythm was somewhat soothing. Then she heard the slam of the front door behind her; she flinched, the key was turned in the lock, she stopped, Dylan's footsteps came behind her, and then she felt his encouraging hand in the small of her back push her towards the car.

***

Joe Dylan was fifteen weeks and four days when he was delivered naturally. His tiny, lifeless body was the same weight as a classic bar of chocolate, he measured the length of ball point pen. He was surprisingly well formed. Dylan looked into Jen's teary eyes and shook his head. He swallowed hard. For the longest, deepest moment, the silence was awesome. Jen tenderly took her baby from the midwife. Half blinded by her own tears, Jen gazed at the small face then she put him to her bare chest and, digging her head back in her pillow, her heart-wrenching cry bounced off the walls of the small delivery room, striking fear into Dylan's heart. This long serving police officer, negotiator, hadn't got the words of comfort for his wife – he had never felt so inept. Half an hour later Dylan took their son from his wife, in his strong, safe hands and, saying goodbye, he handed Joe back to the nurse who tenderly took him away. Dylan lay on the bed and held his wife in his arms. Sobbing, she clutched at his shirt as if she would never let it go until she was exhausted. When he pulled away from her and tilted her red, tearstained face up to his he looked into her stricken eyes. 'I'm so proud of you,' he said. She raised her clenched hand and laid it open on his face.

'You look tired,' she said, as a little sob that sounded more like a hiccup escaped from her lips.

Dylan put his hand over hers and squeezed it tightly. He shut his eyes for one brief moment and felt her warm breath on his face. Kissing her forehead, he brushed away damp tendrils of hair. 'Try to rest for a while. I promise we will never, ever forget our little Joe.'

Jen smiled at him wistfully. 'I know we won't. I love you,' she said closing her eyes.

'I love you more,' he said softly.

***

As Dylan walked in the office early the next morning Vicky walked in behind him. 'Am I dreaming,' he said. Then he looked her up and down. 'Or haven't you been home?'

'Sarcasm doesn't suit you. Actually, I thought I'd come in early and make you a morning cuppa, make sure you're okay?' her voice trailed into nothing but a whisper. 'Talk to me?'

'There is nothing to say,' he said. His lips formed a straight line. 'It's over. He was a beautiful little baby boy.' Dylan dismissed her sympathy to keep his self-control. 'So, I know why I'm in early.'

With suspicion written on his face he said, 'What's the real reason you are?'

Vicky took a deep breath. There was no point in pushing him, Dylan didn't want to talk. 'Dean McIntyre, we got a positive identification for the robbery at the garage. So I want to make sure everyone is doing their bit, myself included, so he can be locked up this morning.'

The briefest smile crossed his lips. 'Good news,' he said, his words punching the air. 'That's a positive.'

'Too right. Am I right in presuming that you're going to switch the kettle on then?'

'Why not, I called in at the butchers and got some pork dripping.'

'By 'eck you know how to treat a man. When I were a young detective it was common place at briefings, a plate full of toast and dripping. Even the local pubs used to have it on the bar alongside black pudding.'

Vicky pulled a face. 'Black pudding? Pig's blood and fat. That must be a real artery clogger. I don't know how you're still here.'

'And then there was the salt... No doubt to ensure we ordered plenty to drink to quench the thirst.'

'As if detectives needed an excuse to drink.'

'True, it's a good job you weren't born earlier. We lived off tripe and elder, pigs trotters, sheep's eyes and brains on the farm when I was young. Pigs ears were for the dogs as well as all the bits we didn't eat, and that fed the cats too. There was no waste; not with a family of seven and the grandparents living with us at one time.'

'My dog would have been obese.' Vicky laughed out loud.

'Yeah, well people do say that dogs look like their owners.'

'And some people might get burnt toast if they're not careful.'

Ned Granger threw open the door from the outer office. 'Get a move on Sarge, we're about ready for morning briefing. Are you making that dripping and toast or not?'

'Not, you are.' Vicky proffered a fake smile.

Ned shuffled off towards the kitchen mumbling to himself as he did so.

Vicky turned to Dylan, took the papers from under her arm and hurriedly slid them across the desk to him. 'I've done you a précis of events that took place yesterday.'

There was a pause. When he looked up his face was pained. Dylan nodded his appreciation. He sat back in his big old leather chair and picked them up. 'I'll be with you as soon as I've read through them.'

***

Dylan found work a welcome distraction. Feverishly he went through the notes, and then standing, he looked at his clock before heading out of his office and into the corridor towards the briefing room. Standing in front of the kitchenette mirror he saw dark circles under his eyes and wisps of unruly hair protruding from behind his ears, he looked a sorry state. Slicking back clumps of hair, he fastened the buttons on his suit jacket and straightened his tie, turned and marched into the meeting -fully prepared for what lay ahead.

Despite the turmoil inside he noticed a cloak of silence fell over the room as he entered. He nodded his reassuring smile. The mask of a detective once again served him well. Everyone present moved to find a seat, and when all the seats were taken others leaned their backs against the walls, door and filing cabinets. Dylan took a seat at the front of his audience beside Vicky and Raj. He noted that a few had started softly speaking, while others remained silent. All had one purpose in mind: to catch a killer.

An hour later the meeting was over and he felt as though they were making progress, Dylan was pleased. Dean McIntyre was today's target, his bail address was 4 Radlee Terrace, where he lived with his father. It was hoped he would be at home. There was the hustle and bustle of many people in one room moving, scraping chairs, and the shuffle of footsteps. A hubbub of noise ensued and the delegates filed out in an orderly fashion through one door - all with a renewed purpose and eager to get the day started.

***

Frank McIntyre was one of those men you heard long before setting eyes upon him. Bad language spewed from his mouth in a torrent of abuse when the police knocked at his door. The image Vicky had of this man was confirmed as soon as she saw him, and she was glad to have Ned at her side.

Dark skinned, he stood flexing his heavily tattooed, body builder muscles at her when his child-like, painfully thin girlfriend called him to the door. With a roll-up in one hand she stood in front of his six foot seven towering frame, wearing a skin tight baby pink T-shirt, that showed off her skeletal frame. Her faded jeans rested on her protruding hip bones. She shook like a leaf.

Vicky and Ned were at the front door aware that two uniformed officers were at the rear as planned, just in case Dean McIntyre tried to do a runner.

'What the fuck do you want now?' Frank spat at Vicky's feet. He leaned heavily on the door frame that he filled with his bulk. 'Is Dean the only person you know on this fucking estate? He's been here all night, hasn't he Raquel?'

Vicky cleared her throat and began to speak. 'We want to talk to Dean about a robbery at the Elf garage.'

'You've already interviewed and bailed him. When are you going to get it into your thick skulls, it ain't him?'

'Surprise, surprise, we found out he was lying to us?' she said with a little smile. 'So we take it he's in then?' she said firmly pushing her way into the house.

Showing the whites of his eyes Frank McIntyre stepped back and Ned followed her inside.

'Don't you need a warrant or something?' Raquel said finding her voice.

Vicky scanned the room before turning her gaze back to Raquel. 'No, where is he?'

'Where he always is at this time of fuckin day, in his pit,' said Frank collapsing into a leather armchair.

Vicky looked at Raquel questioningly.

'Upstairs, first on the left.' she said, her eyes turning towards the back of the house.

Under a grubby, grey duvet in a darkened room that smelt of damp and mould Dean McIntyre was found in his bed. 'Come on Dean. Time to wake up?' Ned said in a raised voice.

'Fuck off,' Dean said as he lifted his head and saw, through eyes half shut, the police officers standing at the foot of his bed. He pulled the bedcover over his head and curled up in a ball.

Vicky spoke to the two uniformed officers who were still outside the house, over the airways. 'We've located the target in his bedroom. At this time, he's being uncooperative. Can we have some assistance please?'

Dean McIntyre kicked out. 'You can't go dragging people out of their fucking beds. I've done fuck all wrong,' he shouted from under the duvet.

A hush came over the room. There were raised voices downstairs and in a short space of time, to the annoyance of his father, two uniformed officers had joined Vicky and Ned in Dean's bedroom.

Standing over the bed, Vicky Hardacre took one look at her colleagues, 'Due to new evidence coming to light, you are being re-arrested in connection with the Elf service station robbery.'

He continued to be unresponsive so he was unceremoniously hoisted from under the covers by the two uniformed police officers, handcuffed and taken outside to their marked car, where he was placed in the rear of the vehicle.

'Where are you taking him?' said Frank joining the detectives in his son's room.

'Cell area, Harrowfield Police Station,' said Vicky. 'Now if you don't mind we need to search his room.' Ned ushered Frank out onto the landing where he remained, watching.

There was nothing obviously of relevance in the room but there was a laptop computer and a mobile phone which they took possession of. Bagging and tagging them immediately in evidence bags before they removed them.

Frank followed Vicky and Ned down the stairs.

'What're you doing I paid for them?'

'That maybe,' said Vicky over her shoulder. 'But they might hold evidence in the stored data. I'll write a receipt for you, don't panic.'

'Clever cow.' Vicky heard Raquel say. 'Who does she think she is?'

Vicky walked down the front path to the car. 'Will he be in Court tomorrow?' Frank shouted after her.

'Probably,' she called back. Ned was already sat in the driver's seat.

Arriving back at the police station a sense of urgency prevailed. 'I hope the computer geeks can get us something from this laptop,' said Vicky. Her eyes were bright. 'Who knows it might show us the purchase of the knife, now wouldn't that be the icing on the cake for us right now?'

'The data from his mobile should give us the information we need to find out who he's been hanging about with and where, but we aren't going to get any intelligence back before he's due for an interview,' said Ned.

'He's under arrest for the robbery so we'll concentrate on that first. We'll not know if he's going to talk to us until his solicitor gets here,' said Vicky.

'Let's face it, Sarge, he's not going anywhere for the foreseeable and then he'll be up for a remand in custody at court after we charge him with the robbery.'

'And that will afford us some time to do some more digging into any subsequent revelations from his belongings.'

'We can still talk to him under caution in the interview about his movements around the time that Freddy and his dog was murdered though can't we?' said Ned.

'Certainly. He's not under arrest for the murder, so we would automatically eliminate him, if possible, like anyone else we talk to. But, he may not want to talk to us at all, especially knowing he's going down for a stretch.'

'Thought we weren't doing negative today Sarge?' Ned frowned.

Vicky eyed Ned suspiciously. 'Are you taking some sort of happy pills?'

'No, why?' Ned grinned.

'You don't seem your usual, annoyingly, frustrating self today.' Ned chuckled sheepishly.

'Don't tell me. The wife's forgiven you?' Vicky said. Ned nodded.

'More fool her,' she said opening the door and letting it slam in his face, locking it behind her. He looked through the window and raised his middle finger. 'Swivel,' he mouthed.

'That's more like it,' she said.

'What you grinning at?' Dylan asked as she walked into the CID office. He was stood over Andy who was sitting at his desk, sleeves rolled up. They were both looking at Andy's computer screen. Dylan stood straight.

'Where's Ned?'

'He'll be here in a minute,' she said as the double doors opened and Ned marched in muttering under his breath.

'What've you two got for me?'

'Computer, mobile phone and Dean McIntyre is in the cells boss!' she said.

'Do you think he might want to clear his slate and admit to what he's done?' enquired Dylan.

'Let's say you've probably more chance of discovering the moon is made of green cheese,' Vicky replied.

***

Two hours later Vicky and Ned were sitting in an interview room with Dean McIntyre and his solicitor Yvonne Best, from Perfect & Best Solicitors who resided in Harrowfield's old Co-op building.

Formalities of the caution took place and everyone in the room spoke their name in turn for the purpose of voice identification.

'Dean you were previously arrested for a robbery at the Elf service station and granted police bail whilst the witness completed the identification process known as VIPER, as your solicitor Mrs Best is aware. The witness positively identified you as the robber. Do you have anything to say about this?'

He gave a long impatient sigh. He was looking down at his hands that were resting on the table that stood in-between the officers and his solicitor. After a few silent moments he slowly raised his eyes to look at Vicky. 'I'm fucked, aren't I?'

'That's one way of putting it.'

He shrugged his shoulders. 'Shit happens.'

'Do you want to tell us about it?'

'What's there to tell? You know all about it, that's why I'm fucking here isn't it?'

'We don't know everything. You had a knife. Where did you get it from?'

Dean McIntyre shuffled in his seat. 'It's legit. I bought it. Straight up.' Dean turned his hands palms up.

'Where did you buy it from?' Ned asked.

'Army surplus, Queen's Street. Owner's top shelf.'

'Why did you want a knife like that? Couldn't you have taken one from home? Let's face it, any knife is going to frighten someone if it's pointed at them,' said Vicky.

'I wanted a proper one.'

'It wouldn't have been cheap?' asked Ned.

'Twenty quid,' he said showing his bottom lip. 'Not much.'

'Where did you get the twenty quid to buy the knife?'

Looking down at the floor between his legs Dean McIntyre shuffled his feet. 'Frank has a tankard where he puts his money. He doesn't know I know about it. He'll kill me when he finds out I've nicked off him.'

'Where's the knife now?' asked Ned.

He was unresponsive.

After a few minutes Vicky tried. 'Is there a problem?'

'No,' he said, with a scowl. 'I chucked it when I saw all the blue lights. I didn't want to get caught with it on me, did I?'

'You chucked it where?' Vicky leaned towards the table and nearer to him. He responded by sitting back. He waited a moment before answering.

'I threw it by the dustbins that belong to them flats by the park.'

'And you expect us to believe that? It cost you twenty quid and you threw it away? Did you go back to look for it?'

'Yeah, the next day but it had gone.' Dean's mouth opened wide and he yawned noisily.

'So, you went back to the place where you'd thrown it and it had gone, disappeared?'

McIntyre nodded.

'Okay. What did you do with your clothes you were wearing on the day of the robbery?' said Vicky.

He had a smirk on his face. 'Went in next door's bin. I'm not daft.'

'How much did you get from the robbery at the garage?' asked Ned.

'Fifty.'

'Pounds or pence?' snapped back Ned, his face deadly serious.

'Fifty pence. As if?' Dean scoffed.

'What did you do with the money?' Ned continued.

McIntyre shrugged his shoulders. 'Spent it.'

'What on?'

'Beer, a bit of weed.'

'You'd threaten a woman with a knife and almost scare the living daylights out of her for fifty quid? The knife cost twenty and the rest goes on beer and weed?' Vicky said raising her voice slightly.

'I wasn't gonna hurt her was I?'

'She didn't know that.'

'Well, whatever she said, I never touched her.'

'What's troubling me, is that it doesn't make sense to nick twenty quid from your dad, who you admit will kill you when he finds out, and throw the knife away that you bought with it?'

'I didn't know the woman would only have fifty in the fucking till did I?'

'Where's the knife Dean? I don't believe you threw it away... did you?' Vicky pushed on.

'Well, I did.'

'You got away from the scene of the crime without being caught. You weren't being chased. So, why throw the knife away?'

'What's the use in asking me, if you don't believe me when I tell you the truth?' It was Dean McIntyre's turn to lean towards the table and for Vicky to sit back. 'Look, I've admitted to doing the crime, so I'll do the time. It'll be a piece of piss. I'll catch up with me mates inside,' he said nonchalantly. 'I don't care.'

'What colour handle did the knife have?' asked Ned.

'What colour? I'm not sure.' McIntyre looked confused. He shook his head. 'I'm tired. I don't want to answer any more questions,' he said turning to his solicitor.

Vicky shuffled the papers on the table and held them in her grasp. Her face showed her annoyance.

'Okay,' said Ned, terminating the interview. 'We've got what we need for now.' Sliding his chair back, he stood, and the others took his lead. 'If you'd follow me, we need to charge Mr McIntyre with robbery.'

'Harrowfield Magistrates tomorrow morning?' said Yvonne Best to Vicky as they walked out of the interview room. They walked along the corridor in the cell area and to the charge desk where the custody sergeant was busy at his computer.

'I guess so, with an application to remand him in custody,' replied Vicky.

Charged, Dean McIntyre was taken back to his cell.

'That'll give him time to come to terms with what he's been charged for and then we'll bring him out later to ask him what he knows about the Knapton murder,' said Vicky.

'It'll be interesting to find out where he says he was when Knapton was murdered.'

'I wonder if he'll have anyone who can verify where he was, that's the most important question,' said Vicky raising her eyebrows at her colleague.

Later that evening, a further interview took place with Dean McIntyre. He didn't want his solicitor present, he said. He didn't need a solicitor and it quickly became apparent his reason, as he confided in the officers that he had information that would help catch who had murdered Freddy Knapton. In return he wanted to do a deal which amounted to the charges being dropped against him, with a condition that he was released immediately from police custody. Then and only then, would he tell them what he knew, and to no one other than the man leading the investigation.

The detectives went back into CID. 'I'll ring the boss at home,' said Vicky forging ahead. As she entered the office she could see the light was still lit in Dylan's office. Dylan was sitting, shirt sleeves rolled up, at his desk, a half-eaten pork pie in one hand and a file he was reading in the other. She knocked at the door and walked straight, in. 'What are you still doing here?' The top button of Dylan's shirt was undone and his tie was askew.

'Working, the same as you, I hope.' Still without looking up he fumbled to find the can of coke situated in front of him. Locating it, he put it to his mouth and took a sip.

Ned came to stand in the doorway.

'McIntyre tells us he has some information that will lead us to the killer of Freddy Knapton,' Vicky said. Dylan's red, rimmed eyes looked up at her.

'And?'

'He wants a 'get out of jail' card,' said Ned.

'He can whistle, but I'll listen to what he has to say,' said Dylan.

'Perhaps he won't say anything?' said Vicky.

'Or perhaps he has nothing to say and he's just trying it on.' Dylan sat up, stretched his arms skyward and then ran his hands through his hair. He looked worn and weary.

There was a pause as he dropped his arms to rest on the desk. He narrowed his eyes. 'Why do I sense a *but*?' he said looking from Vicky to Ned and back. Ned looked towards Vicky and gave her a nod to encourage her to go on.

'He says he'll only speak to you; and he won't do so until he's released.'

'Is he credible do you think?' said Dylan.

Vicky wrinkled her nose. 'Don't know.'

'Why would anyone roll over so easily on an armed robbery charge, and then offer information on a murder investigation as a get out of jail card free?' Dylan asked quizzically as he sat back in his old leather chair tapping its arm with the base of his pen. 'He's not so thick as to think we'll drop all charges, surely?'

Vicky's face flushed. 'That's what he's looking for.'

'What?' Dylan said, his voice rising, his mouth twitched.

'He did offer the information on the murder enquiry without any prompting boss,' said Ned. Vicky looked grateful for him backing her up.

'Mmm. I guess there was no point in him mentioning it unless he has something. Maybe it is his last ditch attempt for freedom?' said Dylan.

'I don't think he's naive enough to actually think that anything he tells us will not be checked and double checked before we agree to anything,' said Vicky.

'I think the penny's just dropped that without turning into a grass he's definitely going down for a while this time,' said Ned.

Dylan gave a wry smile, pushed his chair back from his desk, and stood up. He fastened the top button of his shirt and straightened his tie before plucking his suit jacket from the back of his chair 'Well, in that case there is only one thing to do. I'll go and see what he has to say. But, I'm telling you now they'll be no charges dropped,' he said putting his arms in the jacket sleeves. 'The best he might expect from me is a letter to the judge when it comes to his sentencing, to say how much, if the information is genuine mind, he has helped us.

Minutes later Dylan was in the interview room sitting opposite their prisoner, Dean McIntyre. 'You wanted to see me?' said Dylan.

'You the man in charge?'

Dylan nodded.

McIntyre sat forward, his body language aggressive. 'I'm not saying anything until charges are dropped and I'm out of here understand.' He pointed at Dylan when he spoke.

'You've got some information about the murder of Freddy Knapton I believe?' Dylan's face held a blank expression.

'Yeah, I have,' he said cockily, slouching back in his chair. There was a pause as Dylan waited for him to continue. 'And what I know would help you solve the case.' McIntyre's eyes were bright, teasing.

Dylan stayed silent, looking at him questioningly, but still not showing an ounce of emotion on his face. It prompted McIntyre to continue, 'I'm being straight. I know what happened,' he said, his tone more reasonable.

Dylan nodded. 'Okay, I'll be straight with you. I'm afraid things don't work quite how you think they might. You see, I can't simply open the door and let you go, even if I wanted to. It's my job, as a police officer, to put you before the courts and what happens next - well, that's down to the judge.'

McIntyre looked uneasy, his expression darkened.

'Of course I'd like to hear what you've got to say, but you're not going anywhere and the charges won't be dropped, it just doesn't work like that. Nobody has that power. You'll have to answer to the robbery charge.'

'So you want me to turn into a grass, and I get nothing for it?'

'No, I didn't say that. If you're willing to share what you know with me, and it checks out, then I'll agree to write a letter to the judge who is sitting in on your case. The letter will say, that since your arrest, you have gone out of your way to assist the Police in an extremely violent murder investigation.'

'And?'

'And, as a result I would hope he would reduce any sentence he was thinking of giving you.'

'So, let me get this straight. I tell you what I know, and then I have to trust that you will keep to your end of the bargain?' McIntyre scoffed. 'You could be feeding me a right load of bullshit?'

'I told you, if you want to talk to me then I'll listen. Then, if what you tell me subsequently turns out to be true, you have my word that I will send the letter to the judge.'

McIntyre screwed up his face, shook his head and looked at Dylan out of the corner of his eye. 'You're trying to trick me aren't you?'

'If I'd wanted to trick you I could have taken you into one of the outside interview rooms and let you think you were going to be released, although you wouldn't be. But I'm not that kind of person. Look, you can see my predicament, I won't know whether or not what you tell me is the truth unless I have it checked out. You can trust me, if I say I'm going to do something, then I do it.'

'And if the judge gets this letter from you and he does nothing?'

'Well, to be honest I'd be as shocked as you. Let's face it people get reduced sentences for pleading guilty these days, and giving important information is worth more than that. Think about it. The judge might decide to reduce your length of custodial sentence drastically, who knows. You could be out of prison in no time. I've no doubt you can do the time. But it depends what's important to you?'

McIntyre sat, head down, studiously biting his bottom lip. Suddenly he lifted his head to face Dylan. 'I need to think about it. I'm no nark.'

'Hey,' Dylan said holding up his hands in mock self-defence. 'Nobody said you were. But I can assure you that what you tell me, if you decide to tell me anything will remain confidential.'

Dylan stood up. 'A lot of people that get locked up have information that will help them. But it's not until they realise they're going down do they consider sharing it with us. You know my name, it's Jack Dylan.'

McIntyre muttered under his breath as he was taken back to his cell. At the door he turned and looked at Dylan for a long moment before going inside and sitting at the centre of the thin, blue, plastic mattress.

Dylan leaned against the door. 'Ask the gaoler to contact me if you want to speak to me again and I'll gladly listen to anything you've got to say if it helps me lock a murderer up quicker. Think about it. Why don't you do some good for once?' As Dylan closed the door slowly, McIntyre silently looked up and in that instant Dylan saw fear creep across his face. The echo of the cell door firmly closing followed him down the corridor. Like he had said, he would listen to what Dean McIntyre had to tell him but he wasn't in the market for playing cat and mouse. The investigation into the Knapton murder would continue at pace with or without the help of McIntyre. In Dylan's experience, if a prisoner had information they usually shared something of relevance to suggest they were in the know which McIntyre hadn't.

Vicky was eagerly waiting in the incident room for Dylan's return. She followed him into the kitchen, where Dylan switched on the kettle.

'Any joy?'

'No, not at the moment, I've left him to think about what I said. Do you want a drink?'

'Do you think he knows anything?' enquired Vicky opening a cupboard and removing two cups. She put coffee into both and took the milk from the fridge.

Dylan sat down at the small, wooden table. 'Not sure, but our investigation doesn't and wouldn't just rely on what he might tell us anyway, so nothing lost, nothing gained either way.'

Vicky handed him his drink. He took a sip and put it on the table in front of him with a deep sigh.

'I agree, but it'd be good if he could point us in a certain direction, don't you think? Let's face it we're getting nowhere fast.'

'I'm well aware that the direction he may point us in could send us on a wild goose chase. Let's leave him to sweat a bit and see if he asks to see to me again. I won't be rushing back. Dean McIntyre needs to know we're in control - not him.'

Chapter Eighteen

Dylan found Jen sitting on the floor in the darkened lounge, next to the fire that had long since died.

'What on earth are you doing? Are you okay?' Dylan leaned down to help her to her feet. She looked dazed and slightly disoriented.

'What time is it?' Jen said negotiating the edge of the sofa and sitting. Dylan sat beside her. She folded her arms across her chest and was visibly shaking. Dylan took off his jacket and put it around her shoulders. He held her hand that was like ice. 'Where's Maisy?'

'She's in bed. I only sat down for a moment by the fire. I'll get you your dinner, you'll be hungry, its dark, it must be late.'

'You'll do no such thing. I'll run you a bath and when you're in bed I'll bring you some soup.' He had left her home alone for far too long.

When the sobbing took hold of her Dylan held her, comforting her as best he could. Half supporting, half carrying he helped her up the stairs. 'It's going to be alright Jen,' he said as he tucked her up in bed after her bath - a hot water bottle slid under the duvet at her feet. Bathed and warm Jen appeared calmer. She noticed Dylan's face looked grey and his eyes all but sunk into his head as he lay down beside her. A tray sat on the bedside cabinet. 'Come on love, try and eat something, you like Asparagus soup and I've warmed the roll,' he said. 'Just as you like it.'

To his relief Jen, propped up on two pillows, managed a few spoonfuls, her colour had returned. Setting his coffee mug on the dressing table he offered her a mug of tea, which she took and held with two hands. All was silent as she had a few small sips, the only sound in the room being the tapping noise the radiators made. When Jen finally spoke her quiet voice was thick with emotion. 'Today for the first time I think I understand why people take their own lives.' Dylan's eyes grew wide.

'I don't understand how you could even think of that.' He said angrily. 'What about Maisy?'

'Don't worry, I couldn't. I wouldn't. I'm not brave enough. But, if it hadn't been for you.' Tears once again spilled over onto her cheeks. 'When I'm on my own I feel so down.' Her face crumpled. 'I try to snap out of it. I really do. But I know I can't do this on my own.'

'I'm not sure I understand. What is it you want me to do?'

Jen turned to him. 'Try spend more time at home.' Dylan looked at her with a world of understanding in his eyes. 'I'll try my best,' he said with a tired smile. As Jen's eyes closed to him his smile instantly slid away and in its place came a bitter-sweet look of regret. 'I promise with all my heart I'll will try to be the husband and father you want me to be,' he whispered softly.

When Jen had fallen asleep in his arms, he lay still, although sleep evaded him. Watching the patterns from the headlights of passing vehicles move periodically across the ceiling the minutes turned to hours. The world outside was silent and still - his earlier promise weighed heavily on his mind. How on earth could he spend more time at home with the two murder enquiries gathering pace? He knew he had to try.

***

Immediately he walked through the door of the incident room the next morning a voice made him look over his shoulder.

'DI Hawk is chasing you, sir.' Shelagh MacPhee was sitting at her desk in the corner. 'Would you like me to get you a drink?'

'Two sugars for me,' shouted Ned. Tipping his chair back on two legs, he rocked to and fro.

'Thanks Shelagh,' said Dylan. 'Shouldn't you be out on enquires Detective Constable Granger? Break that chair and you'll pay for it.'

'I wish, I'm trawling through this bloody lot,' said Ned holding up a stack of computer printouts.

'Anything?'

'Nowt to write home about yet.'

Leaning forward over his desk Dylan pressed a key on his keyboard and his computer instantly fired into action with a melodic sound. He sat down in his big, old leather chair with a bump.

Vicky's eyes were fixed upon the Merton Manor appeal posters pinned to his dry wipe board. 'Do you think we'll catch the bastards who did it?' she said, leaning against the wall by the door.

Dylan lifted his head to her. 'The fire?' he said. She nodded. Dylan drew in a deep breath through flared nostrils. 'Well, it won't be for the want of trying if we don't,' he said as he peeled the post-it note from his computer screen with DI Hawks number upon it.

It appeared that North Yorkshire police were having more success with their appeals than Dylan's team. Terry Hawk had been contacted in confidence by a woman who ran an escort agency. One of her girls had reported that she and another girl had been hired by two men who took them to a race meeting, where they had been treated to a day in the VIP enclosure.

'Why didn't the girl contact us?' said Dylan impatiently.

'She was concerned about her job,' Terry said.

'Ah, client confidentiality. The credibility of the agency.' Dylan muttered. 'Of course.'

'I assured the lady boss that the information would be treated in strict confidence. In fact, I'm going to see her this afternoon. I was just checking in with you to see if there was anything else that may be relevant from your enquiry?'

'Credible, do you think?'

'Don't know why she'd call in if not, but that's another reason why I'm going myself. If the information is as good as I think it might be, then she doesn't know how invaluable she could be to us.'

A smile spread across Dylan's lips. 'Perhaps you should take a chaperone?'

There was humour in his voice. 'You're probably right, but people do say two's company, three's a crowd? And, you never know, if there's just me, she may be more forthcoming?'

'That's what worries me.' Dylan laughed out loud. 'Just remember not to get distracted.'

'Don't worry if you don't hear from me for the rest of the day. These things can take time.'

'If I remember rightly you don't rush. Didn't you get a commendation from a crown court judge when you were on the vice squad? How did the acknowledgement go?

'For devotion to duty, during prolonged exposure to female strippers. Indecently assaulted whilst gathering sufficient intelligence to raid and close a brothel,' Terry said, self-satisfied. 'Well, something like that. It was a dangerous job, one of the strippers stuffed my head down her cleavage and by 'eck she was a big girl. I nearly bloody suffocated. Straight up sexual assault!'

Dylan raised an eyebrow. 'I still don't know how you managed to get the bosses to allow you to keep returning. How long did you manage to drag it out, must have been a year?'

Shelagh tapped at Dylan's door and he beckoned her in. She handed him a folded piece of paper. 'Thank you,' he mouthed. Without speaking she turned on her heels and walked out of the office, shutting the door quietly behind her.

'There you go exaggerating. It took me eleven months and fifteen days.' There was a smile in the old timer's voice. 'Ahh... I remember it well. The torment I had to endure and the sights I was subjected to. I deserved that commendation, and as for the boss endorsing the continued visits. Well, you can sort a lot out at Lodge meetings.' Terry chuckled. 'Anyway, better go, I need to spruce myself up. I don't want to keep the lady waiting.'

Dylan sighed. 'You certainly haven't changed Terry Hawk. I bet you still have a bottle of Brut aftershave in your desk drawer.'

'Always prepared me, Dylan. I learnt a lot from police training school but more from your detective training course.'

Dylan put the phone back on its holder, his mood lightened. He hadn't mentioned the Mercedes to Terry but he wouldn't hesitate to do so once he had conformation of the details. Dylan unfolded the piece of paper that Shelagh had handed him. Our crime prevention officer DC Rupert Charles has been identified on one of the CCTV tapes at York races, he read.

'Interesting,' Dylan thought. But, it was a local race meeting so it didn't surprise him if officers from West Yorkshire were having a day out at York. What would be of interest to him would be if he was seen in the VIP lounge, and in Cedric Oakley's company.

'Apart from Cedric Oakely and DC Charles who else have we identified present?' Dylan asked Jon.

'They're working through the tapes. It's proving tedious. There were hundreds of people there on that particular race day.'

'Typical!' Dylan couldn't hide his frustration.

'We've just received these stills from the CCTV footage sir. They might be of interest to you?'

There was no doubt that on the slightly grainy images of the VIP lounge was Detective Constable Rupert Charles.

'It's difficult to say whether he's with Oakley's group or not,' said Dylan pulling a face.

'They've both got a raised champagne glass, sir.'

'And a race card in the other,' said Dylan.

'Maybe they'd just backed the same winning horse?' said Jon.

'Rupert appears to be at home with a pair of binoculars round his neck, and he's dressed for the part.' Dylan looked up. 'He needs to be interviewed, we need to know from him thread to needle about that event. This might just be the break we've been waiting for.' Dylan felt a surge of adrenalin.

'I'll get him in as soon as possible,' said Jon.

Dylan's eyes were staring. 'No, better leave him to the North Yorkshire team.'

Jon's face was serious as he continued to scan one picture after another. One by one he passed them to Dylan. 'Look there,' he said pointing his figure at a photograph he held tightly in his hand. 'He's standing next to Cedric Oakley.'

Dylan craned his neck to take a look. 'That said, they are standing at the bar. It doesn't prove that he knew him. We can't speculate. We have to rely on the evidence.'

From behind his desk in the outer office, Dylan could hear the team buzzing, and that's how he liked it. One thing he detested was an enquiry he was working on becoming stale, which made every action to be completed a chore, although a necessary one. It was at those times that the team's moral was always at its lowest and he found one of the most important qualities of a good manager was keeping the troops upbeat and positive. Dylan's way of doing that was to highlight a particular part of the enquiry where they had had some success, and seek to build on it.

'I've just been speaking to the officers that interviewed the witness who saw the vehicle leave Merton Manor on the day of the fire, and in the lay-by. She's adamant the vehicle was a royal blue Mercedes, with a high shine finish.'

'Good, to ensure that information remains high priority I'll share it with North Yorkshire now to see if there is a similar vehicle of interest on their data-base. Increase the number of officers that are viewing the CCTV we've taken possession of, and circulate a bulletin internally, so that every police officer, traffic warden, community service officer, and special in the force are aware of our interest in it. I want every speed camera checked, any automatic number plate recognition checks in the area located. Anything at all that may give us the registration number of that Mercedes.'

Jon scribbled notes as Dylan spoke. 'I've initiated enquires with local hotels with a view to finding out if any guests who stayed with them, on or around the date of the fire were in possession of a blue Mercedes.'

'Excellent.' said Dylan.

'I know it's a long shot but...'

'I'll suggest it to the North Yorkshire team to copy that initiative.'

'Maybe the Mercedes is on CCTV at the race meeting?'

'If we could only get hold of that car and match it to the paint sample that was taken by CSI from the Manor's gate pillar, that would be great.'

Feeling more positive and on top of things at work, but exhausted after completing copious amounts of paperwork that had accumulated on his desk over the previous few day, Dylan left work for home. It was nine o'clock. At the start of the day he had intended to leave earlier, and as he drove along the long, dark, country roads of the Sibden Valley the adrenaline that had kept him going all day turned to a feeling of deep regret that he had not tried harder. The balance between his home life and work was never going to be easy while he was an SIO, but neither was the task of identifying the whereabouts of the Mercedes, placing it at the scene of the crime at the relevant time of the fire, and identifying the occupants inside. He smiled, it seemed all quite straight forward when he thought about it like that. The database on the computer system in the incident room showed him that no one that had been seen by the team had a similar vehicle to the royal blue Mercedes, and he knew that because he'd had Ned go through every computer printout in relation to vehicles. There was an awful long way to go.

As he pulled the car into the driveway he noticed the main light was on in the bedroom and the curtains were open. 'What on earth is she doing?' he said out loud as he saw Jen standing on the top rung of the step ladder leaning backwards and holding on for dear life.

He took the stairs two at a time. A hand seemed to grab at his chest and his heart filled with love to see her face speckled with tiny yellow coloured dots and the smell of paint greeted him.

'I didn't hear you come in?' she said climbing down to meet him, clutching a paint brush in her hand.

'Have you lost your mind?' he said with a little laugh as she stood in front of him and put her face up to his for a kiss. He tried to brush the paint away from her lips but it only resulted in spreading it across her face.

'I needed something to do,' she said turning away from him suddenly. 'The tablets the doctor gave me seem to be working and this seemed like the obvious thing - a new look. Do you like it?'

'Well, I loved the old and I love the new but, I absolutely love that colour,' he said admiring the newly painted walls.

Chapter Nineteen

Dylan looked at the stranger in the mirror. Unshaven, thinner and a look in his eyes that he didn't recognise. He looked away. Picked up his toothbrush, and brushed his teeth with a ferocity that wasn't necessary. When he spat the toothpaste out there was blood. How long had he been putting work before his health and family, he was ashamed to not be able to remember a time when that wasn't so. That had to change. It was about time he started to put Jen and Maisy first. There was a noise behind him and he turned. Jen set a warm drink on the dresser in the bathroom and walked away. He stared at her retreating figure but said nothing. She had managed to climb out of the abyss she had been sinking into.

***

The details of the vehicle seen leaving the driveway of Merton Manor at the time of the fire were discussed at the morning meeting.

'To-date we don't have information regarding any contacts of the Isaacs driving a royal blue Mercedes. It's therefore top priority to identify this vehicle as soon as we can.'

Meeting over, Dylan returned to his office, his phone was ringing and he picked it up.

'DI Jack Dylan,' he snapped. The person on the other end of the line was obviously walking. Dylan could hear footsteps and heavy breathing. 'Dylan, Terry. I thought I'd just let you know that I met with Nadine, the escort agency boss. She is a smart, intelligent business woman who also appears to be quite wealthy.'

Dylan allowed himself to relax a little. 'So, the escort agency business is a lucrative one you think? And I see you're on first name terms already.'

'You know me Dylan.' Terry chuckled.

'Get on with it man,' said Dylan. 'I haven't time to listen to stories of your conquests.'

'Ah, you're jealous?'

Dylan felt a flaccid smile tighten his lips. 'Not a bit,' he said wholeheartedly.

'Never say never. And, if you ever?'

'I won't,' Dylan interrupted. 'I am interested in what she had to say though?'

'Two of her girls were hired the night of your job at Merton Manor by a couple of men, and the day after by the same two who took them as their escorts to the races. The name the man gave to book the girls was a Mr Debbin, according to the paperwork, and they met them on both occasions at The Wellington Hotel, Harrowfield. The working names of the girls who turned out are Nancy and Shani. Their post-date sheets submitted to Nadine say that they met the guys, stayed the night, left the following morning and were contacted again to return the same day when they were taken by the two men to York races. There were no untoward incidents to report. The girls told Nadine in conversation that the men were splashing wads of cash around like no tomorrow. What we found interesting was one of these girls, Nancy, appears on CCTV to be speaking to our deceased Cedric Oakley at the bar and it has been suggested to me by Nadine that he gave Nancy a 'hot tip' and one of the men bet heavily on it. Two furlongs out, it was held back and it wasn't even placed.'

'Nothing more than that? No words exchanged between this man and Cedric Oakley?'

'No, apparently not, the punters continued to spend their cash and at the end of the day paid and tipped the girls well. Nadine is going to speak to Nancy and Shani again for us and then we're going to meet up. From what she's told me, there doesn't appear to be any threat to their safety and the girls didn't report anything that needs to concern the police. Our team will be updating yours today.'

'Interestingly we've also had a bit of a development. A witness has come forward to say that, on the day of the fire, they saw a royal blue Mercedes leaving the driveway of Merton Manor as the building was alight, and another witness who possibly saw the same vehicle parked in a lay-by on the road overlooking Merton Manor. The lay-by has been searched and exhibits collated. While they both give a good account of the car, neither can say anything about the occupants. They both say that the car had a showroom finish which is what primarily caught their attention.'

'The registered number?'

'Ah, that's what we're missing at the moment but, as they say, leave that with us. Checks are being made with CCTV, ANPR etc. and both our databases will be updated accordingly should we get any result.'

'We don't have any similar vehicles in the system as yet?'

'No, but it's early days. What sort of car did our pair of race goers pick the girls up in, just as a matter of interest?'

'All Nadine could tell me was that they said it was luxurious transport. So, no idea of make or model as yet. Did I tell you Nadine used to be a bunny girl?'

'No, but I do know a rabbit that's been hypnotised by her headlights.'

'Makes a change dealing with the living.'

'That bad?' Dylan winced.

'Worse, and the wife's taken herself off on holiday with kids. Says they might as well be invisible. Thing is, I know she's bloody right. But if I can just get one more rank under my belt it'll make so much difference to my pension. I wish she could see that.'

'That's what the hierarchy do isn't it? Dangle the carrot of a higher pension as a reward for obtaining the next rank?' Dylan was quiet and thoughtful for a moment.

Terry sighed. 'Yes, they do. I'll highlight the information regarding the Mercedes on our briefing sheet.'

'And, something else I'd like you to be aware of; our CPO, DC Rupert Charles, is one of the people who we have identified in the VIP lounge at York races.'

'I'm sure the CCTV will turn up a few Yorkshire coppers at the York meeting.'

'I've asked that your staff interview him. I think it's more appropriate than someone from Harrowfield nick. I've also highlighted the fact that he recently visited the home of the deceased at Merton Manor and advised them about security. Sadly, it appears that they were still waiting for estimates for the work required.'

'It's interesting that DC Charles had a connection to both locations. Do you know if he knew Cedric Oakley?'

'No, but he can be seen on the CCTV next to him at the bar. His dress code suggests perhaps that he is also no stranger to the races.'

'How well do you know this Rupert Charles?'

'Not at all, in fact, I've only just come across him on this enquiry. He hasn't been working at Harrowfield that long.'

'Leave it with us. I'll speak personally to whoever gets the enquiry and ensure that they do a thorough job, including having a look at his financial background. He hasn't by any chance got a royal blue Merc has he?'

'I'm not sure. He doesn't use a royal blue Mercedes to travel to work as I'd have seen it in the station car park.' Dylan stood and walked toward the window. He scanned the yard. 'Good point though, I'll find out.'

As soon as he put the telephone down Dylan marched out into the CID office. Vicky was returning with a pile of papers she had just retrieved from the post-room. 'Beaky wants to know when Jen will be returning to work?'

'Never mind Avril Summerfield-Preston. The Divisional Administrator can bloody wait. I want to know if DC Charles's vehicle is on our database?'

'His red Fiat Panda?' Vicky screwed up her nose. 'Why would it be?'

'That rusty old thing. Is that his?' he said.

Vicky nodded.

'Does he own another?' he said. Dylan sounded irritated.

'How would I know. He's married to a teacher so maybe she's got a car?'

'Find out, and I want to review the CCTV we have from the racecourse again to see who DC Charles speaks to. I'm pretty sure there is nothing to show us that he was with anyone in particular that day in the VIP lounge, but that's not to say we haven't got more footage of him elsewhere at the meeting.'

'I'll ask Jon Summers, boss,' she said with a flaccid hand salute. She could see Dylan wasn't in the mood for jokes by his expression.

'Have you got me any updates on the Knapton enquiry?'

'I'll bring you the latest intel. Do you want a drink?'

Dylan nodded. 'Yes. Thanks,' he said gruffly.

As Dylan waited for Vicky to return, his eyes fell on the photo of Jen and Maisy on his desk. He picked it up and studied it closely for a moment. It was a picture he had taken. Jen's mouth was open, laughing out loud at Maisy. He remembered it well and a lump rose in his throat. Their little girl, in return, was looking up at Jen with a cheeky grin on her face showing off her dimples. The memory of her running across the grass and into his arms after he had taken the picture brought tears close to his eyes. Putting the photograph back in its place he booted up his computer and looked up on the internet the phone number for a local florist, there was so many, which did he choose? Dylan gave a deep sigh as Vicky walked back in the office.

'What's up?' she said handing him a package. 'Knapton update,' she said with a scowl as she scanned his tired, grey pallor.

'I wanted to order Jen flowers but I can't work out how to order on this bloody site.'

'Better get them local. Leave it with me.' She held out her hand and he dug into his pocket, found his wallet and gave her a £10 note. She beckoned for more. His eyes grew wide. He put a further £10 in her hand.

'Triple it and it might just cover it.'

'Sixty quid for a bunch of flowers?'

'She's worth it isn't she?' Vicky raised her eye brows and cocked her head to one side questioningly.

'Make sure they're delivered today,' he said pressing the notes in her hand.

'And the card?'

Dylan shrugged his shoulders. 'You do it. I don't know what to say on stuff like that. Something that will cheer her up.'

Vicky shook her head. 'I suggest you learn, boss.'

More than aware that, although it was relatively early days in both murder investigations, if they didn't have any positive leads soon a review team, led by an assistant chief constable, assisted by a senior investigator and a team of other police personnel, would be soon breathing down his neck.

It was his hope that the latest enquiries, both in West Yorkshire and North Yorkshire, would prove fruitful and ultimately negate the need for a review process to be carried out now, or indeed in the future.

His head was feeling less cluttered, his mind clearing. But he ultimately needed the killers caught before they could strike again.

It was time for Dylan to go into the Knapton enquiry debrief. He had hoped he would have heard from Jen to say that she had received the flowers - but there had been nothing.

'Did you order the flowers and tell the florist I wanted them delivered today?' he asked Vicky when he caught up with her in the corridor to the briefing room.

'First thing. She hasn't rung you?'

Dylan shook his head.

'That's serious?' Vicky's face held a grimace. 'You're definitely in the dog house.'

'It would appear so,' said Dylan rolling his eyes.

Vicky flopped down in the seat next to him as the troops continued to gather.

'Rupert Charles' wife's car, is a Merc,' whispered Vicky to Dylan.

Dylan's eyes grew wide. He opened his mouth as if to speak.

A grin spread quickly across her face, 'It's old and silver,' she said, turning to face the assembled with a playful punch on his arm. 'Gotcha!'

Dylan raised his hand. 'Quiet!'

The Knapton enquiry team personnel were immediately silenced. 'I won't keep you long,' he said. 'The purpose of this debrief is to share the intelligence we have gathered so far and to discuss the way forward.' Dylan gave a little cough and cleared his throat. 'We've had some success in gathering intelligence, identifying, and housing most of the group that used to hang around Groggs Park prior to Freddy Knapton's murder. It is apparent from what people tell us that there was a growing tension between them and Knapton, and verbal threats had been made on both sides. This group, for your information, now congregate in the bus shelter outside the railway station. We are looking at the logistical arrangements to carry out multiple arrests so we can bring in as many of the group as possible. We should have the action plan out in the next twenty-four hours so we can do the raids the day after tomorrow. Questions?'

'What age group are we looking at sir?' came the question from the back of the room.

'Late teens, early twenties,' said Vicky. 'Uniform will be assisting due to numbers.'

Another hand was raised and Dylan lifted his chin in the officer's direction, to acknowledge him. 'Are we arresting or just tracing and eliminating?'

'Arresting, but all will be made clear in the action plan which will be distributed in advance,' said Vicky.

There was a sea of nodding heads before Dylan, and a low murmuring spread like an incoming tidal wave rapidly around the room. Once again Dylan put his hand in the air which brought about silence. Vicky spoke. 'We have nothing in writing but we have had a few anonymous phone calls to the incident room which point us in the direction of this group and we have a statement from Madge Teal who walks her dogs in the park twice a day. She's no time for "foul mouth Freddy" as she named him. She tells us that Knapton's dog nearly knocked her over and she would have been in a bit of a state had a kind gentleman not come to her assistance. This lady states that on the day before Knapton's murder she witnessed angry shouting from this group. Due to the loud noises coming from inside the park - a dog barking and growling, accompanied by bad language, she decided to stay on the grass close to the entrance to let her dogs do their duty, rather than venture inside the park,' said Vicky. Vicky took a glance in Ned's direction. 'Duty, that's crap to you.' She carried on without drawing a breath. 'Madge then says she saw Freddy being chased, stones were thrown and she heard a dog whimpering before she saw Satan limp out of the park, obviously injured. The group were apparently laughing raucously and at this point she tells me she felt sorry for the dog, but not for Knapton, never for Knapton. She said she was in fact glad that he was getting a touch of his own medicine.'

'Is she aware if the gang caught up with Knapton on that occasion?' said Dylan.

'No, she said not and she was frozen to the spot as she watched this from the snicket that runs at the side of the park to the retirement flats where she lives.

'Any news from forensics regarding the knife?' said Dylan.

'No,' said Ned. 'I'll chase it up.'

'Why didn't this woman come forward before now?' said Dylan.

'She lives on her own and was worried about the possible consequences. But she changed her mind when she read about the dog being beheaded.'

'It's interesting that Freddy Knapton's death didn't prompt her to come forward but his dog being killed did.'

'She's an animal lover boss. She tells us she's no time for the yobs. Bad on bad, she says,' said Vicky.

'We will be arresting the day after tomorrow, not tracing and eliminating,' said Dylan to the audience.

There was a distinct notable rise of morale in the room.

Chapter Twenty

The adrenalin that had rushed through his body at the debrief had petered out driving home. The delay in the town traffic that normally frustrated him, he welcomed. It gave him time to think. By the time he reached home he felt unusually anxious. He hadn't spoken to Jen all day. The change in her mood last night had been welcomed but her distance today unprecedented. For some unknown reason he felt like he was on shaky ground.

As it happened, when he reached the house he couldn't have been more surprised to see from the driveway the bedroom curtains had been rehung, the lights inside were welcoming. He let himself in with a cheery call. Dylan hung his jacket up at the bottom of the stairs and put down his briefcase. There was a wonderful smell emanating from the kitchen. The house was unusually quiet, but as he peered around the living room door he could only see Maisy bathed and dressed for bed, lying on the rug enthralled in her favourite movie that she'd seen a million times before. It was as if, however, he was invisible to her. She didn't turn to greet him, or run to give him a hug. He watched his daughter for a minute or two in silence. The stove in the lounge radiated a pleasant heat. She tittered at the movie characters' antics, sung along to the words of her favourite tune, threw her head back in spontaneous laughter and when she sat up and reached for her glass of milk her eyes remained fixed on the TV screen.

Max came wandering out of the kitchen, licking his lips. There was only one thing that would stop the Retriever from greeting him at the door, he must have been eating his dinner. Walking the few steps to greet him, Dylan bent down and ruffled his soft, tan fur and was rewarded by a slobbery lick with his tongue. When Dylan stood up he was greeted by Jen wielding a knife in her hand. Shocked for an instant he stepped backwards, lost his footing and stumbled into the bannister. Jen's eyes looked surprise but, pulling himself upright, Dylan was relieved to catch the makings of a smile cross her face. 'I thought I heard the door,' she said abruptly, before turning back into the kitchen. 'Dinner won't be long.' Dylan followed her wondering if he should be so bold as to kiss her on the cheek, but seeing her upright stance at the worktop as she pumped the knife up and down on the chopping board with an overeager fever, he decided against it.

'Can I do anything to help?' he said.

'You can pour me a drink, and then tell me what you think about that letter on the table,' she said without turning to face him.

Dylan picked up an envelope with the police logo on it. Before he had chance to read it Jen stopped him in his tracks. 'Avril, she wants to know when I'll be back at work.'

'Ah, Vicky said she'd been chasing an update. But, I didn't think...'

'Well, why would you think about me? You've got Vicky running errands for you these days?'

'That's not... I only... It was just today... I didn't get chance to...' Dylan filled two glasses with wine from the fridge. His eyes caught sight of a large bunch of flowers still in their polythene wrap, all ribbons and bows, in the utility room basin. He gave a little sigh, At least they weren't in the bin. He took the wine glass to Jen and popped it next to her on the worktop before sitting down at the table. A small glass vase was at the table's centre that held a few wild flowers.

'The flowers,' said Dylan. 'They're lovely.'

Jen turned her head sharply in his direction. She saw him touching the delicate yellow petals that were already wilting. 'Yes, aren't they? Maisy picked them for me on our walk in the park.'

Dylan didn't mention those he had sent and neither did she, but she reverted to silently stirring the white sauce in the pan. Moving from work top to table the clanging of the cutlery she took from the utensil drawer made the silence in the room more profound. Jen continued to prepare dinner. Now satisfied that the sauce was sufficiently thickened she took the wooden spoon out of the pan and looked back at the plate of parsley on the worktop that was just out of her reach. Dylan, watching his wife's every move, saw where her eyes lay. He jumped up and took the chopped herbs to her.

'Thank you,' she said swiftly taking the plate from him.

'Smell's lovely,' said Dylan appreciatively as he hovered over her. He stared down at the sauce, his stomach rumbled. He hadn't eaten lunch. He took a gulp of his wine.

Jen frowned. 'You hate fish, and even more you hate parsley sauce.' she said turning to face him. They were skating around each other as if on thin ice, and they both knew it.

'Are you ready to go back to work do you think?' Dylan said with trepidation in his voice but his steps were more confident as he walked back to sit down in his chair at the kitchen table.

'As ready as I'll ever be,' she said curtly. She stopped and turned around. 'I wish Avril Summerfield-Preston had the decency to speak to me instead of chasing you, or sending me a letter. I know she's stupid but that's absolutely ridiculous and a waste of public money!' Briefly sounding agitated, she turned back to what she was doing, putting the sauce on the fish in the ovenproof dish. The potatoes were ready to mash and the green beans on the boil.

'Tell you what? Shall I put Maisy to bed and then we can eat dinner, in peace, together for once?' said Dylan as he drained his wine glass. Jen raised her eyebrows at him. Her expression remained the same.

'Come on, give me a break, I know I don't deserve forgiveness but I just don't know how to.' Dylan's eyes were pleading. In that moment Jen felt sorry for him. He'd lost a baby too.

'She'll need a wee before she gets into bed and just one story mind - she'll keep you upstairs all night if you let her.' Jen's voice was softer and Dylan took that as a good sign.

When Dylan finally came downstairs he noticed that Jen had put the flowers he had sent her in a vase on the dresser and lit the candles in the lounge. She had laid two places on the dining room table and the feeling of unease that he had felt before started to ebb away.

Dylan sat at the table and watched Jen as she went to and fro with food and drinks. Eventually she sat. There was still an uneasiness in the air and the lack of conversation was more obvious as they spooned their own food out of the serving dishes, onto warm plates. Jen looked hot and tired as he watched her looking around the table for the salt pot and, realising she had forgotten to put it out, she made to stand. Dylan put his hand on her arm and went into the kitchen, returning with it. Their fingers briefly touched, they both flinched as if electricity had passed between them, but each chose to ignore it. Jen didn't recoil from him but as their eyes met she didn't allow the contact to linger. Picking up her glass of wine she put it to her lips and, downing it in one, her shoulders dropped and she put her head back and gave a big sigh. When she looked at Dylan he saw she was smiling but the smile didn't reach her eyes. He reached for her hand and she let him take it in his and when their eyes met he gave her an apologetic smile. 'I know I don't always get it right. I'm only human,' he said.

'It would have been nice if you'd sent the flowers,' she said sadly.

'What do you mean,' he said. 'I did.'

Jen shook her head. 'Okay then. What did the card say?'

Dylan's face flushed. He opened his mouth as if to answer. 'I... I...'

Again there was silence. Jen picked up her knife and fork. 'Why did you get Vicky to send them?'

Dylan looked bemused.

'You did ask Vicky to send them for you didn't you?'

Dylan was clearly uncomfortable.

'Even if you'd dictated the words for the card to the florist, a stranger, but for Vicky to write those words, words that came from her not you. For goodness sake Jack.'

He looked wounded. 'When have you ever called me sweetheart?' she said.

Dylan shrugged his shoulders. 'Sweetheart?'

'I know I've been all over the place,' she said. 'One minute I feel angry, the next I'm in tears. I'm not daft. I understand you're busy. I knew what your job entailed when we met. I'm under no illusion. It's easy for you to ask someone to do something for you. You and your team, you can rely on each other, help each other, cover each other's back but remember I've only got you and Maisy.'

Dylan nodded. 'I'm sorry.'

'I don't expect you to understand how I feel but I don't want grand gestures, you know that's not me.'

'I'm sorry. I just thought flowers might cheer you up. And I've ended up upsetting you more. It was my idea to send you flowers, honestly, I couldn't work out how to order them on the website, and if I'm being honest I didn't know what to say. Joe was my son too,' he said with tears in his eyes, and I have to carry on.

'You didn't carry him, he lived in me. He was part of me.' Jen pleaded understanding. 'Why won't you open up to me? Do I mean so little to you that you can't trust me with your feelings?'

Dylan put down his knife and looked straight into Jen's eyes.

'Do you want to know how I felt when Joe was being taken from us?' Dylan eyes were red haunted looking. 'I felt like my heart was being torn out of my chest. These hands...' he said showing her his palms. 'These hands are supposed to look after you and our children. His open hand became a tight fist that he banged on the table. 'And yet there was nothing on this earth that I could do to save him, or you from the pain you went through. I might catch murderers, which in turn might bring closure for others, but I could do nothing. Do you know how that makes me feel?'

'When I close my eyes I can see Joe's little face, his eyes that were nothing more than a blue ink spot on blotting paper. The bloodied transparent threads of flesh that would have been his limbs.' Jen's voice cracked. 'The shape of a bow of his lips. His tiny ears.'

'And you think I don't have them same thoughts? He was our son.' Dylan pushed away his plate and he reached out for her hands. They sat with tears running down their faces, but this time was different in as much as they clung to each other.

***

'The two independent witnesses have confirmed that the Mercedes was this royal blue paint colour,' said Jon. 'I have been speaking with the North Yorkshire team this morning and they tell me that the escort girls both confirm in their statements that the men who hired them, they believed, were staying at the Wellington Hotel.'

'Get your coat,' said Dylan. 'We're going round there now.'

Dylan and Jon parked in the hotel car park that was quickly filling up with coaches full of visitors to the picturesque location. Jon's face was etched with grim determination.

'Let's hope someone can shed light on the two men.'

***

'And there is no doubt that the two men that stayed at the hotel were called Devlin?' Jon directed his question to the hotel receptionist.

'No doubt whatsoever sir, brothers, and they did look alike. They caused a bit of a stir, two big tattooed men like that bringing two young leggy blondes back to the hotel. The manager was away so, not wanting any trouble, we decided to turn a blind eye when they took them to their rooms. Not only that, but we had two coach parties of posh people staying for the Festival. The hotel was busy, the last thing we wanted was a fuss, hence I am absolutely certain that on that day the only two men who booked in together were the two Mr Devlin's.'

'Is it possible that you took a registration number from them when they booked in?'

'I am sure we would have as it's mandatory for our booking in procedure if the guests are leaving a vehicle in our car park.'

'Is the manager here now?'

'No, he's on later today. But if you'd like to make an appointment to see him I can gather all the information available for you by the time you return?'

'We need the registered number urgently. Do you think you would recognise the men again?'

The receptionist grimaced. 'Probably, but I can't say for sure.'

'Anything else that you can tell us about the men?'

The receptionist started to chuckle. 'Our doorman, bless him, he's not got two pennies to rub together, those two, bad as they looked, made his day by giving him a substantial tip for getting their car brought around to the front of the hotel. It paid his rent for a month, he said. I'm sure he won't ever forget them. He's off for the next three days.'

Jon made a note for someone from the incident room to see him later to get statements.

***

'Declan and Damian Devlin have previous convictions as long as my arm boss,' said Shelagh. 'Nothing as serious as murder but they had a good teacher in their errant father.'

'PNC shows them both with a warning for violence,' said Andy Wormald.

'Are they flagged for being known to carry weapons?' asked Dylan.

'No,' said Andy.

'Have we got any reference to them being connected to a blue Mercedes?'

'No sir, nothing as grand as that.'

'We need to house them, as soon as we can,' Dylan said with grim determination.

Sitting alone, Dylan was busily typing the Devlin brothers details into his computer while listening to the dial tone of the phone.

'What do you want?' came the angry growl of a voice on the line.

Dylan scooped the telephone off the desk and put it to his ear, relaxing back in his chair as he did so. 'That's it Terry, what did the bosses used to tell us? If you're officious enough you'll have a quiet life?'

'Ah, it's you?' said Terry cheerily. 'What's new?'

'We can now confirm that the name of the men wasn't Debbin it was Devlin, they are brothers. Declan and Damien stayed at the Wellington Hotel and it would appear the car they were using was the car they took the escort girls in to the races. Let's get our HOLMES supervisors to talk to each other so we don't duplicate enquiries. What baffles me is why they'd used their own names at the hotel if they had intentions to kill Oakley?'

'Perhaps Oakley upset them that day?'

'There's no denying we've got two bad bastards driving an identifiable royal blue Mercedes, stopping in a top notch hotel, flush with cash - they've had a pay day from somewhere, haven't they, and what worries me is what plans have they got for getting their next fix?' said Dylan.

'As for using their own names, I think we can put that down to arrogance and the fact that they knew they were in a different county, relying on the police forces communication being like it was in bygone years.'

'We need hard evidence, but it does feel like a giant step forward. It smells right,' added Dylan.

The call ended and Dylan looked at the duty roster to see which officers were working that would be available to assist him with his enquiries. He was more than aware that Vicky needed staff to round up the group seen hanging around in the park about the time of the Freddy Knapton murder. After liaising with the community officers, the team had identified seven who, after subsequent monitoring, were known to be the gang that had previously been frequently meeting in Groggs Park. But he also needed to make headway with the Merton Manor enquiry.

'Vicky,' he called to his Detective Sergeant in the outer office. Vicky came and stood leaning on the door frame of his office.

'You okay?'

Vicky raised her eyebrows. 'course, why shouldn't I be?'

'I'll be contactable at all times tomorrow morning you know.'

Vicky nodded her head.

'Make sure you're tooled up, stab vests on, baton's, spray. I don't want you taking any risks.'

'Would I?' she rewarded him with a little nervous smile.

Dylan cocked his head and gave her one of his best serious looks.

'Don't call me Woodeye.' Vicky mimicked Dylan as she backed away. She turned and waved her hand above her head. 'Laters boss.'

Dylan saw her clip Ned Granger about the head as she passed him. 'You coming for a mucky curry?'

He got up without a word, threw his jacket over his sleeveless arm and followed her out of the door.

Dylan was shaking his head as Jon entered his office.

'You wouldn't want them two waking you up at half-five tomorrow morning would you?' The gang have no idea what they've got coming,' said Jon laughing.

'She'll not back off until she's got them all under lock and key, that's for sure. Too much pride at stake. What worries me is that she thinks she's got something to prove, and she couldn't be more wrong.'

Dylan's mind was instantly distracted by Jon as he sat down opposite him. He seemed eager to talk. 'I've just spoken to the manager at The Wellington,' he said, waving an envelope in front of him which he passed over the desk to Dylan.

'Did he say how the Devlin's paid?' said Dylan.

'Cash, they paid everything in notes.'

'Damn!' Dylan slapped the flat of his hand on his desk. 'I was hoping they might have used a credit card so we could trace its use. Do we know if the notes have been paid into the bank?'

'No boss, I've just got a breakdown of their bill,' Jon said, passing Dylan a copy of the invoice.

'Just a thought, if the hotel cashier hasn't paid the money into the bank, if there is a god, which I am doubting very much these days, we might get Jake Isaac's finger prints on it. Give them a quick call Jon will you...to check?'

Dylan, head down, studied the copy of the brother's hotel invoice as Jon put the call in. 'Bottle upon bottle of Bollinger champagne? Is there CCTV in the hotel?' he asked Jon as he ended the call.

'Yes, the vestibule. It's secreted in the oak panelling above the fireplace where a priest hole still exists. Also you'll be pleased to know they haven't paid the money into the bank and they will retain the remainder for us to collect. They couldn't tell me the amount at this time.'

'Good.' Dylan looked up, his eyes narrowed. 'So, to clarify that means for security purposes the CCTV most probably faces the reception desk?'

'Yes, and they have another camera that covers the entrance to the hotel.'

'Please tell me they're working?' Dylan held his breath momentarily.'

Jon nodded his head. 'They are indeed sir, and I've got the tapes here, all four of them, labelled, timed and dated.'

'Excellent!' Dylan was smiling. 'Did you warn the manager it may be some time before we would be returning them?'

'Yes, I told him they would potentially be exhibits for court. He was more concerned about attracting bad press for the hotel but I told him, at this stage, it's about eliminating people from the investigation. Unless you're going to tell me otherwise?'

Dylan shook his head. 'Any news on the registration of the vehicle they were in?'

'Yes, and I've had the registration number checked out on my way back to the station, it's a hire vehicle.'

'You've saved the best till last, tell me more?'

Chapter Twenty One

'The hire company is over a hundred miles away,' remarked Andy Wormald who was sitting around the desk in Dylan's office with Dylan and Jon. It was dark outside and the incident room was reduced to a skeleton staff due to the early morning raids the next day for the Knapton murder.

'Two counties boundaries to cross no matter which direction you travel,' said Jon studying the map.

'Unfortunately it tells us nothing more than the name and address of the company who own the Mercedes,' said Andy.

'It's a good lead,' said Dylan. 'But now I want to know everything there is to know about Redchester Regal Hire Cars, and the vehicle, and any update we have on the Devlin brothers.'

Jon and Andy scribbled the actions down on their notepads as Dylan relayed them. He could feel their spirits had been lifted by the new lead, and there were positive vibes all round.

'I don't want any contact with this hire car company over the telephone. This enquiry needs a personal visit and that won't happen until I'm satisfied that all the background checks have been done, and every ounce of intelligence has been squeezed from the databases at our disposal. Find out what local police know about them?' he said with gusto. A fire burning in his belly at the thought of feeling the collar of these men. 'Where is the vehicle now? Flag it up on PNC and ANPR, to show as 'of interest' to the incident room. I want it known that Detective Constable Andy Wormald is collating, as a priority, any intelligence in respect of the Mercedes in question, and any information about its whereabouts at the time of the murders. Has it been seen in the county before, Andy? Was it caught on a speed camera, stop/checked by patrol, had it collected a parking ticket at any time and if so, who were the occupants on that occasion?'

Dylan talked with Jon when Andy had gone. 'This latest development will keep the review team at bay, won't it sir.'

'For a while. Arrange for the cash to be collected from the hotel, against receipt. Then the fingerprint bureau can make a start. There is no doubt it will be a long process, but just maybe a fruitful one. We'll leave nothing to chance. Did you speak to Vicky before she left?'

'No boss,' Jon looked at his watch. 'Time I was off to my bed too. The wife will wonder where I've got to.'

***

Dylan's bedside clock numbers flipped over one by one, hardly audible but it was apparent in the still, darkened room. He turned his pillow. The illuminated numbers said 5:30. The night was over for him but Jen was still snoring softly. Dylan turned the duvet cover down carefully so as not to disturb her. He threw his legs out of bed and walked to the bathroom. With minimum noise and fuss he showered and shaved. He left Jen a brief note before leaving.

The traffic was sparse as he had expected in the valley, so early in the day. It was a little after six-thirty when he passed through the crested gates of Harrowfield Police Station. The sight of a near-on empty back yard where the meat wagons (transit vans) were usually parked, sent a rush of adrenalin through his body - the team were out, raiding houses. Slowly and smoothly he steered his car into his parking space, situated directly under his office window next to Detective Sergeant Rajinder Uppal's car. He might have known she would have gone with them to cover the younger sergeant's back and he was glad.

Inside the bowels of the building atmospheric anticipation enveloped him. Those working in the artificially lit incident room had heads down scanning printouts, reading logs, feeding information into computers, researching live enquiries and looking for leads to others. Stood in semi-darkness at his office door; a partitioned office within the large lower level open plan area of the police station, he impatiently rolled his eyes waiting for the strip-light to give him light. His first point of call, once he had dumped his briefcase at the side of his desk and taken off his overcoat, was to collect a radio. Eagerly pressing the button on the device he asked Control to pass a message to DS Vicky Hardace, that he was in the office if she wanted to contact him with an update. They were using a dedicated channel so that it didn't interfere with daily operational policing and enabled officers to speak freely to each other on talk-through.

Just before ten o'clock Vicky and the rest of the troops wandered back into the incident room. Dylan had listened in to radio conversations but wasn't aware exactly how successful or not they had been. The DS knocked softly at the door to his office.

'How did you get on?' asked Dylan, eagerly searching her face for a sign.

'Fine,' she said, Vicky's expression was buoyant. 'We managed to locate all seven. They're being booked into the cells.'

'That sounds encouraging. I just knew when I saw Raj's car this morning she wouldn't be able to resist going with you.'

Vicky gave a little laugh. 'She's like a mother hen, she's already instructed the teams to interview as soon as the on-duty solicitor arrives.'

Dylan tutted. 'It's impractical for one solicitor to sit in the interviews for all seven. Unacceptable.' He winced.

'The custody sergeant has been on to the duty solicitors Perfect and Best informing them that, due to the numbers in custody, they'll need help to prevent delays,' said Raj who joined them.

'Good, any notable reaction from anyone arrested?'

'Some of them were cocky clever, others in shock, as are some of the arresteds' families,' said Raj.

'Did you arrange for the custody officer to do the chart on the dry wipe board showing the names of those brought in for all to see?'

'That boss...,' she said, cocking an eyebrow. 'That was done by my fair hand this morning, before we went out on the raids. It's displayed behind the charge desk so none of them can miss it.'

'Great, while that tactic has been used many times before, it still works. It's good to let them see who else is locked up, especially when they're all in it together.'

'Let's hope that today, seven is a lucky number for us, I've got search teams at this moment seizing everything that might link them to Freddy Knapton's murder, primarily they are instructed to look for bloodstained clothing and footwear, mobile phones and computers.'

'I'm impressed, well done. It's going to be a laborious task interviewing seven but we don't have a choice - we need to find out what went on.'

'I'm just hoping at least one of them opens up in the first interview. There is no reason not to if they're on the periphery of what's happened,' said Raj.

'I'd like to think so too, when they've no reason to face a charge. But you and I know that misguided loyalty or the thought of being tagged as a nark is one hell of a barrier,' said Dylan.

'It's amazing what talk of prison does. Most of this lot are first-timers.' Vicky winked as she succumbed to one almighty yawn.

Dylan lowered his head and peered at her through half closed eyes. 'You better enjoy the short break; it's going to be a long day.'

Vicky belched. 'I know, and I also know that I shouldn't have had that mucky curry last night,' she said grimacing.

'Yes well, you'll learn. Remember the interviews need to be thorough and you don't get extra time added to their detention purely on the basis that you've arrested a large number of people at once. You've got twenty-four hours to interview seven people, less their statuary sleep and break times – I suggest you hit the ground running.'

'Vicky slid off her chair. 'You've not got an energy drink in that drawer of yours have you?'

Dylan shook his head.

'A strong large black coffee it is then.'

***

Dylan was speaking to his opposite number in North Yorkshire. 'Do you remember when we joined up Dylan,' said Terry Hawk. 'It all seemed so easy didn't it - none of this performance shite?

We took more people home than we locked up, and we put the wrong 'uns away and threw away the bloody key!'

'Yes, well I'm turning a blind eye to the paperwork tomorrow and going with my DS Jon Summers to speak to them at Redchester Regal Hire Cars.'

'And we've arranged to see your crime prevention officer DC Rupert Charles here today so I'll let you know how we get on.'

Dylan's eye strayed to the Merton Manor bible; the SIO's policy log that was a daily reminder to him of what decisions he had made on the job, why he made them and why he discarded other lines of enquiry. It was stuffed full of his thoughts and actions that all seemed such a pain to have to document at the time, but eighteen months down the line when the investigation had finished and he was stood in the dock of a court swearing on oath, it would be his saviour. It was hard enough to remember these days what he did yesterday never mind in two years from now and with several more investigations under his belt.

As the day progressed he and Jon worked diligently on the information the team had collated regarding the background for the car hire company. According to local police, the car hire business had not caused them any concerns in the past. It was a known coffee spot for some police officers, a company used by others, but their uninvited visit would never-the-less take place as planned. As Dylan was preparing to leave the station he got a message from DI Terry Hawk that troubled him. DC Rupert Charles had failed to turn up for his interview with the North Yorkshire Police officers.

Dylan wondered why? He looked at his watch, it was late but he didn't want to leave the station until he had an update from the team on the Knapton murder who were still interviewing. He rang Jen to check that her and Maisy were okay.

Due to the artificial light and the continued buzz of staff in the never-sleeping incident room he hadn't realised how quick the evening had passed until he heard the CID office doors swing open and his eyes shot up to the clock that read ten-thirty. Damn, he would be apologising to Jen again. Vicky arrived back in the incident room with some of the team.

'Reading your body language you seem positive,' he said.

'Raj and Shelagh were late going into the last interview. But we're getting there. It's the right group and they're talking at the moment. Some more than others.'

'It's down to this lot boss,' added Ned

'Jason Paul seems a reasonable lad. He tells us there has always been this ongoing aggravation between Knapton and the group, but recently he'd been telling the dog to attack them. This really pissed them off. McIntyre and Farah Ruwal came up with an idea to teach him a lesson. In simple terms some would throw stones at Freddie, and then run into the car park getting Freddie to chase them, where the others would be waiting for him,' said Vicky.

'According to Jason, on the day of the murder Martin Lister brought along a dog pole that his dad, apparently, had been given when he worked as a dog warden,' said Ned.

'So, to be clear, two lads bait Knapton, they run into the car park and he and his dog give chase?' asked Dylan.

'Jason Paul and Joe Grayson were the ones acting as bait,' added Vicky. 'The lad using the dog pole and attack sleeve is Martin Lister, Jason says it was all about scaring Knapton till Farah Ruwal took the knife off Dean. She fronted Knapton up while everybody else surrounded him and the dog was held on the pole. Knapton gave her a load of verbal and others were egging her on to dig him with the knife. Suddenly she stabs him. McIntyre apparently shouts, 'get him down.' She stabs him in the legs. Everybody then sticks the boot in and Dean McIntyre eventually gets on top of him and cuts his throat. Knapton is left motionless, like a rag doll. He says everyone was just euphoric and Dean and Farah went off for a quickie.'

'Really?' Dylan's face was unbelieving.

'That's what he says,' said Vicky.

'Okay, whatever, so why throw Knapton off the roof, do we know?' asked Dylan.

'Apparently McIntyre's idea, according to Jason, just in case Knapton wasn't already dead. And before walking off into the sunset with Farah and the dog, he warned the others they'd be killed if they ever spoke of it,' said Vicky.

'No doubt they will all try to minimise their involvement,' said Dylan.

'Probably. But the suggestion is, more than one of them used their mobiles to film it.' Vicky looked at her watch and frowned. 'Where's Raj, she should have finished fifteen minutes ago?'

'Are we presuming that Dean and Farah beheaded the dog?'

Vicky shook her finger at Dylan. 'We never presume boss,' she said with a smile like a Cheshire cat. 'But, if we are to believe the others then it was them who took Satan out of the car park.'

'Have you found the restraining pole and sleeve?' said Dylan.

'Yes, it was located in the garage at Martin Lister's house. So somebody returned it.'

DS Rajinder Uppal entered the office with a tray of drinks.

'Where've you been?' demanded Vicky reaching up to take a mug of tea off the tray.

'Washing up the dirty pots left in the sink! My first job tomorrow is putting a notice in the kitchen. Pots that are left dirty will be thrown out!'

Vicky and Ned looked at one another and grimaced.

'I've been interviewing Martin Lister. He said he hasn't slept since the incident and cried throughout. He brought the pole along to restrain the dog as he tells me it had bitten someone he knew previously and his intention was that the device would keep everyone safe. He says it was his understanding that the gang were going to let the dog chase them, then kidnap it to teach Knapton a lesson. He says he had no idea that they intended to harm it - he loves dogs. He likened the attack to a violent video game, his words not mine.'

Dylan clapped his hands together and sat forward as if to rise from the chair. 'Okay, let's call it a day. We've made great in-roads. It looks like our main players, if we believe what they're saying so far are Dean and Farah. Dean's locked up but before we release any of the others and the word gets out, we need to lock Farah up. I'll get Uniform to do it for us. Do your team briefings in the morning as usual and we'll have another scrum down at six o'clock tomorrow night, if that suits everyone?' There was a resounding nod of tired heads. 'I'll speak to Chief Superintendent Hugo-Watkins, explain to him that enquiries are progressing diligently and we need extended detention on each of these individuals, which will give us up to another twelve hours, but what a shame, that means he'll have to be up early for once.' Dylan's smile was forced. 'By then we should be able to clarify who has done what, or not, as the case maybe, and we should also be clearer as to what else happened and what we need to do next. I'll chase forensics re the knife examination.

'Have any of them mentioned anyone else being present that we haven't arrested?' said Dylan.

'No,' the others said in unison.

'Thanks everyone for today. It's difficult when there is such a large number of people involved but you've done a fantastic job so far, well done. In the next round of interviews, I want you to ask each of them to name all those present just to ensure there is no one outstanding, other than Farah.'

Dylan arrived home, dragged himself up the stairs, got into bed and snuggled close to Jen.

'Progress? Is that why you're late?' she said.

'Yeah, things are bubbling.'

'Try get some sleep Jack.'

'Are you okay?'

'I'm fine, honestly, I don't want you being poorly.'

***

The following morning the office was once more a hive of activity by seven o'clock. The atmosphere was electric, as it always was in an incident room close to a breakthrough in detecting a murder.

The next interview team on the Knapton murder had their work cut out. So far they'd had only had one interview with the seven arrested. Ideally they aimed to interview them at least twice. The number of people in custody allowed them the opportunity between interviews to liaise with each other to understand what was being said and therefore the intelligence continued to gather momentum. The Chief Superintendent had been in the cells earlier and extended the detention times on all those arrested without any objections from solicitors or prisoners.

'Poor chap, you had to feel sorry for him, he was exhausted after doing all those extensions,' said Vicky.

'And he was quick to tell me as much in the message he sent me,' said Dylan.

'He didn't? I was taking the piss. He should try interviewing them, then he'd know what bloody exhausted was, the knob!'

'Hey be careful. He could be sitting on your next promotion board,' said Dylan.

'Yeah, we'll I'm showing enough of my arse up the bloody tree at sergeant level, I'll not be going for no more boards, I can assure you.'

'Never say never Vicky,' said Dylan with a knowing look.

Dylan was eager to speak to forensics. Traces of blood had been found on the knife blade which they were able to match with Freddy Knapton's. Surprisingly another unidentified minute trace of blood had also been found, where the blade met with the handle. What forensics required from Dylan was any further suspects DNA samples sending for comparison.

'The owner of the knife we believe is a Dean McIntyre. He's a violent individual who is already in custody. He's got previous convictions so if it's him you should get a hit on the national database. Another arrest is also imminent so I will arrange for swabs to be forwarded to you from that person too.'

The hunting knife was the murder weapon. Dylan looked upward to his ceiling. 'Thank you, God.'

The news was like a breath of air to Dylan's starved body. He stood and walked the few steps to look out of his window drinking in the daylight, and as he did so he noticed DC Rupert Charles strolling across the yard to his car. He rapped on the window to catch his attention but, apparently unhearing, the detective constable got into his car and swiftly drove out of the yard. Dylan dragged his fingers through his hair and a moan escaped his lips. 'Ned,' he shouted at the top of his voice. 'Here now!'

Chapter Twenty Two

Dylan sat in on the morning briefing for the Knapton murder. He had a list in front of him of the seven arrested so far. He glanced at the names. Jason Paul, Phillip Masters, Joe Grayson, Harry Withers, Martin Lister, Paul Bishop and Tara Cabe.

'It's like dealing with a football team. We need to make sure we have all their DNA because forensic have found blood on the knife, apart from Freddie Knapton's. Also because it is inferred that they all 'stuck the boot in' let's ensure we have seized their footwear,' said Dylan.

'I think I can speak for everyone when I say that all footwear from our suspects have been seized and the mandatory DNA taking has been done,' said Raj who looked around the room for confirmation. 'Sixteen-year-old Tara Cabe, in the presence of her mother, basically confirms what Jason and Martin told us about the attack. She also tells us she was so frightened that she ran away as fast as she could from the car park. She states that she hadn't been aware before the attack that Dean McIntyre had a knife.'

'How reliable do you think her account is?' said Dylan.

'I believe her. She appears genuinely shocked, frightened and upset but we are now aware she has a drug problem, and she could easily be confused. She confirms to us the word has been passed around since Knapton's murder that nobody should say a word, or they'd end up dead.'

'Who's putting the word out?'

'Ruwal and McIntyre, of whom she says everyone is terrified.'

'Paul Bishop is a cocky twat. He's nineteen years of age and he knows it all. He is adamant that Knapton needed sorting before him and his dog badly hurt someone. He says that they had done the rest of us a favour by getting shut of Knapton.'

'Did he know about the knife?' said Dylan.

'Yes, he said that he knew Dean had a knife but he says that he thought it was just to scare Knapton.

'Great work everybody, I think we now have a good idea of what took place that night. We are missing Farah Ruwal at the moment and Dean McIntyre whose already on remand, and that makes nine of them in total, or is anyone else mentioned as being there at the time of the incident?' The room was instantly quiet.

'So can I take it by the silence, no one else has been mentioned?' Dylan continued, 'Uniform are out at the moment to arrest Farah Ruwal on suspicion of murder and search her flat. Tomorrow I'll contact the prison and arrange for McIntyre to be produced to the police cells within the next couple of days, and we will arrest him for murder and interview him. We don't want to be keeping this lot any longer than the thirty-six hours' detention we already have authorisation for. We need forensic results, we need mobile and computer results and we aren't going to have them in the next few hours. So reluctantly we'll bail them for a couple of weeks after the next round of interviews and by that time we might have all the information we need. This also allows us to concentrate on our two main players, Dean and Farah.'

'I'm day-off tomorrow sir, do you want me in? The kids have an eye sight test booked in after school that's all,' said Raj.

'Not unless you need to come in?' Dylan said.

'Overtime? I'm in!' said Vicky. 'That'll pay for the designer handbag I've got my eye on.'

'You've been around long enough to know I can't authorise unnecessary overtime.'

Vicky slouched back in her chair and pouted.

'I'll no doubt be pulled over the coals already by the Chief for the cost of the two investigations.'

'Yeah, well he isn't the one doing all the bastard work is he?' Vicky mumbled under her breath.

'Incidentally, Paul Bishop admitted to being the artist,' said Ned diplomatically changing the subject. 'His grandad was in the war and drew 'wot no' Chad cartoons for him when he was a kid.'

'Get stuck into his ribs about the damage.'

Ned nodded.

'Okay everyone, meeting over.'

Vicky raced to her desk, threw her pen and pad inside her drawer and locked it in quick time.

'Going somewhere?' said Ned.

'I'm nipping out to put a deposit on that handbag before it's sold,' she said in a whisper and with the wink of an eye. 'If Hugo-Watkins can have new furniture in his office. I can have that bag.'

Overhearing, Dylan shook his head. Sitting at his desk he leaned back in his chair, laced his fingers together and put his hands behind his head, and for a moment, he closed his eyes. When he opened them and sat forward his focus was on the pile of enquires he had written off as 'no further action' earlier in the day. The result of wasted man hours on hopeless pursuits and unproductive enquiries. He leaned forward picked the paperwork up and carried it to the outer office placing it firmly in the HOLMES incident loggers tray before finishing for the day.

Lack of sleep was beginning to be a regular occurrence. Information from interviews and enquiries spun around in his head. Not only was the Freddy Knapton murder enquiry keeping him awake but also the Merton Manor. He was spinning plates and the pressure was on - he could almost hear the review team knocking at his door. On hearing Maisy call in her sleep he put on his trousers, pulled on a sweatshirt and shut the bedroom door quietly behind him, so as not to wake Jen. By the time he reached Maisy's bedside the dream had passed and she was peaceful so he went downstairs in search of a warm drink.

Max sat by the kitchen table, his head rested on Dylan's thigh. His beseeching eyes looked up at his master. Dylan felt the dog's powerful jaws at his fingertips as he rubbed the fur under his chin. Dylan opened his laptop and Max, now devoid of his attention, lay down with a deep groan and positioned himself purposefully, it seemed, across Dylan's foot. As dawn broke, Dylan had completed his schedule for the day. His head, although feeling foggy, felt much relieved for downloading his thoughts onto paper. When Jen appeared he smiled at her. Jen's face scrunched up in a yawn. She looked pale. He gave a gentle kiss on her cheek as he spooned coffee into the cups. She put her arms about him and, feeling the cold skin of his hairy stomach under her warm hands, she snuggled up to him tight. 'I didn't hear you get up?'

'My mind was running ragged with what needs doing so I thought it best to get up and write it all down.'

It was Dylan's turn to yawn. 'And now I have, I could quite easily go back to sleep.' Jen looked up at the clock, squinting as she did so in the half-light. 'What time you due in?'

'Half-six.' Dylan suddenly tightened the grip on his mug.

'Careful,' she said as his lack of concentration nearly saw the drink spill on the floor.

'I think I'd better get you some sustenance,' she said concerned. Dylan sat down with his drink and Jen moved around the kitchen, gathering the breakfast things and putting them on the table. 'Banana, Porridge?'

'Thanks. Whatever. I want to grab a shower before I go to help me wake up.' He drew a hand across his face and rubbed his red eyes with fisted hands.

'You look absolutely shattered.'

'I am, but the Knapton job is coming together. We just need to secure the evidence to prove what we suspect took place before we submit the file to CPS. We need to put each and every one of the gang before the courts for their involvement. The last thing anyone in the team wants is for those responsible to walk free.'

'And how's things coming along on the Merton Manor fire investigation?'

'Slow. We're systematically working through the information we've being given and waiting for tests to come back from the experts. Frustratingly, as you know, some take longer than others and it's a waiting game for us right now. I'm across to Lancashire this morning making enquiries about a hire car and its users.'

***

At six o'clock Dylan was sitting in his car in the driveway. He started the engine and looked up to see Maisy and Jen waving at him from the bedroom window. His heart took a leap of contentment.

Vicky Hardacre was sitting at her desk looking focused. When Dylan reached her she was tapping her pen on her notepad, seemingly oblivious to him. 'Any startling news?' he enquired.

'By the time I got to the shop the handbag had sold out,' she said solemnly. Dylan rolled his eyes. And with that she got to her feet and headed for the kitchen. 'Brew,' she shouted as Dylan continued to his office and opened the door. He'd just taken off his coat and was hanging it up when Vicky walked in with two mugs.

'Farah Ruwals been arrested.'

'And?' he said as he leaned forward, pressing a button to boot up his computer.

'They had to smash the door in.'

'What was the problem?'

'There wasn't a problem. She couldn't be bothered to answer it.'

'I'm glad they made use of the door ram. I'd have been bloody annoyed if they'd walked away from an unanswered door.' Dylan sat down behind his desk and unlocked his desk drawers.

'They'd hardly do that on your shout, now would they?' she said raising an eyebrow. 'Apparently she kicked-off big style, ended up in hospital feigning illness but she's in the cells waiting for us this morning.'

Dylan looked across at her from his computer screen. 'You'd think people would know by now that we'll do whatever it takes to arrest someone who's wanted.' Dylan's eyes went back to the computer screen.

'What're you reading,' Vicky said after a moment or two.

'The night report,' he said absentmindedly. 'I'm off into Lancashire with Jon Summer on a Merton Manor murder enquiry, but before I set off I want to have a quick scrum down with the team.' As if on cue the doors started banging in the direction of the outer CID office - the team was starting to arrive for duty.

'For a young lass Ruwal does a pretty good impression of an ill-treated carthorse this morning according to the custody staff.' Ned shuddered as he entered the room. 'Not a pretty sight.'

'Hark at you. Have you looked in a mirror?' said Vicky.

Ned stood before them, his unbrushed curly hair was tucked behind his ears. His shirt tail out of his trousers. Vicky looked down at his feet to see he wore odd socks. 'Did you get dressed in the dark?'

Ned's lip curled and he stuck out his tongue.

'Children,' growled Dylan. 'We don't have time.'

'Ruwal has some risky selfies on her mobile phone and they're not for the faint hearted. Do you want to see?' said Vicky.

'Has she really?' Ned said his eyes widened.

Dylan scowled. 'I'll take your word for it if they're not from the scene of the murder.'

Vicky shook her head. 'No they're not.'

'I'll delegate that then - privilege of rank. I'd like a résumé of all yesterday's interviews, in brief, for each prisoner, stating what they admit to, on my desk before the end of the day. So when I get back from Lancashire I can catch up. If you need me, I'm on my mobile,' said Dylan.

Late morning brought a curtain of fog down in Harrowfield as Dylan and Jon travelled through Tandem Bridge en route to Redchester. It was a struggle to see six feet ahead. But as Jon drove the vehicle out onto the moors the wind that had picked up moved the fog along and the sky was dark and threatening rain. The Yorkshire weather was displaying its repertoire of changeable conditions. Before long the heavens opened and a deluge of rain fell.

As they arrived at the local police office closest to the garage, fortuitously, a police officer was just entering the usually unmanned police station. Dylan knew that local knowledge may assist them but also it was courtesy to let the locals know of a visit. You never knew when you might need backup.

Redchester Regal Hire Cars had no less than six high-powered, luxury cars on their forecourt. Dylan had to admit to being disappointed not to see a royal blue Mercedes amongst them. A professional eye on the extent of the security, told him that money had been heavily invested on the premises. Security fence spikes to deter and prevent intruders and a banner advertising 'Redchester Regal Hire Cars' sponsored by a security company spanned the frontage of the white, corrugated roofed building.

Jon parked the car directly in front of the mesh-panelled reception windows. Before the two detectives had reached the door a tall, well-groomed man opened it and greeted them. Standing on the door step, he towered over the two six foot detectives, offered his hand and a welcoming smile. The thin faced, clean shaven salesman was of slim build, he wore a pinstripe suit, brilliant white shirt and a blue silk tie.

'Good day gentleman, Mike Talbot,' he said shaking Dylan's hand. He had a strong grip. 'Men in suits? I recognise the walk of a police officer, my dad was in the Met. You're not local I presume with that number plate.' Mr Talbot gave a slight nod of his head in the direction of the plain clothes police vehicle.

Dylan introduced himself and Jon, who both automatically produced their warrant cards. 'Harrowfield CID, West Yorkshire,' Dylan said.

'Come in.' Mike turned and led the way into the building. The fan heater above the door in the narrow corridor blew out a dry heat and instantly Dylan undid his outer coat. Mike turned directly left through an open door and into a furnished office. He sat behind a desk in a leather executive chair; a desk top computer faced him. Two high backed chairs were strategically placed in front of the desk and he beckoned the men to sit. He went to pick up his phone. 'Can I get you a drink?'

'No, thanks we've just had one,' said Dylan. Mike put the phone down.

'How can I help?'

'We need to have a chat with you about a triple murder that's recently occurred in our area.'

'A triple murder? Bloody hell, and how do you think I can help?' Mike Talbot's healthy pallor had turned slightly ashen.

Dylan outlined the circumstances of the fire and how the occupants had been discovered, he included the fact that the couple had both been shot in the head and also told him the wife had been pregnant and the child had been killed.

'Who'd they upset?' Mike Talbot blinked rapidly, picked up a glass of water and took a gulp. The swift action brought about a fit of coughing. He loosened his tie.

'We need to trace and eliminate the users of a royal blue Mercedes, registration number is TTI 155 which was seen in the immediate area at the time. It's the only vehicle connected to the enquiry that is registered out of our force area, and to here, hence the visit.'

'Yes, that's one of our cars. Blood and sand, I've been here a number of years but never before have any of our vehicles been the subject of an enquiry for murder; speeding, parking tickets by the bucket load. But murder, that's surreal. Wait here a minute.' As he spoke he stood, excused himself, and disappeared out of the door. Dylan and Jon could hear voices coming from down the corridor, the opening and closing of drawers and moments later he returned with a bright yellow pocket file. 'Thought so, this is relatively easy,' he said, his face looking brighter. 'That particular car was booked out to a Mr Devlin. He paid in cash, up front.

'Mr Devlin? What do you know about him?' said Dylan.

'Nothing much, other than he hires a car from us every now and then. Most of our business clients hire a prestigious vehicle when they are out to impress - whether that be a woman or business.'

'What's he like?'

'Them, Declan and Damien Devlin are brothers. They both look very much alike, big, burly chaps. Not people you want to argue with, if you get my drift.' Mike handed documents that he pulled from the folder to Dylan. Here, this is all the information that we have. I can copy it for you if it'd help?'

Dylan scanned the pages before handing them Jon. Mike Talbot sat upright, rigid, watching the officers intently. He tapped his pen rhythmically on the desktop.

Holding a copy of the invoice in his hand Dylan lifted his head. 'That hire charge is a bit steep isn't it?'

'We offer top class cars with no added cost for the amount of miles the vehicle might cover - within reason of course.'

'Is it usual for your customers to pay you such large amounts in cash?' said Dylan.

'Depends what they're hiring the car for,' said Mike touching the side of his nose. 'If it's to take the mistress away, it's usually cash.' Mike tittered.

Dylan considered his answer. 'Five thousand pounds still feels a lot to me to pay out in notes.'

'I guess what's a large amount to you and me is chicken feed to others - just depends on your lifestyle.'

'And do the Devlin's always pay cash?'

'I've never given it a thought before but yes, yes they do.'

'Do you know what line of business the Devlin brothers are in?' asked Jon.

Mike Talbot scratched his chin. 'I don't think we've ever had that conversation but they're always well dressed.' He looked thoughtful for a moment or two. 'Look, I hire cars. I only ask the questions that are on the booking forms. What does it say under occupation?' he said pointing to the document Jon was holding.

'Self-employed, that could cover a multitude of sins.' Jon said.

'We will need to take away these original documents in relation to the hire of the vehicle. If you want to take copies, we'll get the originals back to you as soon as possible.'

'Not a problem.'

'Where is the vehicle now? Has Mr Devlin still got it?'

'No, the car's been hired out for a wedding but it should be back with us shortly.'

'There is no home address given by Mr Devlin?'

'No, come to think of it every time they come to hire a car from us it seems they have either just come back from abroad, or are going. Damian Devlin told me when he returned the car this time they were going away again for a bit of sun.' Mike Talbot looked at his watch.

'Did he say for how long?'

'No, but he did say they would be in touch on their return so I assumed that his brother was going with him - they seem to be joined at the hip. Perhaps they live abroad?'

'How many times has the Merc been out since Mr Devlin returned it?'

'Once,' he said. As Mike was speaking he seemed to be distracted. He looked out of his window. The same window that he must have spotted Dylan and Jon from when they entered the big iron gates. 'Thought I caught a reflection of a car in the mirror facing the entrance. I can see the vehicle in question's just being driven back into the parking lot. You couldn't have timed your visit better if you'd tried.' Mike Talbot pushed his chair backwards and it scraped noisily on the wooden floor. 'Do you mind if I go and deal with this customer, it will only take a couple of minutes?'

'No, not at all. We'll wait for you here.'

'Once I've checked the vehicle over with the client you might like to take a look over it yourself?'

With the Mercedes car keys in Mike Talbot's hand, a short time later he led Dylan and Jon outside. The first thing Dylan noticed was that the vehicle had the immaculate showroom finish the witnesses had described.

Jon whistled. 'How do you get a shine like that?' he said. 'That's impressive.'

Mike bristled with pride. 'We have experts,' he said indicating with the nod of his head towards the workshop. 'They work hard at keeping the bodies of our cars in that condition. It's all part of the service. Our customers come to us because they want something a bit different, something a bit special and that's why they're willing to pay that bit extra.'

Mike unlocked the vehicle for the detectives. 'This will need a good valet. Not everyone wants confetti in their hire car.' He opened all the doors wide. 'Help yourselves, have a good look around and I'll go and get a copy taken of the file.'

'Don't forget we'll need the original paperwork of the agreement.'

'Not a problem,' he called over his shoulder before vanishing into the office building.

Dylan was more concerned about the condition of the exterior of the car and both him and Jon walked very slowly around it looking for any damage that appeared recent.

'Genuine do you think?' said Jon to Dylan as they circled the vehicle.

'Possibly.' Dylan's mouth formed a straight line. He breathed in deeply. 'What worries me is that he isn't offering information, although to be fair, his answers to the questions put to him are plausible. He doesn't strike me as daft enough not to keep legitimate records either.' He stood still and looked about him at the numerous different high spec models on display. 'It's obvious he makes a reasonable living out of renting quality cars, but who does he rent them all out to? You wouldn't have thought there would be the call for so many in this area, would you?'

Jon stopped at the nearside wheel arch and spent a moment or two looking at one area in particular with interest. 'See that,' he said pointing out a shallow indentation that wasn't readily visible unless viewed at a specific angle, at close quarters. 'I'd say someone has been to work on that. And I wouldn't call them an expert as our man suggests. Jon looked up at Dylan who bent down by his side. 'Can you see it now sir?'

'I can now you've pointed it out. Remind me to take you with me when I change my car will you?'

Jon smiled.

'We'll see how genuine our Mr Talbot is in a moment or two. It might have been some time ago since this car left Merton Manor but I want CSI all over it ASAP. Get on the phone. Arrange to get a low loader down here pronto. I want a forensic examination, paint samples, as well as debris samples taken from inside the wheel arches. The so called experts can do what they will but hopefully no one has touched the under-carriage. I'll break the news to our host shall I?' Dylan said as Mike walked towards them. Jon was straight on the phone making the arrangements, he turned and walked out of ear shot.

With a smile on his face and the expectation of a swift exit from the detectives, Mike had a spring in his step and a large brown envelope that he was waving at Dylan. 'Here you go,' he said. Dylan took the proffered paperwork.

'Just one thing,' Dylan said pointing to the near side wheel arch. 'I understand you check your vehicles thoroughly when they're returned?'

Mike looked a tad uncomfortable. 'Yes, we do why?'

'When did this vehicle take a hit on the front nearside?'

Mike reddened from his neck upwards. 'When it was in the hands of Mr Devlin,' he said slowly. 'But it was no trouble. Damien Devlin gave me a grand to cover the cost. They're good customers. It really is no skin off our nose - it's not like we don't have an in-house body workshop.' His laugh was false to Dylan's ears.

'So you're telling me this vehicle was fixed up after Mr Devlin returned the vehicle to you?'

Mike nodded.

'Then tell me again. How well do you know the Devlin brothers if you're now saying what good customers they are?'

Mike's arms were open, his hands splayed. 'I don't, really I don't know them at all, they're just customers. They come in, hire a car, pay me and bring it back. I've never had any trouble from them. Honest! Look, they were even upfront about the damage -now that's a first.'

'I'm surprised and disappointed you didn't mention the damage to us though,' said Dylan with a shrug of his shoulders. 'It's going to have to go for forensic examination.' Dylan was angry that he hadn't been more forthcoming with that information in the first instance, but he remained calm. He needed Mike Talbot on their side.

'I'm sorry, I honestly never gave it a second thought. I'm obviously never pleased when a car comes back damaged but when the customer pays for repairs without a fuss what more could I ask? Accidents happen. Look, I understand if you have to take the car away to be examined, I'm not objecting. Take it, take it for as long as you need it.'

'Good, we do have the power to seize the vehicle anyway, but it's always nice to do it with the co-operation of the owner. I'm aware it has been re-hired since the Devlin's used it, but since they had it at the time of the incident we'll be leaving nothing to chance as far as obtaining evidence goes, not when we're running an investigation into such brutal murders.'

'I know, I totally understand. Please, all I ask is that your guys don't leave it in some compound somewhere for years. It takes ages to get a shine on it like this.' Mike ran his fingers lovingly over the bonnet. 'Thankfully it's not the only car of its kind I've got in the fleet.'

Jon was still talking on the mobile phone. 'Invoice the incident room for the low-loader sir? The local lads are asking,' he said taking a moment to look Dylan's way.

Dylan nodded.

'You're bringing a low loader?'

'It's a necessary expense, we don't want any potential evidence lost en route,' Dylan said matter-of-factly. 'Should the Devlin brothers be in touch; I want you to say nothing of our visit or the examination of the vehicle they hired. Is that clear? Otherwise you may be assisting offenders.'

'I promise. Is there anything else I can help you with?'

'Actually yes, if either of them contacts you, you could obtain an up-to-date phone number for them - just in case they have ditched their mobiles and have new ones, since they filled in the forms.' Dylan waved the brown envelope in front of him. 'And, if you do get it, you could ring me, that would be very helpful, and I'd be extremely grateful.' Dylan handed Mike his business card. 'Someone will be in touch shortly; we'll need a full statement from you regarding the hiring of the vehicle by the brothers, and incorporated in that statement will be the exhibiting of the documents you have given us today. Details of the damage to car, and work that was done to rectify it by yourselves.'

It was just over an hour later before the detectives left the garage and headed back to Harrowfield. As Jon drove, Dylan spoke on the phone to the on-call crime scene investigator, Mark Hamilton. 'I want photographs of the vehicle when it arrives with you. It would be great if you could find something, anything to connect the vehicle to Merton Manor. Damage has been repaired to its front nearside and we'll need paint samples for forensics to compare with those recovered at the scene.'

'We'll do our best sir,' Mark said.

'Can you finger-print the interior of the car. For your information it has been hired out once since the Devlin brothers returned it and it appears the car hire place does a bloody good job valeting the cars. So, I'm well aware they may have been wiped away and only if we're extremely lucky will we find any marks belonging to the Devlin brothers now. We can prove they hired the vehicle but without Mike's evidence, disputed or if he refuses to give evidence at a later date, we will need to put the Devlin's in the car, for continuity.'

Just before four o'clock Dylan and Jon arrived back at the Harrowfield police station. 'I'll leave you to complete the necessary paperwork Jon, and let's see what we can find out about the mobile phone number given on the car hire agreement,' Dylan said, as the two walked across the car park towards the outer door of the CID office. 'Including updating the incident room staff for the database. I'll give DI Hawks a call to let him know we've seized the Merc. But before I do…' he said, holding the door open for Jon to enter the office before him. 'I need to see how they're doing with the Knapton murder.'

Chapter Twenty Three

Within thirty minutes, all those working on the Knapton murder enquiry team, including civilians and office staff, had assembled in the incident room.

'First,' Dylan said. 'How far have we got with Farah Ruwal today?'

'We've only managed one interview.' Vicky sipped from a can of Red Bull.

'Is that your dinner?' Raj asked.

Vicky looked surprised. 'Breakfast, dinner, tea and probably supper.' She pulled a face.

Raj frowned at her.

'When the hell do you think I'm going to get out of this god forsaken building today to get something more substantial? I've said it before and I'll say it again, the shiny arses at headquarters have a lot to answer for. Never once did they give a thought to the shift workers when they closed the canteen - can't you have a word?' she pleaded with Dylan. 'Tell them we don't all have bloody nine-to-five jobs and chuffin lunch breaks?'

Seeing the look on Dylan's face Raj quickly interjected. 'Still, my thoughts are that they'll all be charged at the absolute minimum with threatening behaviour, public order or affray, but who knows what forensic will find on their shoes or what their clothing may reveal. It could be that more of them will be facing a murder or an attempted murder charge.'

'And, don't forget we have mobile video footage which promises to corroborate some evidence, if not all,' Vicky said as she peeled the skin off the banana that Raj had handed her.

'For now we have the majority who tell us they knew about the plan to taunt and scare Knapton, and they admit to going along with it. But it's what we can prove, as to who did what, that really matters. We may have a clearer understanding when we have viewed all the mobile footage, which should also help us in discussions with Jackie Stanley at the Crown Prosecution Service,' said Dylan.

'Farah Ruwal admitted to me in interview this morning that she knew about the knife,' said Vicky.

'They are all consistent in saying that Farah Ruwal started the stabbing of Knapton, and then Dean took the knife off her to finish him off. There is corroboration from some of them that these two also dealt with Knapton's dog Satan, although this is only circumstantial,' Ned added.

'Let's not forget what the pathologist said, Knapton was dead before he was thrown over the car park wall. None of them admit to knowing he was dead, but they no doubt intended him to die when they threw him over the edge,' said Dylan. 'So, any more from Farah?' he added.

'She's more concerned about her flat door being smashed off its hinges than being arrested for murder,' said Vicky. 'We dropped it straight on her toes and her response was that, like I said earlier, she knew Dean had a knife. She tells me and Ned that she was more than up for teaching Knapton a lesson with Dean because, "it was about time somebody stood up to him." She says Dean wasn't scared of him. She says he isn't scared of anyone. She even goes as far as to say that they had every intention of, scaring the shit out of Knapton. She fully admits taking drugs that day with Dean and being so high that after the attack on Knapton her and Dean had sex in the car park. She puts herself there at the time of the incident with the others and she says she knew what was going on, but states she didn't see who did what as she was otherwise occupied.' Vicky raised both eyebrows. 'It was only when they had finished canoodling, she says, they walked back to the group and Knapton wasn't moving and that is when they picked him up and dumped him over the edge.'

'I don't think we expected anything other from her did we?' said Dylan.

'Okay, we have her clothing and footwear let's get that checked. Do we have her DNA?'

'Yes, we swabbed her. The only time she has come to our attention in the past has been for possession of a small amount of cannabis, she claimed at the time was for personal use and the more recent shoplifting incident.'

'We need their mobile phone evidence back as soon as possible. I want to see not only who's been saying what to whom but also who has been ringing who, when and from where. Don't forget to check their social media accounts. I want you, Vicky and Ned, to continue interviewing Farah Ruwal. I'm hoping she might relate more to you two than strangers. I've heard the saying "the more the merrier" but not on a murder enquiry. It's bad enough when there's one or two suspects, but nine?'

***

Farah Ruwal had her solicitor present. Keith Parkin, new to the Harrowfield district, had previously worked on the Redchester circuit. They commenced the next interview.

'Farah, you're aware that seven other people have been arrested in connection with Freddy Knapton's murder aren't you? And, they are all people who know you.'

'So what? Lots of people know me.' The big woman sat reclined in her chair her arms folded atop of her very large stomach.

'We've been told by some of those that it was you that had hold of Dean's knife, Knapton was calling you names, so you were the first to stab him.'

'Well they're lying. I were in't car park but I weren't nowhere near Knapton when he was stabbed. I were shagging Dean like I said before. It were the rest of 'em that were messing about with Freddy Knapton and his dog.' Farah's facial expression resembled that of a bull dog.

'You told us it was your friend Tara that fancied Dean McIntyre and that's why you were hanging around with the gang in the park in the first place, to keep her company. Why lie?'

'I told you I ain't lying. Just because he ended up with me, not her, I can't help it can I?'

'First time you had sex with Dean was it, in the car park on the day Knapton died?'

Farah ran a sleeved arm under her running nose. 'So what if?'

'Just asking. Can you tell us what's been going on between Dean and Knapton leading up to his murder?'

Hands flat on her thighs she leaned forward and spoke in a quieter voice. 'Look, Freddy was a little shit. His dog was the Devil. He set his dog on us. We'd be like doing nothing, minding our own business in the park but he went out of his way, every bloody day just to annoy the hell out of us. He thought he was some sort of tough guy. Well he weren't.'

'We understand from the others that there was some sort of plan, can you tell us about what the gang intended to do to Knapton on that day?'

Farah slouched and looked up to the ceiling, then back at Ned a moment or two later. 'Well, my boyfriend Dean...'

Ned's eyes were wide. 'Ah, so he's your boyfriend now?' he said teasingly.

'Yeah.' She shook her head from side to side and her jowls wobbled.

The interviewers knew that although she had replied in the affirmative her body language was suggesting it was perhaps an untruth.

'You can ask him,' Farah continued. 'He told me he loves me.' She stuck out her tongue.

'Okay, let's carry on,' said Vicky.

Farah's demeanour changed. She prickled like a proud peacock. 'My Deano's scared of nothing, or nobody. He said we should teach Knapton a lesson.'

'By we, do you mean the others in the gang too?'

'Yeah, but like, Deano's the leader of the gang.'

'So, you were going to tell us about this plan to teach Freddy Knapton a lesson?' said Vicky.

'It were sort of a plan,' she said tossing her head from one side to the other. Tendrils of her dark greasy fringe fell over her face and she flicked them out of her eyes. 'It started when Knapton started throwing stones at us and we threw them back. He ran away but he were so thick the next day he came back for more and this time we were waiting for him with a cart load of dog shit we'd gotten out of the bin. He still didn't get the message so we agreed a plan to get him into the multi-storey where he couldn't run away so easy and where we were going to scare the crap out of him once and for all.' A little smile flickered upon her lips and mischief danced in her eyes.

'So, you just wanted to scare him then, right?' said Vicky.

'Yeah,' she said labouring on the word. 'But, scare him good and proper - you know so he shit himself.' She gave a little laugh. 'Enough so he wouldn't mess with us or anyone else again - if you know what I mean?'

'Tell us, what happened the day he died?' Vicky continued.

'Well most of us went on to the top floor. There were no cars about, and we larked around half-hiding, waiting while a couple of the others hung around in the park. Their job was to get him to chase them - which he did. He didn't let his brute of a dog off the lead until he got to the car park and he told it to "find 'em". But we were ready for it and caught it with Martin's dad's gear.'

'So Martin is good with his dad's gear is he?'

Farah whistled. 'Good? He's bloody fantastic. Council should hire him as a dog catcher. He brought the gear to the park one day and showed us how good he was with Bish's dog.' All was silent for a moment or two. 'Martin got the dog in the loop at the end of the pole. The others surrounded Knapton and the next thing I know he was on the floor not moving. I didn't see what happened y'see coz me and Dean were...'

Vicky quickly interrupted. 'I think we are all aware of what you say Dean and yourself were up to Farah you don't need to tell us again.'

'I can't help it if he finds me sexy, can I?' she said as she scratched her head. Pulling her hand away she looked at her hand and put her fingers in her mouth chewing what she had removed from under her nail.

'What did you do when you saw Knapton lying on the floor not moving?'

'We threw him over the wall.'

Vicky looked at her questioningly.

'He were dead.' Farah said, her voice rising a few octaves. 'You don't need to look at me like I'm a bloody criminal.'

Ned cleared his throat. It was his turn now to challenge everything she had said.

'Farah, that's not true is it?'

Farah frowned. 'Yeah it is, ask anybody. They all saw us at it.'

'I'm not disputing that you two had a thing going on in the car park with Dean, but what we are disputing is that you threw Knapton over the wall after he was killed.'

'No fucking way! I'm not having that. You're making me out to be a murderer,' she squealed.

'Why don't you just tell us the truth, all this excited you?'

'Is he some sort of perv?' she said turning her attention to Vicky. She looked back to Ned. 'You're a sad bastard you are. And the drugs were only legal highs for your info.'

'You knew Dean had taken a knife with him to the car park, didn't you?'

'I'm not saying I didn't, but he gave it to one of the others when we went off to...'

Ned stopped her. 'Who, who did he give it to?'

'Who?' Farah screwed-up her face, 'I don't know who?'

'Who did Dean give the knife to? People we have spoken to say it was you who grabbed the knife from Dean and stabbed Knapton.'

'Well they're fucking lying then aren't they?' Farah splayed her legs and her gaze fell to the floor.

'Dean stabbed Knapton after you didn't he?'

'Fucking lies. I told you what happened.'

'Why, then, when we called to see you at your flat did you tell us you knew nothing about Freddy Knapton's murder?'

'Okay, but that was then. I'm locked up now aren't I? So what's the point in me lying to you?'

'We've recovered the knife that Freddy Knapton was stabbed with. Apart from his blood there are also traces of someone else's blood on it. Is that going to be yours?'

Farah looked momentarily shocked. She shook her head. 'No, no way!'

'Dean is going to be brought here from prison and arrested in connection with Freddy Knapton's murder, which means there were nine of you in total, against one.'

Her face lit up. She sat forward. 'Will I be able to see him?' she asked eagerly.

'No, I'm afraid it's not possible for you to see Dean.'

Farah groaned and sulked like a child.

'What's he going to say when questioned about the murder do you think?'

'How the hell should I know, and if you won't let me see him how am I going to find out?' she mumbled under her breath.

'As you are aware we have seized your clothing and footwear and it will be checked for Knapton's blood.'

'Well there might be some there mightn't there coz, like I said, I've admitted to helping the others lift him over the car park wall.'

'Are we going find his dog's blood on your clothing too?'

'No.'

'But there are others who say you and Dean took the dog away and we know it was beheaded, and if that's so it's very likely you'll have its blood on your clothing isn't it?'

Farah threw her head back and laughed out loud.

'You think that's funny, why?' Vicky's eyes narrowed.

'That nasty fucker without its head, now that was funny. So what you going to do about it?'

Keith Parkin gave her a quizzical look over his half-rimmed spectacles. 'I think I'd like to talk to my client if we could stop there for a break please,' he said to the detectives.

Farah turned her head sharply towards him. 'Why would you want to do that? I'm just starting to enjoy myself?'

'This interview is terminated at sixteen-hundred hours for the purpose of the tape,' Vicky heard Ned say.

The break was short lived when they got a call from the cells to say that Farah Ruwal was ready to be interviewed again. During the free time that had been forced upon them, Vicky and Ned had updated the team with the fact that she admitted being at the scene, knowing about the intention and the knife but denied she or Dean stabbed Freddy Knapton.

The door of the interview room had been left ajar during the recess but the repulsive odour still lingered on their return. The interview resumed with Farah Ruwal.

'When did you first know Dean had a knife?' asked Vicky.

Farah shrugged her shoulders. 'A few days before? He showed me first because he knew he could trust me.'

'Can you describe the knife for me?'

'He told me it were a proper soldier's knife. It had a yellow handle. In fact...' Farah paused, 'If you find blood on it then it's probably from then, I remember, he told me not to touch the blade because it were so sharp, it cut my finger badly and I bled buckets.' Farah held her finger up in the air.

'You've still got the scar?'

'Scar?' Farah looked from Vicky Hardacre, to her solicitor, and back.

'A scar on your finger where the knife cut you?'

Farah held out hands, palms up, on the table that sat between the detectives, and her and Keith Parkin. 'Nah,' she said with a little laugh. 'I'm one of them folk that heal quick obviously.'

'Why are you lying to us?' said Ned.

'I'm not, it's what happened, trust me.'

'The trace of blood we are talking about was found beneath the base of the handle. You see when someone stabs someone else their hand slides down onto the knife, this is how sometimes they happen to cut themselves accidentally. You have a cut, but on your right hand. Is that how that happened?' Vicky asked.

'No,' Farah said picking at the scab. 'That's from a sharp stone I think.'

Ned took over the interview. 'Farah, you're not helping yourself by continuing to lie. Freddy Knapton was murdered and your friends say you and Dean stabbed him. Some of them admit to kicking him and apart from Tara and Phillip Masters they also admit to tossing him over the edge of the car park. Tell me, how did you know he was dead?'

'Dean said he was. Everybody said he was. He was,' Farah's voice rose.

'I'm not saying he wasn't,' Ned said calmly. 'But let's suppose for one minute that he was just unconscious, and you helped throw him over the edge knowing that the drop from that height would kill him?'

'But I told you. He was dead.'

'If he was dead, then why did you need to throw him over the wall? You could have just left him lying on the car park floor couldn't you?'

She was silent for a moment. 'We did it to make sure he was dead.'

'So you wanted Freddy Knapton dead, why?'

Farah opened her mouth to speak but her solicitor interrupted her. 'I think I need time to advise my client further. Could we stop the interview?'

Ned glared at him, 'I think it's only fair that we allow Farah to answer the question.' His eyes went back to Farah's pale, jowly face. Keith Parkin shrank back in seat.

'Farah?' Ned said softly.

'I guess we were frightened that he could tell you about it.'

'How could he if he was dead?' It was Ned's voice that rose.

'If he was alive.'

'So your intention was to help make sure he was dead?'

She looked at her solicitor, the corners of her mouth turned downward. 'No reply,' she said.

Terminating the interview seemed like the most sensible thing to do. Vicky and Ned left the cell area and walked back in silence to the incident room. Vicky headed for the kitchen and Ned followed. He stood with his back to the wall. 'Everyone present says she stabbed him. She tried to kill him for god's sake and she admits she thought they had. One way or another by throwing him off the top floor of the multi-storey, she was making sure he was bloody dead.'

Vicky's face was set. Taking three mugs out of the cupboard she banged them each, in turn down onto the worktop. She kept her eyes on the kettle as she spoke. 'You're right Ned, but I still wish she'd just drop Dean in it.'

'But she luvs him,' he said in a stupid voice.

Vicky tutted. 'Who said romance was dead.'

***

Dylan had just put down the phone to Detective Inspector Hawk to update him on their visit to Redchester Regal Hire Cars and the seizure of the Mercedes when the pair burst in his office.

'Do you want coffee?' asked Vicky.

'Is the pope catholic?' Dylan grinned. He lifted the drink that she had placed down on his desk and looked up at them apprehensively.

'Go on, what've you got for me?'

'Not much, Farah's still trying to make out that her and Dean only joined in the attack after the stabbing, when Knapton was laid flat out on the concrete floor of the car park, unresponsive. We pushed her. She admits she knew about the knife. Dean showed it to her but she tells us he handed it to someone else in the car park, and guess what?' Vicky raised her eyebrows. 'She doesn't know who.'

'She admits her and Dean helped toss him off the roof of the car park. Of course she says they thought he was dead,' said Ned.

'What was the point if he was dead?' said Dylan.

'That's what we said. She couldn't answer that one. So we dropped it on her toes that the only reason to push him over the edge was to make sure he was dead and she agreed that was true,' said Vicky.

'So she doesn't deny helping to throw him from the car park onto the pavement, just to the stabbing,' said Ned.

'We told her about the second blood trace being found on the knife and she came back at us with an excuse. She's lying her arse off but she's implicated herself in the process.'

'Did you ask her about Knapton's dog's death?'

Ned nodded. 'We asked her if we would find the dogs blood on her clothing. She denied it. But she found it highly amusing.'

'Like I've said before let's wait until we have gathered the data from all their mobile phones to see if it implicates them any further,' said Dylan.

'Her solicitor is a new kid in town,' said Vicky. 'He's from Lancashire, a Keith Parkin have you come across him before?'

Dylan shook his head.

'He tried to jump in when he realised she was incriminating herself,' said Vicky.

'And?'

'And Ned...' Vicky sniggered looking his way, 'wasn't having any of it was you tiger?'

'Good, so what happens now?' Dylan looked from Vicky to Ned and back to Vicky.

'We're going to have another interview with her and then bed her down for the night.'

'I'll chase up forensics and mobile analysis,' said Dylan.

'I'd love to place the knife in her hand, which of course would support everything that the others are saying,' said Vicky.

'I still think it's bloody annoying that we have to wait so long for information to come back from the mobile phone providers. All we've got so far is people telling us what footage they took at the scene?' said Ned.

'Well if we view it, we might not be able to retrieve it and then we've lost what potentially could be damning evidence. So, we'll just have to be patient and wait for the experts to present us with the evidence,' said Vicky.

'I'll liaise with Jackie Stanley again after the next interview. I think we should charge Farah with murder and go for a remand in custody, there is nothing to keep her around here and let's face it she would certainly intimidate the others involved if she was on the outside.' Dylan's smile was satisfying. 'Well done. I'll catch up with you tomorrow. Any problems later call me.'

Chapter Twenty Four

Dylan's mobile rung the next morning. It was Vicky.

'Hello boss,' came a muffled voice.

'Vicky, where are you?'

'Farah decided she wanted to speak to us so the early-turn sergeant gave me a shout and me and Ned came in. We've just been in and done a quick interview.'

'Are you eating?'

'On the hoof again, cold bloody toast while I'm writing up the charge sheet. Sticks in your throat when you see the prisoners' getting hot food delivered to the cells.'

'What did she want to speak to you about that was so urgent?'

'Let's say a night locked up still works wonders. She's now remembers holding the knife and lashing out at Freddy Knapton in the car park. But she still denies stabbing him. She tells us she dropped the knife when Dean took her away for a...'

'Slowly but surely; that's enough to charge her in my book. Liaise with CPS will you and let's charge her and get her to court for a remand in custody. Like I said yesterday, I don't want the others intimidated and I don't think for a minute she'll hang about if she gets bail.'

'Will do.'

'Dean McIntyre is being produced from prison today so if you're available, you and I will interview him. It'll give me a break from paper shuffling,' said Dylan.

'I'll leave Ned to charge Farah, and I'm all yours.'

***

After the formalities had been completed in the presence of Dean McIntyre's solicitor, Dylan told him that he was under arrest for the murder of Freddy Knapton. His reply was direct and straight to the point.

'Not fucking guilty!' His stance was robust and aggressive. Dylan gave a wry smile. He was more than a match for the prisoner and, in the mood he was in, he was going to enjoy the interview.

'Not fucking guilty, eh?' Dylan mocked. 'I should remind you that you are not in a court room yet Mr McIntyre, you're in an interview room at Harrowfield police station. Eight other people have been arrested and interviewed in connection with this murder and have given us their accounts of the incident. And, surprise, surprise...' Dylan's eyes were bright. 'They all say Dean McIntyre, you, were in the car park when Freddy Knapton was killed.'

'Just because I'm on remand, inside, of course they'll blame me. Are you thick? Let them tell me that to my fucking face?' McIntyre showed his teeth and growled.

Dylan couldn't hide a snigger. 'Or maybe, they're just saying it as it is. You're a bully, that's why you'd like to be in their presence when they speak to us. Even your girlfriend Farah Ruwal says you were there.'

McIntyre looked bemused. 'Fat Farah? Are you taking the piss? She's not my girlfriend.'

'Well, she says she is. Although, why anyone would boast about having you as a boyfriend I've no idea.'

McIntyre scoffed. There was a pause as he shuffled his legs apart, slumped back in his chair and concentrated on picking the skin around his nails.

'It is our understanding that more than one person in your group took video footage on their phone of what took place that day, the mobile phones of your friends are being examined by the experts as we speak.' Dylan leaned forward.

Dean stopped and lifted his sullen eyes to meet Dylan's. He remained silent.

'We are satisfied that your prized hunting knife was the weapon used to kill Freddy Knapton,' said Vicky. 'Perhaps it's time you thought about telling us the truth. What do you say?'

McIntyre's solicitor demanded the interview be terminated. 'This is new evidence about possible mobile phone footage that I was unaware of. Therefore, I cannot possibly advise my client until I have seen it. This feels like an ambush.'

'No problem,' said Dylan. 'We'll terminate the interview and give you time to digest the evidence, although I'm sure your client is well versed on ambushes.'

Vicky and Dylan went back to the incident room. 'You knew the solicitor would do that so why didn't you disclose the fact that we were examining the mobile phones for film footage before we went into interview?' asked Vicky.

'I wanted to see the look on McIntyre's face when he heard about it.'

'I didn't think I'd ever say it but I feel a bit sorry for Freddy now, he didn't stand a chance did he?'

'And the killers, just an angry mob of young adults who thought they could do what they want when they want. Led by a thick bully who can only speak with violence.'

'Apart from Tara, she's only a minor.'

Ned came to the door. He was waving a piece of paper. 'Sorry to interrupt. This report's just come through from forensic that I'm sure you'd like to see.'

'Good news?' asked Dylan.

'Yes, sir,' he said with a rare smile as he offered the paper to Dylan who immediately started reading. 'And the Chief Super wants to see you,' he said to Vicky.

'Me?'

'Yep! What've you been up to, he didn't sound too happy,' said Ned.

'Me?' Vicky said again pointing to her chest.

'Yes, you numbskull, and he said it was urgent so look sharpish.'

Dylan's attention was on the report: – Traces of blood on the knife positively identified as belonging to Farah Ruwal. Traces of blood on the knife that belonged to the deceased Freddy Knapton. Examination of Dean McIntyre training shoes revealed two traces of blood one being that of Freddy Knapton the other belonged to his dog (Satan). Traces of blood on Farah Ruwal's clothing identified as Freddy Knapton's and his dog. Traces of blood on

Paul Bishop's shoes belonging to Freddy Knapton. Traces of blood on Phillip Masters shoes belonging to Freddy Knapton.

Dylan eyed Vicky over the report. 'Anything you want to share?'

Vicky looked sheepish. 'I might have upset Beaky, a bit.'

'How much is a bit?' said Dylan. He turned to look where Ned stood at the door, looking very comfortable, with his back against the wall. 'Shut the door behind you will you?'

Begrudgingly, Ned left them alone.

'Well?' said Dylan.

Vicky tilted her head to one side. 'I called her a twat,' she said quietly and grimaced.

'You did what?' said Dylan slamming the report down on the desk. 'Avril Summerfield-Preston is the divisional administrator, you might not like the woman, few of us do, including the staff under her supervision. My advice - stay clear of her in future.'

Vicky dropped her gaze to the floor. 'Okay! Okay! I hear you!' Vicky held her hand up as if to stop the verbal assault.

'You know she has Hugo-Watkins ear,' Dylan said a little calmer. 'You're not stupid. You've been in the job long enough now to know how it works. What did you call her a twat for?'

Vicky's cheeks flushed. 'She was being judgemental.'

'Judgemental? And you got upset by someone being judgemental in a police station, why?'

'Let's just say she had something inappropriate to say about Jen and the baby.'

'What?' Dylan said in a way that she thought he'd misheard. He felt a cold shiver run through him. He had often wondered at some of the things that he had seen her do, and heard her say, but he couldn't believe even she could be cruel - until now.

'So, as usual, you guessed it, I jumped in feet first and called her a twat amongst other things.' Vicky paused. In all honesty she was lucky I didn't deck her.' Dylan's silence encouraged her to continue. 'She said she'd report me. So, I let her have it with both barrels. You know me in for a penny, in for a pound,' Vicky screwed up her face. Her shoulders dropped. 'You might as well know I also asked her if it meant I would be the subject of her and Hugo-Watson's pillow talk that night? Stupid, yes, I know, but I couldn't help myself. I was so bloody angry. I told her sleeping with the boss was the only way she'd got where she had and kept her job, at which point she started hyperventilating.'

Dylan's lip curled up at the corner.

'You're going to tell me I deserve to get a right rifting.' Vicky bit her lip.

The fact was she knew him so well. It was exactly what he was going to say. But in all honesty he didn't know what he would have done if he'd been there. 'Is there anything you haven't told me?'

'No, I left her screaming for someone to get her a glass of water and her pills.'

'She'll be out to get her own back,' said Dylan. 'You know that?'

'Yeah, well she can do her damnedest. Unless you've been in that situation no one could even begin to guess how you feel.' Dylan sensed a knowing in Vicky.

'Frighteningly you remind me of me in my younger days. And I think I should be thanking you for sticking up for Jen, not reprimanding you. So, go on then, what did she say?'

'You don't want to know.'

'I do.'

Vicky lifted her arm and showed Dylan the flat of her hand. 'Please, trust me on this, you don't.'

'In reality, I'd have liked Jen to be a little stronger before the news got out but, it's out there now and there isn't a lot we can do about it is there. People like Avril will always have an opinion.'

'Jen's my friend and that, that woman, she's pure evil.'

Dylan smiled at her as his telephone rang. Hearing Hugo-Watkins voice he put his finger to his lips.

'Hello sir. Detective Sergeant Hardacre is at present very busy. Yes, she's interviewing a murder suspect. No, I don't think it would be helpful for her to be distracted. If my officer has spoken out of turn to the divisional administrator then I will personally speak to her and find out the facts. And sir, if this is about what I think it is Detective Sergeant has already spoken to me about it, and I'd appreciate you doing the same to Avril Summerfield-Preston who I believe made some inappropriate comments about my wife and the baby? I'll deal with my officer's outburst if I feel it necessary and I'd be extremely grateful if you'd do the same with Ms Summerfield-Preston but, right now you'll appreciate I'm dealing with two murder enquires. I have to go and deal with a lot more pressing police matters. Oh, and by the way, thank you for enquiring about my wife who is sadly having a great deal of trouble coming to terms with losing our unborn child. I am sure you'd like me to pass on your condolences?' Dylan dropped the phone on its cradle. His nostrils flared, a sign, Vicky knew, that showed how angry he was.

Vicky didn't know whether to smile or not.

'That took the bloody wind out of his sails. And I am in no doubt she was with him. I hope he had his phone on speaker so she could hear what I had to say. By the way, before I forget consider yourself bollocked,' he said with a wink of the eye. 'We've some results from forensic but not for everyone yet, I guess they'll still be examining clothing etc. belonging to the others that were arrested and bailed?'

'Yes, we prioritised or 'best guessed' the items of clothing that we thought they were most likely to get forensic evidence from and they've been sent. It's so wrong that we can't afford to send all the exhibits. How anyone can put a price on convicting a murderer I'll never know.'

'But they do. If only the public knew how it really is.'

'Absolutely, guess it was no good sending a pair of Farah's knickers off to forensic when the most likely evidence would be on a training shoe though eh boss?' Vicky laughed heartily.

'Trust you. McIntyre and Ruwal had to be our priority because of the evidence we have against them. Bishop is not a surprise,' he said passing the forensic result document over his desk to her. 'But Masters is. Masters, the footballer said he left when Tara Cabe ran off and she didn't deny it, but if he did, then he obviously stuck the boot in early on, before he left.'

Vicky scanned the forensic results received so far. 'I'd better disclose this information to McIntyre's solicitor before we go into the next interview otherwise he'll only stop it again.'

Dylan and Vicky walked at pace together down the corridor towards the stairs that lead to the cell area. As they did so, Avril Summerfield-Preston wandered out of the typist office, saw the two heading towards her, and promptly did a U-turn back inside, shutting the door behind her.

Neither Vicky or Dylan made a comment but remained focussed and walked on by. Once McIntyre's solicitor had digested the latest revelation from forensic they were soon back in the interview room sitting facing the pair.

After the relevant formalities had been adhered to before the start of an interview could commence, Dylan spoke.

'Okay Dean you have now seen some of the evidence we have against you and we are waiting for more results. Is there anything you want to say to us at this time?'

Dean McIntyre was in the mood for talking, it was obvious from the start.

'Alright, I hold my hand up, I was there,' he said holding his right hand above his head. 'But Knapton was fucking threatening me so it was self defence?'

Dylan hoped his face hadn't given anything away but what a stupid and unexpected comment he thought. 'But Dean, there were nine of you and you had a knife that you'd taken with you.'

'That were only because he had that fucking nasty dog that he used to set on us. That thing was more dangerous than any fucking weapon.'

'Did you stab Knapton?'

'There is no good denying it is there? But I only did it because he was going fucking mental.'

'So, can we go back to the beginning. Is it true that there was a plan to get Freddy Knapton into the car park to 'teach him a lesson'?'

'Yeah, he was a fucking nutter and his dog was a vicious git.'

'Who thought up the plan?'

'Dunno, all of us I suppose,' he said screwing his nose up as he stared into the corner of the room as if searching for an answer.

'Once you enticed him into the car park what was the plan? What were you going to do next?'

'Dunno, suppose we were just going to scare him into stopping threatening people. He should have been locked up ages ago.'

'So you managed to get him into the car park then what happened?'

'We surrounded him, pushed him around a bit. Fat Farah Ruwal was shouting and screaming at him. She's a fucking mental bitch.'

'Who had the knife at this point, you?'

'I did. Knapton were laughing and spitting at her like he was possessed. He wasn't a bit bothered by all of us being there. He liked to be the centre of attention I think. Then Farah grabbed the knife off of me and was like jabbing it at him, then she stabbed him with it.'

'She stabbed him?' Dylan asked

'Yeah.'

'How many times did she stab him?' Vicky took over.

'I don't know. He was staggering about.'

'Did you take the knife off Farah?'

'Yes, she was going berserk.' Deans lips parted slowly. He grinned.

'Is that when you stabbed him?'

'Everybody was agitated. Like I said he was going mental.'

'Was it you who cut his throat?'

'He wouldn't stop, he kept threatening us. Everyone was running at him, he went down, everyone was jeering. '

'He fell to the floor did you say?'

'Yes, there was a lot of blood everywhere. Then he went quiet, stopped moving. His dog was barking and barking and he wouldn't shut up.'

'Where was his dog?'

'I don't know. I could hear it. One of the others had caught it and held it in a snare thing that they use for mad dogs.'

'Then what?'

'We decided it best to throw him over wall.'

'But he was dead?'

Dean nodded. 'To make sure.'

'Whose idea was that?'

'Dunno, but it seemed like the right thing to do at the time.'

Dylan took over again.

'You have the dog's blood on your clothing. Is that because you killed it?'

Dean snarled. 'It were a nasty git. Just like its owner. We sorted it and left it for people to see in the park so that they would know it wouldn't bother them or their dogs again. What're you gonna do to me, ban me from owning a fucking dog?'

'We?'

'Farah.'

'So, that's what you thought did you? That if you killed him and his dog that they wouldn't bother anyone again?'

'Yeah.'

'So you did intend to kill Freddy Knapton? And, in your eyes that was teaching him a lesson?'

'It went a bit ... got a bit out of hand I suppose.'

'Out of hand? But when Freddy was laid on the floor, not moving, I suspect, was it only then that you decided to make sure he was dead by throwing him from the roof of the building?'

'That were never planned,' he said with a nod of his head.

'Anything else you want to tell us, or say to us?'

'No,' he said shaking his head this time. He lowered his head for a moment or two. But just as Dylan was about to terminate the interview he sat up straight in his chair. 'Oh yeah, if I get charged with this will they drop the robbery charge I'm on remand for?'

'That's for the Court to decide,' said Dylan. 'I can't comment.'

***

The Knapton murder team were getting ready for the debrief. The team gathered consisted of uniform officers, detectives, CSI, HOLMES teams and anyone else who had been involved.

'Boss,' said Vicky leaning forward to catch his attention as he walked past. 'Do you know what McIntyre's reply was when I charged him?'

Dylan leaned forward to hear what she had to say, 'Go on?'

'It was self defence.'

Dylan smiled. He took up his position at the front of the room. He told the assembled, 'Dean McIntyre has been charged with murder. Which means, for those who aren't aware, we have two people charged with murder and seven others who are on police bail, likely to face serious charges. A lot of you in this room will have known or even had altercations with Freddie Knapton and his dog, perhaps both. Whatever our personal thoughts are about him, he and his dog were subjected to a violent attack which resulted in their deaths. It appears this gang simply wanted to teach him a lesson. Well, they certainly did that! Let's hope the law will now teach them a lesson.

This isn't a full debrief. I have called in everyone, not simply to update you, but to thank each and every one of you for your sterling efforts in bringing these people to justice. Thank you. On a date in the future I am sure we will have a small celebration to which you will all be invited. Also, would you please pass on my personal thanks to your partners and family for their patience and understanding.'

Dylan stood up and left the room heading straight for the Merton Manor incident room.

Chapter Twenty Five

He looked at his office clock. It was six-fifty. He smiled to himself as he booted up his computer. Once again, on his pillow, he'd left Jen a note to tell her how much he loved her, with his signature smiley face and a kiss but also he added, 'One of these mornings I will still be here when you wake.' Maisy was regularly waking up during the night crying. It had been happening more frequently of late. Earlier that morning it had taken them an extra-long time to settle her and he hadn't been able to go back to sleep afterwards. He wished he knew what was upsetting her and how he could help. She obviously thought he could, as it was daddy,' she called.

Now the Knapton murder was no longer a mystery Dylan could focus his attention back on the serial killers. He sat quietly trawling through the database housing the enquiry to date. The word staddlestones for some unknown reason grabbed his attention. He pondered the fact that if they had gone to the extent of finding out if the staddlestones at Merton Manor were identifiable and valuable, then why hadn't they checked those mentioned on past reports? Hadn't Vicky mentioned a distinctive staddlestone she had seen in the garden of a neighbour of a complainant on the Knapton enquiry? Yes, he remembered, the elderly man who had been so angry when his neighbour had been knocked over by Freddy Knapton. He had threatened he would not be responsible for his actions should the police do nothing about the villain. Not that the officers had taken his threat seriously considering his age, size and ill health. Maybe staddlestones were just more common that he had thought? Never-the-less Dylan made a note to get that, and others, mentioned on the system, checked out as to their origin.

It wasn't long before Dylan's peace and quiet was shattered. The team began to arrive and the noise of their jovial banter bounced off the walls and filtered into his office. A successful ending to an enquiry breathed new life into the station, not just the incident room. There really was nothing like 'feeling a collar' for Dylan or getting 'a cough for murder'. And, no matter how many times he had done it, or what rank he achieved, he knew he would always feel the same thrill.

At exactly nine o'clock Dylan's office phone rang. He picked it up and answered in his usual way.

'Hello, Mr Dylan, this is Mike Talbot from Redchester Regal Hire Cars.'

'How can I help you Mike?'

Dylan doodled on his notepad waiting for the anticipated question about the release date of the Mercedes they had seized from his garage, so his next words came as a bit of a surprise.

'You told me to ring if I heard anything from the Devlins?'

Mike Talbot had Dylan's full attention. 'I did indeed.'

'Before I say anything, I want you to give me your word that you won't tell anyone that I've called. I have a family and the last thing I want is to bring trouble to my door.'

Dylan sat upright in his chair, his tone changed. 'Be assured Mike,' he said, standing so that he could close his office door. 'Anything you tell me will be dealt with in the strictest of confidence.'

'We've had a call from Mr Devlin. I don't know which one or where they are but he requested a car, I am told for a week on Monday when he told my secretary that they would be coming back into the country. She told him that the Mercedes he had previously used was out and he was offered a black Jaguar for the same price.'

'And did he approve?'

'Yes he did. He couldn't confirm a pick up time but said he would be here that day and could she have it, and the paperwork, ready for him to sign to avoid delay?'

'Good. Thank you for ringing me and sharing that.'

'Nobody likes murderers,' Mike said. 'I've got a young family too.'

'Do you have the Jag on site?'

'Yes, why?'

'We'll need to borrow it for a short time before they collect it. Is that okay with you?'

'That'll be two of my cars you'll have. I'll be out of business if this carries on. What do you call a short time?'

'Just a few hours between now and a week on Monday. Tell me have you got any plans to hire the jaguar out between now and when they collect it?'

'It's not booked out to anyone at this moment in time, no. But I can't turn custom away.'

'I understand. Look, I'll see what we can do about giving you something so you don't lose out. We may have to modify the car slightly, but the modification won't be visible, or cause any damage, I promise.'

'I guess the less I know the better,' he said. Mike Talbot took a deep breath.

'I'll get back to you later today,' said Dylan. 'I want the car to be ready just in case the Devlins' plans change and they want it earlier. One other thing, I don't suppose you know what the phone number Mr Devlin rang on do you?' asked Dylan.

'No, sorry, the call came direct into the admin office and I was passed the message.'

'Never mind. Thanks again for ringing. I'll be back in touch.'

Police officers needed the eyes and ears of the public, always have, always would, that along with a bit of luck and tenacity he knew got results - if only every police officer took that into account when dealing with the general public.

Dylan could feel the adrenaline pumping and in quick time a list was written. Get hold of the technical department to fit the following to the Jaguar, tracking device, camera, microphone. The Devlins would have to strip the Jaguar to find them. These men were suspected serial killers and therefore he would get the necessary authorisations written up and signed quickly, for this necessary and intrusive surveillance. The last thing he wanted was to put Mike Talbot in danger. He would not risk that anything could be traced back to him. If Dylan thought it would be, he would stand down the operation. Thanks to Mike he now knew that the main targets for operation Artichoke, the name given to the Merton Manor murder enquiry, would be back in their sights soon. He didn't know where they were at the moment but it was a gift that he had time to plan and, as Inspector Stonestreet always told him, 'failing to plan was planning to fail.' There was no time to lose in ensuring covert observations commenced at the garage a couple of days prior to the given date. He would leave nothing to chance, in case the targets turned up sooner than anticipated.

Dylan would have to discuss the strategy with Terry Hawk to locate both men using surveillance. A meeting needed to be imminent to work out a joint approach to arrest the brothers, and recover evidence. No time like the present, he picked up the phone.

'Now then mate. How you doing?' Terry's voice was upbeat. 'Sorry to hear about your and Jens loss. Bad news travels fast. How are you both?'

The hairs on the back of Dylan's neck rose. 'How on earth did you hear about it?'

'Another bloody mandatory course for management, would you believe they are re-inventing the health and safety wheel. Why they can't just let us get on with real police work these days I'll never know. The lovely Avril Summerfield-Preston made a beeline for me, she knew that I was working with you. She soon scurried off though when I made it obvious I wasn't in the business of gossip.'

'Ah, enough said.' Dylan's nostrils flared. 'It hit us like a thunderbolt Terry to be honest. Jen's still... Well you can imagine. Knocked us both for six. In our job we have to make tough decisions but when they affect the people you love... it's... well it's not good.'

'Contrary to some people's belief we are still human beings, even if we are a bit damaged. Look forward not back is my motto. We've no choice but to go on...'

'Talking of going on, I've just had a phone call. It appears the Devlin's are about to surface. We've no intelligence that suggests where they are at the moment but I think it'd be good to meet up to discuss our approach in dealing with them when they do. They've reserved another hire car from Redchester.'

'Great news! I agree. It'll be good to set eyes on those two bastards. What d'you say we meet up for brunch about eleven o'clock tomorrow in Harrowfield? That hotel, just off the M62 where you took me before, The Waterfront Lodge, Prego in Brighouse. I'll see you there.'

'Looking forward to it.'

When he put down the phone Dylan's thoughts turned to forensics - he hadn't had a call regarding the findings in relation to the Mercedes. He was impatient. He wanted results. Unwittingly his fingers tapped the desk. This evil pair were the slaughterers of a young family and they may have gone on to kill Cedric Oakley. His evidence would have to be indisputable to ensure the CPS would think the case acceptable to take forward. Budgets were tighter than ever, court dates months away, prisons full. They hadn't recovered the weapon which had been used in the murders, he hoped and prayed it still existed. Even if it was recovered, he knew they would still have to evidence it in the hands of the Devlin brothers.

En route to the CPS office meeting Dylan looked down at the car's fuel gauge. Seeing it at under a quarter full, he made for the nearest garage. From there he drove on the back road past Sibden Park. The day was bright and fresh and he looked down the parkland to the boating lake, his eyes scanning the empty swings for Maisy. Seeing a Golden Retriever racing across the grass he instinctively knew it was Max. He steered the car into the entrance of the grounds. From where he parked he could see Maisy pushing her dolls pram, every couple of steps she stopped to tuck baby in as she had a habit of doing and it made his heart swell with love. Jen walked slowly a few steps behind encouraging their little girl with a tap of her hand on her shoulder, every now and again, to walk on. Her head was down, her demeanour sad. He wondered if she was thinking how it would be, if only... Dylan got out of the car and whistled long and low, the whistle he used to call Max. It brought a smile to his face to see the dog stop suddenly in his tracks, stand perfectly still - his ears standing tall. He looked around and then to Jen's obvious surprise, Max started running. He ran long, he ran hard, he ran fast in Dylan's direction and no amount of calling from Jen could stop him. Maisy saw Dylan before Jen did and, leaving her pram behind, she too ran stumbling over grass sods and twigs in his direction.

Dylan felt once again like a boy as he ran in her direction, arms open wide. Fussing Max with one hand he held Maisy up in his arms in another. 'Boy, you are getting heavy young 'un,' he said as Jen reached them. He gave Jen a crushing hug. 'Hello missus,' he said.

'What are you doing here?' she said smiling broadly.

'I was just passing and saw Max in the park so I thought I'd pull in and see how you were?'

'I'm fine.'

Dylan scowled at her. Maisy seeing her daddy's face put two fingers either side of his mouth and upturned his lips in a smile. He tickled the little girl and made her laugh.

'No.' Jen laughed. 'Really I am,' she said at his furrowed brow. 'I need to get back to normal. Aren't you supposed to be busy? Maisy hasn't seen you properly for days.'

'On my way to a meeting at CPS; you got a problem with me stopping to buy my favourite girl a coffee and,' he said turning to Maisy, 'If I'm not mistaken yours might be a chocolate milkshake m'lady?'

He stood Maisy on the floor at his feet. 'A big one!' she said sticking out her tummy. Grinning broadly, she hot footed it towards the cafe entrance which was part of the Sibden Hall building.

It was the first time since losing the baby Dylan had seen Jen's lips form a real smile, a smile that reached her eyes.

'You sure you've got time?' she said, seeming a little flustered. She bent down and put her handle on Maisy's pram. 'Hey, come back here for your dolly,' she called.

Dylan lay a reassuring hand upon Jen's shoulder. 'Everything else can wait,' he said, guiding her gently toward the cafe. Jen hooked up to him and rested her head on his arm as they walked. 'This is nice. We come here every afternoon after Maisy finishes at the childminders.'

'Do you really? You never said before.'

'You never asked. It's something that I will miss when we move.'

'So we are still moving then?'

'I'd like to. If the right house comes up for sale.'

'I think it would do us all good.'

'Maisy's been asking where you are every night before she goes to bed. She misses you. And sometimes when she gets up in a morning she looks all over for you, calling out your name.' Dylan felt uneasy. Maisy was growing up fast, becoming more observant. It wouldn't be easy for her to understand his work. How did you explain to a young child that someone else needed their parent more than they did when there was a bedtime story to read, or a scratch to kiss better? It was hard enough for a partner of a police officer to come to terms with never mind a youngster.

The cafe in the park was clean and tidy and empty of customers. The tranquillity, pretty linen embroidered table cloths draped over the small square tables, china tea cups and homemade cupcakes, were a world apart from the hustle and bustle of the incident room and talk of murder. The 'normal' anyone in the job needed from time to time to stay sane, including Dylan, he thought sinking his teeth into a warm homemade buttered scone with jam. He chuckled with Jen to see Maisy chasing a Malteser around her plate with a teaspoon, the decoration from the piece of chocolate cake she had already devoured.

'It's like a party isn't it?' Maisy said joyfully without taking her eye off the sweet, and the spoon. The tip of her little pink tongue showed itself between tight little red, bow lips. Something she had taken to doing when she was concentrating.

'Yeah, it is,' said Dylan with a smile in his voice.

Capturing the prized sweet and crunching it happily her smile turned to a frown when she lifted her eyes to his. 'Daddy, why are you not smiling?'

Dylan looked from Maisy to Jen. 'I am smiling, look.' Dylan showed his teeth his smile was so wide.

She shrugged her rounded shoulders. There was a moments pause. Maisy looked back at him. 'When you're on the telly, and in your newspaper you're not smiling,' she rolled her eyes. With that she looked at the chocolate cream on her finger and she licked it clean. 'It makes me and Max sad.'

Dylan and Jen looked across the table at each other puzzled.

***

The faces of Declan and Damien Devlin were displayed on Dylan's computer screen. He sat for a moment staring at the mug shots. The cold blooded killers? The task ahead felt as though the team were about to snare wild animals, and snare them they would, no matter what it took. These two had cut their teeth on petty crimes, and crime had always been their way of life it seemed. Progressively, their records showed they had become more and more violent. Was it inevitable that one day they'd turn to murder? When the killing starts they had reached the climax of their careers and there was only one way now for them to go and that was down.

'Do you really think we've enough to link the incident with North Yorkshire,' said Andy Wormald as they walked across the car park together to their respective cars, Dylan en route to meet the North Yorkshire Detective Inspector.

'Not yet Andy, but I've got a gut feeling that it won't be long in coming.' I'll see you in the incident room later,' he said as the two parted company.

***

'I like my full English breakfast Terry but looking at that stacked plate of yours I'm ready to admit defeat.'

'Hash browns, black pudding, full bag of bangers, Jack, sets me up for the day.'

'Did you manage to speak to our crime prevention officer?' said Dylan as he tucked into his bacon and eggs. I saw him in the yard the other day but by the time I got outside he'd got into his car and driven away.'

'No not yet, he's still outstanding. Don't worry he's not a priority we'll get around to seeing him. He can't evade us forever. It's a pity we can't house the Devlins though,' Terry said while he ate.

'We have no intelligence whatsoever of a permanent address. Mike Talbot at the car hire company seems to think they might live abroad.'

'It's worrying that they might be planning to carry out another job, hence their need for this car,' said Terry.

'Once they pick the car up we'll have surveillance on them around the clock?'

'I don't think we have any choice Jack. Let's hope they lead us to an address or a collection point to pick up a weapon.'

'Twenty-four-hour surveillance is going to be expensive but it's got to be done, and we must be in a position to strike at any time,' said Dylan.

'You and I know we've got circumstantial evidence but by no means enough to hold and charge them without catching them in possession of firearms. Both forces of course will share the cost of surveillance but let's agree if they remain in your county, you take precedence as the SIO and we'll swap if they enter North Yorkshire.'

'Agreed. What a bonus it would be to catch them with the gun they've already used twice.'

'Are we going to be that lucky Dylan do you think?'

'Time will tell. Now, I just have to persuade the Assistant Chief Constable that we don't have an alternative but to have twenty-four-hour surveillance, and since the last time I saw him was when I had him over the desk after the promotion board fiasco, you'd better wish me luck.'

Terry chuckled. 'I'll back you up.'

'Not even he can let two suspected armed killers wander around the county looking for their next prey without doing all we can to protect the public.'

'I think as long as the paperwork is in place, just in case the wheels come off, he'll be happy Jack. The killing has started now we need to stop it.'

'I propose we'll have the team doing back to back twelve hour shifts once we're up and running and work the senior cover between us? That'll mean you might have to spend a few days down here.'

'Not a problem, I'll stay here,' he said as young Kelly the waitress came to clear up the plates.

'You up to no good Jack Dylan?' she said with her typical smile. 'Wait till I tell Jen I found you in here having a full breakfast on a weekday.'

Chapter Twenty Six

'We're going to have to think of some way to make it easier for Maisy to understand,' Jen whispered to Dylan as she stroked the head of the sleeping child.

'Understand what?' Dylan said softly.

'She noted you didn't smile when you were on TV again today.'

It was nine o'clock and Jen was checking on Maisy. Dylan was still in his suit having just returned from work. He held his tie to his shirt as he bent down to kiss Maisy's brow. She flinched at his featherlight touch. 'They'd have been reporting on the Knapton enquiry from court I guess.' Dylan murmured. He followed Jen out of the room. Dylan walked across the landing towards their bedroom and taking one last look at their daughter Jen pulled Maisy's door too.

'I turned the TV off immediately and then the evening paper came through the letter box,' she said walking into their bedroom. She pulled the curtains too. 'Half past two in an afternoon and the evening paper is on the doormat. She ran and picked it up and your picture was on the front page - guess what?'

'I'm not smiling.' Dylan pulled on his slippers.

Jen nodded. She walked in front of him down the stairs.

It was nine-thirty when Dylan and Jen sat down to the evening meal.

'She asked me why I wasn't smiling before, that day at Sibden in the cafe, do you remember? I wonder why it upsets her?' asked Dylan, picking up his knife and fork and stabbing a chunk of meat in the meat and potato pie. The warm, homemade meal tasted good. He hadn't eaten since his brunch with Terry Hawk.

'I think I know. Little Jude and Holly across the road, who go to the childminders with Maisy?'

'Mmm...'

'His mum, Joanna was on breakfast TV the other week and she waved and said, 'Hello' to them. All the children watched it together with Chantall. It's crossed my mind that when you're on TV you're more often than not appealing for witnesses to a murder, or the like, so I guess you have a similar look on your face as when you're sad or cross?'

'When I'm talking about murder I can hardly smile, wave and say, "Hi Maisy" can I?' said Dylan lifting his glass to take a long drink of his water. He put the glass down on the table and held the cool drinking vessel in his hand for a moment. 'What do you suggest I do?'

'I don't know. I've been wracking my brains to try and think of something. I can stop watching the news and leaving the TV on when I'm not in the lounge, in case there's a newsflash. Then, like I say she sees you in the newspaper. I can try and stop her seeing that but that's not the answer is it? What if she'd seen you with that bloody great bust lip the other year? She's only going to get more observant, more inquisitive and more sensitive to other people's expressions and moods as she gets older. One of her favourite games when she can see herself in a mirror is pulling faces, shocked face, happy face, sad face... I've tried explaining to her that you're at work and Jude's mummy was not at work, but that just went over her head. She's just too young to understand why you act differently at work.'

They ate in silence until Dylan had finished his plate of food and Jen had pushed half of hers to one side. She stood up. Cleared the table and brought him a slice of cake and a cup of coffee. Dylan had been reading the headlines of the evening newspaper. Acknowledging her return to the table by touching her hand affectionately, Jen smiled sleepily at him.

'Nobody said being a parent was going to be easy,' he said. He looked thoughtful when she sat down next to him on the sofa. 'Penny for them?' he said cuddling up to her.

She shook her head. 'I feel like a useless parent.'

'Look, I've had a thought,' he said. 'How about we make up a sign for Maisy to look out for? Something that I do for her so that she knows that I'm sending her a smile,' he said.

'Like what?' said Jen, sitting up to look at him.

'Well, I guess it's got to be something that I can do that doesn't look out of the ordinary to anyone else watching. What about if I check the knot on my tie?' Dylan put his thought into action. 'Like this.' He put his hand to his neck and pretended to straight the knot in his tie, and that's our secret smile.'

'Do you think you'll remember to do it? If not, she's going to be upset. You don't need any more pressure than you already have when you're conducting a press conference. It's hard enough remembering all the facts, especially since you absolutely refuse to use cue cards.'

'And what sort of an idiot would I look like if I needed a cue card to remember the details of the job I was in charge of?' Dylan looked perplexed.

'Well, we can give it a go,' said Jen. 'If you're sure?'

'I'm sure,' he said. 'Anything is worth a try. Now, can we go to bed please and we can explain our plan to Maisy tomorrow.'

***

DI Jack Dylan's team for operation Artichoke was all but ready to roll. He had hoped that there may have been some intelligence in respect of the mobile phone number on the hire agreement but nothing had been forthcoming.

It was a nervous time for any SIO when observations were in place and even more so when surveillance teams, combined with armed support, were active. A mobile operation such as the one on the Merton Manor enquiry utilised a vast amount of resources.

The Jaguar car, now modified, was back on the forecourt of Redchester Regal Hire Cars awaiting the pick up by the Devlin's. This expensive operation had no guarantee of being fruitful but it was worth the risk. Nothing had moved, as expected, over the weekend so it was hoped that the Devlin's would stick to the plan.

On Monday afternoon the target vehicle was still at the garage and Dylan was feeling the pressure. At half past three came the call that the target had moved. The observation team were unable to say which Devlin brother it was that had collected the vehicle, they looked too much alike and the distance that they had to keep between them and the Jaguar, to be sure they were not seen, didn't assist. However, having pulled out of the garage the other brother was collected a few yards down the road outside the newsagents.

The car travelled in the direction of Yorkshire. As it arrived at the border between Lancashire and West Yorkshire it pulled into the car park of a Hotel called The Quarry Stone.

Surveillance officers pulled into the car park at the rear, and they confirmed over the radio that they had sight of both the back and the front entrance. Dylan watched the clock in his office, his eyes hanging on each movement of the minute hand. Two hours past and the men were still inside. When they left the hotel there was no doubt in Dylan's mind that they were heading in the direction of Harrowfield. The Surveillance officers confirmed Dylan's fears and he felt a fire running through his veins.

The officers' commentary told him that the target had stopped on the main road, a few yards from a large period house that stood in its own grounds. Thornton House was the name in black lettering on the grand brass plaque on the pillars at its entrance.

The team were picking up no conversation between the brothers inside the vehicle, the radio was playing too loud. The car however was not to stay there. Five minutes later the Jaguar set off and travelled a further seven miles, and now they were in the countryside. They parked up next to observe a large country estate Dylan knew as Filby Hall, again they were static. This time for some eight minutes before moving off. Frighteningly, they were heading towards the Sibden Valley, and it became clear that Sibden Hall was their next stop. 'Where are Jen and Maisy this afternoon?' said Dylan quietly. His words unheard he picked up the phone to call home but the dialling soon went to voicemail. With a shaking hand he rang Jen's mobile but again there was no answer. Had they gone to the park as 'they did most afternoons'? As much as Dylan wanted to jump in his car and ensure they were okay, the job in hand meant he had to stay put, in a warm, windowless room with artificial lighting. He couldn't leave the command room - as SIO - the man in charge, his job was not done.

The target vehicle came to a halt outside a garden flat, number eleven, The Maltings where both men got out and went inside. Dylan could feel his heart beating in his chest. Thirty minutes he waited to hear that they had emerged and were now carrying a small holdall. There was only one place near that would have the goods that might bring them huge rewards, and that was Sibden Hall, but without any intelligence or being able to hear what Declan and Damien were talking about, the surveillance team was Dylan's only source of information. The commentary from the surveillance team continued. The Jaguar was on the road Dylan regularly travelled to and from work. His breathing was quick and shallow. Radio reception in the area was notoriously bad and they lost the surveillance team for what seemed to be the longest moments of Dylan's life as the car pulled into Sibden Hall car park.

The surveillance team plotted up some distance away. There was only one vehicle with eyeball on the target. In the car park the two men had got out, had a look around, taken a toilet break against the walled garden of the fourteenth century house, got back into their vehicle and were out of the car park and on the move again. They were now travelling back in the direction they had come.

Returning to The Quarry Stone Hotel they went inside.

To those observing, it appeared that the two men were bedding down for the night; sitting in the bar Dylan was told, they were enjoying a meal and drinking heavily. 'How long were they planning to stay at the hotel?' Dylan wondered. It was Dylan's call, should he get some covert enquiries done now, or wait until they left the premises? Was it possible while the two were otherwise engaged to take a look in their room?

There were lots of thoughts running around Dylan's head, while the surveillance team were busy feeding him updates from strategic observation points. None of them had any idea what the holdall contained. The area where the holdall had been picked up Dylan knew well. It had been visited numerous times on the Knapton enquiry when statements had been taken from witnesses in the old peoples' residences that Knapton had harassed. 'I need to know who lives in number eleven, and I need to know now!' Dylan said. Vicky had previously been to the flats at number nine, The Maltings to see an Arthur Carson on the Knapton murder investigation he was informed. 'That's right I remember it well, we talked about a staddlestone being in one of the neighbouring gardens to Mr Carson's home. But, how could that be connected to the fire? Surely not, surely that distinctive staddlestone that she had seen couldn't possibly have come from Merton Manor?' Dylan said.

Dylan grabbed his phone. 'Vicky, where the hell are you?' he said as the phone went directly to answer phone.

As soon as he put his phone down, it rang. 'You checking up on us boss,' Vicky said with a lazy laugh. Dylan could hear Ned in the background.

'Abort the enquiry you're dealing with and come see me,' said Dylan. The line went quiet and he knew she was listening. 'A location you visited on the Knapton enquiry features in the surveillance for operation Artichoke but we don't have the necessary intelligence.'

'On our way boss,' she said with a matter of urgency in her voice. The phone call was terminated immediately and in Dylan's mind's eye he saw her direct Ned instantly back to the station.

'Before they went to the Maltings to collect whatever is in the holdall have the two eyeballed their next target Jon?' Questioned Dylan.

'Damn car radios,' Dylan muttered under his breath, hitting the table with a fisted hand, just as Vicky walked in the room. 'If it wasn't for the darn music we might have listened in on their plans.' But without any information to aid them, there were lots of risks to assess for the public's safety, for the owners of the properties and for the officers. Should Dylan get someone to book into the same Hotel, or should they stay away? 'I need what intelligence we have on the houses they've perused Jon,' he said. 'Who are the occupants? Sibden Hall is a Grade 11 listed building; I know it well. It's situated in a public park and therefore differs from the others as it opens to the public and is only part lived in on an ad-hoc basis by the family who own it. There's also a lot of in-depth information on the internet about the thirteenth century manor house – I know because I've looked at it many times, the property is on our doorstep.'

'Fucking hell,' said Vicky. 'The crime prevention officer - did he visit recently?'

'I don't know. I know North Yorkshire haven't managed to tie him down to interview him yet.'

'I told you, he's a gambler. You don't think he needs money?'

'We can't rule anything out, nor assume but it has to be all hands to the pump, I'm going to need you working with us on this. Don't worry, you won't be involved when they're locked up, you've more than enough on your plate with the murder file for Knapton but can you do some of the urgent background work?' requested Dylan.

Vicky raised her eyebrows. 'I can work my day off?'

Dylan's head tilted. 'Go on then,' he said.

'Yes!' she said with a little jig. 'New handbag here I come!'

'Do me a favour and see if you can discreetly check Charles's appointment diary, will you? DI Hawk will be taking over from me for the night cover and I want to bring him up to speed with the developments before I leave for home. I'll ask him if his team have done the financial background checks on Rupert Charles yet and if not, we'll get them done immediately.'

Vicky left the office with a spring in her step. 'Tell Andy I want to see him,' he shouted after her.

'For the time being I don't want Rupert Charles wandering in and out of the incident room,' Dylan advised Andy. 'Speak to the resident Holmes computer team in confidence so that if he enters, one of them can tackle him as to what he's doing there and why?'

'I will sir.'

There was a lot of work to be done. With the threat of weapons in the holdall, at the hotel, Dylan was working against the clock to secure the evidence required to put the two known criminals behind bars for good, without, in the meantime, endangering the public. It was apparent to the detectives that the Devlin brothers were planning their next job, but which one of the houses they had briefly recced was to be their target?

Dylan discussed with his counterpart the positive and negatives of kicking the door in on their hotel room and locking them up. 'If we're extremely lucky we might find firearms, and there again we might find nothing, and more than likely end up having to release them and then they'd know we were on their case.'

The majority of the surveillance team were now bedded down for the night, ready to react should a call come in if the targets moved.

'I'll speak to the firearms tactical advisor to prepare plans for armed entry to the hotel room, or for the best approach to a vehicle stop if required at any of the recced houses,' Terry said.

The two Detective Inspectors considered a covert entry to the houses and officers changing places with the occupiers so there was a welcoming committee for the brothers. But the resources that would be required were not possible to sustain, for they had no idea when the Devlin brothers intended to strike, if at all. The detectives plan had to be fluid, which meant that they had to be ready to react to any change, at any time during the operation.

Dylan's mind was buzzing as he headed for home. His consolation was that he wasn't doing the night watch and would be able to warn Jen to stay away from Sibden Park. At least he was at home in his own bed, for now. The last thing he wanted to do was to leave Jen alone overnight with the threat of an operation about to take place nearby.

It was a restless night. Dylan couldn't settle and Maisy dreaming called out for him in the night. However, when he went to comfort her she wanted Jen. 'It occurred to me today that when a big job breaks she rarely sees you. You leave the house before she's awake and don't get home before she's in bed, fast asleep. She misses you - we both miss you, but at least I'm able to understand why you're not here,' said Jen when they were back in bed.

The next morning Dylan was up and ready for whatever the day held for him. He was pleased Jen seemed upbeat which made it easier for him to focus on the job in hand. The last thing he wanted when armed criminals were about, was to make the wrong decision due to his mind not being on the job - once in his career was enough. He knew today when he took over from Terry Hawk that his priority, once again, was to ensure the public and police officers lives were not in danger. He would be acting on information he was hearing, not seeing, from the surveillance team and he wouldn't hesitate to make decisions instantly as was required of him at his rank.

Maisy was eating her porridge sitting opposite Dylan. When he stood to put on his suit jacket she turned her chin upwards and gave him a toothy smile. 'Will you be smiling today daddy?' she asked. Her face was pale her eyes tired.

'I'm smiling at you because you're my girl.' Dylan walked around the table and knelt down beside her. She put her arm around his shoulders. 'I love you, daddy.'

'I love you too,' he said. 'To the moon and back, remember?' Dylan had a lump in his throat as he pulled away from her.

'You should be leaving if you're going to get to the morning briefing,' said Jen, one eye on the kitchen clock.

Dylan lifted Maisy from her chair and sat down sitting her on his lap. With an arm around her he put his finger under her chin and she looked up at him. 'I want to share a little secret with you,' he said. Jen, who was washing up at the sink stopped and turned to see Maisy put her finger to her lips. 'Okay,' she whispered. 'What is it?' Her eyes were wide.

'When you see daddy on television next I will touch my tie like this.' Dylan put his hand to the knot on his tie and tightened it slightly. He cleared his throat. He was unsmiling. Then he ran his hand down the length of his tie and pulled his jacket together. 'Now, when you see me do that, you know what I am doing?'

'No,' she said with a little giggle.

'I'm telling you I love you and I'm sending a smile to you but I'm working and I'm not allowed to smile at work, I have to be very serious.' Dylan deepened his voice. Jen smiled.

Maisy appeared to think about what he said. 'You mean like when I'm pretending to play doctors and nurses with Jude,' she said.

'Yes, just like that.' Dylan glanced across at Jen who nodded and smiled as she walked towards them.

'Can we tell mummy our secret,' she whispered.

He stood with her in his arms. 'Yes, we have to tell mummy so she doesn't forget to put the TV on. Look out for me won't you?' he said tapping his nose as he handed her over to Jen.

Dylan bent his head to kiss Jen and Maisy.

Maisy lay her head contentedly on Jen's shoulder. 'Phew,' Jen sighed. 'Fingers crossed. Don't forget!' she whispered.

Dylan picked up his briefcase and walked towards the front door, looking backwards and giving Maisy a little wave.

'So, mummy,' Maisy said. 'We have to remember Daddy is only pretending to be a policeman when he's on television,' she said seriously. She shook her head in little jerky movements and put her finger to her lips. 'Shh. Don't tell anyone,' she whispered. 'It's our secret.'

'Don't worry, I won't,' Jen said.

Dylan could sense Jen's amusement. 'Innocence really was bliss,' he thought.

At the station Dylan headed straight for the command room. Terry Hawk's eyes looked sore from lack of sleep. The command room was very warm, mostly due to the size of it, the close proximity of the people working in it, and all the computers. The entire system was here at their fingertips, the Commanders sat with their small team of staff. It was eight a.m.

'They haven't moved,' Terry said. 'I've had a meeting with the manager away from the hotel. They are booked in for two nights in what he describes as an executive suite. They asked for their best room and they paid upfront with cash. They had their passports which meant there was no concern from the hotel management. It's a first floor room at the rear which looks out onto the grounds, and is relatively secluded to afford anyone using that particular room privacy. They have opted for no room service, preferring clean towels to be left at the door and requested the local and a national newspaper. I've updated the tactical firearms advisor and I'll leave you to brief the ACC I'll get my head down for a couple of hours and I'll be back around lunchtime.'

'Did you manage to get any sleep?'

'A couple of hours, it wasn't too bad.'

Dylan could feel the anticipation of the team who were ready for a strike at any time. Things were bubbling. The intelligence was being gathered on the three houses they had been seen observing yesterday. Dylan liaised with the firearms team to discuss as to where it might be possible and safest to carry out an armed stop or challenge on the vehicle if the opportunity arose. It was about neutralising the threat, the severe threat that the two potentially armed men posed. Together, they looked at the aerial pictures of the three properties that were available to them from the police database. Of the three properties the Devlins had shown an interest in, Dylan, with the firearms tactical advisor discussed the locations. It was decided that Filby Hall was the residence to make an armed challenge to ensure the safety of the public and those involved.

'If we arrange to have a police car parked up on the driveway of Thornton House and at the entrances to Sibden Hall – this will deter the brothers from pursuing action at those properties,' Dylan said.

'I get it, that will give the impression to any outsider that the police are in attendance,' said Andy.

'Exactly, and hopefully force their hand towards Filby Hall?' said Jon.

'Of course that could be the intended destination anyway, but best to be prepared,' said Dylan. 'I want plain clothes officers to make contact with the occupants of Filby Hall and get them out of there to a place of safety for at least the next forty-eight hours and confirm back to us when that's been done. I want Sibden Hall closed to the public and that includes the car parks.'

Time was passing Dylan was aware, and it wasn't long before he got word that the two Devlin brothers were in the Jaguar and leaving the car park of the hotel.

The constant feed from the surveillance team revealed that they were once again at the Maltings, and whilst one of them remained in the vehicle, the other had gone into number eleven. What Dylan or the team didn't expect was that he would return to the vehicle with an elderly man.

'What the fuck's going on?' said Terry Hawk when he walked in and was given the update that the three were at The Rising Sun Public House.

'I'm told they're celebrating a birthday,' said Jon looking bemused.

'The old man, he must be related?' said Dylan. 'Vicky, you and Andy go and visit number eleven. Can you get to the rear garden without going through the house do you think?'

'I could at number nine and I think they are all built pretty much to the same design,' she said.

'Examine that staddlestone and see if there are any markings on the underside which could possibly be the same as the ones that remain at Merton Manor.'

Vicky and Andy were en route when Dylan got the word that the Devlins had left the pub with the elderly man. His heart missed a beat. 'Tell Vicky and Andy to abort the enquiry, we can't risk them being seen at the property at this time, it's too risky,' said Dylan

Dylan felt his breathing return to normal. Surveillance following the vehicle gave a running commentary that the car had driven past Filby Hall, slowing down approximately fifty yards from its entrance and stopping for a full five minutes. The men didn't get out but seemed happy to survey from where they sat. Then they dropped the old man off at home and returned to the hotel.

Planning, for the SIO had to be meticulous, including building into the arrest plans which police stations the men would be taken to when they were arrested and detained. Also which addresses would be searched afterwards, and by whom. Officers were briefed.

The firearms team had covert officers in the grounds of Filby Hall and in the hallway of the house, and Dylan had confirmation that the occupants had left for a place of safety. If the Devlins turned up as expected, the plan was to allow them to vacate the car, then they would be challenged and officers would immediately immobilise the vehicle. Dylan's priority was to neutralise the threat and protect lives, which also included the Devlin brothers.

Dylan's information from Vicky told him that over a year ago DC Rupert Charles had attended Filby Hall, according to his diary, in his role as crime prevention officer. There was nothing on record to say he had been to Thornton House but he had been to Sibden Hall numerous times to advise. The North Yorkshire team, DI Terry Hawk, assured Dylan they would pursue him as a priority, after the Devlin's arrest.

When he arrived home Jen knew by Dylan's demeanour that something was afoot. She could always tell by how alert he appeared. At times like these he didn't eat much. At the start of their relationship she would think he was ailing but no. Just another side-effect of the job and the after effects of the regular adrenaline rushes. He wasn't ready to sit down and put his feet up. He didn't want to nod off in the chair and, as the evening meal was put in front of him, he refused a glass of wine. She looked at him questioningly. Late as it was when he arrived home, Dylan wasn't ready to put his head to the pillow just yet either. Jen lay in bed at his side. She lowered the lighting and cuddled up to him as he lay propped up, watching the TV with no sound. A classic sign to Jen that he was shutting out the world but she wouldn't allow him to shut her out too.

'Tell me about it?' she said softly.

'You don't need to know.'

'I do need to know if something is worrying you.' She paused for a moment and waited. He remained silent. She could see the set determination on his face. His breathing was shallow.

'I worry more when you don't tell me,' she whispered. 'I don't know what danger you're in?'

Dylan turned his head to face her. 'I don't take risks, not now, not now I have you and Maisy. But, when I know where people are who I know are capable of murder and we're on the cusp of feeling their collar, everything feels like it's on the edge... I'm anxious. We don't want any casualties.'

'That's good isn't it? You're anxious in a good way then?' Jen's voice sounded relieved.

'I always wanted to be the man in charge. The person who made the ultimate decisions. That way I guess I know I'm in control of my own destiny. After the firearms incident I was involved in all those years ago, when someone else took the choice out of my hands to shoot to kill...' Dylan took a deep breath. 'Well, I never wanted to be in that position again. But, with that great responsibility comes the destiny of others too, and I can now understand the angst my commander faced that day. The rank, my role, comes with its own pressure. We think... we know our targets are planning another job, and we're on their trail. I've got the whole circus on instant response alert. The threat to life is severe. And it's on our patch.'

Once Dylan started telling Jen the history of the evil pair, the developments and what they anticipated, it was as if the flood gates had been opened in his mind. Eventually, while he dropped in and out of sleep, it was Jen's turn to lay wide awake watching the shadows on the ceiling long into the night. Firearms, would the mention of that word haunt her forevermore after she had found his file on that dreaded day and learned what he had experienced in his past? Maybe he hadn't been the one to kill the criminal in the act of committing the crime, but then again maybe he had. No one would ever know - and it was his job that fateful day, along with his colleagues, to protect with the use of firearms, the lives of innocent people.

To Jen's surprise Dylan suddenly spoke to her, as if he hadn't been asleep - although she knew he had. 'Jen, I won't be near any firearms, not this time - well not if I have anything to do with it. Remember, I lead from the back now, in what the hierarchy love to call the theatre of operations - a lovely windowless, artificially lit room full of computers. Sweaty, highly charged officers all with the same adrenaline rush are my only threat in there - so don't worry.'

When sleep looked like it was a consideration, she kissed him softly on the cheek, turned over and nestled in his strong arms that turned to envelope her. 'Jack Dylan,' she said softly 'I do love you.'

He smiled to himself and held her until the alarm at five thirty separated them.

Dylan was sure if something was going to happen, it would be today.

Chapter Twenty Seven

Detective Inspector Terry Hawk managed to get some good quality sleep on his watch overnight, so much so, that he wasn't ready to head straight off to his hotel. It was apparent when Dylan got to the station that everyone had the same feeling of imminent action - today was going to be the day. The Devlin brothers were due to book out of their hotel room. Would they end up coming face to face with the officers on operation Artichoke? It was highly probable. Hopefully their next room would be the police cells.

The police were prepared and their firepower collectively was far greater in number than the criminals. However, it didn't always follow that things went to plan. Everything had been done that could be done to prevent harm to the public. Members of the firearms team, volunteers in the role, were highly trained and tested regularly. Confrontation was something they consistently trained for. Firing their weapons was the last resort in life-threatening situations, but there were never any guarantees. Each and every one of them had a part to play. The camaraderie was palpable in the briefing - the tension and adrenalin was almost tangible. Some officers had years of experience under their belt, for others, it was their first operation, each hung on the firearms tactical advisor and detective inspector's words.

The officers deployed were in situ, ready and waiting for the confrontation should it arise. In the command room, the wait for any movement seemed like an eternity. Dylan's mind took him back to the day he took the oath to be a police officer. He had stood in the Court room, in full uniform, stiff collar, shiny shoes, helmet in hand - the helmets, when new, left a red ring around the forehead, as it had that day. His trousers, back then, had razor sharp creases. His shoes bulled-up so that he could see his face in them; bible in hand in front of the magistrate, 'I Jack Dylan do solemnly and sincerely declare, that I will well and truly serve the Queen, in the office of constable, with fairness, integrity, diligence and impartiality, upholding fundamental human rights and according equal respect to all people; and that I will, to the best of my power, cause the peace to be kept and preserved and prevent all offences against people and property; and that while I continue to hold the said office I will to the best of my skill and knowledge discharge the duties thereof faithfully according to the law.' He had known the words verbatim although on that occasion, nerve-racking as it was, he had read them from a cue card.

Side by side, Dylan and Terry stood in the command room adjacent to the incident room waiting for the events to unfold with trepidation. Terry had hit the nail on the head when he said, 'We might all be police officers Dylan but above all we are human beings. Can you feel the adrenalin starting to build?'

'Not quite like the old days Terry. We would have been out there waiting for instructions, with others, ready to strike. Rather than back here in the safety of these four walls.'

'Somebody's got to do it Dylan and I bet the teams are glad it's me and you in here and not some university graduate who may understand the theory, but never had the sweat run down their back in a life threatening situation. Mind you, if I'm honest, knowing what I do now I'd rather be here. I don't miss the hours in the back of a police van waiting for the command to strike do you?' Terry gave a nervous laugh. Dylan knew the pressure was on.

'What did they use to call the mobile command unit, Enterprise, wasn't it? It was no bloody starship though was it?'

A voice came over the radio that silenced them.

'An unmanned police patrol car is positioned in the driveway at Thornton House, as requested sir,' said Jon.

'Have we managed to get any units freed up for high visibility at Sibden Hall Jon,' Dylan asked.

'I'm being told we don't have a free police vehicle at our disposable to cover both the Sibden Hall entrances.'

Dylan knew the helicopter had been up in the skies over Keighley that morning, assisting a search for a vulnerable missing person. The mounted branch had also been called out to assist. They were able to cover the ground at pace and had been successful in locating the missing man in a semi-conscious state behind a drystone wall.

'Jon, looking at the log, I see there were two mounted officers in attendance, a PC Dodswoth and PC Lawrenson. Do we know if they are en route back to HQ? If so, they shouldn't be far from Sibden Hall and could do us a great favour. We desperately need some visual presence at the Hall, and quick. Get control to give them an urgent call will you, that way I can keep this channel free?'

'Will do sir.'

'Another marked car might've looked a bit suspicious anyway,' said Terry.

'I was worried the activity overhead might spook the Devlins but the flight path was not within our proximity fortunately,' said Dylan.

'Too true, that could've knackered everything.'

The radio cackled. 'Sarah and Marie are diverting to Sibden to do the high visibility for us. They are presently on the A58 and their ETA is five minutes.'

'That should give the Devlin's a shock to see police on horseback at Sibden Hall should they choose to go there,' Dylan chuckled.

'John and Duncan have arrived with the dogs and are in situ at Filby Hall sir,' said Jon over the airways.

Dylan was taking the lead as agreed, since it was in his force area, and both he and Terry sat in silence, listening intently, senses alerted to any radio message. Officers were disciplined and there would be no unnecessary chat over the airways.

The next message came over the radio: 'Mounted police parading in Sibden Hall.'

But the second message was what they were waiting to hear. 'Targets one and two out of the hotel in possession of a suit carrier and small black bag.'

The commentary continued. 'Targets one and two are in the Jaguar. Suit carrier placed in the boot. Small black bag inside the vehicle. We have an off, off. Targets on the move.'

'Armed, Jack, do you think?' said Terry his brow furrowed.

Dylan nodded once. 'One of those times Terry when we do make assumptions, and we're more than ready for them. I won't put our officers in danger. If they are not armed, which is highly unlikely, it will make the challenge so much easier. I'm putting the designated evidence securing team for the Quarry Hotel on standby, now ready to move in.'

The radio crackled only with commentary from the surveillance team on the dedicated channel - that no one other than the officers on the operation could hear. Officers on the teams could talk to each other - but only if necessary.

The black Jaguar was heading in the direction of Thornton House; a matter of minutes away. The main road was the one that the Devlin brothers had travelled the day before. Traffic was sparse.

'Target vehicle slowing down at the entrance of Thornton House, it appears that they have eyeballed the police car and have pulled away. Dylan took a deep breath; he could see relief on Terry's face.

The radio playing loud music in the Devlin's car was suddenly turned off and at last the officers could hear the brothers converse - although they said very little.

To ensure those present in the command room didn't miss anything, the room remained silent. The surveillance team leader was also able to listen in and gain early indications of what the brother's intentions were.

At times like these Dylan realised how difficult it must be for a visually impaired person, reliant on what others could see and relay to a third party. In the past the command room would have been full of smoke from cigarettes. Officers chain smoking to help them cope with the tension. Dylan had to rely on the clarity of the information he was hearing because, from it, he would have to make instant decisions. The images he had in his mind's eye were being created by others as he sat staring at four stark, grey walls.

'We have a left, left into the entrance of Sibden Hall, vehicle stationary, hold your positions, be aware target vehicle reversing back out onto the carriageway.

It was obvious from the occupants of the car's conversation that they had immediately seen the police horses.

'Fucking hell they've sent the cavalry after us!' Dylan heard them say loud and clear.

He turned to Terry and they shared a brief smile - one of relief.

Clifton was a large piebald full shire police horse who was positioned in the centre of the driveway after traversing the park, experienced police officer Sarah Dodsworth on his back. PC Marie Lawrenson, her colleague, was riding Dylan's favourite chestnut, Fimber. Marie's 'little ginger friend.' Police horses and dogs were great ambassadors for the force as well as doing a great job saving lives and helping to prevent crime. The force didn't have any better profiles.

'Thank god the Devlins reversed out of there, Sarah and Marie had no armed support,' said Dylan.

'So only one place left on our list Jack.'

'If we have read everything correct our diversions should push them towards Filby Hall where we are ready and waiting.'

The commentary was now continuous. 'All officers at Filby Hall be aware target vehicle is now heading in your direction.'

'Vehicle right, right from carriageway into the driveway at Filby Hall. Jaguar accelerating down the driveway, passenger may be holding a hand gun. Jordy, Silver commander you should have eyeball, the commentary is yours.'

'All units, target vehicle skidding to a halt outside the front door. Both driver and passenger out, out. From visual both armed with handguns and walking swiftly towards the front door,' said Jordy, the firearms tactical commander, who spoke quickly to keep up with the Devlin brothers' movements.

Dylan's heart was in his mouth.

'Strike! Strike!' came the call.

Dylan held his breath as armed units sped down the driveway. Armed officers housed within the building showed themselves. Shouts could be heard as armed units pulled up behind the two men and took up their positions using their vehicles as protection.

'Armed police! Armed police! Put your weapons down now! Armed police, weapons down now!' The challenge was loud and clear. The Devlins were surrounded on all sides. 'Put your weapons down now!'

The next thing that Dylan heard was gunshots. Bile rose in his throat, his heart raced. Terry looked at his colleague without speaking. There were a few seconds delay before he heard.

'Bronze Commander shots fired, one suspect down not moving, one down moving very slightly. Officers moving in. Threat neutralised. One suspect confirmed dead. Ambulance required urgently to the scene, please.'

In readiness for a rapid response, paramedics had been in a vehicle nearby, secreted behind a high hedge along a nearby country lane. They were called forward to Filby Hall to deal with a man with gunshot wounds.

'One injured suspect arrested, one suspect deceased, two nine millimetre handguns recovered.'

Dylan and Terry relaxed back in their chairs. Dylan joined his hands together and put them behind his head. 'Threat neutralised,' he whispered, blowing air out of pursed lips. 'Thank the lord. Can I have an update from Silver and Bronze commanders please?' he said sitting upright once more.

'Bronze commander, both suspects opened fire at the officers when challenged, fortunately no police personnel injured. All events recorded on video. We've got the police helicopter up monitoring events. Can we have it to transport?' Dylan heard them say. He looked at Terry puzzled. 'Don't look at me,' he said.

Jon asked for talk through. 'We're going to need at least one of you to take charge of the homicide scene until professional standards arrive.'

'We've got a vehicle on standby,' said Dylan who was already on his feet and heading to the door.

'Roads are blocked in the locality I'm being told due to a pile up on the main road. We've no choice but to fly you in. Can you be prepared to join the helicopter on the helipad in the next few minutes, sir?'

Dylan's heart dropped immediately to his stomach as panic set in. He felt hot liquid running through is veins belying the cold sweat that formed in beads on his brow. 'You'll never get me in the air,' he heard himself saying the words to Jen, over and over again. Dylan looked back at Terry, his eyes wide.

'The scene needs to be protected. It's going to be an independent investigation team from outside the force area on behalf of the IPCC,' said Terry. 'You go to the scene and I'll see to things here at the station, and also let your assistant chief constable know you're up in the clouds.' He gave Dylan a sarcastic grin.

'The scene is secured. Secondary teams are on standby to carry out enquires at the hotel and also at the Maltings.' Jon updated control.

***

'I'm hearing that at least three shots were fired by the two men before one of the targets was shot dead and the other injured. Tac advisor's raging that they managed to fire any rounds,' said PC Rothwell. Dylan followed her up the stairs. He felt numb. 'The pilot is already in the aircraft waiting. There's no time to get you into a flying suit,' she said at the door to the roof of the building where the helipad was located. 'The rotors are running; we will approach from the front right of the helicopter. I will indicate to you when the pilot has given me the thumbs up to escort you to the aircraft. Have you ever been in a helicopter before sir?'

Dylan's mouth was so dry, he couldn't speak. He licked his lips. 'I don't fly,' he finally managed to say.

'What never?' she said, a little smile lifting the corners of her lips.

Dylan shook his head. 'Never, ever.'

'Don't worry, just follow me, I'll escort you to the aircraft as I said, and place you in a seat at the rear, strap you in and close the door. You will have a communication lead attached to your helmet,' she said passing him the helmet she held loosely in her hand. 'Once that's attached we will be able to communicate. Until then, the noise that you can hear outside will be so loud we won't be able to speak to each other from the brief time when we open this door, to when we connect via comms. When we get outside be aware of the strength of the wind the rotors produce, it will, I promise you, nearly knock you off your feet. Dylan looked from her five-foot-six, slight build to his six-foot solid stature. 'Mark my words sir, it will knock your socks off. My advice, push into the backdraft and you'll be fine.' Dylan looked at her and felt more reassured. 'Are you ready,' she said with her hand on the door. 'Before we go. Have you any loose items in your pockets, cash?' she said.

Dylan fumbled in his pockets.

'If so just make them secure.'

He nodded his head.

'We're off then,' she said as she flung the door open.

Lisa headed towards the front of the helicopter and Dylan followed. Even with the helmet on, the wind strength powered by the rotors surprised him.

The aircraft was smaller than he anticipated, never before being up close. Once inside and the door closed, just as Lisa had said, she indicated a seat and he sat down. She attached the comms lead to his helmet and he felt a lot easier and reassured knowing he would soon be able to hear her voice, and she him.

Lisa smiled as she made herself busy by turning on her computer. Conscious that he was nervous she constantly glanced in his direction. When she was able to speak to him she would reassure him. A well-oiled cog, the procedure was now in motion, and there was no stopping it.

'Just ensuring the radios are on the correct channels,' he heard her say, her voice, such a relief to his brief unhearing world. 'Follow our instructions in case of an emergency,' she said. 'An emergency?' Dylan's heart beat faster, his temples throbbed, his blinking was frequent, his swallowing often. He couldn't remember when he was last so scared. Probably when he was that little boy facing the enraged bull at his grandparents' farm. And, as then, he had no place to hide but face the fear head on.

Dylan could hear the pre-flight checks; doors and harnesses secured, radio checks done, both engine control switches confirmed at 'fly'. In-between liaising with the pilot and control to confirm they were preparing to take off, Lisa reassured Dylan that all was well.

The helicopter was airborne. What seemed to take an age had in fact taken but a few minutes according to Dylan's watch. These guys were good, very, very good and not for the first time that day was he was impressed and proud to be part of such an elite team of professional people - the police service.

To settle his nerves Dylan didn't take his eyes off Lisa, looking for any change in her facial expression or body language. Safely en route, and with constant reassuring glances from Lisa, she liaised with the units on the ground, who'd started planning with the pilot a suitable landing site.

'Don't worry sir, you're perfectly safe, do you think I'd be sat here if you weren't?' She stretched her neck to look out of the window. Dylan closed his eyes and swallowed hard. His stomach was churning. Look at that dreadful traffic down there it's like a car park. One, two, three, four, five, six cars in that pile up,' She turned back to Dylan. 'See what I mean? You're much safer up here than you are down there.'

Dylan heard Jon's authoritative voice over the airways. 'The grounds are large enough to land the helicopter.'

'We need a place free from wires, animals, and fairly flat,' Lisa said.

'Plenty of room here, the garden is like a football pitch. In fact,' he said seeing the goalposts at either end, 'it is. The house has a football pitch would you believe?'

The helicopter was circling the location and the descent began. Only now could Dylan bring himself to look out of the window.

The landing was as smooth as the take off and Dylan knew the sense of the word relief when the pilot gave the authority for them to exit the aircraft. Lisa unstrapped herself with ease and leaned towards Dylan to unstrap him, she removed his communication lead from his helmet. She motioned him to follow her and she helped him get out of the helicopter. He was grateful for her reassuring hand holding onto his arm to guide him out of harm's way. At a safe distance from the rotor blades she stopped. 'That's it sir, you're all done, you can give me your helmet now. Unless of course you fancy coming back with us?' Lisa gave him a cheeky grin. Jon Summers was walking towards him. Dylan took off his helmet and handed it to Lisa. 'I'll pass, but thanks for the offer,' he said. 'I really couldn't have done that without you.' He looked about him as siren's rung out loud and clear.

'The firearms commander's not happy, one of the Devlin's managed to fire three rounds before he was dealt with.'

'Ambulance on site?'

'Paramedics are working hard to keep who we believe to be Damien Devlin, alive.'

'Don't try too bloody hard,' Dylan said. The wind created by the helicopter rotor blades, preparing for take-off, carried his words with it.

'Sir?' Jon said cupping his hand around his ear.

'I'm eager to see if the weapons are ones that were used for the killings at Merton Manor,' shouted Dylan as the two men ran towards the house.

'And the murder of Cedric Oakley,' said Jon.

'I'm told they're the right calibre,' said Dylan.

'Patience is a virtue sir. Ballistics' will be on it straight away.'

'Sadly I don't possess patience. We can't even touch them for now. Where's the CSI Supervisor?' As he said the words he saw crime scene investigator Mark Hamilton. 'Good, once we've got the guns photographed in situ, made safe and recovered, we'll be able to move forward. Continue videoing everything in situ ready for Professional Standards. IPCC will be involved.

Terry Hawk stood down the units at the other locations. 'Sarah tells me we owe the horses an apple,' he said to Dylan.

'Order them a sack of apples!'

The scene was a busy one. An established approach to secure evidence and protect the scene was in motion. The firearms team had re-grouped, Dylan knew the officers would be waiting for their debrief - their job done. Weapons fired were being retained as exhibits. 'We'll have a debrief with all concerned at Harrowfield nick at five o'clock tonight,' said Dylan.

'Yes sir.' Jon scribbled down actions as instructed by Dylan, updating him after each were completed.

Dylan was more aware than most, from personal experience, of taking part in the shooting of a man albeit several years ago, how rigorous these type of investigations were.

'The chief superintendent from the Professional Standards Unit is on his way, stuck in the traffic,' said Terry Hawk on talk-through.

Dylan would be pleased to hand it over to him. He would be the liaison with the IPCC. These guys were ruthless, but fortunately Dylan and the team had had the foresight and time to enable them to capture the events of this incident on camera, for the safety of all concerned. He never wanted anyone under his command to go through what he had - and years later still be suffering the consequences of. The footage from equipment that they had in place would stand up in any court of law to show a lawful killing.

It was a massive relief to him that no police officers had suffered any injuries during the armed assault. If any had, he would have carried the guilt with him forever.

'The secondary teams have moved into action sir,' said Jon. 'The team at the hotel searched the room where they had stayed but it revealed nothing other than to confirm they had stayed there.'

'One less scene to worry about,' said Dylan. 'Find out if Vicky has an update on the Maltings?' Dylan barked the instruction. 'She knows what she was looking for.'

Dylan made his way across the lawn to speak to officers at the scene. His phone rang and he excused himself.

'Vicky, what have you got?'

'The old man who lives at number eleven only turns out to be the grandfather of Damien and Declan Devlin. He's a frail old man. Wanted to know if they were in trouble because, he tells me, they're good lads. They brought him the staddlestone in his garden as a present for his birthday.'

'If only he knew the full story. And he will,' Dylan sighed. 'Did you get chance to check the staddlestone out?

'Yes, the identification marks on it are clear, it came from Merton Manor.'

'Fucking brilliant!' Dylan said rather louder than he intended. Those around him lifted their heads from what they were doing to turn his way.

'And you'll be pleased to know we've had confirmation of fingerprints found on the bank notes seized from The Wellington Hotel.'

'That's great. If Clancy Mason at Ballistics can confirm that the two nine millimetre hand guns recovered today are the ones used at Merton Manor and to kill Cedric Oakley, like we think, we've hit the jackpot. We will have enough to piece together irrefutable evidence. One of them might have got away without going to court but I can't wait to see the other going behind bars for the rest of his bloody life.'

'You've not heard then?' said Vicky, her voice lowered.

'Heard what?' Dylan was walking around the exterior of the crime scene. He leaned against a fence post.

'I'm with Terry Hawk in the command room boss, I believe he wants to speak to you.'

Dylan heard muffled voices and Terry took over.

'What haven't I heard?' said Dylan.

'The injured brother, believed to be Damien Devlin died en route to the hospital mate. The Paramedics tried hard to save him but they couldn't.'

Dylan banged his fist on the gate. He felt a fire cursing through his veins. 'Twat! Bastard! How dare he fucking die?' But deep down he knew it was justice.

'In all honesty listening to the running commentary, those guys had probably planned to die should they get cornered by the police. There was nothing we could have done that would have changed the outcome of this incident I fear. They were happy to have a shoot-out.'

'Yeah, well it was a lot less painful for them than I'd have liked it to be. I can see the news headlines tomorrow, can't you – Harrowfield police gun down two armed criminals? The investigation into the shootings will leave nothing to question, and sadly for the officers involved - that won't be quick and painless. Each one of them will be under suspicion until the enquiry is over.' Dylan spat the words out.

'That's the nature of the beast,' said Terry. 'We live and die by our sword, or our decisions as it were, as police officers.'

Dylan ended the call and dropped the phone in his pocket.

The area was out of sight of the general public, and the scene would be kept secure and sterile until the investigations had been completed. This location was quite rightly chosen, after discussions with the firearms tactical advisor, because it was the only place to neutralise the threat of two armed criminals without putting the public or the surveillance team in danger.

Post-mortem's would have to be carried out on both deceased. Two murderers and would-be robbers off the streets. Was their motive purely money this time or were they looking to kill again at Filby Hall? Dylan knew that questions would be asked of him, as to why the brothers weren't intercepted en route, and he would be accused of setting a trap for the deceased. The enquiry into the shootings would leave nothing to question. It would be lengthy and thorough. As far as DI Dylan was concerned he, and his opposite number at North Yorkshire had made the right decisions. Dylan knew when there had been a homicide, there had to be a thorough investigation. He felt keenly for the firearms officers, they carry weapons so that they can confront this sort of situation. Sometimes they have to use their weapons, which still remains a rare event, and they should have the full support of the police force and the public in such difficult life threatening situations.

Dylan realised he hadn't heard anything about DC Rupert Charles. He asked Terry whether his team had any update.

'The property he lived in was rented apparently and according to his landlord he did a moonlight flit. They've checked with your duties clerk, Dorothy Brown, and he hasn't turned in for work since his last rest day, neither has he rung in sick. They are searching the house but it is revealing nothing at this moment in time. What we do know is that he owes money. So it looks like he's done a runner.'

'And his wife?'

'She's being notified through her work as she's been working away. Well, at least he won't be looking over his shoulder for the Devlin brothers when he reads about their demise in the newspapers.'

'We have a duty of care Terry to him and his wife. I'll get him circulated as missing and vulnerable.'

'As if we haven't enough to bloody deal with.'

The incident room was full to overflowing at Harrowfield police station. The noise from within could be heard across the back yard. The fire doors were thrown wide open to allow North Yorkshire DI Terry Hawk and DI Jack Dylan accompanied by ACC Wendy Smythe in. As they entered the large open space that had been cleared as much as possible to house the amount of people attending, the talking amongst their audience stopped. The senior officers walked to the front of the room and sat in the seats that had been put there for them. The debrief was also being recorded.

'I want to thank all those involved in this investigation and for the assistance given to us by Terry and his North Yorkshire team in what turned out to be a combined effort to trace and arrest those responsible, we now know, for four sadistic, violent murders. The outcome was not the one we intended but fortunately we were prepared and reacted professionally to a violent armed confrontation which, as you are aware, left two armed criminals dead. I want to praise the firearms officers for their actions in such difficult circumstances. I too have been in the position you are in, several years ago, but be assured justice will prevail. These enquiries are far from over. There is a lot of work still to be done over the forthcoming weeks. But, we can all sleep soundly tonight knowing that two violent armed criminals are no longer roaming the streets of this county.'

Dylan sat down and the ACC stood up, also to thank the officers. 'I have to inform you,' she said. 'That there will be a more detailed debrief, and a review in due course. Also, the IPCC are overseeing the investigation into the deaths of these two men.'

The debrief was over and the officers were dismissed. Each individual team would have their own debrief and record lessons learnt for future incidents. 'Lessons will be learnt from this,' Wendy Smythe said to Dylan and Terry on her way out. 'I'll speak to you later Dylan, I want an update in respect of our missing detective.'

'Detective Constable Rupert Charles Ma'am, but first they are asking me for a quick interview for the news. I need to speak to Connie Seabourne at the press office regarding the contents of a short press release but I will have to do it live.' Instinctively he looked at his watch.

'What sort of content were you thinking?' said ACC Smythe.

'Along the lines of, *"Earlier today officers from two forces were involved in confronting two armed criminals. They were challenged by armed officers in an area away from the general public. The two men fired at the officers who* had asked them to drop their weapons. The officers returned fire when their request was not complied with and, as a result, both armed criminals lost their lives. A sterling effort was made by the team and paramedics but they were unable to save either of the two men. Obviously there is a major enquiry underway by the IPCC." That should suffice for now don't you think?' he said.

'I believe it will, yes. In fact, I'll be at your side, we'll do this together. I'll endorse the efforts of everyone.'

Dylan reluctantly agreed. But managed to text Jen letting her know everything was over and he was doing the press conference with the ACC and to get Maisy to watch. When he did the interview he over exaggerated the touching of his tie.

After a brief live interview, the two detective inspectors sat alone in Dylan's office when Wendy Smythe had left.

'Two-nil to the home side Jack.' Terry was jubilant.

'What a couple of bad bastards they were; they even wore bullet proof vests I am told,' added Dylan.

'Thank goodness the firearms officers hit with a neck and head shot, otherwise it may have been a different scenario.'

'Fingers crossed ballistics match up the weapons with both our murder scenes Terry.'

'They will Jack, they will. Look I have to debrief the team back North, they're going to be waiting for my update. So let's take a rain check on a drink tonight and we'll catch up early next week shall we?'

'That sounds good. Thanks mate for the assistance,' he said and, as the two men stood, they shook hands.

Terry turned at the door. 'And I hope your lass is feeling a lot better soon, and the missing detective turns up safe and well.'

'Me too Terry, Take care mate.'

'I better go, otherwise you know what they're like, they'll be spending my overtime budget - that's already in the bloody red.'

'Yours and mine alike,' Dylan said with a faint hint of a smile.

Dylan sat alone quietly for a moment, all he could hear was the ticking of the clock on his office wall. The telephone rang and ended the moment. It was dark outside. It had been a long day but the killing had been stopped.

'Glad it's all over,' said Jen. 'You and the ACC are headline news.'

Dylan was eager to know. 'Did our Maisy see it?'

'Yes, she did and she was over the moon that you did that thing with your tie.'

'Good. That's all that matters... I'm heading home.'